THE
LIFE-GIVER

JASE PUDDICOMBE

ISBN: 978-1-956136-17-3

The Parliament House

www.parliamenthousepress.com

Cover Art by: Shayne Leighton

Edited by Cindy Kilbourne, Mary Westveer, & Malorie Nilson

To my dad,
For giving me my love of books
And for everything else afterwards

PART ONE

PART ONE

THE LOST DREAMER

H ot. Everything was hot.

She didn't know when it had happened, but she was Dreaming. She must have slipped into sleep much faster than usual. Had she had time to reassure Lyam? To pull her favorite red blanket up to her chin? To complete the ritual in full?

Too late either way. She was already floating before the wild expanse of the Sun.

The air crackled with heat around her. Sweat broke out on her forehead, her arms bruising from the intensity of the flames, the entire field of her vision overtaken by oranges and reds and yellows too bright to look at directly. She put her hands up before her eyes, sheltering behind them, familiar with this scene but still shaken to her core.

The awe never diminished, no matter how many nights she returned here.

Faintly, she could feel the distant thrumming of the other Dreamers. They appeared like small glowing orbs floating somewhere in her periphery, fourteen in total, including her. Their presence was comforting. She reached out to them; felt them thrum back, familiar. Emery; Islah; Rayah; Nethan. People she had known almost her whole life, despite having never met them.

Another popped into view to her left, the orb slightly smaller than the others and quivering, a fresh smell bursting through the fiery, smoky scene. A new Dreamer. Of course, Annelie knew that another had been Chosen recently, bringing their number to fifteen. She felt the other Dreamers reaching out to the newcomer, thoughts floating warped through the rippling air.

Welcome.

You are one of us.

Join us, sister.

The new orb was flickering in-and-out of view, clearly uneasy, until a larger orb floated closer, blazing confidently. Nethan, the oldest among them. At his approach, the newcomer seemed to relax, her orb brightening and becoming more solid.

Elinah, *a new voice murmured.* My name is Elinah.

Welcome, Elinah. *A chorus of voices rose to their new sister, and Annelie joined them, remembering how terrifying her own first Dream had been when she'd only been six years old. She wondered how old Elinah was.*

The quivering flames rose up on either side of Annelie as she drew nearer and nearer to the surface of the Sun, her fellow Dreamers by her sides. The roaring flames echoed in her head, emanating around her, resonating dully in the ageless vacuum she floated in. Her skin crisped in the searing heat, her curly hair sticking to her forehead. She felt everything physically, and that's how she knew she was Dreaming.

Her feet landed suddenly. The flames shot up around her, terrifying in their height, three times the size of her. But she didn't cower. This was their Life-Giver—their protector. She felt comforted, cradled in their midst. The embers matched the warmth surging up inside of her, the power she could feel at her fingertips and thrumming deep within her. Power gifted to her here by the Life-Giver. The surface under her feet was solid and sturdy. It burned her bare soles and raised the hair on her arms, the heat almost painful against her skin.

The other Dreamers had grown distant, suspended somewhere behind her. She didn't think any of them had landed this time, other than her. She could understand why. The Life-Giver's surface was boiling hot, flames draining the corners of her vision. And yet, she felt at home. Protected in the love of her Life-Giver.

She crouched amid the flames; touched her hand to the white-hot surface underneath her. The surface jumped in response, flames curling up her fingers and wrapping around her wrist, dancing along her skin like a soft caress, a welcome back. She smiled.

The familiar pressure started inside her head, rattling at her skull. She didn't shake it off, instead embracing it with closed eyes and a steadying breath. Her blood throbbed through her veins, spots dancing behind her closed lids, joining the flickering flames before her even when she closed her eyes.

The voice that greeted her was one that inspired apprehensive awe.

You have returned.

She licked her lips, her throat parched. Hello, Life-Giver.

The flames jumped wildly. Annelie always worried that one day she would offend the Sun God because she was terrible at remembering all the rituals and formal words she was supposed to use during the Dreams. She preferred to speak from the heart. Slowly, she opened her eyes to see the flames unfurling, curling around her small form, the air crackling. She swallowed.

There was anger in the air.

I warned you, the voice whispered, still strong enough to shake her skull. **You should not have come.**

Tense, Annelie rose back to her feet, diminutive compared to the flames. The smell of crisp fire shifted slightly, acrid smoke blurring her eyes and burning her throat until she felt the need to cough. This was rare, but she still wasn't afraid. She was sure that the Life-Giver would protect her.

You should not be so sure. The voice caressed the inside of her mind, rubbing against her innards, twisting around the corners of her person. She shivered with it, trembling under the sheer power present around her.

Dreaming always felt so real.

It is real. The voice echoed, shaking the burning ground, sending *the flames scattering. Shadows danced around her, engulfing her.* **Far more than you know. This is the way things should be, daughter.**

She swallowed, taking an involuntary, trembling step back. Something was different this time, in the way the air crackled, sizzling between her fingers. Flames curled around her arms and legs, twisting with her skin to create mottled shadows, bright orange against silken brown. She stared for a moment, wondering at the crisping of her arms, how she somehow remained intact despite the sheer weight of power squeezing at the edges of her being.

You remain whole because I will it for you, child, *the voice murmured, and she remembered herself enough to reply, slowly, quietly.*

I know. I know I'm lucky to be here with you. I just want to make you happy.

My happiness is yours, *the voice answered softly, swirling around her again, cradling her like a child.* **But it is not so easy. Darkness is coming, my daughter.**

She didn't know what that meant. The Life-Giver's riddles were not hers to understand. She was simply a messenger. She should know better than to try and overstep her boundaries.

The air crackled louder, something growing sharp. The acrid smell returned until Annelie's eyes were watering and her face scrunched up. She blinked furiously, lifting a hand again, sheltering herself.

You should not be afraid of me, *the voice continued sadly.* **This is not the way. This should not be the way.**

Tell me what you want, *she begged, doing her best to salvage something. She could feel the other Dreamers nearby; hoped one of them was having greater success than she was.*

This is not how it should be.

If you're not happy—

There is no other way. *The voice lashed out, a quick whipping strike of flames reaching out before her, and she flinched back with a cry, throwing her arms up over her head. The flames hissed around her, their wicked laughter filling the air as she stumbled back, tripping* over and landing on the scorching surface with a yelp. Her skin smarted.

I have been left with no choice, the voice whispered. Sharp blackness flickered at the edges of Annelie's vision, overtaking the bright intensity of the flames, creeping closer and sending cold shivers chilling down her spine. She folded her knees into her chest, curling herself into a ball as the blackness rippled closer, reaching out in spidery lines that contaminated everywhere she looked.

This was wrong. Blackness had never existed on the surface of the Life-Giver before; even shadows appeared like flames in the Dreams.

She couldn't believe what she was seeing, and yet, she couldn't deny how solid the black tendrils were as they crept in front of her, chilling cold in their dreadful wake. They seeped across the Life-Giver's flames, dulling them, until eventually, the horrid dark webbing reached the base of one of the glowing orbs of the other Dreamers.

It happened so fast. The black crawled up and around the orb, absorbing it within seconds despite how the orb thrashed. A faint scream echoed through the air, and Annelie jumped to her feet and rushed forwards, reaching out to the orb in a rush of desperate adrenaline.

Rayah. It was Rayah who was screaming and suffocating in blackness.

After less than a second, the orb winked out.

Annelie stopped abruptly, eyes wide, staring out towards the empty space where her fellow Dreamer had just been. A disgusting tang of rotting, burning flesh sat heavy in the air. This was wrong. The way the ball of light had just winked straight out as soon as the cruel inky blackness touched it—it was wrong. She could feel it in the panic of the other Dreamers, clamoring for their lost companion, the one of their number who was no longer there.

There is no other way, murmured the voice again, this time with a tinge of regret. The flames curled around Annelie, gently lifting her, cradling her in the air, and wrapping around her. A final embrace for the night. **The time has come.**

She slipped backward, feeling the familiar tug at her ankles, *under her armpits, pulling her up and out. She struggled momentarily, reaching back for the warmth. No...*

You should not have come. *The voice was fading, no matter how she reached for it. Her feet left the solid surface and she floated again, weightless, fading into the flames.*

The Dream was over.

CHAPTER
ONE

For the Dreams are fundamental,
And in their practice and harmful delight lies our destiny.
The Dreamers are our salvation.
Should any harm come to them, plague will fall upon us all.
The Book of the Life-Giver, Vol. I, Chapter I

The knocking was the loudest sound in the room.

It startled Lyam awake, jolting him upright in his chair and blinking rapidly until the world swam into focus around him. He pushed his glasses up his nose, grimacing when he saw that he'd fallen asleep on last night's notes. The ink ran across the parchment, leaving a sticky, grainy, drying mess. He was going to have to clean that up quickly.

The knock sounded again. Lyam stirred, glancing towards the trapdoor in the floor before turning back to the messy surroundings of his desk. He'd left a face-print in the ink from his write-up of Annelie's latest Dream. Lyam drew in a tight breath, then let it out in a lingering sigh. His one job, and he couldn't even do that right. He shouldn't be falling asleep on watch after so many years caring for Annelie.

Running a hand through his dark hair, he turned towards the pendulum clock sitting tucked away on a shelf, his eyebrows rising when he saw the time. It was still the middle of the night —still sacred. No one should be knocking on the trapdoor right now.

No one should really be knocking on the trapdoor at all.

Finally waking up enough to take in the situation, Lyam leaped to his feet, his stool almost toppling over. He righted it just before it could crash to the floor, wincing at the sharp scrape of the legs against the ground, and turned instantly to the chair behind him to check that he hadn't made too much noise.

Annelie was still Dreaming.

She lay back in the luxurious lounging chair that took up more than half of the small hut, her eyes creased shut. Every so often, she would twitch, her fingers clasping or her feet flinching, small soft whimpers escaping her lips. Lyam held himself back from waking her, much as the desire rose. He'd been her Scribe for nine years, and yet he still couldn't completely repress the instinct to stop her. The Dreams always looked so painful.

There was another knock, louder this time, and Lyam was drawn back to the matter at hand. He spun instantly, his bare feet catching in the soft red rugs covering the floor. The trapdoor in the corner that led down to the tunnels was only opened to bring them supplies, or for when Lyam went to report the latest Dream findings to the other Scribes, or to his one-on-one private meetings with his Designer. There were never any visitors. No one ever came *in*.

Lyam's muscles tensed, fear rushing through him.

His gut tightened, his heart pulsing uncomfortably in his chest. He knew better than most that ignoring problems tended to only make them grow, so he shoved aside his fear as best he could, swallowed down his nausea, and strode with as much confidence as he could muster, as little as it was, to the trapdoor, opening it just as another knock began.

Crouching to glance down the drop into the tunnels, he was met with the dark, worried figure of another Scribe. She was wrapped in a long cloth, everything but her face covered, lit only by the lantern in her raised hand. The long, shadowy expanse of tunnels stretched out beyond her.

"Scribe Lyam," she hissed, and he recognized her voice—Jemme, a Scribe only slightly older than him. The dusty, stale smell of the tunnels drifted up around her. "Come down. I need to talk to you."

Lyam blinked. He glanced behind him instinctively—back towards the chair where Annelie was lying—and shook his head. "Annelie is still Dreaming."

Surprise entered Jemme's tone. "Still?"

"Of course; it's the middle of the night." Lyam frowned down into the circle of lantern light, folding his arms over the front of his robes. His calves burned. He didn't imagine he looked particularly imposing when his clothes were sleep-rumpled, his dark brown hair sticking up everywhere, and his glasses wonky, but he knew he had the upper hand here. Nothing was supposed to disturb the sanctity of the night. Nothing.

"I'm sorry to come like this," Jemme answered in a low, rushed murmur, "But I really have no choice. It's important, Lyam, if you'd just come down here—"

"Annelie is *Dreaming*," he reminded her, voice tight and low.

"That's what worries me. Please?"

Lyam was about to refuse, but he could hear the desperation in Jemme's voice, see the tension in the line of her shoulders. Her hand was trembling around the lantern, making the light flicker haphazardly, shadows leaping around the rocky tunnel walls. She was still in her night robes.

Lyam hesitated, glancing back towards Annelie. She was mid-Dream, her expressions shifting with each passing moment, and it was risky to leave her. Dreams were the fabric of their society, and the only way for the Designers to access them was through the notations of the Scribes. Lyam had to be there when she woke. But it was still deep night; she'd sleep for a while yet. Jemme wouldn't have come here without good reason, right?

Sucking in a breath, Lyam fetched the ladder and lowered it carefully into the tunnels.

Jemme let out an audibly relieved sigh as he began descending to her level. The minute he was safely down in the dusty, cramped space, she grabbed for him, hissing, "Something's happened to Rayah."

Lyam blinked. Rayah was Jemme's Dreamer; they'd been working together for some six or seven years now, and they were both experienced. He frowned. "What do you mean?"

"I don't know what's happened." Jemme was still shaking, her fingers painfully tight where she clung to Lyam's robe. "She was Dreaming like normal; everything was going well. I was about to sleep as well, but then she—she *screamed.*"

"That happens sometimes," Lyam murmured, but Jemme was shaking her head, speaking over him.

"She shot straight up, burst awake, screaming. I thought maybe it was just a nightmare, or the Life-Giver hadn't accepted her, or something. B-but then there was the *smell.*"

"Smell?" Lyam asked, perplexed.

Jemme shuddered. A look of revulsion passed over her face. "Like...rotting, or...something smoking. I can't describe it. The most—" She swallowed. "No words would do it justice. Acrid, burning. It was horrible. And then I saw—on her skin...there were *scars.*"

"You mean burns?"

"No, no," Jemme shook her head quickly, the whites of her eyes wide in the lantern light. "I'm used to burns. This was— they were *black.* Black scars, all over her skin, spreading the longer I looked."

Lyam stared at her, astonished.

"I tried to help her," Jemme continued, her voice shaky. "But when I reached for Rayah, she screamed and...and—"

"You left her?" Shock leaked into Lyam's tone before he could school himself.

Jemme's eyes clouded, her expression tightening. "I had no choice. I didn't know what to do, she just—she was screaming so loudly, and the black scars were spreading, and the *smell*... Even her eyes turned black."

Lyam's blood ran cold, chills rippling down his spine.

"She sent me to warn the others," Jemme said shakily. "Your Dreamer. She's still Dreaming?"

With effort, Lyam nodded. He glanced up at the trapdoor again, to where Annelie was still twitching away in her sleep, and made straight for the ladder, panic building in his gut. "I shouldn't have left her alone."

"I'm sorry." Jemme caught his arm just before he could ascend. "I had to. I have to warn the others...in case something happens to them too."

Lyam glanced down at her from halfway up the ladder. He could hear the fear present behind the brave voice she was putting on. Lyam swallowed, digging his fingers into the rough edge of the ladder, his expression softening at the desperation in her expression. Slowly, he said, "I can't leave Annelie now. But when she wakes—or when she is no longer Dreaming—I'll help. I can get to the West tunnels."

The relief from Jemme was palpable. "Thank you."

"Of course," Lyam answered and watched her back away into the encroaching darkness, her lantern sending shadows leaping wildly against the dusty mud-brick surrounding them. The weight of the unseen outside pressed down against her.

Lyam didn't wait to watch her go. The minute her back was turned, he scaled the rest of the ladder, the rough wood splintering under his palms, and scrambled back into his hut, pulling the ladder up and closing the trapdoor behind him. Panic rushed his movements.

In the warm light filtering from the lanterns on the walls of their hut, Annelie was still Dreaming. She lay splayed out on her chair made of pale wood and built to recline. The chair was designed for comfort and swaddled in cushions and blankets that Annelie had collected over the years. It took up most of the space in the center of their small hut. Lyam's bench, desk, and cot were squished in the corners.

Sweat encrusted her forehead, her eyes screwed shut. Her fingers had frozen into half-formed fists, clutching at the edge of her favorite red blanket, her bare feet kicking on occasion. Her white robes were crumpled and stained, and the warmth of the Life-Giver emanated around her, seeping out of her brown skin in a visible golden glow. The smell of smoke and ash lingered.

Lyam leaned forward, gently touching the back of his hand to her forehead. She was burning fever-like, so he went to fetch the bowl of water and washcloth and gently dabbed cool drops to her forehead and the back of her neck. She eased a little, though she did not wake.

Lyam settled himself onto the bench by her side, ready to watch over her until she awoke. She was shifting and muttering under her breath, her eyes darting rapidly behind her closed lids, and the scent of burning sat thick in the air. Her legs were curled up tight, muscles clenched, and he knew she'd be cramping when she woke. They'd have to take time to unwind her slowly, massage her sore legs, and he'd take her for a short circular walk around their hut. He tried to help her exercise when she could, but it wasn't often. Dreamers had a hard life, and it took a toll on Annelie's body. She couldn't walk unaided at all.

Lyam removed the cloths when Annelie began to twitch more often. Her stiff fingers leaped into life, clutching at the blankets, and she rocketed upright, drawing air into her lungs like it was her first breath in this world. Her hair frazzled out around her, and she made the smallest little whining noise, eyes flying open wide and wild.

Lyam grasped for her hand, grounding her. "Welcome back."

She turned to him, eyes still wide, breath still heaving. Her gaze was unfocused, sliding over him with bare recognition before turning to the corners of their hut and then finally settling back on him. She blinked, shaking her head.

He squeezed her fingers gently, her skin searing under his

touch. "It's barely morning. You're still on your chair, no falling this time. I'm here."

Annelie glanced around again, swallowing with effort. She looked down at where her red blanket was twisted around her, the soft, threadbare cotton still warm. She flexed her free hand; watched how her fingers still trembled. "I'm back?"

"You're back," Lyam affirmed. "Home again, like you always will be."

Annelie smiled then, like a reflex. Her head lowered as her eyes closed, her breath slowing down. "Was it a long one tonight?" She asked, eyes still closed. "It felt like a long one."

"It was," Lyam confirmed, releasing her hand in favor of reaching for the cool washcloth again. "And it looked intense. Lots of twitching, not much peace on your face."

Annelie laughed bitterly, rubbing her hands over her eyes. She was still trembling, but as Lyam gently wiped her clean and ran his fingers through her tight curls, she began to settle, leaning back and lowering her hands, opening her deep brown eyes to turn and look at Lyam. There was a wrinkle in her brow.

"One of the Dreamers," she voiced slowly as she came more and more back to herself. "Something happened. I think—was it Rayah? Something happened..."

Lyam's throat closed up. "How much do you remember?"

Annelie shook her head, letting out a little frustrated groan. "Not enough. Something happened, though. To one of them. There was this... black... I think it was Rayah? We have to find out! When you go to the meeting—"

"No need," Lyam interrupted gently, switching the wash-cloth to her forehead and pushing at her shoulder to get her to lie down again. "Jemme came by."

"Jemme?" Annelie resisted him until her questions were answered. "Rayah's Scribe?"

"Yeah. She said Dreamer Rayah was... I don't know, attacked? Or hurt?"

"What?" Annelie leaned closer, rolling onto her side with a soft rustle of the blankets. "What do you mean, attacked?"

"I don't know, but Jemme said... something about a burning smell, and these, these *scars*. They were—"

"Black," Annelie breathed. "Black scars and rotting flesh."

A chill ran down Lyam's spine. He stared at Annelie, perplexed. "You saw it?"

"Yeah... I think?" Annelie squeezed her eyes shut, bunching her fingers into fists around the frayed edge of her favorite blanket. The lantern light flickered over her features, her wide round eyes, her snub nose. "It's like... I've told you, right, how in the Dreams I can sense the other Dreamers?"

Lyam nodded, familiar with this idea even if he couldn't exactly imagine it himself. Dreams were far beyond him.

"They're like... these lights," Annelie continued, her voice soft and a small smile tugging at her lips. She described it to Lyam, and Lyam did his best to follow, imagining the floating balls of warmth that Annelie always said her fellow Dreamers felt like in the Dreams. He was awed by the Life-Giver's power. The Dreamers had never met in real life, after all, each of them confined to their separate huts. Yet Annelie seemed to know them like old friends. She could tell them apart in the Dreams sometimes, but it depended on the strength and intensity and her personal relationship with each one.

'So, when Rayah..." Annelie swallowed, biting her lip. "I saw it, you know? Like...this blackness swallowing her whole. It felt... unnatural. I don't think it was part of the Dream."

A moment of silence rang through their little hut as Lyam absorbed that information. His first reaction was to state that it was impossible. The Dreams were sacred and controlled by the Life-Giver so that nothing that they didn't permit could enter. Only the Dreamers were allowed to communicate with them. If something else had got in—well, it simply couldn't have. It was impossible.

After a moment, Lyam said quietly, "Jemme went to the other Scribes. After me, I mean. I said I'd help once you're settled."

Annelie nodded immediately. "Yes, you must. Rayah shouldn't be left alone. It was..." She took in a breath, leaned back, and closed her eyes. "You were right, earlier. Intense. It was intense."

Lyam took her hand again, gently smoothing his thumb across her knuckles, watching the way it helped her to relax. She melted back into the chair with a dark chuckle. "I'm not even sure anyone else landed on the surface, you know?"

"But you did?" Lyam asked, leaning back and reaching for his parchment. He always kept a stack under Annelie's chair for moments like this when she remembered things in the immediate aftermath of the Dreams.

"Yeah," Annelie confirmed, her voice regaining some life to it. "It was... awe-inspiring. The same as always—comforting, warm. Terrifying. But the Life-Giver was upset about something. I couldn't...there was no answer when I asked. They wouldn't tell me anything."

Lyam was scratching away at the parchment as she spoke. He looked up at her words, feeling his forehead crease, confused. His glasses had slipped down his nose a little. "Nothing? Not at all?"

Annelie narrowed her eyes, clearly thinking. She looked faraway. Lyam always wondered where her mind went when she thought back on her Dreams. Some strange in-between space, maybe. Certainly, a place where he was unable to follow.

"They said I shouldn't have come," she said eventually. "It was strange. The Life-Giver definitely heard me, but they seemed more bothered about making sure I was listening to them than actually answering any of my questions."

"Mirah won't like that very much," Lyam muttered from behind his pen.

"Either way, it isn't important right now." Annelie leaned forward and nudged insistently at his shoulder. "You need to go. The other Dreamers need to be warned."

"Any hints as to whether the rest of them are ok?"

"I think they're all fine," Annelie answered thoughtfully, chewing on her lower lip. "Or they were when I woke up. But I don't know. Something could have happened after I'd already left."

Cold washed over Lyam at those words.

"I'll report back," he said, getting to his feet. He gave her hand one last pat. "You sure you'll be alright here? I shouldn't be too long."

Annelie waved away his fussing with a small, fond smile. "I'll be fine. Just go."

"Make sure you rest. There's tea by the side—"

"Just *go*, Lyam," Annelie chuckled warmly. She closed her eyes and stretched out across her chair, her usual bright smile softening her round face. "I'll still be here when you get back."

Lyam looked at her uncertainly for one more moment.

"If you don't go now, I'll hit you," she said without opening her eyes.

Lyam huffed, amused, and turned on his heel to head to the trapdoor. He was always dampened by a sense of unease when he left Annelie's side. She was untouchable inside their hut, he knew, but it didn't make him feel any more comfortable about leaving her alone when he knew first-hand just how vulnerable she could be. Physically, at least. He had no doubt that she could fight off an intruder by shouting curses at them alone.

He made sure to leave the lanterns with enough fuel to burn for a couple more hours, just in case, before lowering the ladder down the trapdoor and dropping into the tunnel.

It was warmer down here than in the huts. Stiflingly warm. The air could get difficult to breathe, the fuel from the intermittent lamps clouding what little free space existed. Lyam turned west, following the rocky, twisting wall carved out by Designers long before his time so as not to lose his way. This route was far less familiar to him than any other. After all the only places out this way were other Dreamer huts, and usually, he was forbidden from going there.

Tonight called for desperate measures. Jemme had looked so terrified earlier, and Annelie seemed more shaken by this Dream than usual. Lyam himself still couldn't entirely let go of his feeling of unease. Darkness closed around him as the lanterns grew fewer and farther between, the scent of the fuel becoming a little more bearable as he descended the uneven floor. The quiet was eerie; no other footsteps besides his own, no other sounds apart from his breathing and the odd scampering of the tunnel cats, their pale eyes reflecting when they caught the lantern light. It must still be very early.

When Lyam came to the first turn for the Dreamers' huts, he stopped for a minute, swallowing. He knew he wouldn't be wanted. No one should ever come here, not for any reason, but he was left with little choice.

Spreading bad news had never been one of his gifts. Still, he took a small breath and turned down the passage, squaring his shoulders as best he could.

The next trapdoor was hard to see, barely lit at all. He should have brought his own lantern. Too late to go back now, Lyam pushed his glasses up his nose and felt with fumbling fingers along the jagged roof not far above his head until his nails scraped against wood, and then he stopped.

Took a deep breath.

Knocked lightly against the wood.

This was so unheard of that Lyam actually wasn't sure what the punishment would be if he entered another Dreamer's hut. He was staying down in the tunnels, of course, but what if one of the guards caught him here? They would report back to Head Guard Tomas with no hesitation, and Lyam didn't want to think about what that grim-faced man would do to him. Probably not the death penalty, not if the Dreamer's Scribe was present, but then again, probably not much lighter than that.

Lyam waited anxiously in the stuffy, dusty tunnel. The air was perfectly still around him, not even a muffled noise to be heard. The slinky shape of a tunnel cat slipped through the shadows to his left.

He knocked again, a little louder this time, gathering as much courage as he could.

Still silence, but something far-off shuffled, a little loose sand falling from the tunnel roof.

Lyam held his breath, screwed his eyes shut for a second, and knocked once more. His knuckles stung.

Finally, eventually, there was movement. More loose sand crumbled down around him, some falling into the creases of his robes as he waited with a slow sense of dread for the door to open. Sure enough, a sliver of lantern light slipped through the slowly opening crack above him until an unfamiliar face peered down at him.

Lyam paused, blinking. He didn't recognize the boy looking down at him, and he was only a boy. Barely twelve years to him, Lyam would guess.

The boy stared at him, terrified.

Lyam smiled as reassuringly as he could. "Uh...hi. I'm looking for the Scribe—"

"You can't be down there!" The boy hissed, his face hidden in shadows but his tone giving away his fear.

Lyam withdrew a step but stopped himself from turning away completely. The boy was hardly threatening, so he steeled himself and replied, "I know, but it's an emergency. Unfortunately."

The boy remained silent other than his harsh breathing.

"I don't really want to be here either, believe me," Lyam added, but it appeared to be the wrong thing to say because the boy jerked so violently that he tripped over his own feet, landing on his back with a thud that shook the packed sand above Lyam's head.

"Ok, ok, it's ok." Lyam rushed forward. "I'm not here to cause harm, and I don't want to come up. I have to warn you of something that's happened, that's all."

The boy, still prone on the floor of the hidden hut above Lyam's head, swallowed audibly before crawling back over to the entrance, peering down. For the first time, Lyam got a proper look at his face, and by the Sun, he was young—his face round and chubby-cheeked, brown skin soft, sandy hair floppy. The trapdoor hung awkwardly half-open, and through it Lyam caught a glimpse of a hut just like his own, with wooden walls and rug-covered floor.

Forbidden for anyone's eyes but the Dreamer and the Scribe who lived inside.

"Something's happened?" The boy asked eventually in a voice so tight and thin that it almost got lost in the stale air.

Slowly, Lyam nodded his head. "To one of the Dreamers. Rayah. She was attacked."

The boy's mouth dropped open and he visibly trembled. A confused silence held.

"I don't understand it either, not yet," Lyam continued carefully. "All I know is that I had her Scribe come tearing to my hut in the middle of the night, terrified that something might have happened to someone else. Is your Dreamer ok? Nothing unusual happened?"

The boy swallowed, turning his head to look further into the hut. "I-I don't think so? Sh-she's just... sleeping, it looks like. I don't know. I'm..."

Suddenly, it clicked. The boy's uncertain words: the fact that Lyam didn't know his face, had never seen him at any of the meetings.

"You're newly chosen, aren't you?" Lyam asked gently.

The boy whipped back around to look at him, fear and shame written all over his face.

"It's alright," Lyam soothed. He remembered well enough what it felt like to be new and alone the first night with a Dreamer, and this had to be one of the boy's first nights. The news of the new Dreamer had only reached Lyam's ears a day or so ago. He straightened up, lifting both hands palm-out in a placating gesture. "I'm not here to judge you. I'm really just another Scribe. My name's Lyam. What's yours?"

The boy swallowed thickly, crouching down by the trapdoor to better meet Lyam's gaze, which impressed Lyam slightly. The first week was the toughest. "Jorin. But you—are you really Scribe Lyam? *The* Scribe Lyam?"

Lyam bit his lip, taking a moment to answer. He hated when

his reputation preceded him, but sometimes it was unavoidable, and Jorin must have been aware of the rumours before he came here.

"You *are*." Jorin leaned closer, something like wonder entering his tone. "Your eyes. I've never seen real gold eyes before."

Lyam glanced down and away; a learned gesture. Sometimes he hated his reflexes.

"Why is Scribe Lyam visiting me?" Jorin continued in a wondrous voice. "Is this some kind of test? Do I have to pass before I can attend the first meeting?"

"No, no," Lyam hastily answered. "Like I told you, it's just to check on your Dreamer, to make sure they're alright. Rayah— well, we need to make sure nothing like that happened to anyone else."

"But how do I tell?" Jorin glanced away again, back into the hut. "Sh-she's sleeping, it looks like?"

"Has she been shifting at all? Disturbed?"

Jorin sent him a confused look.

"Like, wriggling around?" Lyam tried to explain. "Making noises, maybe crying, looking like she's about to wake up but then her eyes are still shut?"

Slowly, Jorin nodded.

"Good. That's good," Lyam explained gently. "That means she was Dreaming. You should write down what she remembers when she wakes, in careful detail. It may be important in figuring out what happened to Rayah."

"So, she's ok? I mean...I didn't do anything wrong?"

"Nothing at all," Lyam reassured as best he could. He pushed off the wall, readying to leave. "Watch over her until she wakes and look after her. I think it was a hard night for them."

"Wait!"

Lyam turned back, a crease in his brow.

Jorin squatted by the trapdoor, his expression nervous. "How do I—every time she's woken up so far, she's been crying, and I don't—I don't know what to do?"

Lyam softened. He gave Jorin a small smile. "You're her Scribe. You were chosen for a reason. You know what that means?"

Silently, Jorin shook his head.

"It means that the Life-Giver knows you." Lyam's smile grew. "They chose you for your Dreamer because you're the perfect person to help her. She needs you, and you're there for her. You can't do anything wrong as long as you stay by her side."

Jorin didn't look convinced, but Lyam was short on time. He turned with a wave of his hand and continued deeper into the tunnels, but he didn't hear the trapdoor close behind him for a long time.

At the other huts, Lyam received a better welcome. The Scribes all knew him by sight at least, and he found it easier to explain his presence with each repetition, easing their suspicions. According to the Scribes Lyam spoke to, none of the other Dreamers had experienced anything strange, which was good, but left Lyam with a sense of heavy dread.

If only Rayah had been attacked, then what was the reason? Had she done something wrong? Lyam couldn't imagine it. Jemme was a good Scribe, always sparing a few kind words for Lyam when they crossed paths. Plus, Annelie's night had been a difficult one.

He arrived back at his hut to find Annelie sitting up in her chair, eyes narrow and brow furrowed, some of his most recent writings spread out around her.

"Find anything helpful?" Lyam asked through a yawn, closing the trapdoor behind him. The smell of musty parchment welcomed him home just as much as the sight of his desk.

"I'm just trying to find anything odd," Annelie answered, not lifting her eyes from the various writings surrounding her. The rustle of the paper under her fingertips was familiar, and it eased Lyam a little as he settled himself back onto his bench by her chair. "How are the others?"

"Everyone is fine," Lyam reassured, only getting a grunt in response. He leaned over and fetched the bowl of water again, pouring some carefully into a glass and holding it out for Annelie to take. "Anything catching your eye?"

"Not enough." Annelie ignored the glass and instead turned a page. Her bottom lip was caught between her teeth. "Something's *off* recently, I know it, I just..."

"We'll look together," Lyam placated, holding out the glass again. "Drink. You need it."

She made a face at him but took the water anyway. Once she started drinking, Lyam leaned over and took the parchment from her fingers, scanning over the documents she'd picked out. They were his writings of her most recent Dreams, only the past few days' worth spread out on the bed around her. They'd been fairly standard as far as he could tell; not that coherent, just a few descriptions of the Life-Giver's surface and the Life-Giver's voice giving the usual cryptic statements. There was a slight warning tone to them, which was perhaps a little odd. *Darkness is coming. You should not be here.*

"It's still not *right.*" Annelie set the now-empty glass down on the side and leaned over next to him. "The words, the messages. They don't add up like they should."

"The Life-Giver likes to be cryptic," Lyam pointed out. "I don't think this is anything new."

"But usually I can pick out *something.*" Annelie sat back, pursing her lips, a deep frown creasing her brow. "I'm sure I'm forgetting more details, too, like I wake up and try and grab for them but they just... scatter. I haven't got a hope of giving you anything decent."

"It's enough," Lyam reassured her. "Mirah can pick out more than us, anyway."

"I hope so," Annelie muttered.

Lyam hummed, glancing back down at the parchment. He could see what Annelie meant, but the sparsity of the Dreams lately wasn't anything unusual to him. Still, if it was troubling Annelie, then it was worth noting. He reached for his pen.

Annelie watched him with narrowed eyes. "Are you seriously writing about our lack of writings?"

"Yes."

"...Isn't that a bit of a paradox?"

"It's important," Lyam insisted. "Your instincts are usually right, Anni. I'm not about to stop trusting them after all these years."

She sat back a little and Lyam grinned at her. She rolled her eyes back, saying, "Doesn't mean there's anything useful. I'm afraid your meeting might not be very fruitful this week."

"That's alright," Lyam answered more confidently than he felt. He already found his meetings with their Designer nerve-wracking enough; he didn't need Annelie making this one sound any worse than it had to.

Annelie frowned. "Something is just *off*. That's all I know."

Lyam nodded, the scratch of his pen against parchment the only comforting sound in the room.

CHAPTER
TWO

For the Dreamers to remain sacred, they must be isolated,
And therefore, they require a link to the people.
The Scribes act as that link.
The Book of the Life-Giver, Vol. II, Chapter I

A note came to their hut via the guard later that day from the Head Scribe calling an emergency meeting. It didn't give any further information, but they both knew what it was about. Annelie hadn't stopped talking about Rayah's attack, and Lyam was finding it difficult to forget Jemme's terrified expression when she'd come to their door in the early hours of the morning. There was no news of Rayah's condition now.

Lyam wrapped his heavy official Scribes' robes around his shoulders, making a face when he found a stain by his right elbow. It was probably just ink, but he didn't have time to wash it out before the meeting if he wanted to be on time, and the thought of walking in late in front of all the other Scribes had him shuddering.

Annelie caught his expression from her chair and gave an exasperated sigh. "You look fine. Just go."

"I hate these things," Lyam muttered about his robes, shifting awkwardly in the stiff green material.

Annelie chuckled. "Good job you don't have to wear them often, then. Go. You hate being late."

"I know." He dropped his sleeve and picked up his notebook, sliding it into his inner pocket as he approached Annelie to drop a swift kiss to the top of her head. "I'll be back soon. Don't break anything."

"I'm not *that* bad. Don't bring any more tunnel cats home."

"No promises."

Once in the tunnels, Lyam pushed the hood of his robes down, sweat already plastering his hair to his forehead. The route he took this time was far more familiar than the path he'd had to cover in the night, better populated and properly lit, but he still took his own lantern with him.

The tunnel sloped steeply downwards as Lyam headed towards the main city, the roofs of the underground houses slowly coming into view as the ceiling moved sharply upwards. The cavern that contained the main city was a vast, open underground space, with lanterns flickering from every available surface. The clamor and noise of the city echoed, bouncing off the distant rocky walls, the liveliest place that Lyam had ever been. The tunnel path continued down the side of the cavern, leading up to the Southern Gate, tall and ostentatious marble carved with a fearsome sun, its rays fanning out above where the large doors were propped open.

As Lyam approached the gate, he was joined by a throng of people traipsing the widening passage, walking their carts or tugging donkeys along, heavily laden with their wares. Footsteps and chatter and the squeals of playing children bounded up from the city below them, and as Lyam drew closer, the scents of the morning market wafted towards him, fresh fruits grown in their special underground farms and vegetable dishes cooked in spices making his stomach rumble. Lyam spotted a couple of other green robes among the crowd on the way to the Southern Gate and breathed a sigh of relief that he wasn't the only Scribe running late.

Walking through the city always came as a bit of a shock to Lyam, jolting him out of his comfortable world of solitude and silence with Annelie. Noise racketed off every corner, echoes mixing together in a confusing whirlwind roaring throughout the loud cavern. He passed under the giant Southern gate, avoiding the black-clad guards, and wove his way between the crowds. The road was thronged with carts and donkeys, contrasting the finery of some of the well-off people, a couple of palanquins marked with the Citadel symbol passing him by. The buildings were close together, crammed in as much as possible, some four or five stories high, especially as he came closer to the central square.

Eventually, the path opened out, the crush of the crowd thinning slightly until Lyam felt like he had room to breathe again. He walked with as much purpose as he could muster, his head ducked low to avoid the stares of other people. He always hated the attention his eyes drew.

The Scribes' Hall was near the central square of the city, under the heavy stare of the Citadel, housed in an enormous marble building with vast pillars on either side of the grand door. On closer inspection, the pillars and the lintel of the giant, heavy stone doors were covered in writing. Lyam knew the words depicted some of the most famous Dreams throughout history, continuing all the way around the sides of the building and right to the back of the Hall. Eventually, every blank space would be covered.

There had been a time when Lyam was desperate to read every word. He still held that curiosity, despite life doing everything it could to suck that enthusiasm out of him.

Lyam took the steps up to the building quickly, nodding once to the guard standing at the door before he ducked inside.

Instantly, he was plunged into darkness. His footsteps echoed against the flagstones of the dimly-lit foyer as he hurried on into the corridor, following the path to the meeting room. The walls were lined with bookshelves; dust and mildew heavy in the air. It was familiar, comforting. Aside from the hut that he shared with Annelie, this building felt the most like home.

The meeting room was already mostly full by the time Lyam arrived. The other Scribes stood grouped together in small clusters, the tense air filled with worried chatter. A ring of seats upholstered in green circled the outside of the room.

Lyam bit his lip, pausing in the doorway. He was thankful that no one had spotted him yet and turned to sidle as quietly as possible to one of the seats.

He almost got away with it.

"Lyam!" A broad shout sounded from Lyam's left, and then a very familiar face came bounding into view.

Lyam braced for the shock and grunted when he was drawn bodily into a hug. "Hello, Adan."

"So pleased to see me, as always." Adan's grin was evident in his voice, his reddish hair sticking up from his head. Thick brows sat over hooded eyes, his jaw square. He crushed Lyam against him for half a second too long before drawing away and looking him over. "You've got thinner. Stop saving your leftovers for the tunnel cats, honestly."

"Shut up," Lyam grumbled good-naturedly. "How have you been?"

"Oh, not so bad. Could do without the added worry. You heard about Rayah? Oh, of course you did; I heard you were the one going around telling people."

Lyam screwed his face up, embarrassed. "Jemme came to me first. I just offered to help, that's all."

Adan grinned wickedly. "I'm sure you did. The new Scribe is terrified of you."

"What?!" Lyam hadn't acted that badly, had he? He didn't think he had it in him to be intimidating.

Adan burst into laughter. "I wouldn't worry too much. From what I've seen, he's terrified of pretty much everything. Tasmin welcomed him to the meeting room, and he all but screamed."

"Hey," Lyam murmured. "Remember what we were like when we were new."

Adan just shrugged. His dark eyes met Lyam's for a moment, tense behind his usual laughter lines.

"Seriously, though," Adan dropped his voice. "Is Dreamer Rayah ok?"

Lyam shrugged a little helplessly. "I don't know. Have you seen Jemme? She was really shaken when she came to me."

Adan shook his head. "I'm not sure she's coming. Whispers are that she's stayed by Rayah's side since morning and refuses to leave, even for Tasmin's summons."

Lyam winced. Not that he was surprised. If he was shaken by the night's events, then he couldn't even imagine what she was going through. The thought of Annelie being attacked in the night, of her eyes turning black and her skin rotting...

Lyam shuddered and pulled his thoughts away. It didn't bear thinking about.

At that exact moment, a door opened to their right, and Tasmin herself strode into the room. Her greying hair was pulled back in a sharp bun, her robes straining against her curves. Her motherly features, covered in worry lines, were welcomingly familiar to Lyam. She glanced around once, and the room fell quiet.

Then she broadened her shoulders and stepped into the center of the circle of seats, taking up her place as Head Scribe.

There was a flurry of movement, Scribes rushing to take their seats. These meetings were usually held weekly, even if this one had been called with urgency.

Lyam wasn't surprised. They would need to discuss what to do about Rayah before taking the matter to the Designers.

Once everyone was seated, Lyam himself sliding into a soft-cushioned chair on Adan's right side, Tasmin cleared her throat. She stood in the center of the circle, her green robes lined with gold to show her status as Head Scribe. Her dark eyes were sharp as she spun slowly to catch everyone's attention, and when she met Lyam's gaze, Lyam recognized the familiar warmth to her that had been there ever since he first joined the Scribes' ranks, back when he was no more than a child. She'd been a constant presence by his side the whole time, right from just after his choosing when he'd been terrified to so much as enter the Hall.

Now, Tasmin remained a charismatic, calming presence, standing in the center of the circle with a welcoming smile.

"My Scribes," she began once everyone had quieted, her voice soft but commanding. "You're all aware of the purpose of this meeting. Dreamer Rayah was attacked last night while she was Dreaming."

The silence in the room was tangible.

"I know that Jemme went to most of you with help from others." Lyam shifted in his seat. "And you all know the serious nature of the matter. You'll notice that Jemme is not among us. She has chosen, and I agreed, to stay by Rayah's side until we understand the situation further."

Lyam swallowed. Tasmin spoke clearly, her expression unreadable, but Lyam could see the tight stress lines around her eyes. She might be holding it together, but he'd known her long enough to see that she was worried.

"We must discuss what to do. I open the floor." She stepped back, took her own seat in the circle, and gestured to the middle. "Anyone who wishes to speak may do so."

There was an instant scramble as several Scribes attempted to stand, but the fastest was Seth, who all but threw himself into the middle. He pulled his robes around him as he turned to face Tasmin. "What happened to Rayah? Is she ok?"

Lyam instantly grew tense. Despite never having physically met her, Lyam felt like he knew Rayah, the same as he felt he knew all the Dreamers. Annelie talked about them, and he knew all of their Scribes well. Their community was small.

There were murmurs of agreement all around, and Tasmin got back to her feet. "Dreamer Rayah is recuperating. The attack was damaging."

The mutterings grew.

"But I have every faith that she will recover." Tasmin's voice was tight. "Head Healer Lara has seen her, and Jemme is with her. She is as safe as she can be, for now."

Hardly reassuring, but Lyam supposed Tasmin couldn't say anything else yet. It was scary, though, the prospect that possibly not even Tasmin knew what to do.

Once Seth had taken his seat again, another Scribe got to his feet. Avery. Lyam only knew him a little. "How do we make sure this doesn't happen again?"

Tasmin rose back to her feet. She looked at each of the Scribes one by one, and Lyam shivered when her gaze met his before she moved on.

"We must be watchful," she said. "Until we understand the exact nature of what has happened to Rayah, we cannot predict whether or not it could happen again."

"So, what do we do?" Called someone else from the circle.

"We watch," Tasmin answered calmly. "We watch our Dreamers, and we wait. And when we have news, we take it to our Designers."

"What are we even watching *for*?" Avery wailed.

There were a few murmurs of agreement, the sounds very close to being panicked. Lyam dug his fingers into the edge of his cushioned seat.

"We're Scribes; we know the signs." Tasmin's commanding voice cut through the chaos. "We know the signs, and we know our Dreamers. I'm proposing a Vigilance tonight, and we report back here tomorrow morning."

Lyam groaned, and he wasn't the only one. *A Vigilance.* The last one of those had been years ago, and Lyam still remembered the struggle of staying awake all night, of functioning the next day on no sleep. Scribes got little sleep as it was, needing to be constantly alert for their Dreamers. Lyam honestly couldn't remember the last time he'd had a full night's sleep.

A Vigilance would hardly be welcome.

He was right; there was an instant clamor of complaints, but Tasmin held one hand up and spoke firmly, her sharp tone once again cutting through the crowd.

"Be vigilant, and return here in the morning. Do not leave your Dreamers' sides unless it is absolutely necessary. We don't yet understand this threat, so be watchful, be calm, and report back here tomorrow at first bell. Understood?"

There were still murmurings of dissent, but Seth stood back up, his jaw clenched. "Understood."

Others joined him, and Lyam quickly scrambled to his feet as well, dipping his head in Tasmin's direction and murmuring his agreement along with everyone else.

Tasmin remained in the center of the circle until everyone had got to their feet, and then she nodded to them all, wrapping her gold-lined green robes tight around her. "Then I will see you all at first bell."

With the dismissal, the crowd of Scribes broke back into small groups, talking to each other with murmured breaths. Some left immediately, others lingered, and Lyam hovered awkwardly in the corner.

Tasmin caught his eye quickly, thankfully, and beckoned him after her. He followed her to the other side of the Hall, back towards the door, where Tasmin paused and grasped the shoulder of a nearby Scribe standing hunched under the lintel.

"Scribe Jorin," she said, and Lyam recognized him as he turned.

Jorin. The young Scribe he'd met last night.

Jorin spun to face Tasmin, and his eyes widened at the sight of Lyam standing next to her. He was tall, Lyam noticed, almost taller than him already, but hunched over, his shoulders bending forward. His sandy hair flopped into his eyes as he looked at Tasmin, and an expression of something close to panic crossed his round face.

"Don't worry," Tasmin told him gently. "You're not in trouble."

"Oh." Jorin's voice wobbled just a little, and he followed them over to a quieter corner of the room. He visibly swallowed. "Right. Um. How can I help you?"

"I wanted to introduce you to Scribe Lyam," Tasmin said and gestured Lyam closer.

Lyam felt a crease form in his brow, confused, but stepped up by Tasmin's side anyway. He gave a short bow to Jorin, keeping his features as smooth as he could.

Jorin bowed back, fumbling over his robes. "Oh, we actually already met last night."

"I'm just giving a formal introduction," Tasmin soothed, though Lyam sensed a bit of humor to her tone. "I actually want you two to get to know each other better."

Lyam shot her a look.

"Scribe Lyam," she addressed him directly. "I'd like for you to mentor Scribe Jorin."

Oh. Nerves tightened in Lyam's gut. Despite Lyam having been a Scribe for so many years, beaten only by Tasmin herself in his longevity, he'd never actually mentored someone before. He'd always been deemed too young.

"Are you sure?" He asked Tasmin uncertainly.

She nodded once. "You're eighteen now. You're ready."

Lyam wasn't so sure he agreed with her, but he had little room or time to complain. Mentoring was a great responsibility; he would have to teach Jorin everything, from the basics of how to watch over a Dreamer to how best to order his hut.

It was just the kind of added work that Lyam didn't need right now.

But he still turned to Jorin with a smile, remembering all too well his own first Scribe meeting, all those years ago when he'd only been a child. Jorin was older than Lyam had been then, most Scribes were, but he was still very young.

"In that case," Lyam said with a small smile directed at Jorin, "you'd better come with me."

Jorin's face crumpled in fear.

Tasmin grasped Lyam's shoulder, clutching on a little tighter than necessary. He turned to see her with a crease in her brow, her warm features marred by a frown.

"Be careful tonight," she murmured to him. "Things are darker than they seem."

Before Lyam could question her, she turned and walked away, back through the flickering lantern light into the darkness of the corridor.

Lyam bit his lip. There was an uneasy feeling in his gut, twisting up his insides.

"Um," Jorin spoke from next to Lyam, and Lyam turned to see him hunched over with his lower lip caught between his teeth. The air around them was warm from the lanterns, but the meeting room had practically emptied, most Scribes gone back to their work already. The call for a Vigilance would have changed everyone's plans, Lyam knew.

"What do we do now?" Jorin asked, his voice small.

"We wait," Lyam said, beckoning him to start walking towards the corridors. "We have until last bell to prepare. Tasmin just called a Vigilance, do you know what that is?"

Jorin shook his head.

"That's alright." Lyam led them down a familiar corridor in the Scribes' Hall, heading towards one of his favorite places; the library. "I can explain."

"Please," Jorin answered, his voice still small. "I really don't understand anything so far."

"When was your choosing?"

"Three days ago." Jorin bunched his hands in the front of his green robes, letting out a small laugh. "It feels like a lifetime ago, though. I don't even remember what I was like before Elinah's Dream."

"Elinah's the name of your Dreamer?"

"Yeah. She's eleven, and she's terrified. I didn't know her at all before we were chosen, so I don't know why the Life-Giver put her with me. I don't have a clue what I'm doing."

Lyam glanced sidelong at Jorin, considering, before he said ruefully, "You're not alone. When I was first placed with Anni, I thought she was so irritating. The knobbly-kneed, scabby little girl who lived around the corner from me and was always trying to make me play chase instead of reading was my Dreamer? It didn't feel real. I was sure there must have been a mistake."

Jorin sounded taken aback. "Really?"

"Really."

"But you and Dreamer Annelie are the youngest ever chosen!" Jorin stared at Lyam, pausing in the corridor open-mouthed. "I mean, aren't you the ones who've had the most Dreams Designed out of anyone? You've had the most influence over the Council aside from Dreamer Nethan, and that's only because he's older."

Lyam scratched awkwardly at his head, glancing away. He could feel the heat creeping up the back of his neck. Admiration wasn't something he was used to. His gold eyes had always marked him as different, and differences here equaled suspicion. He'd been quiet and reclusive his whole life. The absolute opposite of Annelie; she was vibrant and full of life, bouncing around demanding that he play with her or explore the tunnels with her or feed the tunnel cats morsels from their dinner. He felt a stab of affection at who she used to be before the Dreams took her away.

"I'm just saying," Lyam answered gruffly after an awkwardly long silence. "If Anni and I can do this, then so can you and Dreamer Elinah. It just takes time. The Life-Giver knows what they're doing, so trust in them and get to know her. It gets easier with time."

Jorin stood still for a moment, taking in those words, before Lyam started up the corridor again, beckoning Jorin after him. The lanterns were low here, flames protected so near the precious books, the green walls covered in shadow.

"Have you been back to see your family yet?" Lyam asked after another awkward silence as they approached the library door.

"I, uh...I wasn't sure if I was allowed."

Lyam paused in opening the door, turning to face Jorin completely. Jorin was looking down at the ground, his fingers bunched together. Lyam's heart went out to him. It wasn't easy being chosen, but to go through it at a time like this, when one of the Dreamers had just been attacked...

"You are allowed," Lyam answered patiently. "You have free rein to go anywhere in the city, but at night you have to be in your hut by your Dreamer's side. You have a meeting with your Designer once a week. You should arrange that directly with them. Have you met your Designer yet?"

Jorin nodded.

"Good." Lyam pulled open the door, beckoning him forward. "We'll have to be quiet in here, but I can explain everything a little easier if I have some references."

Jorin nodded again, following Lyam through the door. Lyam was proud at the look of astonishment that crossed Jorin's face as he entered the library for the first time.

The library was set in a cavernous room with stone walls and a glassy rocky finish, rising right up to the high ceiling sailing far above their heads, shrouded in darkness. Rows and rows of bookshelves, going in every direction, far higher than the top of even Jorin's head, lined the floor. There were chairs and benches and tables set at every turn, some filled with Scribes bending over books. Other Scribes were standing atop precarious ladders to reach the higher shelves. The earthy scent of ancient books accompanied by the rustling sound of pages being turned filled the air, but otherwise, the silence was oppressing.

"Here," Lyam whispered, reaching over to take one of the specialized lanterns for the library, adapted so that the flame was sheltered against the risk of fire. "Follow me."

Lyam's footsteps were loud, echoing between bookshelves. Jorin followed after him, sticking close, which Lyam was grateful for because it would be all too easy to lose him among the rows and rows of confining shelves.

Lyam took them through a confusing, twisting pathway, but one he knew all too well until he reached his favorite corner table. He set his lantern down and turned to Jorin. "Sit here while I get the books."

Jorin sat down uncertainly, perching on the very edge of the seat. Lyam hid a soft sigh and turned to the shelves.

It didn't take him long to gather what he needed, and he soon returned, setting a small pile of books in front of Jorin. "These will tell you the basics, but I'm going to talk you through it first and answer any questions."

"I have lots of those," Jorin mumbled, almost too quietly to be heard.

Lyam hid a smile. "I bet. Here." He slid a book across the table to Jorin, one of the smaller volumes. "This is your new best friend. It's a basic introduction for new Scribes. It runs through things like how to record Dreams and make sure your Dreamer is comfortable, how to make sure you get the right rations, and ensure your hut stays safe. No one enters the hut apart from you and your Dreamer, and you mustn't leave your hut at night except in exceptional circumstances."

A confused furrow appeared on Jorin's brow. "Excuse me, but you were out of your hut last night, weren't you? When you came to me?"

"Uh," Lyam hesitated, then gave a small laugh. "Exceptional circumstances. What happened to Rayah—that's highly unusual. With the Vigilance tonight, it's extremely important that you record everything that happens to your Dreamer, even down to the tiniest detail. Anything could help us at this point."

Jorin looked a little lost. "How do I even *do* that? How do I record her Dream?"

"You write it down. Everything that happens, you write it down."

"Everything?"

"Everything," Lyam agreed and handed him another book. "This one tells you some of the most frequently used systems for recording Dreams, but ultimately every Scribe is different. You write in the way that makes the most sense to you, and then you take it to your Designer."

Jorin looked down at the two books in front of him and took a deep breath. Lyam noticed that his fingers were trembling.

38

Lyam felt a tug near his heart. He wasn't cut out for this. He'd never mentored before, and he honestly wasn't very good at talking to anyone who wasn't Annelie, and yet Tasmin had given him this job *now*, at the very moment some unknown force had attacked one of their own. Right before a Vigilance, too. Lyam didn't know how to do this; he didn't know how to calm Jorin's nerves when Lyam's own fears were clamoring all-too-loudly in his ears.

But he had to try.

Taking in a slow breath, Lyam pulled up a chair beside Jorin and sat down next to him. "Look," he said softly. "I'm not going to pretend this is easy. Being a Scribe is hard, but it's worth it. We're the link between the Dreamers and the world, and we're their only connection to anything outside the hut. That, first and foremost, is our role—looking after our Dreamers."

Jorin stared at Lyam, fear creasing his smooth forehead. "I have no idea how to do that."

"It'll come with time," Lyam told him with confidence. "You were chosen for a reason. You're the only one with the right tools to care for your Dreamer, so you really can't get it wrong."

Jorin bit his lip, looking unconvinced. But Lyam didn't know what else to tell him.

"Tonight," Lyam continued, gruff with awkwardness, "things are a bit different. This isn't the easiest time to become a Scribe, but, well...I suppose we're going to have to work through it together." Lyam took in another slightly shaky breath. He was so bad at doing this. Annelie was going to laugh so hard when he told her about this later.

Jorin was looking terrified again. "What's so special about tonight?"

"It's a Vigilance."

"Everyone keeps saying that word to me, but I have no idea what it means."

Lyam allowed himself another small smile before he leaned over, extracting another book from the pile and flicking through a few pages. "It's a special ritual, one held only by Scribes. We watch over our Dreamers with even more care than usual, and we make sure to write down everything from the words they say to the slightest twitch of their fingers. We stay awake all night during a Vigilance."

Jorin swallowed. "You mean we don't stay awake every night? I thought you said we have to watch our Dreamer?"

"We do," Lyam explained gently. "But there's a difference between sleeping and Dreaming. When your Dreamer is asleep, you sleep. But when they Dream, you stay awake."

"How am I supposed to tell the difference?" Jorin asked despairingly.

Lyam thought back to Annelie, to her sweating and crying out in her sleep, to her back arching and the strange, suffocating heat that seemed to fill their hut whenever she Dreamed. The encroaching sense of not being alone and the knowledge that Annelie was somewhere far beyond his own reach.

Lyam swallowed. "You'll know."

Jorin still looked unconvinced.

Lyam closed the book again and gently leaned over, placing a calming hand on Jorin's shoulder—or at least, Lyam hoped it was calming. "Look. A lot of this seems overwhelming, I know, but most of it is just instinct."

"But I have no idea what I'm doing," Jorin whispered.

Lyam squeezed his shoulder. He didn't know how much comfort he could give, not when he didn't really feel like he knew what he was doing either, but Jorin was reminding him so starkly of Lyam himself when he was a new Scribe that he knew he had to try. Everything had been so new and frightening, and he'd been missing his family terribly, and he was supposed to care for someone who was basically a stranger.

He had to help however he could.

"Every Dream is different," Lyam started to explain quietly, eyes on his lap. "Every time Annelie sleeps, I'm scared that I'll miss something. And if I do miss something, then I could ruin the Designers' work and block the Dream from becoming reality, and that is terrifying.

"But I have to remember that it isn't my role to make sense of the Dreams. That's up to the Designers. They're the leaders, along with the Council members, and they're the people who make everything else run smoothly. All I have to do is write down what Annelie says and does."

Jorin opened and closed his mouth, clearly considering his next words carefully. "But you... I mean, you know what you're doing, right? You've been doing this for so long...."

"I wish I could tell you it gets easier," Lyam answered with a low chuckle. "It's just—it's hard. But you'll get to know your Dreamer and your Designer, and I promise you that it will come naturally. And in the meantime, I'll be here to guide you through."

Jorin sat quietly as he seemed to digest that, looking from Lyam back to the pile of books sitting in front of him.

"You'll be fine," Lyam said as confidently as he could, finally releasing Jorin's shoulder. "Be careful tonight, write down everything you possibly can, and come back to the meeting room at first bell. Tasmin will tell us what to do then."

Jorin nodded slowly.

Lyam didn't know what else he could do, so he just smiled back. "Come and knock at my hut if you need anything else. I'm there most of the time. Otherwise, just read these books. They should tell you most things you need to know."

Jorin managed a smile back at him. "Thank you. It really is an honor to meet you, Scribe Lyam." Jorin bowed his head formally.

Lyam smiled back awkwardly. "Um. Thanks, but I'm just— I'm just like any other Scribe here, really."

Jorin looked back up at him. He fidgeted for a moment before asking, "Were you really only nine when you were chosen?"

Lyam released a slow, careful breath and nodded.

Jorin let out a low whistle.

"It isn't that big of a deal," Lyam said, looking away awkwardly. Annelie caused more of a stir than he had, after all. She was only six when she had her first Dream.

"How did you cope with all this so young?"

"Tasmin was a good mentor. Besides, you can't be much older."

"I'm twelve," Jorin confirmed. "And I'm finding this hard enough."

"Having a good mentor is everything. I hope—I hope I can be a little help to you, at least in the beginning." Lyam fixed his gaze on the pile of books so he wouldn't have to meet Jorin's eyes. "Please, do ask me for anything you need, and I'll try my best to see to it."

Jorin nodded, still staring up at Lyam with something like awe.

Lyam tried not to grimace. He didn't like being the center of attention for long. He got to his feet. "If that's all for now...."

"Yes, yes, sorry," Jorin said hastily, spinning to reach for one of the books. "I'll just—I'll come to your hut if I have any other questions?"

"Yes," Lyam said thankfully, mustering up a smile. "I'll be there most of the day."

Jorin nodded, and Lyam watched him turn back to his books before making his own way out of the library.

CHAPTER
THREE

Most ancient of all are the Water-Gatherers.
They walk in the Sunlight to sustain us,
And we should worship them.
The Book of the Life-Giver, Vol. III, Chapter IV

After leaving Jorin in the library, Lyam dropped in to visit his own family, who lived in the western outskirts of the city in a small village, more like a suburb to the main city. The community was close-knit, and Lyam found himself being greeted with a nod and a smile by the few people he saw as he walked its familiar streets. He kept his eyes down; even here, their gold color still attracted stares.

As soon as he approached his childhood home, the door flew open, and his littlest sister, Kirah, came flying out to meet him.

"Lyam! Lyam!" She tumbled into him, her entire weight thrown into his stomach, so he doubled over with a muttered *oof*.

"Hey, Kiri. How're you doing?"

"Sairah took my meerkat!" Kirah's lower lip was wobbling,

but she was warm against him as he scooped her into his arms and started walking back towards the house.

"Your meerkat?"

"Daddy made him for me last week, and he's *mine*, but she took him!"

"That doesn't sound very fair."

"Mama won't listen," Kirah sniffed, and Lyam hummed in response as he ducked into the little home, smiling at the familiar surroundings.

The scent of baked bread and spices was present as always, permeating the air. The walls were sandy-brick and rough, dust always present despite his mother's best efforts, and the lanterns were lit and evenly placed, keeping the small rooms bright.

Lyam headed straight through to the kitchen, Kirah still attached to his hip. He found their mother standing at the stove, her back to him, hands busy over a pan. Sairah, older than Kirah by two years but still several years younger than Lyam, was sitting reading at the table. A glass figurine of a meerkat crafted with exquisite detail sat before her.

Kirah squealed as soon as she saw it. "*Mine!*"

"No," Sairah said patiently. "Daddy said it's for both of us."

"*Mine!*"

"You can't just take everything!"

"Girls," their mother tutted, turning with hands covered in flour, and broke into a wide smile when she saw Lyam. "By the Sun! You turned up out of nowhere!"

Lyam grinned, finding himself gathered into a tight hug while still holding a squirming Kirah. He was always shocked by how much taller he was than his mother now; she barely came up to his chin, and Lyam was by no means tall.

"How have you been?" His mother asked as she pulled away, instantly fussing over his hair and snatching his glasses off his face to give them a clean on the edge of her apron. "How's dear Annelie?"

"Well," Lyam answered, hesitating for a second. He put Kirah down to take his glasses back, watching as she immediately ran to Sairah to try and get a peek at her book, her dark hair done up in two buns bobbing as she went. Sairah sighed but made space for her and offered her the next page.

He didn't want to worry them with tales of what was really going on.

So he put on his best smile and bowed to his mother. "Really, mama, everything's going well. Anni's Dreams are tough, like always, but we're managing."

"Eating well? Sleeping?" His mother tutted, tugging at his green robes. "You've lost weight again."

"I'm fine, really. Where's dad?"

"In his workshop. You could pop your head in. He's always happy to see you."

"I'll do that."

He stayed in the kitchen for a little while, helping his sisters figure out some of the longer words in their book (one of the old myths; it was nice to see his father instilling the same love in them that he'd had as a child) before he kissed his mother on the cheek and went to his father's workshop, tucked out of the back of the house in its own self-contained little shed.

Lyam knocked lightly on the sandy door before he stepped inside. It was dim apart from the few furnaces blaring, the heat almost unbearable and smoke making him cough. Once his eyes adjusted, Lyam could make out his father's old workbench, placed where it always was, covered with sheets of glass waiting to be molded. Sand littered every surface, and his father's touch was everywhere—the delicate lantern cases, figurines at the desk, and detailed mosaics piled carefully in the corner.

"Hey, dad." Lyam leaned against the wall, watching as his father turned from where he'd been leaning over one of the furnaces.

His father hummed, as unruffled as ever, even while handling temperatures beyond anything Lyam could imagine. He watched as his father removed the glass and set it in the cooling tray, a hiss of steam rising up into the air, helping to clear Lyam's lungs from the smoke.

Only when the glass was fully secured did he turn to Lyam, his face kind, and his eyes warm. He held out a hand, and Lyam went to him instantly, wrapping him in a hug. His father had always been thin, but now he felt frail in Lyam's hold, almost like paper waiting to come apart.

"It's been too long." His father's voice was as even and gentle as ever, and Lyam grimaced with guilt.

"I know, I'm sorry. It's busy at the moment."

"Always busy, your life." His father smiled wryly, turning back to his workbench. "Tell me your stories. Everything."

So Lyam did. He settled on a bench beside his father and watched while he worked, entertaining him with tales of Annelie's latest Dreams. He wasn't technically supposed to talk about them other than with Mirah, but Lyam's father had been the one to encourage Lyam's love of stories. The least he could do was give some of his own back.

When he'd recounted everything up to the previous night, Lyam hesitated. Sharing his current worries with his father might not be the best idea. As much as Lyam wanted advice and someone to talk to, he didn't want to worry him. He knew his family already felt like the Dreams had ripped Lyam away from them. Lyam felt it too, at times like this when he came home and felt like a stranger. So, he didn't want to provide any more reason for them to fear for him.

His father always seemed to know when something was wrong.

"Tell me," he murmured into the silence, hands still patiently working the bellows.

Lyam swallowed. "It's nothing, dad, really. Ignore me."

"Doesn't seem like nothing when you're worrying about it so hard I can feel your thoughts from here."

Lyam bit back a laugh. He bunched his fingers in the stiff material of his robes and caved, telling his father about how Rayah had been attacked by something that no one seemed to understand and how he had to go through a Vigilance that night.

He also told him about Jorin and how Lyam was nervous about being a role model for someone else for the first time.

At that, his father chuckled. "You've been a role model for years, whether you know it or not."

"I have?"

"Your sisters think you single-handedly light up the Citadel, so I'd say so, yes."

Lyam stuttered. "Ah, that's just—that's just them, though."

"And your mother and I," he disagreed gently, pausing to meet Lyam's eyes. Lyam's father had brown eyes, as did his mother and sisters. Lyam's gold eyes were something of an anomaly. "We're proud of you—how hard you work, how much you clearly love that little rascal Annelie. She looks up to you too, I expect."

Lyam snorted. "I look up to her, more like."

"You're a team," his father agreed. "And like a team, you solve problems together. Work together, and you'll uncover what all of this is about. I have complete faith in the both of you, as the Life-Giver showed by choosing you. Trust in them, my child, and you won't go far wrong."

Lyam let those words linger in his mind as he said his good-byes and headed out of his family home. He let them take hold, growing firmer until he could maybe believe them. He trusted Annelie with his life, and the Life-Giver was their guide and protector; his father was right. As long as Lyam believed that, then everything would right itself again. It had to.

Lyam also dropped by Annelie's parents, as had become routine for him over the years. Their little house, set back behind one of the main tunnels through the city, felt as much his home as his own parents' house did. They asked him about their daughter, and he comforted them with what news he could.

It was a cruel, hard life, being a Dreamer. They knew it, and so did he, but he told them about how he'd caught Annelie sneaking another portion of her favorite snack and how she'd thrown a pillow at him when he told her off, and left out the parts where she writhed in the night, sweating from her Dreams.

It was when Lyam left the city through the South Gate and started the trek back to his hut that he heard a noise he shouldn't have.

Lyam paused, the lantern in his hand swinging. Shadows leaped across the tunnel's sandy walls, jumping up around him. He shrunk into himself and took a deep breath.

There was the sound of footsteps coming from his right.

Lyam stayed as still as he could, listening hard. No one else should be this deep in the tunnels; the only place this passage led was to his and Annelie's hut. Lyam's breath sounded loud in his ears, his chest tightening, his hand clenching around the handle of the lantern. He cradled it close to his body, sheltering it from sight, his own shadow looming behind him.

There was a scuffle, then a rustle, and then the definite sound of footsteps. Heading directly towards Lyam.

Lyam froze for one heart-stopping second, and then he was scrambling backward, feet slipping on the rough ground, stones stabbing his feet through his sandals.

A shape turned the corner in front of him, looming large.

Lyam squeaked, trapping a scream between his teeth. His back met the wall behind him, and he flattened himself against it, staring as the shape came closer and closer.

"It is true, then," sounded a low, booming voice, bouncing loud around the tunnel walls. "A Scribe with gold eyes."

Lyam stared in shock as the figure came closer, stepping into the lantern light. Strong features came into sight, a proud nose and a mouth set in a grim line, black skin darker than any Lyam had seen covered in long blue robes that billowed out around him as he strode determinedly forward.

As he came closer, Lyam noted that his eyes shone a bright, fierce gold.

The breath stopped in Lyam's throat.

Another one. Lyam had never seen anyone but himself who had gold eyes.

"Scribe Lyam," the man said, that low booming voice echoing around him again.

Lyam shivered. He forced his dry mouth to move, his voice sounding shaky and quiet. "Wh-who are you?"

A low chuckle. "Of course, you wouldn't recognize me."

Lyam stared at the man's giant, hulking form, bewildered, his heart thudding so loud in his throat he thought he might faint.

The man looked down at him, gold eyes glinting in the dull flame from Lyam's lantern. "You do not know the Water-Gatherers?"

Breathlessly, Lyam shook his head. He'd heard the name before, vaguely, read it somewhere in old books in the library, but not in common texts.

Another low chuckle came from the man. He took a step forward, and Lyam pressed as far back against the wall as he could, clutching his lantern in front of him.

The man paused. "Are you afraid of me?"

Lyam swallowed and nodded before he could think better of it.

Silence held for a moment while the man stood there, studying him. Lyam froze under that sharp, discerning gaze and held himself as still as he could, every limb trembling, his fingers clutched tight around his lantern. The heat swirled around him, the scented smoke from his lantern tickling the back of his throat. *Gold eyes. He has gold eyes too.*

"You don't need to be afraid," the man said slowly.

Lyam worked enough moisture into his mouth to ask again. "Who are you?"

"Enoch. You may call me Enoch."

The name was unfamiliar. Lyam wracked his brains, trying to think if he'd ever heard the name spoken anywhere, written anywhere, and couldn't recall it at all. *Strange.*

"I am the last of the Water-Gatherers," Enoch said lowly, his deep voice echoing in Lyam's bones. "Though I don't suppose that means anything to you. I had hoped—ah, well. The old ways grow ever distant."

"I'm sorry," Lyam replied, then paused to clear his throat. He

49

didn't believe it for a second; the Water-Gatherers existed only in myth. His mouth felt full of sandpaper. "Why did you come here?"

"Just to see you," Enoch answered easily. "To see if it was true. A gold-eyed Scribe."

"Is that important?"

Enoch studied him, his proud features softening just a little. For a moment, he looked like any other man Lyam might see around the city, aside from those fierce, piercing gold eyes.

"Do you know the old stories, Scribe Lyam?" Enoch asked quietly. "Of those with gold eyes?"

Lyam bit his lip. He'd heard the myths, of course, just like any other child, the stories of the ancient people who had lived above ground directly under the Life-Giver's beams. That was when everyone had been able to speak to the Sun, not just the Dreamers, but it was a myth and nothing more.

Lyam narrowed his eyes a little, taking his time with his answer. "I know the myths as well as anyone else."

"Oh, no," Enoch disagreed, "I think you know them better. I think you ask the right questions, or you will very soon."

Lyam stared, confusion creasing his brow.

"I came to give you this," Enoch said and stretched out his hand. His fingers were thick and long, completely enveloping Lyam's hand. Something heavy dropped into his palm.

"You'll find it in the library," Enoch said, taking a step back. His blue robes billowed around him as he turned. "Come find me once you've seen it."

Lyam swallowed, watching as Enoch walked through the tunnels in long strides, the shadows leaping around him. He had no idea what had just happened or who Enoch was, but something was making Lyam's heart thud loudly in his throat, his hands clenched tight around the lantern and whatever Enoch had given him.

Slowly, Lyam turned his hand over and opened his fingers. A key lay heavy in his palm, old and rusted, digging roughly into his skin.

He had no idea what it was for.

Slowly, Lyam closed his fist around the key again and turned to the passage that would take him to his hut and to Annelie. Maybe she knew something of this, although Lyam wasn't sure how. All he knew was that he didn't like the key; he didn't like that he had it when he had no idea what it was for. For all he knew, it could be dangerous.

He wet his lips nervously and headed for his hut.

§

B y the time Lyam got back, he found Annelie sitting among piles of parchment, a furrow in her brow. She had a scroll open in her lap, others scattered around her chair with still more rolling on the floor.

Lyam rolled his eyes as he hauled himself up the trapdoor, sitting on the ground for a moment to catch his breath.

"Shush," Annelie mumbled from her chair, eyes still fixed on the parchment in her lap.

"I haven't even said anything yet," Lyam grumbled good-naturedly. He felt weary, despite knowing he was going to have to stay up all night.

But one look over at Annelie reminded him of why it was worth it. Lyam's throat tightened as he remembered Rayah and Jemme's conspicuous absence from the meeting earlier. That could have been him. It could have been Annelie attacked, writhing in agony, or whatever had happened to Rayah. He couldn't even begin to imagine what that felt like.

His chest ached.

"There's something missing," Annelie mumbled, eyes fixed down on the scroll in her lap.

Lyam rolled himself over and got to his feet, taking care to close the trapdoor behind him. Then he moved to her side. "What do you mean?"

"I don't know." Annelie's lower lip was caught between her teeth, her hair in wild curls around her face. She had soft

51

features, a small frame, a body that wasn't built for the hard task it underwent every night. But Lyam knew not to underestimate her. There was strength behind her eyes.

He moved to sit next to her on her chair, and she shifted naturally to make space. Her soft blanket was comforting against Lyam's legs. He was tired from wearing his heavy robes all day.

"Look." Annelie shoved the scroll in her lap under Lyam's nose, gesturing to a passage. "Doesn't this sound... bad to you?"

Lyam read it back over. It was a note from one of Annelie's Dreams, one from late last week going by the date Lyam had written neatly in the margin. *I have seen you, but you have not seen me. There is no way forward.*

"I guess?" Lyam said and then placed a hand over the scrolls. "I need to tell you about what happened."

"I want to know. I just—this is really itching at me. We're missing something, I'm sure of it."

"Like what?"

Annelie shook her head. She placed the scroll down and picked up another one, her eyes flickering over the page faster than Lyam could follow. "I don't know. But there's *something*."

Lyam nodded, taking the scroll and glancing through it himself. He knew not to ignore Annelie's feelings. "Which part is bothering you?"

"I don't *know*." Annelie threw the scroll down and fell back on her chair, frustrated. "Just...all of it. None of it. Something's just *wrong*."

Lyam hummed, reaching out to run his fingers soothingly through her hair. She shifted until her head was laid in his lap and her eyes fell shut as she curled into a ball.

"What happened?" Annelie asked miserably. "Did you find anything out?"

Lyam shook his head with a sigh. "Nothing useful. Jemme wasn't at the meeting. I can tell that Tasmin is worried, though."

Annelie perked up at the mention of the Head Scribe. "You saw Tasmin?"

"Yes. You'll never guess what she's done."

Annelie twisted her head until she could look up at him, her eyes flicking open. "What?"

"Made me a mentor," Lyam answered and chuckled at Annelie's startled gasp.

She flew upright off his lap, twisting to stare at him. Then she burst out laughing. "*You*? A mentor?"

"I know," Lyam said wryly.

"*Why*? Did they finally decide it was time to reward all your years of hard work?"

"Hardly," Lyam grumbled, though he couldn't help but smile at the way Annelie was grinning, her crooked tooth glinting. "Punishing me for getting away without it for all these years, more like."

Annelie laughed again, the sound bright in the closed-off room. The heavy blinds at the window trapped the sound inside; with the trapdoor closed, the only source of light in the room were the two lamps that Lyam had set up in the corners, one by Annelie's chair and one by the trapdoor. His desk was next to the trapdoor on one of the colorful rugs.

"There's more," Lyam said quietly. "There's a Vigilance tonight."

The change was immediately noticeable. Annelie's face dropped, her soft features hardening, a furrow appearing in her brow. She turned to him with a deep frown. "*What*?"

"You can see why," Lyam tried to placate her. "Tasmin's worried about what happened to Rayah. There's no way of knowing that it won't happen again."

Annelie jutted out her jaw. "But exhausting all the Scribes isn't going to help! You're our best minds. we need you working on this!"

"I know. But think about it. A Vigilance will show us what really happens at night. If we all keep watch, then hopefully, we can find a pattern about what on earth is going on."

The words he'd left unsaid hung in the air between them. That he'd see exactly what happened to Annelie every night; that he'd have to witness her screams and writhing, her suffering, and be unable to do anything about it.

Lyam hated it. Annelie knew he did. There was nothing either of them could do about it.

"It'll be ok," Lyam continued, watching the furrow deepen in her brow. "I'll be fine."

Annelie let out a frustrated sigh, turning to him, her hands balled into fists in her lap. "You *won't* be, though, Lyam. You know you won't be."

Lyam bit his lip. The last time there'd been a Vigilance, he'd been absent for days, his mind wandering as he tried to catch up on sleep. It took almost a full week for him to recover.

But still. He had little choice.

"I'll be fine," Lyam said again.

Annelie didn't believe him. Lyam wasn't one hundred percent sure he did, either.

৯

T he Vigilance was hard.

Annelie stayed awake for as long as she could, staving off sleep to sit up with Lyam instead. They played games, cards and stones and marbles littering the floor. Lyam helped Annelie off her chair and over to his desk, her leaning heavily on his arm as he gently steered her across their small room, taking most of her weight. She beat him fourteen out of seventeen games.

But eventually, sleep caught up with her. Lyam could see it in the tightness of the skin around her eyes, the way she stooped a little in her seat, back bowing under the weight of the day. Night had crept in around them, the candles in the lanterns burning low.

Annelie held it off for as long as she could, but eventually, Lyam called a halt. He placed down his hand of cards and reached across to prod her lightly in the arm. "Come on, Anni. It's time."

"I can stay awake a little longer," she argued, but the croak in her voice was audible.

Lyam shook his head. He got to his feet, dressed back in his simple tunic, and crossed the table, holding out his arm to her. "Come on."

"I'm fine."

Lyam looked at her, feeling his eyes soften. She seemed so determined, her arms crossed across her chest, her eyes fixed firmly on the table, the game splayed out between them.

"It's ok," Lyam insisted. "I was losing anyway. Come on."

It took another few moments of Annelie staring at him stubbornly before she relented. She got to her feet with his help and leaned on him heavily, almost stumbling. Lyam waited until she had her feet under her before steering her back towards her chair. Parchments rolled away from their feet; Lyam made a note to clean them up later.

He got Annelie back up onto her chair and leaned her backward, lifting her feet for her when she grew too tired. He drew the blanket up around her when she reached for it and placed a glass of clear water by her that she could reach without sitting up.

Annelie watched him tiredly as Lyam set about tidying their hut, bringing the piles of parchments back together and placing them on their shelves (out of order, but he'd sort that out later). "Are you really going to be ok?"

Lyam could already feel his eyelids itching, but he nodded his head anyway. "I'll do my best."

Annelie bit her lip, watching him as he came to settle back by her bedside. "At least change your clothes."

"I'm comfy enough in this. Worry about yourself, not me."

Annelie shook her head. She glanced away, her fingers tangling in the soft blanket. "Promise me one thing?"

Lyam looked up from where he was peeling a fresh sheet of parchment out of the pile. "Of course. What is it?"

"Stop if it gets too much." Annelie's tone was low but commanding. "If you need to look away, look away."

Lyam paused. He glanced over at her, noting the way her brow was furrowed, her hair—tamed a little—falling down around her shoulders, the soft white robes she slept in hanging around her collarbones.

He reached over and took her hand.

"It's my job, Anni," Lyam murmured. "I want to look out for you."

"Just promise me," she insisted, looking him right in the eyes.

Despite caring for her since they were children, Lyam still found it difficult sometimes to hold Annelie's gaze. There was a burning behind her eyes, a strength to her expression that it could be difficult to hold.

Lyam held it this time. "I promise."

"Good." Annelie lay back, balling her hands into tight fists around the blanket. "I'll know if you don't."

"You'll be too busy Dreaming," Lyam disagreed, but he was smiling as he reached out to tuck her in, not too tight, so she had the freedom to move. "We've got to try for some answers. Maybe something to help Rayah."

"I know." Annelie's voice grew heavy as she stared down at her hands. "It's hard, though. Lately, it's like—"

Lyam watched her closely and noted the way her eyes were downcast, how her shoulders bowed.

"Like what?" Lyam prompted softly after a moment.

Annelie sighed. "I don't know. Like the Life-Giver is further away. Not displeased, I know...not displeased. Just... distant. It's hard."

"Hard to Dream?" Lyam asked. "Could that be what happened to Rayah?"

Annelie shook her head quickly, shuddering. "No. Not that. I felt that. This is just..." she sighed, shaking her head. "Never mind. I don't know yet, but I'm hoping I'll find out."

"Be careful," Lyam warned and squeezed her hand once before releasing it.

Annelie smiled at him faintly.

It took a long while for Annelie to sleep. She drifted in and out a few times, her eyes falling closed and her body curling inwards for only a few minutes at a time before she was blinking awake again. Lyam tried to encourage her, softly humming her favorite lullabies, and eventually, it worked.

He knew she was in deep sleep when she went almost completely still. With a heavy heart, Lyam pulled the fresh parchment towards himself and reached for his pen.

The Vigilance had begun.

PART TWO

PART TWO

THE THREE FALLEN

The scene was familiar almost as soon as Annelie opened her eyes.

She hung suspended in the black vacuum, the Life-Giver's burning surface looming before her. The flames shot high in the air, reds and oranges and yellows and pinks. From here, she couldn't feel their heat or smell the incensed smoke they gave off.

Around her, the other Dreamers popped into view. She took pleasure in their familiar presence, feeling the glowing orbs close by, sensing their emotions. Charis, who was nervous, and Kiran as bold as ever, ready to dive straight for the surface. Nethan was one of the first to pop up, the new Dreamer Elinah closely following him and sticking to his side.

Annelie stayed with them, waiting for all of them to pop into view. As soon as they were all but one in number, she could feel the sense of anticipation, the urge to wait a little longer in case the impossible happened and Rayah reappeared.

But they all felt what happened the previous night.

Annelie swallowed down her fear and started to inch her way closer to the Life-Giver. Movement was easier in the Dreams than it was in reality; her body responded more easily to her commands, flying *through the vacuum until she was close enough that the tops of the highest flames were brushing her bare feet.*

Annelie paused and tried to remember the ritual. Life-Giver, Great One, I seek entry—

No, child.

The voice rocked Annelie to the core, as it always did. She took a deep breath, absorbing the voice, letting it rattle in her ribcage as she welcomed the Life-Giver in. I just want to come and talk to you.

You are always welcome. But you don't need such false words. Come to me as you are, daughter; that is all I ask.

Annelie swallowed. Breaking ritual wasn't allowed, technically, but... she hated remembering the lines anyway, always feeling false when she spoke them. So she spoke from her heart. I want to talk to you about Rayah.

Ah. *The voice grew heavy with sadness.* **I wondered how long it would take.**

What happened? Can you tell me?

I fear the answer.

You? Fear?

Gods have as much to fear as mortals, my child. Perhaps more. I am nothing without you.

That's not true.

No? *The Life-Giver almost sounded amused.* **Have you ever wondered what I do when you are not here?**

Annelie went still. ...No. I suppose I haven't.

That's the problem. I am nothing when you are not here.

Annelie swallowed, struggling to believe what she was hearing. She moved a little closer, the flames parting under her, making a safe pathway for her to descend. She sensed a few of her fellow Dreamers drift down, too, Nethan and Kiran and even Elinah. Just three seemed to hang back.

Her feet landed, and she felt grounded, surrounded by the delicious heat and powerful, incensed smoke of the Life-Giver once again. Her skin crisped, the flames licking up her arms, curling around her fingers, and she smiled, running the tip of one of the flames across her knuckles.

This is how it should be. The Life-Giver's voice was almost full of... yearning.

It can be like this whenever we Dream.

The Life-Giver's sigh rocked through Annelie's body, weariness seeping into her very bones. She crouched on the surface, cradled by dancing fire. What happened last night? Is Rayah ok? Will she heal?

She may.

Why was she attacked? What even was it that attacked her?

Search for answers among your own. The Life-Giver's voice became almost harsh. Annelie flinched. *The ones you need to question are not here.*

What do you mean?

Do not seek your salvation here. I am not responsible for the actions of my people.

I don't understand?

I fear you don't have much time left.

As those ominous words vibrated through Annelie, the air shifted, seeming to change again. Dread shuddered through her when she saw that same inky darkness as before pulsing at the corners of her vision, wrapping between the dancing flames like unnatural shadows. Cold seeped through the air, such a stark contrast to the achingly bright heat of the Life-Giver that Annelie shot straight to her feet, backing away.

What is that?

The fruits of many years' corruption. The Life-Giver sounded sad—distant. *Go now, daughter. It is no longer safe for your kind here.*

But...but Life-Giver—

Go. The Life-Giver's voice turned harsh, the flames becoming thin and whip-like, lashing against Annelie's skin until she was literally beaten back. *Now. Leave, daughter, and do not come back.*

But—

GO.

The power that jolted Annelie out of place was stronger than anything she'd felt before. She was knocked off her feet, her joints rattling as she was wrenched up and out from the Life-Giver's surface and back into the vacuum. Annelie shrieked, writhing against her invisible bonds.

All around her, she could see her fellow Dreamers in similar states. Nethan seemed to be calm, but Elinah was crying, and Kiran was shouting if the brightness of his orb was anything to go by. Annelie tried to reach out to them, but the clamor of their cries was too great.

The three who hadn't landed on the surface—Charis she recognized, and one might have been Imri—were the only ones not fighting. They must be far enough away to remain unaffected.

The inky blackness that swept across the Life-Giver's surface followed the Dreamers as they were ejected. Annelie shuddered in horror, watching as thick, dark tendrils reached up into the vacuum, blacker even than the vacuum itself. She could feel their cold power even from this distance. The tendrils moved rapidly, climbing like vines up invisible poles, following paths that she couldn't trace. She shot backward as fast as she could, everything in her begging to get away from them.

The other Dreamers withdrew, scattering in disarray, but the three that hadn't landed on the Life-Giver's surface weren't quick enough.

The blackness reached them before she could even cry out a warning.

NO! She shouted with all her might, feeling her fellow Dreamers calling out too, clamoring for their own who were disappearing rapidly as the tendrils took hold. Blackness wound around their orbs like snakes, leeching all the light from them until they grew dimmer and smaller, terrifyingly quickly.

It was over in seconds; the blackness had swallowed them whole.

Annelie screamed until her throat was raw, and she was still screaming as she was pulled out of her Dream and back into the waking world.

CHAPTER

FOUR

The System is essential:
Dreamer – Scribe – Designer.
These are the three sacred tasks to serve the Life-Giver,
And none shall disturb the perfect balance between the three.
The Book of the Life-Giver, Vol. I, Chapter I

The Vigilance was tough on Lyam.

Tiredness weighed him down until it was difficult to physically move. His limbs felt full of lead, his eyes itching behind his glasses, the pen slipping from his hand as he caught himself nodding. The hours of the night seemed endless when he was the only one awake.

Things changed when Annelie began Dreaming.

Lyam always struggled to watch Annelie Dreaming. Lyam knew it was a thousand times worse for her to go through it and was forever thankful that his choosing had placed him as a Scribe instead, but it was never easy to watch.

Her body started to twitch, her hands curling and uncurling

into fists so tight that she would have scratched herself if it wasn't for Lyam gently catching them in his. She writhed in her chair, face screwed up in pain.

Sometimes, on strong nights, Lyam could sense the Life-Giver's presence. He could see it in the hazy glow that sometimes appeared to wrap around Annelie's body or the faint smell of ash and incense that occasionally filled their small hut.

On normal nights, Lyam would watch over her and write down what words Annelie mumbled to herself, but he wouldn't have to stay awake and watch over her when she wasn't Dreaming. He could catch his own sleep, only waking if she cried out for him, and after so many years, his body was attuned to when she needed him.

But not during a Vigilance.

He was yawning after the first few hours, his head feeling stuffed full of cloth, but he forced himself to remain upright. He noted down every single detail—every time Annelie so much as twitched, or muttered, or let out a little cry. Dreaming took a toll on her.

And then she started to scream.

Instantly, Lyam leapt off his bench and leaned over her, eyes wide. Annelie's face was screwed up, her eyes still shut tight, her lips pulled back in terror. Her back arched, spine bending at an almost inhuman angle until Lyam heard a terrifying crack. Fear gripped him as he reached for her, but she fought him even in her sleep.

She was still screaming.

Lyam tried calling her name, cupping her face between his hands, but nothing helped. She continued to jerk, her features contorting. The sharp smell of burning entered the air, and a light grew around Annelie, coating her in bright white until Lyam was afraid to hold her.

But he didn't let go. He grasped for her hands when she jerked out of his hold, cradling her as close as he could, the parchment forgotten behind him.

She thrashed for a moment more, struggling, before her eyes

flew open, and she launched herself at him, nails digging into his arms. "Go!"

Lyam startled, almost dropping her if it wasn't for her fingers fastened on his skin. She didn't let up for a second, screeching, "Go, go, you have to go!"

"What?"

"You have to!" Annelie was sobbing, her frail frame trembling in his arms. "*Please*, Lyam—Lyam, there were three of them, *three.*"

"Three what?"

"Like Rayah. Three were attacked, just like Rayah."

Lyam felt as if a bucket of freezing water had been thrown over his head.

"Three?" he whispered, hardly daring to believe it. He must have heard wrong, surely.

"Charis," Annelie cried, her breath coming in loud, panicked gasps. "Imri, I think. I don't know—I didn't see the third. I can't —Lyam, you have to *go*, please! Nethan will know. Go to Nethan, *please*. I know he was there. I know he'll know what to do."

Lyam rocked her close, shock holding him in place. Only his natural instinct to comfort Annelie honed over their many years together kept him going.

"Tasmin," he agreed. "I'll go to Tasmin."

"*Please.*" Annelie's tears had made the front of Lyam's tunic damp. He could feel his own eyes stinging, a hard lump sitting in his throat. "You have to help them. Their Scribes..."

Lyam shuddered. He didn't want to think about it; three more Scribes watching their Dreamers rot before them. "I'm going now."

Annelie grabbed his tunic before he could get far. She was trembling, fear written all over her face. "You'll... you'll be back?"

Lyam melted. He gripped her hand tight and pressed their foreheads together, wishing not for the first time that he could just bring her with him. But no, Dreamers were forbidden from leaving their huts, too sacred and fragile to mix with the rest of the world.

Although Annelie was the furthest from fragile that Lyam had ever seen.

"I'll be back by nightfall," he promised. "Before you Dream again. I wish—"

"I know. I want to come with you too."

"One day, maybe."

She hiccoughed out a laugh. They both knew it was a futile wish.

Lyam kissed her forehead, feeling her clutch onto his hand before he stepped back and away, leaving her small and alone on the bed.

❧

T asmin looked exhausted when she answered the door to him.

"Three, I know," she murmured, bent down over her desk. Her office in the Scribes' Hall was quiet so early—Lyam had been half-worried about finding her here, unsure whether or not she'd still be with her own Dreamer. But she'd waved him in as soon as he'd arrived.

"How did you know?" Lyam asked, settling into one of the seats opposite her desk.

"Nethan Dreamed," she answered and drew a hand across her face. "I'm assuming Annelie did too, or you wouldn't be here."

Lyam nodded. His fingers were tight on the edge of the seat. "I know I technically shouldn't have left her during a Vigilance, but—"

"No, no," Tasmin waved him away instantly. "Some things are more important than the rules. What did Annelie see?"

"Three more Dreamers have been attacked."

Tasmin nodded heavily. "Nethan said the same. He urged me here as fast as he could. I think he knew you'd be coming."

"Probably." Lyam scratched at the back of his head and wondered again what Nethan looked like. All he knew was that

Nethan had been Dreaming the longest of any of them, longer even than Annelie, and that Annelie always spoke fondly of him.

"I'm going to call the meeting now," Tasmin said, moving towards the door. "I'll fetch the bell-ringer, but there's no need to wait. You can continue straight from here."

"But what do I do? Three more, Tasmin, *three*—"

"I know," she said in a low voice and met his eyes dead-on. "That's why I'm breaking ritual. Go to your Designer, Lyam, as soon as you can. Now, if you can manage it."

Lyam's heart stuttered. *"Now?"*

"It's a state of emergency. Four of our Dreamers have been attacked by something we don't understand. We can't keep this to ourselves any longer."

Lyam's mouth felt dry. He'd never gone to Mirah outside of their weekly meetings before, not even when he was a child. The rules had always been very clearly in place, and he knew how to follow them, how to keep his head down and stay out of trouble.

He'd never done anything like this before.

"Here," Tasmin told him, pausing to scribble a note from her desk. She handed it to him, her soft features unusually sharp. "Show this to your Designer if she gives you any trouble. She'll be in her office by now, Lyam—go, and quickly. I don't want the whole city suddenly noticing Scribes in places where they shouldn't be."

Lyam scrambled to his feet, taking the note and clutching it in his sweaty palm. "Of course. I'll... I'll be as discrete as I can."

He left Tasmin's office with trepidation sitting low in his stomach.

Exiting the Scribes' Hall was easy enough, but the trip through the city to the Designers' Court was harder. Lyam dodged as many people as he could, walking through as many small alleys as possible and avoiding the main streets that were already filling up with donkey-drawn carts and palanquins despite the early hour. The lanternlight filled his path with leaping shadows, and he hurried his footsteps, keeping his head down low. The green of his robes gave him away, but he hoped not too many people saw him. If anyone was out, they were mostly busy with their own business and thankfully left him alone.

Getting to the actual Designers' Court itself was more difficult. It was a large, grand building situated in the main square of the city, directly opposite the Citadel itself with all its shining, reflective glass. Lyam never enjoyed his visits here, always feeling far too conspicuous when he was walking through the giant grand doors, but after years of visiting once a week, he knew his preferred way in—a servants' entrance near the back.

Mirah's office was up on the second floor. She had a window overlooking the square and the Citadel, letting light into the wide room, thin streams of reflected beams from the Citadel dancing with the shadows in the corners of the room. Mirah herself was seated behind her wide glass desk, her attention fixed on the pile of scrolls before her. She was painfully thin, her straight hair tied back out of her face, emphasizing her hollow cheeks. She looked as present and sturdy as always.

Lyam knocked once on the door, hovering in the frame while Mirah looked up. Her tired expression shifted into one of surprise, and she immediately set aside her parchment and beckoned him in.

Lyam made sure to close the door behind him before taking a seat opposite her.

"Lyam?" Mirah's musical, warm voice was an instant source of comfort to the worries flitting about Lyam's head. "This isn't our usual time to meet."

"I know, I'm sorry." Lyam forced himself to speak slowly, despite the way his fingers were digging into the sides of his chair and how his throat felt like it was constricting. "I have bad news."

Mirah looked at him curiously.

"You might not believe me," Lyam continued carefully, "but something awful is happening to the Dreamers."

"The Dreamers?" Mirah tilted her head, confusion etched into her brow.

"Four of them have been attacked. I don't know how or why —it was Dreamer Rayah first, and then last night three more. Tasmin sent me straight here as soon as I told her."

"Attacked?" Mirah frowned. "What do you mean, attacked?"

"I don't know. They just—Scribe Jemme said it was like rotting."

Mirah leveled him with a serious look. One Lyam had only seen her wear a few times. She folded her hands on top of her desk and leaned in as close as she could. "Tell me everything."

So Lyam did. He told her all about how Jemme had come to him in the night alone, how he'd helped spread word to the other Dreamers—how Tasmin had called a Vigilance, and then that morning, how Annelie had screamed, how he'd gone straight to Tasmin and how she'd sent him here.

Mirah took this all in her stride. She occasionally made him stop and repeat things, and she grabbed her own personal notebook and wrote a few things down. The more Lyam told her, the more relieved he felt. The Designers would be able to fix things.

He was weary by the time he finished talking. Mirah gave him a long, grave look, her thin lips pursed.

Silence held between them.

"Who else knows about this?" She asked after a moment.

Lyam shook his head, sitting back in his chair with a sigh. "I don't know. Tasmin. Dreamer Nethan and anyone else whose Dreamers saw everything. The Scribes from the meeting yesterday know some of it."

Mirah tapped her finger on the edge of her desk, considering, and Lyam felt a weight lift off his shoulders. He wasn't alone anymore.

Except he hadn't told Mirah about his strange encounter with Enoch, the man he hadn't recognized at all. Lyam wasn't sure why, but he didn't want to tell anyone about that yet. At least not until he knew a little more. He needed to figure out what the key Enoch had given him was for first.

"I'll go to the Citadel," Mirah said finally. "Izani will be there."

At the name of the Head Designer, Lyam relaxed. He sat back in his seat, bunching the stiff green material of his robes together. "Do you think he'll help?"

"I think he'll have a better idea of how to proceed," Mirah answered. Lyam watched her as she wrote something else down, her glass pen clicking against the rings she wore.

"Will the other Designers report to him too?"

Mirah glanced up at Lyam, tilting her head. "The other Designers?"

Lyam nodded. "I think Tasmin is going to call an emergency meeting to tell everyone to see their Designers."

Mirah looked horrified. "Why is she doing that? Everyone's going to panic!"

"I-I don't know what else we can *do*. Scribes aren't built to deal with this kind of thing, Mirah. None of us know what we're doing. You should have seen the last meeting. It was chaos."

"I thought as much."

"We just don't know what to do." Lyam glanced away. "We're all a bit scared. Well, more than a bit, actually. Ever since Jemme told me what happened to Rayah, it feels like I haven't been thinking straight."

Everything had moved too quickly. Lyam felt like he hadn't had a chance to breathe, hadn't had a moment to gather himself or properly check in with Annelie. The memory of her screams that morning still tugged at his bones. He itched to return to her.

"What exactly did Jemme say, again?" Mirah asked, pen poised over her notebook.

"There was a smell of rotting, and Dreamer Rayah's skin had turned black," Lyam answered, shuddering. "But it was the look on Jemme's face that scared me more." She'd been so afraid, he remembered, breaking one of their most sacred rules just to warn everyone else.

Mirah placed her pen down and snapped her notebook shut, glancing towards the pendulum clock on her desk. "Do you think Tasmin will have called the meeting yet?"

"Probably," Lyam answered. "She was about to do it when I came here."

Mirah cursed. "Then Izani will be flooded with concerned Designers soon. I'll go to him now. We'll think of something, Lyam, don't worry."

Lyam licked his parched lips and tried to look comforted. He still didn't know what he was going to do that evening when he had to coax Annelie into another sleep and watch her be ripped apart by her Dreams again. Fear clutched at his heart. If more Dreamers had suffered the night before, what was to stop Annelie from being next?

For a moment, his blood ran cold.

"What do I do, Mirah?" Lyam asked miserably. "Annelie has to Dream again tonight. What do I do?"

Mirah sighed, meeting his eyes. The look on her face was drawn and tired, but she reached over and patted the back of his hand, all the same, her skin smooth and cool. "Do your best. Stay with her. How is she?"

"Worried," Lyam answered honestly. "And she was a mess this morning. It was..." he paused, shuddered. "It was one of the worst Dreams I've seen her have in years."

"Get back to her side, then," Mirah responded, her musical voice soft. "She'll need you right now. Give her my love, won't you?"

Lyam nodded. It struck him as odd, then, how Mirah and Annelie had never met, the two most important people in his life, and he acted as a bridge between them—as he was supposed to.

Sometimes, it felt a little cold, how distant Annelie was from the rest of his life when she was his reason for living. He knew she got lonely sometimes, but they'd both been chosen at such young ages that she could barely remember her family. Sometimes, she'd get a distant look in her eye or grow still and silent for a while, but she always returned to her bright, bubbly self without much difficulty.

Still.

Lyam shook his head, smiling at Mirah instead. "I will."

"And stay close to her. I'll go straight to Izani, but it'll be hard to keep this quiet. Make sure not to tell anyone anything yet. Until we know what's going on, we can't risk word getting out. If people knew something is happening to the Dreamers—"

Mirah didn't need to finish her sentence. Lyam knew.

"I won't tell a soul."

"Good. Stay with Dreamer Annelie. I'll summon you as soon as I hear news."

Lyam nodded. He stretched, his eyelids feeling heavy. He'd be lucky to make it through the day without sleep claiming him, but at the same time, his body thrummed with nerves, with the constant underlying knowledge that something was *wrong*. Too many strange things had happened lately.

He rose from his seat, comforted a little by Mirah's parting smile. But nerves still stirred heavily in his stomach as he left her office.

CHAPTER
FIVE

Scribes may be permitted to visit their family only when strictly necessary.
Their role is to serve their Dreamer,
And to assist their Designer.
There is no greater obligation.
The Book of the Life-Giver, Volume II, Chapter IV

On his way back to his hut, Lyam was accosted by an increasingly-familiar figure.

"Scribe Lyam!"

Lyam turned, surprised, and found Jorin running up to him, out of breath, his green robes flapping at his sides.

"Elinah said I'd find you here," Jorin panted as soon as he was within earshot, skidding to a stop on the dusty ground just before Lyam. "She said I had to get you to take me to the library."

Lyam blinked. "The library?"

Jorin nodded. He still looked too gangly for his own body, his wide smile showing a gap between his front teeth. "Elinah said to go there, that it was important. I don't know why, exactly. I mean, I still have some of the books you gave me last time to read, but—"

"You're reading them?" Lyam asked quietly, impressed.

"All of them! Well, I've got through four, but I promise I will get to the others—"

"That's good," Lyam murmured, leading them across the square and back towards the Scribes' Hall, weaving in and out of the crowds. "I gave you a rather large pile."

"They're interesting," Jorin hastened to say. His strides were long, his lanky body already almost taller than Lyam. "I like it. Learning about the history of the Dreamers and how they've shaped our people. The Designers have been working for centuries down here, building our tunnels and our homes. I never realized."

"You didn't?" Lyam asked, surprised.

Jorin shook his head. "My father's a farmer. I thought people like him were the ones who built our world, but I was wrong. It's all the Designers, and because of what the Dreamers tell them."

Lyam nodded, thinking that over. He'd forgotten what it was like, out there in the city away from the Dreams. How removed they were, how much the people of the city could move on with their lives without thinking of the Dreamers on the outskirts who were responsible for their every move, the Life-Giver's gifts the only reason any of them could survive. Apart from the people who had been chosen or their families. Lyam thought of his own little sisters, who he didn't see anywhere near as much as he'd like, and Annelie's parents, who hadn't seen their only child since she was six years old.

Lyam turned his thoughts away before they grew too harsh.

"What about your mother?" Lyam asked Jorin as they approached the Hall.

"Oh," Jorin paused for a moment. "She, uh—she passed away three years ago."

Lyam's heart tugged. "I'm sorry."

"It's ok," Jorin assured him, his voice far too stable. "She had the red sickness. There wasn't anything the healers could do. My father looks after my brother and me—or, he used to. I haven't actually seen them since my choosing yet."

"You haven't?"

Jorin shook his head ruefully. "I, uh—Elinah hasn't been settling very well. I don't like leaving her side."

Understanding settled in Lyam's chest. "Is she having trouble adjusting?"

Jorin nodded.

"That makes sense," Lyam said, leading the way past the black-clad guards at the entrance to the Hall. "But you should visit them. I'm sure you want to, and Elinah will settle eventually."

"I hope so," Jorin answered, his voice lined with worry. "I don't like seeing her like this."

Lyam bit back his answer, thinking back to when Annelie was new to Dreaming. They'd been so young, barely old enough to understand that they could never live in the city again. If Tasmin hadn't been there for him, Lyam thought he would have given up long ago. She checked on him every morning without fail, teaching him how to care for Annelie when she screamed and cried and when she trembled with a power her small form couldn't contain—when she was so afraid of sleeping that she'd try and fight her own body every evening.

"It gets easier," Lyam told Jorin, his voice steady. "The Life-Giver is gentle, as gentle as possible. Elinah will be ok, and so will you."

Jorin turned his head to give Lyam a gap-toothed smile, brightening up his whole face.

Lyam smiled back, though it was small. He wished he believed his own words. It was true that Annelie was a lot better now, but it had taken a long time, and now the fear of the night had returned.

The Hall was quiet, eerily so. Lyam tried to ignore the heavy trepidation in his gut as he led Jorin through the small, winding passages. The lack of other Scribes was noticeable, and Lyam guessed everyone was too afraid to leave their Dreamer at this point.

When Lyam shouldered open the heavy door to the library, no one else was in there. The usually silent room was utterly dead, the air thick and heavy with the musty smell of books. The shelves rose eerily to the ceiling, and a place Lyam usually found comforting caused alarm bells to ring in his head.

With Jorin close on his heels, Lyam carefully stepped inside, his footsteps echoing up to the ceiling high above their heads, muffled by the rows and rows of scrolls and books that met them. Lyam was still weighed down with tiredness as he turned to Jorin, murmuring as quietly as possible, "what did you want to look for?"

"I'm not sure," Jorin spoke louder and flinched at the residual echoes. "I like history, though. Reading about the first Dreamers we have records of."

"History?" Lyam murmured, leading them to that section of the library, in one of the many rows on the left-hand side. "There's plenty of that here."

"Amazing," Jorin half-whispered at Lyam's elbow as they entered the aisle, the books and scrolls rearing up high above their heads.

Lyam smiled, sensing Jorin's fingers itching. "Pick out anything you want."

That seemed to be all the permission Jorin needed, as in the next second, he was off down the aisle, fingers brushing over the titles on the shelves.

Lyam settled himself at a table at the edge of the aisle, content to watch as Jorin marveled over the books. He rubbed his eyes, his limbs heavy, and he was tempted to simply lay his head down on the desk in front of him and close his eyes and sleep. But Jorin was his responsibility, so Lyam forced himself to stay upright, his back stiff and sore.

Jorin was immersed in manuscripts, so Lyam allowed his thoughts to wander, his eyes idly taking in the familiar shelves around them. Lyam had spent so much time in this library over the years that he knew the books Jorin was picking just by sight, had read a fair few of them himself. Sometimes he read them aloud to Annelie, too, to help soothe her at night—at least, the ones he was allowed to take from the library. Some manuscripts were too old or too damaged to leave the Hall. Lyam did his best to memorize his favorite pages from them so that he could tell Annelie what he'd found when he returned.

It felt like a long time since he'd been at peace enough to spend time here, hours melting away in the pages of books. It may have only been two nights since Jemme had come knocking on his door, but Lyam felt as though his whole world had turned upside down. He remembered the fear in Jemme's eyes, the haunted look on her face, and shuddered. He didn't want that to happen to anyone else.

But now, the Designers were taking care of it. Lyam had done his bit, had told Mirah everything, and she was taking it to the Citadel, to the Head Designer and the Council. Perhaps even the Speaker would hear of it. It was out of his hands now.

He just had to do whatever he could to keep Annelie safe.

"Can I take these back with me?"

Jorin's voice broke into Lyam's thoughts, and he gave himself a tired shake, blinking up to find Jorin standing before him with a pile of books in his arms.

Lyam smiled at him. "I see you've found some things you like."

"There's a lot of interesting stuff here," Jorin defended himself, his cheeks darkening a little. "I've never even heard of some of these books."

Lyam scanned the titles Jorin had found, finding them all to be old, telling of the history of their civilization, the old workings of their underground city.

"You can take most of these," Lyam said, standing, "but not this one." He took the one off the top of Jorin's pile, handling it with great care. "It's too damaged. But if you're interested, there's some older stuff at the back of the library. You might find something there you can take back with you."

"Older stuff?" Jorin's eyes brightened. "I didn't realize anything *was* older than this."

"It's mostly myths," Lyam answered. "But I like them."

The shine in Jorin's eyes was all the answer Lyam needed. With an amused smile, he got to his feet and led Jorin out of the aisle, turning left at the end.

It was darker back here, the lantern brackets less frequent in the walls. The texts towards the back of the library were much older, the smell of musty parchment almost overpowering. Their footsteps echoed loud in the empty library, the shadows leaping around them. Jorin held his lantern close.

"Here," Lyam murmured, directing them down the farthest shelf on the left. He hadn't been down here in years, had little reason to. The myths were interesting to read but not terribly relevant to life as a Scribe. His work had led him down more sensible paths, although part of him ached to lose himself in the ancient stories again.

At least he'd be able to introduce Jorin to them.

"Have a look." Lyam gestured ahead of himself. "There's a lot, though, so start small."

Jorin was already pacing down the aisle, mouth open as he scanned the titles.

Lyam didn't bother trying to hide his amusement. He leaned carefully back against the shelf behind him, right at the very back of the library. The myths were tucked away in one of the dimmest corners. Lyam could remember, when he was younger, often hiding away back here when he wanted to escape for a while, just to lose himself in another world; one where people lived above ground, and the Life-Giver was almost within touching distance, and most people had gold eyes, like him.

But it was nothing but a myth.

Gold eyes. Thoughts of his strange meeting with the man named Enoch floated through Lyam's mind. He gave a shudder, automatically drawing his cloak closer to him. Enoch had spoken of the myths as if they were real, and he had *gold eyes like Lyam*. Lyam had never met another who had them, and something deep within him loosened at the thought that he wasn't alone. The strange stares and distrustful looks he received when people caught sight of his eyes seemed to matter less.

But something about Enoch also made Lyam deeply uncomfortable. What had led him to be down in the tunnels so late? Why had he been there? The tunnel they'd met in was supposed to be just for Scribes; it was too close to the Dreamers' Huts. But Enoch had been there anyway.

A Water-Gatherer, he'd called himself. Lyam heard the name a long time ago, in some of the most ancient myths, but there was very little information on them. If he wanted to find out more, he was probably in just about the best place to start.

Lyam pushed off the shelf too quickly, suddenly thrumming with excitement, and almost knocked a set of scrolls off the shelf behind him. Righting them and fearful of the noise they made, Lyam turned to glance at Jorin, who had managed to bury himself behind another pile of books. Lyam smiled at the sight and turned away. Jorin would be alright for a while.

Walking as steadily as he could, Lyam weaved his way past the rows and rows of books until he entered an aisle full of references. He glanced through the titles, passing over most of the more recent ones until he found himself deep in shadow at the end of the aisle. The books and scrolls back here were much older, yellowed, and scuffed, and Lyam had to take care handling them. He scanned the titles slowly. Books about managing the sand and dust, about farming and glassblowing and bellringing and Designing were piled up high upon each other, too much information to sift through.

Biting his lip, Lyam paused when he saw a title that caught his eye. The cover had a piece of art worked into thick pages, an image almost entirely made of blue, forming a long, billowing cloak that enveloped a shadowy figure.

A cloak that looked just like Enoch's.

Heart in his mouth, Lyam reached forward and, agonizingly slowly, drew the book out of the shelf. The titles around it let out a soft sigh of fluttering, yellowed pages, and Lyam watched them with a close eye to make sure none were about to fall.

Only when he had made absolutely certain that nothing was moving did he turn to the book in his hands.

The first thing he could tell was that it was *old*. The parchment was beyond yellow, so thin that Lyam was afraid it was going to break apart between his fingers as he carefully turned it over. The art that had caught his eye was done in intricate swirls, depicting a man in a wondrous blue cloak standing tall and proud, his hands out as if to guide, inviting Lyam in. Mouth dry, Lyam carefully held the book in both his hands and opened it, eyes scanning the pages quickly.

The title was *The Water-Gatherers*.

The Water-Gatherers are the most favored children of the Life-Giver, second only to the Dreamers. They walk under the Life-Giver's rays and perform the most arduous of tasks, spending all day alone cultivating the rivers and streams. Their work is said to be immense and beautiful, although none but the Water-Gatherers may see it. They are reclusive, soft-spoken, but rare to find alone, keeping together. They are strengthened by their numbers. If they speak, their words are to be greatly heeded, for they are as close to the Life-Giver as the Dreamers.

Lyam's heart was beating rapidly. *Water-Gatherers*. He'd only vaguely heard of them before, had no idea what kind of role they could play—keeping the river running? There was no river underground, only the tiny brook that ran through the Eastern side of the city. There were certainly no rivers and streams as were described. This book was old, very old if it even predated the current layout of their city.

Some things didn't make sense. The scroll seemed to imply that there were many Water-Gatherers, but Enoch had told Lyam he was the only one. And he'd spoken in cryptic riddles, something Lyam hadn't been able to make sense out of, whereas this scroll warned to pay attention to their words. Lyam would, if he could, but he had no idea what Enoch wanted from him.

And then there was the part about the Life-Giver. Implying

that *anything* that came as close to the Dreamers' relationship to the Sun was a punishable offense. This book could be labeled as blasphemy; Lyam was surprised it even remained in the Scribes' Hall at all.

Licking his dry lips, Lyam placed the scroll back in its place on the shelf. He shouldn't concern himself with things like this. Enoch was just an old man with strange memories, and Lyam should pay him no mind. It was time he found Jorin and went back to Annelie—he'd left her alone too long.

Lyam glanced once more at the scroll before he turned his back on it and walked away. The sounds of his footsteps echoed in the silence, muffled by the shelves of books but still uncomfortably loud. Lyam hurried, turning back to the aisle he'd left Jorin in.

It was empty.

Lyam frowned, confused. Jorin knew not to wander alone. The library was vast and a maze for anyone who didn't know it. But maybe Lyam hadn't done a good enough job telling him that. He wasn't used to having responsibility like this.

Nerves began to tighten in Lyam's stomach. He pushed his glasses up his nose and near-jogged down the aisle, searching the little nooks along the way.

No one was there.

"Jorin?" Lyam called, confused and a little concerned. He checked the main aisle of the library, but when there was still no sign, Lyam turned to the back of the library—a place he hardly ever went. As far as he knew, only old files were kept there, but perhaps Jorin had wandered that way if he was exploring.

Lyam was about to turn the corner when he jolted to an abrupt stop.

Tucked away in the shadows, at the far end of the dim aisle Lyam found himself in, there was a glisten of something shiny.

Lyam stepped closer to the edge of the aisle, deep in the shadows cast between two of the lanterns. The glint of something shiny remained out of place, beckoning to him.

When Lyam was close enough, he reached out with careful

fingers and grazed the edge of something solid and smooth. Leaning closer, he could just about make out the shape of a large box, square and ornate, the glint coming from the myriad of decorations covering its surface. Two snakes curled gracefully around the edges, their snouts meeting at the top of the box where an ornately designed Sun was sitting, its rays spreading out across the rest of the box. At one side of the box were two hinges, and on the other side was a keyhole made out of the same shiny metal as the snakes. It glistened as the lantern light fell across it, shadows creeping around its edges.

The key in Lyam's pocket, the key given to him by Enoch, burned against his leg.

Lyam swallowed, mouth dry. *You'll find it in the library.* Enoch's words echoed back at him, and suddenly Lyam felt cold to his bones.

It couldn't be.

Heart in his mouth, Lyam edged closer still, one hand reaching out to trace the cold metal head of one of the snakes. The shadows leaped around it, flickering from the dim lanternlight.

Drawing back, Lyam reached into the pocket of his Scribes' robes for the key. His fingers were shaking. The key glistened in the lantern light just like the keyhole as he held it up; they were the same metal.

Lyam swallowed. His hand was sweaty around the key, and he clenched his fist to stop his fingers from shaking. He stared at the box, torn. It looked like some sort of safe, obviously tucked away in the darkest corner of the library for a reason. And he had a key that could have been stolen, for all he knew. The safe might not be Enoch's. If it was, then why wouldn't Enoch have just sent him here himself? Why make everything so cryptic and confusing? No one but Scribes could enter this library, so there was no way Enoch could have put something here. It didn't make any sense.

Lyam licked his lips. His grip tightened around the key. It wouldn't hurt just to test it, would it? Just to see if the key even fit the keyhole in the safe. It might be pure chance that Lyam had stumbled across a strange safe while also having a strange key in his pocket.

Or it could be the workings of the Life-Giver, pulling at strands of his life that Lyam didn't yet understand.

Lyam swallowed around a painfully dry lump in his throat. With his fingers still trembling, he reached out and fitted the key carefully into the safe.

There was a satisfying click.

Lyam's heart began to hammer. *It fit.* The key fit. Had he found whatever Enoch had wanted him to? Could he even *trust* Enoch? He knew nothing about the man. But if the scroll he'd been reading was correct, then Enoch was close to the Life-Giver. Like the Dreamers. Like Annelie.

If there was one thing Lyam knew, it was that he always trusted the word of the Life-Giver.

Fighting down the part of him that desperately, desperately wanted to run away, Lyam turned the key in the lock.

There was another satisfying click, and then the door of the box swung lazily open, creaking just the smallest amount.

Lyam almost daren't look inside.

But he'd come this far already.

Taking in a shaky breath, Lyam crouched, carefully looking inside the box. It wasn't particularly large, its contents heavily shadowed, but Lyam could make out a small pile of scrolls the familiar smell of parchment wafting out. He swallowed. Who would go this far to hide a pile of scrolls, in a *library,* no less? Breathlessly, he lifted a hand and carefully reached inside, his fingertips just brushing the corner of one parchment.

"Scribe Lyam?"

Lyam almost jumped out of his skin. He leaped upright, dislodging the door of the safe as he scrambled to his feet, knocking it back into the wall with an almighty bang.

Jorin was standing in the entrance to the aisle, his head cocked curiously. "Are you... alright?"

"Yes, yes," Lyam hastily answered, reaching behind him to

right the safe, relief slowly washing over him that Jorin wasn't lost somewhere amongst the books. Lyam swung the door of the strange box shut as fast as he could, snatching the key out of the lock as soon as he'd locked it and sliding it instantly back into his pocket.

Jorin was still giving him an odd look. "Are you sure?"

"Yes, sorry." Lyam shook his head, trying for a weak smile. "Where did you go? I wasn't sure you'd find your way back!"

Jorin's eyes widened. "Oh, I'm sorry! I just wanted to look down another aisle. Look, I found this description of the city when it was above ground!" Jorin bounded over to him, nothing but pride and curiosity in his gaze, and Lyam softened.

He remembered being young and enthralled by the library, too.

Lyam slowly took the scroll from Jorin. It was old, too old to take from the library, but its illustrations were beautiful. Lyam smiled at Jorin. "You have good taste. Just tell me next time you want to see something, ok?"

"Of course," Jorin answered immediately and then bowed. "I am truly sorry. I didn't mean to wander off, Scribe Lyam."

Affection curled through Lyam, soothing. He bit back a smile, reached out, and ruffled Jorin's sandy hair. Jorin jumped back, huffing, and Lyam laughed at him.

Jorin smiled back, his youthful face glowing in the lamplight. "I was wondering if you could show me which of these books I can bring back with me? I probably shouldn't take all of them."

"Sure." Lyam followed him out of the aisle, grateful for the added lantern light. Shaking his head, Lyam did his best to push the safe to the back of his mind and focused instead on the rather large pile of scrolls and books Jorin had managed to accumulate.

But the key still weighed heavy in his pocket.

When they were done in the library, Lyam walked Jorin back to his hut, partly because it was the right thing to do and partly because Jorin had picked too many books to carry by himself. They hadn't thought to bring any bags, so they were both weighed down by parchments and scrolls piled high in their arms.

Once they'd stepped through the enormous Southern Gate and out of the city, the tunnels became much quieter until it was just the two of them alone. By one of the dark twists towards Jorin's hut, the tiniest sound disturbed the air—a quiet mewl.

Lyam stopped.

Jorin twisted, a few steps ahead. "Are you ok?"

Lyam didn't answer, frowning. The mewling was so faint that he barely heard it, but he tracked it to the corner, to a tiny cove in the sandy wall. Shifting the parchments and his lantern, Lyam peered inside the little hole and found the source of the sound.

A tiny kitten lay flat inside the small space. It couldn't be more than a few weeks old, its sandy-colored fur matted and its tiny pink mouth wide open as it mewled. It was shivering, and one of its paws was bent awkwardly, its tail barely moving. There was no way such a tiny animal should be alone.

Lyam looked around quickly, hunting for any sign of the mother. Tunnel cats were usually everywhere down here, but there was nothing other than his own quiet breathing and Jorin standing, confused, a few steps away. This kitten must have been abandoned.

Lyam turned back to it, battling with himself. He'd rescued tunnel cats before, but never one this small. There couldn't be much chance it would survive, but standing there looking at this tiny, pathetic little animal mewling for a mother that would never come, Lyam knew he couldn't just leave it.

"It'll be ok," he whispered. He crouched to place his pile of books down on the floor and reached inside the cove, feeling the kitten react to his touch. One of its eyes was slightly discolored, pale, and filmy. Lyam wondered if maybe it was blind.

The kitten licked at his fingers as soon as he was close enough, a small purr rumbling through it. He was careful as he wrapped one hand around its fragile body, lifting it carefully out of the cove and pressing it against his chest, right over his heartbeat—he'd read that young animals were comforted by the sound of a beating heart.

The kitten mewled, shivering in his hands. He could see that she was female, her fur matted and tangled and covered in dust.

There was no way he was leaving her here alone.

"What's that?" Jorin's curious voice sounded closer than Lyam expected, and he jumped, holding the kitten protectively. Jorin's eyes lit up when he saw her. "Oh! It's so small. Where's the mother?"

"I think she's been abandoned."

"That's so sad." Jorin blinked up at him. "Are you... going to keep her?"

Lyam nodded. "I can't leave her here alone."

Jorin, to his credit, didn't say anything. He just nodded. "I'll go and drop my books off and come back for the others. Will you wait here?"

"Of course."

It took a few long minutes for Jorin to make the two trips to his hut and back. Lyam kept his attention on the kitten, cradling her close and examining her as much as she would let him. Her oddly-bent paw might be broken, or she could have been born that way—she really was tiny—and her filmy eye seemed to want to stay shut. She was warm, though, and he could feel the fast pulse of her tiny heartbeat in his fingers.

He walked with Jorin back to his hut, making sure he got home safe, before turning his feet down the passage the rest of the way to his own home with Annelie.

He knocked on the trapdoor as soon as he arrived, cradling the kitten against his chest. It took no time for Annelie to answer, her dark curls falling in her face as she peered down at him. As soon as her eyes landed on the kitten, she raised a brow. "Another one? *Really?*"

"She's abandoned," Lyam defended himself.

Annelie just rolled her eyes and held out her hands, and Lyam carefully passed the kitten up to her before climbing up himself. By the time he got inside and closed the trapdoor behind him, Annelie was examining the kitten closely, holding her up in the air and taking in every tiny detail.

"She's blind."

"Maybe. I'm not sure."

"She has a twisted paw."

"That isn't her fault."

"You said she was abandoned?"

"I think so." Lyam settled next to her on the floor, the rug soft beneath him. "I found her alone, and she's too young to be away from her mother."

Annelie nodded slowly. "We should name her."

"We can keep her?"

"I think you'd hold her hostage if I tried to say no," Annelie laughed, placing the kitten carefully in her lap. "Besides, she's kind of cute, in an unexpected way."

Lyam chuckled. He reached out and stroked the top of the kitten's head, who was purring loudly, her tiny body vibrating. "I think we should call her Mima."

"Mima, it is." Annelie petted her back, the kitten shivering under her touch. "She's cold."

"I'll get a warm towel. We should swaddle her; she's so tiny. I'll do some reading about her eye and her paw."

Annelie kept playing with her while Lyam warmed some water over their hearth. "Did you find out anything else while you were out?"

"Yes, actually." He told her everything about the key and the safe and Enoch. She listened with a grave furrow in her brow that made her look far older than her years, Mima curling up and falling asleep in her lap.

"We've got to look inside," Annelie said as soon as Lyam had finished his story. "That safe could have information."

"What kind of information?" Lyam asked, coming over with a towel and the bowl of warm water. His eyes were burning with sleep, but he still started to gently clean the kitten's fur. "What could possibly be in there that's useful? Something attacking the Dreamers like this has never happened before."

"What if it has, and these are the records for it?" Annelie pressed. "Or what if it's some code, something that could help Izani and the others at the Citadel?"

"Then we should just go straight to them," Lyam answered tiredly. "I don't know Enoch. I don't even know where he got the key *from*. What if he stole it, Anni?" At this, Lyam's voice grew terrified.

Annelie chewed on her lower lip. "But you said that you read a book about the Water-Gatherers being as close to the Life-Giver as the other Dreamers and me."

Lyam paused, Mima purring under his attention. Thinking about it sent shivers down Lyam's spine.

"The book also said that the Water-Gatherers had strength in numbers. Enoch told me he's the last one," Lyam pointed out. "Besides, if the Life-Giver is so close to them, then why is Enoch the only one left? Why have we never heard of him before?"

Annelie blew out a sigh and leaned back, all bony elbows and sharp edges. She looked just as exhausted as Lyam felt. "I don't know. But it feels important. I don't think we can just ignore it, not even if we wanted to."

Lyam bit his lip, his heart growing heavy with dread. "I was afraid you were going to say something like that."

Annelie smiled bitterly at him, leaning back against the wall. When she closed her eyes, Lyam saw how gaunt she looked, how sickly. He leaned closer and felt the back of her head; she was sweating.

Lyam stood to go and get the cloths to dip in water and put on her forehead, but Annelie stopped him when he wobbled slightly. She shifted, keeping Mima the kitten carefully safe in her lap. "You need to rest, Lyam."

"I'm fine," he told her stubbornly, but when he took another step forward, the world tilted around him, and he stumbled.

Annelie closed her fingers around his arm and tugged, and while she wasn't very strong, Lyam still went back the way she was pulling him.

"You need to rest," she said, forcing him back down. "You haven't slept since the Vigilance, have you?"

Deflated, Lyam shook his head. He felt like he'd been on the move non-stop for days.

"Rest," Annelie told him and pointed to his bed in the corner of the room.

"What if you need me?" Lyam mumbled.

Annelie shook her head, a fond smile touching her lips. "Then I'll wake you. But right now, you need sleep. Please."

At that, Lyam broke. He nodded and reluctantly made his way around her chair, pausing just long enough to drop a kiss on her forehead.

She beamed at him, petting Mima, but then pointed imperiously at his bed. "Sleep."

Lyam huffed out a laugh as he slipped out of his official green Scribes' robes, leaving him in the thinner white robe he wore underneath. He took off his glasses and slipped into his bed, curling up under the blanket and closing his eyes.

Sleep came for him quickly.

CHAPTER
SIX

As the city grew, and the People of the Sand grew in number,
There came a need for leadership.
The Council was formed, and at its head the Speaker of the Sun,
Who holds the words of the Life-Giver in their heart.
Listen to them.
The Book of the Life-Giver, Vol IV, Book I

It only felt like minutes later that Annelie was shaking him awake.

"I'm sorry, Lyam," she murmured, and as he blinked blearily, he realized she was kneeling on the floor of their hut beside his bed. Mima was swaddled in her other hand. "You need to wake up."

Exhausted, Lyam groaned. "How long has it been?"

"A couple of hours." Annelie's lower lip was caught between her teeth. She looked forlorn as she tugged at the sleeve of his robe.

Lyam's head felt stuffed full of cotton. He fought his way out of the last remnants of sleep and sat up, reaching for his glasses.

Annelie watched him worriedly. "A message came for you."

Lyam felt a crease appear in his brow. He turned to her, trying to stifle a yawn. "A message?"

"From Tasmin," Annelie confirmed. "The guard just left."

At that, Lyam sat up even straighter, shaking himself awake. He swung his legs out of bed. "Is she ok?"

"I think so. The guard said she summoned you urgently, though." Annelie sat back, cradling Mima close to her. She looked forlorn.

Lyam ducked to meet her gaze. "Hey. What's wrong?"

"Nothing," she answered, too fast. "Just go. Tasmin needs you."

"You need me, too," Lyam reminded her gently.

Annelie bit her lip, her eyes still fixed determinedly on the floor. She looked... weak, for want of a better word. Lyam hated referring to her like that, even in his own head, because he knew she was anything but, that it took great strength to Dream every night and meet their Life-Giver in the flesh. It took a toll on Annelie's body, naturally, but she still wasn't weak.

Just then, though, she looked weak—tired, beaten-down— and her hair fell limp about her shoulders, her eyes dull.

"Anni," Lyam murmured and ran a hand through her hair. "What's wrong?"

Annelie drew in a shuddering breath. Her eyes fell closed for a moment, then opened, and her voice was barely a whisper as she said, "I'm scared."

The words fell between them, shivering in the air, shriveling the distance between them.

Lyam swallowed. Instinctively, he pulled Annelie close, wrapped his arms around her frail frame, and hung on tight. She buried her face in his shoulder, the position so familiar that Lyam relaxed, even though he could feel the tension in Annelie's muscles. Mima, pressed between them, mewled.

"I'm scared to Dream," Annelie said again, her voice almost lost in the silence between them.

Lyam rocked her gently, fumbling his way around his thoughts. She'd never been afraid of the night before, not for years. On the contrary, Annelie often spoke with warmth and gentleness of the Life-Giver, talked about how she felt comforted on the flaming surface of the Sun. Lyam had always marveled at how it was possible—how the select few among his people were chosen to be Dreamers, to speak with the Life-Giver every night on the Sun's very surface. Having them thrown into jeopardy was... unsettling.

Annelie buried her face in his chest as Lyam straightened up a little. He glanced towards the desk, where the candle was burning low. It would soon be night.

"I'll be here," Lyam murmured.

Annelie trembled. "But Tasmin has summoned you, and—"

"I'll be back," Lyam reassured her. He patted her back, rocking her. "I'll be here. And if I'm not, Mima will look after you, right?"

Annelie coughed out a laugh at that, staring down at the kitten cradled in her lap. One tear rolled slowly down her cheek.

Lyam cupped her face and wiped it away. "I'll be here, Anni. I promise."

She shuddered against him but nodded. "I know. You're always here."

"Exactly." Lyam squeezed her once before releasing her. "And if it gets really bad, just cuddle Mima. You won't be alone."

"You just want an excuse to keep her."

"Maybe."

Annelie chuckled wetly, sitting back on her heels on the floor and letting out a slow, shaky breath. She squared her shoulders, gently stroking Mima's head. "Takes more than some weird shadow to beat us, huh?"

"Damn right."

Annelie grinned at him, and he smiled back. "Come on." He got to his feet, pulling her up with him, and helped her back to her chair. She went willingly enough, settling back against her pillows and drawing her favorite red blanket up around her. It was frayed at the edges after so many years of use. Mima settled beside her, her filmy eye shut and her bad leg twisted, but she seemed more than content to lie there next to Annelie and purr.

"I'll be back," Lyam promised as he slipped on his green Scribes' robes. "As quick as I can."

Annelie gave him a wan smile. "We'll be here."

✿

The city was quietening down, shops shutting, and people returning to their homes for the evening. Lyam often wondered what it felt like to live a life in the city with routine and familiarity and without fear of what the night may bring. He'd never longed for it, but he did wonder, sometimes, what it was like to live a life far removed from the Dreamers.

He shook the thought away as he headed on through the town, dodging a handful of dust sprayed up from the back of a cart's wheels in front of him. The smell of spices was hanging heady in the air as people began to cook in their homes, evening meals being prepared for families to enjoy. Lyam quickened his steps; Annelie would need to eat before she Dreamed again.

A knot of worry that had seemed to be there since Jemme's arrival at his hut two nights ago tightened at the thought of the night ahead. He turned his feet down the path to the Scribes' Hall with a heavy sense of trepidation that he did his best to ignore.

Tasmin was waiting for him in her office. Lyam knocked once on the door before ducking inside, finding her bent over several papers scattered around her desk, a heavy frown line apparent in her forehead. She gestured him over to one of the seats before her, and he sat quickly. "You summoned me?"

"I did," Tasmin answered. "Sorry to drag you here so close to the Dreaming, but it's urgent."

"As long as I can get back to Annelie in time," Lyam answered with a smile, but it soon fell off his face at the worry in Tasmin's expression. "What's happened?"

"The Council met earlier," she answered, heaving a sigh as she placed down the parchment in her hands and instead fixed him with a look. Her gaze was searing. "After I saw you this morning, I called a meeting, but I think every Scribe went to their Designer in such a panic that chaos ensued."

"Mirah said something about that," Lyam replied with a soft snort. "But I don't know what else we expected, honestly—everyone's terrified."

"I think so too," Tasmin agreed. "But the Designers were completely overcome. Designer Izani immediately called a meeting to set their minds at ease, and then he went straight to the Council. We've just dispersed from the first emergency meeting in decades."

Lyam's brows shot up. Tasmin, as Head Scribe, had a place on the Council, but they met once a week and no more, not ever. A part of him was satisfied by how seriously the attack on the Dreamers was being taken, but another part of him was terrified. If even the Designers didn't know what to do, then they were all in trouble.

"What happened?" Lyam asked again, more urgently.

Tasmin let out a low sigh. "Designer Izani told us all what the Designers were saying, and then, naturally, I was invited to speak." Her lip curled a little. "I think about half of the Council didn't believe me, but the rest seemed scared enough to bully them into doing something about it."

Lyam's heart jolted in his chest. "So there is a solution?"

"Not exactly." Tasmin placed her hands down flat on her desk and fixed Lyam with a look, her expression serious. "I'll be honest, this situation is completely unprecedented. No Dreamer has ever been harmed whilst Dreaming before. It's caught us all off guard."

The knot in Lyam's stomach tightened.

"There are a few things we can do," Tasmin continued.

"Tomas is increasing the guards' presence. One will be stationed outside every Dreamer's hut, all through the night. And Izani is calling an emergency meeting of the Designers first thing tomorrow where I'm sure they'll come up with something more concrete. But in the meantime—and this is extremely important—we must keep the situation quiet."

Lyam blinked, sending Tasmin a confused look. "Keep it quiet? How?"

"Don't mention the attack to anyone else." Tasmin swallowed, breaking eye contact to look down at her desk. Suddenly, she looked very tired. "We don't know why it's happening, and we don't know what the effect is yet. We need more time, and the Council has decided we can't have mass panic. So, we must keep it quiet."

Lyam bunched his fingers in the corners of his robes. "How? How are we supposed to keep something like this quiet? It's dangerous!"

"Keep your voice down," Tasmin snapped at him, and it was enough to draw Lyam up straight in surprise. He stared at her. She almost never snapped at him, not even when he was younger and made mistakes.

Tasmin seemed to notice, for she toned down her voice and sighed. "It's the Council's decision, Lyam, not mine. They've decided it's imperative that as few people know about this as possible. So far, only you and I know that three other Dreamers were attacked last night. We have to keep it that way."

Lyam blinked. "How come only the two of us know?"

"Only Nethan and Annelie saw it."

"None of the other Dreamers?"

Wearily, Tasmin shook her head. "I don't know why. But it seems the Life-Giver only revealed it to Nethan and Annelie."

Lyam digested this information slowly.

"So, I'm asking you to keep it quiet," Tasmin continued, her eyes boring into him. "It's the Council's wish, or I would not ask this of you. Until the Designers come up with a plan, we need to keep things calm."

Lyam shifted uncomfortably in his seat. The knot of worry in his stomach tightened, making him feel sick, bile rising in his throat. He dug his fingers hard into his robes, feeling the material strain under his touch.

"But what about the other Dreamers?" Lyam asked eventually. "They need to be warned, surely? What if something happens to them too?"

Tasmin remained calm, but her expression tightened. She kept her gaze on Lyam's. "I don't know, Lyam. I don't know."

Lyam swallowed, his throat burning. Tasmin always knew what to do. Fear clutched at his heart, tendrils of it climbing up his throat, webbing out across his chest until he felt frozen in place.

He needed to get back to Annelie.

"I won't tell anyone," Lyam said into the silence. "Not if that's what the Council thinks is best."

Tasmin visibly relaxed in her seat, her back bending forward, her shoulders bowing. She ducked her head once in a nod. "Thank you. I appreciate it. Really."

Lyam swallowed. There was a sour taste in the back of his throat, but he pushed it down and rose from his seat, his robes falling around him. "I need to get back. Annelie's scared. She's never been scared before."

Tasmin rubbed at her forehead with one hand. "Nethan feels the same way. He has an awful feeling about tonight. Be careful and keep watch, Lyam."

Lyam dipped his head once in a bow and then turned to leave the room. His stomach roiled, tension locking every one of his muscles in place so that he walked stiffly, woodenly, his body not quite obeying him. He was left with bitterness as he closed the door to Tasmin's office behind him and walked quickly through the corridor, his eyes fixed on the stone ground beneath his feet.

Urgency was building in his chest. He needed to get back to Annelie quickly before night fell and something could happen to her, too.

He itched to let the other Dreamers know. He thought of the

Scribes, his friends. How afraid they'd all been in the last meeting, how desperate they were to care for their Dreamers. What if it happened to Adan next? Or Jorin? What if it had already happened to them? How were they supposed to cope then?

But he had to trust the Council's judgment. They'd decided to keep it quiet, and the Designers were working on a solution. He had to trust in them.

Until then, he was going to do his utmost to keep Annelie safe.

The tunnels began to grow steep the further he got away from the city, each turn taking him into a narrower space. The air grew staler, the lanterns fewer and further between, darkness creeping up behind him.

He skidded around a corner, momentum carrying him on, and then—

He crashed into something solid and warm and fell heavily down to the ground.

Sand and dust blew up around him, making Lyam cough, screwing his stinging eyes shut. The lantern had flown out of his hand and landed with an almighty crash, glass shattering, and when Lyam blinked his eyes open, he'd been plunged into darkness, his glasses somewhere to the side. He fumbled for them, sliding them back on.

Fear gripped Lyam's heart.

There was the sound of heavy breathing in the tunnel—his own fast panting, but something else beyond them. Something deeper and longer, more solid.

A low groan sounded from somewhere in front of Lyam.

Breath catching in terror, Lyam scrambled backward, his palms, still stinging from catching him when he fell, scrabbling in the rocky, sandy floor of the tunnels. The smell of dust stuck in his nostrils, mixing with his sweat and smoke from the burnt-out candle, sticking in his throat.

Footsteps from in front of him, and then a low, somehow familiar voice, "Who is there?"

Lyam held himself utterly still.

A scuffle, a grunt, and then, "Scribe Lyam?"

Lyam's heartbeat raced in response. He recognized that voice, low and deep and smooth.

Then the sound of a taper being lit and a flame danced into view.

Lyam instantly recognized the man holding it, huge and bulky and with eyes as gold as his own.

"Enoch," Lyam breathed, his pounding heart rate slowing slightly.

Enoch regarded him with a warm gaze, his blue robes rippling around him as he bent down to offer his free hand to Lyam. Lyam stared in response, shivering, but quietly reached forward and took it, allowing Enoch to pull him to his feet.

"We seem to have broken your lantern." There was amusement in Enoch's tone as he turned and held the taper higher, lighting up the rest of the narrow passageway. Sure enough, the remains of Lyam's lantern lay scattered about the tunnel, glass sparkling in the light, the candle, or what was left of it, well and truly broken.

Lyam swallowed.

"Best to step back," Enoch advised as he bent down, producing from somewhere in the depths of his blue robes a small drawstring pouch. He opened it and began picking up the glass directly from the tunnel floor.

"Wait!" Lyam cried out, almost stuttering. "You'll—you'll cut yourself! What are you doing?"

"Can't have you walking on with this still on the ground," Enoch answered, his voice low and gruff. "By shadow's eyes, child, you'll cut your feet to pieces. Stay still and quiet now."

Lyam, despite himself, bristled. "I'm hardly a child."

"You're certainly not an adult," Enoch rumbled. "Stay still, at least until I've cleared this up."

"Why are you here?" Lyam asked, unable to keep all the bitterness out of his tone as he leaned against the wall, watching Enoch carefully pick up each individual shard of glass and place them safely into the pouch. He was *eighteen*, he'd have Enoch know. "I wouldn't have dropped it if you hadn't run right into me."

"Ah." Enoch hung his head a little, collecting the last pieces of the broken lantern and tying the pouch up tight. He straightened, turning to face Lyam, and Lyam couldn't help that he cowered a little. "I was waiting for you, Scribe Lyam. You're out late today."

With a shudder, Lyam remembered the time—remembered that he had to get back to Annelie. He swallowed and gathered enough courage to step forward, closer to Enoch, who was blocking the narrow, dark passage back to his hut. "I have to get back to my Dreamer."

Enoch studied him, immobile. "We're running out of time."

"What are you talking about?" Lyam asked, desperation coloring his tone. "*Please*, I have to get back."

"Have you ever heard of hailstones?" Enoch continued as if he hadn't spoken. "Read about it in one of your books, perhaps? I thought it was a myth until this morning."

Lyam stared at him in confusion. "What?"

"Water, I know well, but hail?" Enoch shook his head. "I've never seen anything like it before. Large, fat drops of ice, some as big as the palm of your hand, falling continuously from the sky. They were hard, look...." Enoch extended his hand, pulling his robes up his arms until Lyam could see several cuts littered about his skin. "Sharp, just like the shards from your lantern."

Lyam swallowed, staring at Enoch's arm. He'd never seen anything like it before. It was similar to when someone fell on broken glass.

"I've never heard of hail," Lyam murmured. "But you—wait. You—" he stared at Enoch and stumbled back two terrified steps. "Y-y-you were *outside*?" The last word Lyam whispered. Even the sound on his lips was horrifying.

Enoch regarded him coolly. "As I told you last time we met, I am a Water-Gatherer."

Lyam swallowed. He remembered the book he'd seen in the library, telling of a people who were almost as close to the Life-

Giver as Dreamers, if such a thing were possible. A people that walked freely under the Sun.

Lyam stared at Enoch and felt fear clutch at the bottom of his stomach. "You're *real*."

Enoch's gaze softened a little. He reached out a hand, then stopped himself, the taper in his other hand flickering shadows across his face, illuminating his broad chin. Everything about Enoch was broad: hulking shoulders, wide forehead, long nose. His gold eyes reflected the light brightly, much like Lyam's own, and Lyam swallowed.

Real. What he'd read in the book, it was *real*.

"But I read that there were lots of you," Lyam half-whispered, his voice still loud in the silent tunnel. "There can't only be you. Can there?"

At that, Enoch released a low, weary sigh. "I wish there couldn't, Scribe Lyam, but it's true. I am the last of the Water-Gatherers. The only one left, though shadow's eye there should be more."

"Then how?" Lyam asked, his voice stuck in his throat. "How can there only be you?"

Enoch's expression darkened. It scared Lyam, the sudden sharpness to his features. Like Enoch was wearing a mask and the weathered, beaten lines of his face suddenly became something to fear.

"That is a question for one of your own," Enoch answered, his voice suddenly cold. "Have you done as I asked last time? Did you use the key?"

Lyam swallowed. The back of his throat felt dry as dust as he remembered the library, almost getting caught by Jorin. He wished he didn't have to sneak around like this. But at the same time, it felt wrong to get Jorin involved, and he'd been told directly to keep quiet about the attacks. It still didn't sit quite right with him, but Lyam trusted the Council enough to stick to it, at least for now.

The key still sat heavily in Lyam's pocket. He reached into his robes and withdrew it carefully, holding it out flat in the palm of his hand. The light from the taper flickered over it, making it glint dully.

Enoch's eyes lit up upon seeing it again.

"I found what it unlocks," Lyam said softly, his voice dryer than he'd like. He coughed to clear his throat but couldn't seem to unstick the lump that clogged his airways.

Enoch stared at him eagerly. "And?"

"And, I don't know yet," Lyam answered, staring down at the palm of his hand to avoid Enoch's piercing gaze. It was uncanny to see gold eyes looking back at him that weren't from his own reflection.

"What do you mean, you don't know?"

Lyam shivered at the loud sound, retreating into his robes. His palm closed tight around the key. "It means I found the safe in the library, but I don't know what it holds yet."

Enoch fixed Lyam with a stern look.

Lyam quailed under that gaze, cowering backward as he tightened his hold on the key, feeling the metal digging into his palm. He couldn't help but feel like he'd disappointed Enoch somehow, and the knowledge of that bristled inside him. He might not know Enoch at all, but Lyam didn't like being a disappointment.

He licked his lips. "I found the safe, though. I know where it is."

Enoch's eyes narrowed. "But you didn't look inside?"

"I tried! I wasn't alone. It wasn't—I didn't feel safe."

Enoch drew back, his features starkly surprised. "You told someone else about this?"

"No!" Lyam swallowed, stepping back once again as Enoch advanced on him. Terror built in his throat, eyes on the taper that Enoch held aloft. It was burning down. Too much time had passed already. He needed to get back to Annelie. "I didn't tell anyone, I just—someone was with me, but I didn't show him the safe."

Enoch relaxed again, stopping his terrifying advance. He stood tall above Lyam, bulky, his shoulders broad enough that he was almost completely filling the tunnel, touching both its sides with his arms. He cut a terrifying figure in the near-darkness, his wildly flickering shadow filling up the space behind him.

Lyam swallowed.

"So," Enoch said after a long, silent moment had passed. "You have found the safe."

Slowly, carefully, Lyam nodded. He wasn't sure what Enoch wanted from him, but he knew for sure that he didn't like where this conversation was going. He didn't want anything to do with whatever Enoch was trying to get out of him. Lyam just wanted to be a good Scribe and look after his Dreamer, and he *needed* to get back to Annelie.

"Please," he tried again, his voice low. "I need to—I have to get back to my Dreamer. *Please* let me pass."

Enoch's gold eyes bore straight into him. "You're out later than advised. Why? Where have you been?"

Lyam felt his throat constrict. He couldn't tell Enoch; he couldn't tell *anyone*. But how else was he supposed to get passed? Terror was making his heart rate quicken. He could feel his blood running fast through his veins. He was supposed to be with Annelie. His lantern may be broken, but he could see by the taper Enoch was holding and how far it had burned down that he was out of time.

What if she'd started Dreaming already? Alone, for the first time, and in danger?

"I have to go." Determination made Lyam's voice stronger, although it still shook. He took a step closer to Enoch despite all his muscles screaming at him not to.

Enoch met his eyes again, looking down at him, and his expression was unreadable for a moment. "Are you still afraid of me?"

Lyam swallowed. Silence beat at him, but he didn't know what to say. Of course, he was terrified, but Enoch seemed to want him to be calm. But Lyam didn't know how to be unafraid of a man he barely knew. A man who walked outside.

The silence seemed to be enough for Enoch, who simply gave

a sharp nod of his head. "I was going to ask that you show me the safe. But I see that your head is in another place tonight."

Lyam clenched his fist around the key. Show Enoch the safe? What utter madness. That would involve taking Enoch into the Scribes' Hall itself, and Lyam wasn't completely sure how much Enoch belonged in their world. He had no idea how he'd explain away the presence of a Water-Gatherer to anyone that might find them. If Lyam had barely heard of them before, then he could guarantee that none of the other Scribes would be any the wiser either.

Lyam shook his head and then desperately thrust the key out towards Enoch. "Please, take it back. I don't want anything to do with this anymore."

Enoch regarded him silently.

"I need to be with my Dreamer," Lyam continued, his voice tight. "It—it's not safe, at the moment. I need to be with her. I can't be part of whatever you're planning. I *can't*."

Enoch didn't move. His eyes remained on Lyam's face, and Lyam cowered a little, unable to hide his desperation. The key remained held out between them, quivering in Lyam's grip.

Slowly, Enoch lifted his hand. Lyam froze, watching as Enoch reached as if to take the key, his warm, calloused palm briefly enclosing Lyam's hand.

But instead of taking the key, Enoch simply folded Lyam's own hand down around it.

"Go," he said, almost gentle, "but return to me tomorrow. You will find me if you follow the southernmost tunnel. I always answer the bell."

Lyam stared at him. His words weren't making sense. Southernmost tunnel? His and Annelie's hut was the farthest south the city went. There was no southernmost tunnel.

"I will see you tomorrow." Enoch's tone brokered no argument, and then he finally stood aside and gestured for Lyam to pass him.

Lyam could have cried with relief. Finally, he could return to Annelie, even if he had nothing good to report back to her. He would worry about Enoch's words later; his first priority had to be getting back to her.

Nervously, Lyam skittered forwards, squeezing himself past Enoch; he had to get so close that he could smell the dust and sweat, feel the warmth radiating from him. Then he was free.

As soon as he was through, Lyam started running.

He needed to get home.

PART THREE

PART THREE

THE GREATER THE LOSS

Hot. Everything was hot.

Annelie tried to shield herself, curling her legs into her chest. The vacuum felt more oppressive than ever, the Life-Giver's flames flickering in the distance. She'd wanted to stay awake so desperately until Lyam came home, but if she was here, then she hadn't managed it. The Dream had already begun.

She was afraid.

She felt it in a shiver that spread through her whole body, the fear choking her, raising goosebumps along her arms and lifting the hair at the back of her neck. But the flames from the Sun's surface licked up towards her, beckoning her closer, and Annelie gave into them easily, letting their familiar warmth surround her and draw her in close. She was safe here, in her Dream. No matter what might have been happening, she knew she was safe with her Life-Giver.

Around her, dimly, she could feel the presence of the other Dreamers—eleven bright growing orbs, herself included, with four conspicuously absent. She shivered again, feeling fear rising from her gut. The flames flickered around her, drawing tighter to her body, and she relaxed.

Her feet landed on the blistering surface of the Sun, but she felt calm. *The Life-Giver's comforting presence surrounded her, wrapping her in a warm, soft blanket of flames that licked up her arms and curled around her middle, her legs enveloped in the same seeping warmth. She closed her eyes, at peace.*

Hello, Life-Giver.

The flames pulsed around her, brightening with pleasure. **My child. You have returned.**

I always will. *Annelie opened her eyes again, glancing around at the tongues of fire surrounding her. White-hot and bright orange and searing red, the colors imprinted onto her eyelids so that even when she closed her eyes she could still see them. The soles of her feet burned.*

The flames pulsed once more. **You are afraid.**

Annelie swallowed. Not of you.

Do not lie to me. *The words were spoken soothingly, a statement rather than a question. The flames surrounding her loosened a little, curling up around her head as well, licking gently at her hair without burning it. The warmth Annelie felt was indescribable, and with it came comfort; safety.*

The Life-Giver would not harm her.

Something's happening, *Annelie said softly, her voice cracking in the sizzling air.* To us. Something's happening, Life-Giver.

The flames molded to her shape. They moved with her, loosening as she stretched her legs out and relished in the lack of pain, and as she held one arm out before her the flames curled around her brown skin, wrapping each individual finger in its own halo of golden light.

Annelie closed her eyes and gathered her courage. Something is hurting us, Life-Giver. Your Dreamers. I don't know what to do.

The air changed. The noise of the flames crackled in her ears, the feeling of them searing against her skin even as she remained unharmed. The Life-Giver tightened their hold over her, and Annelie was powerless to it.

I know.

You...you know?

Instantly, the flames reared up higher, shooting sparks far above her head. **I know.**

Sudden fear made Annelie's blood run cold, despite the achingly hot air that surrounded her. If the Life-Giver knew, then was Annelie safe? Why wasn't anything being done to help the Dreamers? Terrified, Annelie reached out beyond the flames that surrounded her and felt the presence of the balls of light that were the other Dreamers. At least they were still there. At least they were all safe for the moment.

You know? Annelie whispered again, her lips so dry they stuck together. Do you know what's attacking us? Life-Giver, can you help?

Silence met her words, broken only by the roaring and crackling of the flames that were wrapped tight around her, cocooning her, making her feel safe and comforted when the world of the Dream beyond them was terrifyingly dark.

I know, the Life-Giver finally answered her. But I cannot help you. I have been pushed too far.

Annelie drew in a high-pitched breath that caught sharp as glass in her throat. The flames around her loosened a little, and Annelie felt herself slip. Her feet lifted off the blistering surface of the Sun and she was floating.

Listen to your Scribe when you return, the Life-Giver's voice still sounded directly in her ear, reverberating deep in her bones. Things are being set in motion. You must move fast if you are to save us both.

Annelie frowned. Save them both? She was useless outside of her Dreams, and Lyam was already doing too much for her, she couldn't ask him to do anything else. And he hadn't been there when she fell asleep.

He wasn't there.

You are not useless, child, The Life-Giver snapped suddenly. You are my chosen, as is your Scribe. Work together, as you are designed.

Another jolt ran through the Dream. Annelie jerked, felt herself drift further away, the flames of the Life-Giver growing further out of reach. Desperately, she threw her hands forward, trying to get back to the surface, but the Life-Giver was growing ever distant.

I am leaving you, my daughter. The Life-Giver's voice was

quiet, but the words jarred Annelie's bones. **Move quickly. I do not want to lose you, too.**

And then, the Dream jolted again. Annelie felt a drop low in her stomach as she was flung out into the darkness, the flames of the Life-Giver fully leaving her. Annelie could only watch in horror as the Sun retreated, physically moving backward. Wind rushed past Annelie's ears, the roaring of the flames growing further and further away.

She gasped, reaching forward, but her fingers only met empty air.

"Life-Giver!" She screamed, seeking the comfort of the flames again, desperately reaching for the blistering heat rather than the cold air she found herself trapped in. She floated, shivering and crying and screaming for her Life-Giver, but the Sun gave no answer. The flames grew further distant, darkness flickering in the edges of Annelie's vision.

The other Dreamers near her were also screaming; she could hear them distantly, as if listening through a thick door, the sounds warped and strange.

The air shifted again as the Sun moved further out of reach.

The cold grew worse—unbearable. Annelie's bare arms were frozen, her lips chattering and the edges of her fingers turning blue.

And then she saw it.

Inky blackness once again swarming through the air. It filled the vacuum, dark and ominous, leeching hungrily after the orbs. She could hear the other Dreamers, sense their balls of light, but in the darkness—in the darkness, she felt one of them wink out.

And then another.

And then three more.

Annelie drew in a sharp, desperate breath, crying frozen tears. She forced herself to move, trying to get her chilled limbs to do something, whether to fly closer to save them or to flee to save herself from the horrid inky blackness she didn't know. She struggled and cried as another orb of light winked out, and then still more, until seven in total had disappeared.

Seven more Dreamers, leaving only four of them left. Nethan was still there, sheltering Elinah—the youngest Dreamer was quaking in fear, her orb shivering visibly. The other was Emery, she thought, and then...just her.

Just four of them.

Annelie screamed, desperately flinging herself against her frozen restraints, but the cold seeped into her bones and filled up her lungs and clogged her airways, trapping her screams, locking her in place.

She closed her eyes and wept as she felt the Dream slowly leaving her. One last time, she reached for the Life-Giver, tears clinging to her lashes, cold locked in her bones.

Move quickly, child. My people and I are counting on you.

CHAPTER
SEVEN

The bond between Scribe and Dreamer is like no other.
They are each other's world,
And only they may understand each other.
To enter a Dreamer's hut is to commit the worst blasphemy,
And is punishable by death.
The Book of the Life-Giver, Vol VI, Chapter II

L yam was out of breath and panting when he finally made it back to his and Annelie's hut.

He scrambled up the trapdoor, pulling the ladder up with him, and closed it hastily behind him. He could hear Annelie's panting and crying before he even made it inside.

The second the trapdoor was closed behind him, Lyam ran to Annelie's side. She was splayed out on her chair, twisting and turning, her hands clenching into half-formed fists at her side. Her favorite blanket had slipped down around her, leaving her with only the thin white robe covering her. She must have been Dreaming for a while; the candle on the desk had already burned out. Mima was standing over her, having escaped from her towel, her good front paw patting at Annelie's shoulder. The kitten was mewling along with Annelie's cries.

Lyam didn't spare a second to light up the hut, instead leaning over Annelie and smoothing her hair back from her forehead, brushing his fingers across her sweat-ridden brow, murmuring under his breath in a desperate attempt to soothe her. It didn't work, or at least, it had no visible effect; she still lay arching across her chair, her feet kicking, desperate breaths tugged from her chest.

He should have got back in time.

"I'm so sorry," Lyam murmured, catching one of her hands in his own and squeezing tight. He leaned over her until his forehead was buried in her shoulder, and he held her frail, trembling frame in his grip, squeezing tight as if that could get through to her. Mima stood alert beside them, tail flicking.

The desperation to check for signs of blackness or rotting on Annelie's skin overtook him. *What if she was next? What if he was the next Scribe left alone?*

He was leaning across her like that when she came awake with a gasp.

There were tears on her cheeks. Lyam could feel them instantly as she pressed up into him, her face against his chest, her arms reaching up to weakly clutch at the edges of his stiff green robes.

She was sobbing, her breath hitching and wheezing, her fingers scrabbling against him. He hushed her, rocking her, but it didn't work. She was inconsolable, crying into his shoulder, unable to get words out past the panic of her breathing.

Lyam leaned back as much as Annelie would allow and looked her in her eyes, and then he wished he hadn't. She looked utterly terrified. She was trying to say something, that much he gathered, but it wasn't working when she was trembling so badly she could barely speak.

"Lyam. I-I have—There's—"

"Hush, it's alright."

"No, it...it can't—I won't—"

"Count your breaths. Come on. It's alright."

"You don't *understand!*"

Lyam wrapped his arms around her and brought her into his chest again, rocking her gently. She trembled and gasped, but he counted out loud, helping her to time her breathing—in for three, out for five—until she was a little more relaxed.

When she had stopped trembling so violently it was rocking both of them, Lyam laid her back against her chair and went to light a candle. Mima clambered onto Annelie's lap, and she absent-mindedly began stroking her fur, her eyes distant and glassy.

Lyam fetched the bowl of water and damp cloth, gently washing away the sweat that had collected on Annelie's face and neck. She lay limp under his ministrations, her body weak and tired, tear tracks drying on her cheeks.

He wiped those away, too.

"You don't understand," Annelie managed after an agonizing silence, her voice low but tinged with desperation. "Things are so much worse than we thought."

Lyam went still. Before he could ask her what she meant, someone started pounding on the trapdoor. The angry noise rang through the hut, jarring them both.

Lyam jumped. The cloth slipped out of his hand and landed on Annelie's sheets, leaving a wet patch behind it. He muttered under his breath and scooped it right back up, placing it in the bowl. Then he looked back at Annelie, who was staring at him with wide eyes, Mima cradled in her arms.

"So much worse," she whispered, and shivered, drawing her blankets up around her neck. "We've all been fools so far."

The knocking rang through the hut again, followed by a loud, distressed shout.

Lyam stared at the trapdoor, fear gathering in his gut.

When the knocking didn't stop, he shook himself and strode towards the trapdoor. This was so horrendously familiar; the last time this happened in the dead of night, Scribe Jemme had brought him the worst news of his life.

With trepidation curling through him, Lyam pulled open the trapdoor.

"You!"

The shout came from the tunnel below, and Lyam blinked into the sudden glare of a lantern thrust into his face. "You! Has it happened to you, too?"

Lyam recognized the voice like a punch to his stomach. *Adan.* His friend, his best friend other than Annelie, now glaring up at him with eyes widened in the lamplight and rage flying from his lips.

"This isn't supposed to happen!" Adan cried again. "I thought we were going to make a plan!"

Lyam blinked, confused, and reached for the ladder and dropped it down to the ground, preparing to climb down. He'd never heard Adan sound so distressed before. Where was his usual joking tone, teasing Lyam?

"You stay there," Adan growled, and then he did the unthinkable.

He put his foot on the base of the ladder.

Lyam recoiled, horror tearing through him. He threw his hands out, shock rendering him immobile while Adan climbed the ladder, *into the hut.*

Inside his hut with Annelie. A place none but them were permitted to enter.

Even the guards that brought their food and water left them in the tunnel every morning for Lyam to collect. Everyone knew that the hut was the sacred resting place of the Dreamers, to be disturbed by none but their Scribe. Lyam knew that; had it drilled into him during his mentorship. Adan had to know it, too.

And yet he ascended the ladder.

"You're supposed to be on my side!" Adan's voice rang with anger as he hauled himself inside the hut. "We're Scribes, Lyam! A team!"

Lyam rushed to try and shut the trapdoor, but he was too

late. Adan stumbled his way inside, glaring at Lyam, before he turned his gaze to the chair where Annelie lay, blankets pulled up to her eyes, staring wide-eyed back at him. Mima crouched protectively in front of her.

Lyam felt anger rise in a wave through him. He shot forwards and placed himself directly in front of Adan, furious. "What do you think you're *doing*?"

"I thought we were in this together!" Adan interrupted. "But you—you're still here, and your Dreamer...!"

From behind him, Annelie said almost wonderingly, "who are you?"

"Adan," Lyam answered, his entire body shivering with the presence of someone in his hut who shouldn't be there. Fear made his fingers tremble.

"Your friend Adan?"

"Yeah."

"Oh." Annelie smiled at him, lowering her blankets, but Adan's face was as dark as a blown-out wick as he snarled.

"You."

Annelie's mouth opened a little. "Me?"

"You!" Adan lifted an accusatory finger and pointed it straight at Annelie. "You're still ok! Why? *How?*"

Lyam swallowed, staring into Adan's eyes. He looked furious, but there was fear there, too. Something made him deeply afraid. And Lyam knew his friend. Adan might like a joke, but he wasn't one to break the rules, and Lyam could only imagine that something awful had happened to bring him here in his desperation.

Lyam swallowed. "You left your Dreamer? It's still night...."

"I know it is!" Adan was shouting again. "I know, and Kiran —" his voice broke, and Adan tore his gaze away.

Lyam's blood ran cold. Annelie made a pained, distressed sound behind him.

"Your Dreamer?" Lyam breathed, reaching out a hand. "Dreamer Kiran, is he—"

"He was attacked," Annelie confirmed, and her voice was full of horror. "Seven of us were."

Lyam span, eyes wide. *"Seven?"*

She nodded, biting her lip. Lyam stared at her, shock rendering him immobile. *Seven?* That was almost all of them; almost all the Dreamers had been attacked. Lyam suddenly felt very grateful that Annelie had woken up sobbing and crying the way she had, because at least she was still *here.*

With growing horror, Lyam turned back to Adan. "Dreamer Kiran. What happened to him?"

Adan dropped his head into his hands. His shoulders shook, and suddenly he looked small, despite being at least a head taller than Lyam. His body curved inwards, and Lyam felt a tug in his chest.

He stepped closer, hesitantly, and reached out to place a hand on Adan's shoulder.

Adan curved in completely, a small sob escaping from him.

"He's rotting, Lyam," Adan whispered. "He's rotting, and there's nothing I can do about it."

Lyam frowned heavily. "What do you mean, rotting?"

Adan turned to him and there was a haunted look in his eyes. He shuddered. "He won't talk. He won't move. And his skin...the *smell.*" Adan shook his head and pressed his face into his hands, drawing in a long, slow breath. The awful, haunted expression didn't leave his face, not even as he angrily dashed his tears away and turned his back on Lyam.

Lyam stared at him in horror. He'd never seen his friend quite like this before, without a trace of humor, locked in torture. He thought of Jemme, and the terrible look in her eyes just before she left him. He hadn't seen her since that night, had no real idea what happened to her Dreamer. In fact, with all the rush to try and figure out what was happening, Lyam had hardly spared any thought at all to what was happening to the Dreamers who'd been attacked.

Looking at Adan, even the thought of it made Lyam feel sick.

Adan turned back around slowly, his expression so twisted that Lyam barely recognized him. He looked straight past Lyam, over to the bed where Annelie was watching them both, bright and intent.

"Do you know why?" Adan asked lowly, his tone almost threatening.

"I wish I did." Annelie pushed her covers back and made to stand up, Lyam instantly rushing to her side to support her. He helped her to her feet, hobbling over to Adan, who stood immobile and distraught.

Gently, Annelie reached up and placed a hand on Adan's shoulder.

"I'm so sorry," she said earnestly. "Kiran always makes me laugh. He's so outspoken, and he's always challenged everything. He's usually the first to run to the surface."

Adan's eyes were wet.

"I wish I could tell you what happened." Annelie's voice was trembling. "All I can tell you is that I saw the blackness take him and the others, just the same as the past three nights. And we're going to figure out why."

Adan touched Annelie's wrist, holding her hand against his shoulder, and she shivered. Lyam remembered that she hadn't seen anyone other than him in nine years. "Was he in pain?"

Annelie winced. It was enough of an answer.

Adan's face grew grim. He dropped Annelie's wrist and stepped backward, flickering his gaze between her and Lyam. "Wait a minute. What was that about the past three nights?"

Lyam's blood ran cold. Just then he remembered the warning Tasmin had given him to keep to himself that three Dreamers had been attacked. Most people only knew of Rayah, which could have been an isolated incident. No one but he and Tasmin knew of the three. Except Adan did now.

Adan glared at them both. "What are you talking about?"

Lyam swallowed.

Adan took in a cracked, shaking breath, and his obvious distress was breaking Lyam's heart. He wanted so desperately to help, and he was still so overcome by the presence of someone else in their hut, even when it was Adan, probably his favorite person other than Annelie. He'd always wondered what it would be like for them to meet.

"Lyam," Adan said, and his voice was so potent with fear and distress that Lyam broke.

"There were another three Dreamers that were attacked last night," Lyam confessed in a rush. Annelie crossed to him, wobbly on her feet, to take his hand. "Rayah first, and then those three, and now…"

He trailed off, but the silence explained everything he couldn't bring himself to say.

"Eleven out of fifteen Dreamers?" Adan stared at him, but Lyam found it impossible to hold that gaze, so he looked away, timidly staring at the floor like the coward that he was. His heart lay shriveled in his chest, his fingers tight around Annelie's, the weight of Adan's gaze on him heavier than the guilt sitting uncomfortably in his stomach.

"You knew," Adan said into the silence.

Lyam flinched.

"You *knew*," Adan's voice broke, "that the Dreamers were in danger, and you didn't— you didn't *do anything!*"

"I'm so sorry." The words were stuck in Lyam's throat, but he forced them out, thought of his promise to the Council and hated them for a brief second.

He'd only done as he was told.

And it had resulted in seven more Dreamers being attacked.

"Kiran is practically *dead*," Adan spat out, his voice horribly raspy and broken.

Lyam flinched back further, grimacing. Anger swirled in his stomach, making him bold. "We're going to do something about it. We have to. The Council have been lying."

"The Council?"

"They're the ones who told me to keep quiet," Lyam confessed quietly.

Adan stared at him, his thick brows raised.

"I didn't know what to do," Lyam continued. "Clearly not this, but…but I couldn't disobey a direct order. Could I?"

Adan frowned, considering. He ducked his head in a bow. "I'm sorry. I... I shouldn't have come here. Forgive me. I just... Kiran..."

"He needs you," Annelie interrupted.

Adan turned to her, surprised.

"He needs you," she repeated, intense. "You're his only comfort. Go."

Adan swallowed. A fierce expression flittered across his face, and he nodded, turning away.

Just as he was about to leave, Lyam reached for him. "I'm so sorry."

"Don't," Adan replied, holding his hands up and looking down with shame and fear written all over his face. "I know I shouldn't have come here."

Lyam swallowed. He knew he should report Adan for this, for entering another Dreamers' hut, but the idea of handing him over to the Council was... awful. Adan looked broken; a shell of the usual bubbly, joking person he was. Lyam barely recognized him. He couldn't put him through anything else.

He honestly wasn't sure if he could face Tasmin and the Council again. Not after the disaster of more Dreamers being attacked, when Lyam had *known* they were in danger, and yet no one had done anything about it.

It made Lyam feel sick.

"Go back to Kiran," Lyam murmured. "Anni's right. He needs you."

Adan dipped his head in a nod, hesitated a moment longer, but then turned to the trapdoor without a word.

Lyam stayed still just long enough for Adan to have truly left before he rushed to pull up the ladder, slamming the trapdoor shut behind him and locking the padlock firmly. He was trembling, furious with himself for allowing someone else into Annelie's hut, *Annelie's* hut, her one safe place in the world and now it had been ruined. He trembled, curling himself into a ball right there on the floor.

A soft noise from Annelie had him turning. He found her

curled up back on her chair, Mima cradled in her bony elbow, her head bent low over the kitten. He went to her side in an instant, gently touching her arm. She flinched, petting Mima's head slowly with two careful fingers. She was sweating again; Lyam fetched the washcloths and a bowl of cool water.

"I saw them, Lyam," she said dully as he wiped her forehead with care. "I saw them wink out, but I couldn't do anything."

Lyam paused, accidentally squeezing the cloth in his hand too tight so a couple of droplets of water fell onto Annelie's chair. He shook himself and went back to wiping the back of her neck. "I know you did all you could."

"It wasn't *enough*." Annelie drew in a trembling breath, pausing in stroking Mima. The kitten looked up at her curiously. "Nothing is enough, nothing's going *right*, and the Life-Giver..."

She trailed off, and Lyam turned to her with a question in his gaze. He knew he should be writing down everything she was telling him, should be recording everything to take to Mirah in the hope that she'd be able to salvage something from this disaster, but he couldn't hide his worry about Annelie. The Dreamers were in danger, and although she had somehow remained unharmed, he couldn't shake the fear that she could be next.

He patted down her arm and said, "The Life-Giver?"

"The Life-Giver is leaving." Annelie whispered, trembling so much that Mima licked her fingers in an attempt to comfort her. "*Leaving*, Lyam. The Life-Giver told me they're leaving."

Lyam froze, the enormity of those words hitting him slowly.

He couldn't believe it. For the first time, he couldn't believe her. Lyam had always had unwavering faith—in Annelie, in the Dreams, in the Council, in the Life-Giver. It was all connected. The Council members were appointed by the Life-Giver in the Dreams; the choosing of the new Dreamers and Scribes and Designers happened when the Dreamers had their first Dream. Everything resided on the Life-Giver's presence. Everything.

There was no way the Life-Giver could be leaving.

Annelie's fingers clutched onto Lyam's robes, desperately scrabbling at him to look at her in something other than utter shock. He stared at her, hardly recognizing her. Her skin still glowed faintly with remnants of the Sun. She tugged at him again, and finally Lyam moved.

He wrapped Annelie up in a tight hug, holding her trembling frame against him. His voice was hoarse when he said, "Leaving? You're sure that's what the Life-Giver said?"

Shaking, Annelie nodded her head against his chest.

Lyam swallowed. "Then we need to start figuring out what that means. It...it can't mean *actually* leaving, it's probably a metaphor of some kind. The Life-Giver is always cryptic."

"Not this time," Annelie whispered.

"I'll talk to Mirah."

"Lyam, I felt it." Annelie placed Mima carefully in her lap before she clutched tight to his robes, hard enough to scratch him through the rough material. "I felt the shift. The Life-Giver is leaving us."

Lyam's stomach dropped. He felt bile rise in his throat.

Annelie clawed at him, a high sob stuck in her throat. "The Sun is really leaving, Lyam. The whole Dream shifted. I don't know what to do."

Lyam swallowed, clutching her back hard. He wanted to tell her that he didn't know what to do either, that he was lost and confused and terrified, that he didn't know who to turn to. Tasmin and the Council had told him not to say anything, Mirah had gone straight to the head Designer but given him no real advice, and now seven more Dreamers had been attacked. Annelie was in direct danger, and Lyam didn't know what to do.

"It will be ok," Lyam murmured, though he didn't believe it himself. "I'll go to Mirah. We'll fix it."

"How?" Annelie demanded, shaking, her hands bunching into fists. "It's like nobody's *listening*. The Life-Giver is leaving us! And...and seven of them, Lyam! I just...I just *watched*."

"It'll be ok," he said with more force, rocking her against him and letting her cry into his chest.

But would it be ok? He didn't know. He could go to Mirah, hope that she had come up with something better, or could make sense of the words. But nothing made sense to him anymore.

"And you weren't here," Annelie sobbed, shaking. "I slept, and...and you weren't here."

Lyam felt his heart break. He gathered her up in his arms and held her tight, murmuring brokenly, "I'm sorry, I'm so sorry I wasn't here for you."

Annelie let out a quiet sob.

"I tried to get back," Lyam said, remembering the night before all too clearly. "Tasmin told me not to tell anyone about the attack." His brows lowered when he remembered Adan's face earlier, his broken expression, his cries for his Dreamer. What if it could have been prevented if Lyam had said something? What if he'd let the Dreamers know of the danger they were in? Would things have been different then?

What if it had been Annelie, and Lyam hadn't been here?

"And then I ran in to Enoch again," he continued, freezing as he remembered their strange conversation. "He's the one who really delayed me, I'm sorry, I'm so sorry, I should have got passed him."

Annelie tilted her head up to look at him, confusion apparent in her features. "Enoch? The Water-Gatherer?"

"That's what he says he is."

"What does he look like?"

Lyam swallowed, thinking back. "Big. He fills the tunnels. Dark skin, gold eyes like me, and he's bald. His robes are bright blue."

"Blue?" Annelie's eyes widened. "No one has blue robes."

"He does." Lyam shifted, biting his lip as he remembered what Enoch had told him, a horrible connection drawing up in his mind. "He said there was hail. Have you ever heard of hailstones?"

Annelie shook her head.

"He told me about it. It's like blocks of ice falling from the sky." Even the description scared Lyam. He remembered the cuts on Enoch's arms, how angry and red and sharp they'd looked. Like cuts from glass. Undeniably real.

Annelie's eyes widened. "Because the Life-Giver's leaving," she breathed. "Without the Sun, the weather can't balance."

"Enoch wants to go and look at what's inside the safe in the library," Lyam continued, "But I don't know if I can take him. I *shouldn't*. No one but Scribes are allowed in the Scribes' Hall."

"Your fellow Scribe isn't allowed in our hut, either," Annelie answered slowly. "Is it right to tell on him?"

Lyam bit his lip, conflicted.

Adan was in pain. He hadn't meant any real harm. He'd just been desperate for answers. Lyam thought about what he'd do if he was in Adan's place, and he shuddered.

There were no lengths he wouldn't go to if Annelie was harmed.

He looked back at Annelie, noted the way she was staring at him with certainty in her gaze, Mima curled up in her lap, and he felt in his gut what was right. He knew he wasn't going to tell on Adan, especially not when Lyam himself carried some of the guilt for what Adan was going through. There was no telling quite what had happened to the Dreamers, but Lyam didn't like the way the Council had dealt with it so far.

Which was a terrifying thought.

He swallowed, looked back at Annelie, and shook his head.

Annelie relaxed back into her chair, her fingers lightly stroking Mima's fur. She released a low sigh and tilted her head back, closing her eyes. Lyam studied her, noticed the frailty to her thin wrists, her creased brow, her paper-thin skin. He crossed back to her side, taking her hand in his. "What do we do now?"

The quiet desperation in his voice spoke volumes. Even he could hear it.

Annelie blinked her eyes open and turned to face him, her movements sluggish. She reached out and touched his cheek with the tip of her fingers. "I think you should go to Enoch."

Lyam recoiled, shocked.

"If he truly walks under the Sun, then he's our closest link to the Life-Giver," Annelie pressed on, her words slurred together. "When...when I'm not Dreaming, at least. But go to him, and go to Mirah, and go to Tasmin. Warn them. Warn everyone."

A chill settled deep in Lyam's bones. He swallowed, his dry throat working, fear starting a low churn in his belly that rose up through his bloodstream and enveloped his heart in a cold grip. Annelie sounded afraid, more afraid than she'd ever seemed before.

"I don't even know how to find Enoch," Lyam whispered, his voice trembling. "He said the southernmost tunnel, but that's... us. Isn't it?"

"Check the map?"

Lyam squeezed her hand once more before standing up and crossing over to his desk, pulling out the map he kept hidden in the drawer. He studied it closely, and...there. Past Rayah's hut, before Jorin's, there was a tunnel that he'd never been down; he'd honestly thought it was disused.

But it was technically the southernmost tunnel.

They were desperate enough to try anything at this point, and Lyam trusted Annelie's instincts. If she wanted him to go to Enoch, then he would. He just needed to think about how on earth he was going to take Enoch to the Scribes' Library, and whether he even should. He'd be technically committing a crime if he did. Enoch would have to be very convincing.

But what was in the safe that was so important? And how did it link to the danger currently facing the Dreamers at night?

Only Enoch would have the answers.

"Ok," Lyam murmured, crouching back by Annelie's side. She had her eyes closed and was curled up on her side, so he tugged her favorite blanket up around her. Mima clambered her way up to her pillow, wobbling slightly on her bad leg. Lyam stroked her soft fur. "I think I know where to find him, or at least, where to start looking. I'll go to him first, then Mirah."

"And Tasmin," Annelie insisted, her voice raspy. She opened

her eyes and looked at him, and Lyam was shaken by the fear he found there. "But... be back before I sleep?"

"I will," he answered without a second of hesitation. "I promise. This time, I'll be here."

Annelie swallowed. Fear was written all over her face.

Lyam gripped her hand tighter.

"Warn them," Annelie hissed, her words heavy. "Before it's too late."

࿐

T he tunnels were quiet as Lyam made his way through them, head down, lantern clutched determinedly before him.

His official green robes rustled noisily, disturbing dust as he walked, giving him the urge to cough, but he resisted. Everything was too quiet for the noise inside his brain. He couldn't untangle his thoughts. There was worry about Adan, questions about the Council, sorrow for the seven Dreamers who had been attacked, and underlying everything was his constant fear for Annelie.

How could he guarantee her safety that night? When she Dreamed again, what if she was next? They didn't *know* what was harming the Dreamers, but everything in him was burning to protect Annelie. He wouldn't let her be next, not if there was anything he could do to prevent it. For her, and for the others.

Lyam paused when he got to Rayah's hut, staring up at the trapdoor for a moment. She'd been the first, the very first this had happened to. If only he'd taken it more seriously back then, couldn't they have done something more to protect the Dreamers? They were the most precious members of their society. Nothing would function without them. And now there were only four left.

Lyam only paused for a heartbeat before fear drove him onwards again.

He studied the wall to his left as he walked, knowing that according to the map the entrance to the southernmost tunnel should be somewhere along here. It was dusty, a few cobwebs dangling from the ceiling seeing as the only people that ever came back here were the Scribes and the few guards who brought them their food and supplies. A shiver ran down Lyam's spine as he walked, lantern swinging from his right hand, his left carefully feeling along the wall. Sand trickled past his knuckles.

Eventually, as he walked, there was a dip in the wall.

He froze, swinging the lantern forward so he could illuminate the next part of the passage, and sure enough, there was an opening. Narrow, and low, filled with cobwebs that looked as if they'd been recently disturbed. A few scattered piles of sand lay on the ground surrounding the opening.

Lyam gulped. The lantern only illuminated the very beginning of the narrow passage. He would have no idea what he was disturbing if he went through there.

But he had no choice. What if this was his only chance to save Annelie?

Steeling himself, Lyam crouched, pulling the lantern with him, and ducked into the passage.

The tunnel was cramped. Lyam had to walk with his back stooped and his head held low, though there was thankfully enough room that he didn't have to crawl. He thanked his shorter-than-average height as he crept his way forwards. Sand and dust fell down around him, beetles scurrying away from the lantern light, the smell of dry dust clogging up his throat. Shadows swung around him as he made his way forward.

Eventually, the floor of the tunnel began sloping upwards. Lyam blinked, hesitating. The Dreamers' huts were already built on higher ground than the city, so that the huts themselves could be above ground, although of course the windows were always kept tightly covered to protect the sacred sunlight. If the ground was sloping up further...

Enoch walked in the light. He'd told Lyam, shown Lyam the scratches on his arms from the hailstorm.

Lyam's heart pattered away quickly in his chest. He couldn't be about to face actual sunlight. There was no way.

He turned to go back.

But Annelie. The Dreamers. What if this truly was the only way to help? Annelie had said to go to Enoch, and Lyam had never once gone against Annelie's gut.

He wasn't about to start now.

With a scared, shaky breath, Lyam turned back around and pushed on upwards.

The tunnel climbed steeply, so steep that Lyam had to grip the gritty walls, lantern swinging wildly, and heave himself up the narrow passage with his head ducked low to avoid smacking it against the ceiling. Scariest of all, the place was getting... lighter. Lyam could start to pick out details ahead of him, from outside the circle of his lantern light—a spider retreating, the pattern of the mud-brick of the walls, some sand hanging loose.

In fact, the further Lyam went, the less he needed the lantern.

He stopped again, frozen, when he saw up ahead of him something that chilled him to his core.

A streak of light. Pale, thin, almost wispy-looking, it beamed down the passage and stopped just a few centimetres in front of him; a burst of pure light.

A sunbeam.

He'd read about such things, but never in his life did he imagine he'd see one in reality. The farmers grew their crops using reflected sunlight from carefully-controlled cracks in the ceiling, but anyone other than the farm workers were forbidden from seeing them. The sunbeam looked fragile, tangible, as if he could touch it if he dared reach out his fingers.

The fear that had clutched at him over seeing such a sacred thing died in his wonder at the light. He leaned a little closer, glasses slipping down his nose, and he examined the sunbeam closely. It was more awe-inspiring than when he'd read about it. The light from the Sun, from the Life-Giver, was the most beautiful thing Lyam had ever seen, but he felt as if he could break it if he tried to touch it.

Never mind what it might do to him.

Lyam swallowed. He glanced up ahead to where he could clearly see the end of the tunnel, lit up by streams of light similar to the one beam that landed just in front of where he stood. The end of the tunnel looked to have been blocked off by something, potentially a large stone or some kind of rounded object, Lyam couldn't quite make out what it was made from at the distance he was standing. He didn't want to risk going any closer for fear of breaking the careful beams of sunlight that drifted his way.

He scanned the area in front of him slowly, marveling at the singular narrow beams of light, and then he saw it.

A bell.

Enoch's words came back to him, and Lyam knew what he had to do. Working moisture into his mouth, he stepped closer, carefully edging around the one beam of light that almost touched him. For a beautiful, terrible second, he wondered what it would feel like against his skin, but then he pushed the thought away with revulsion.

Once he was safely around the light, Lyam reached out to where the bell was sitting on a little ledge. His fingers just grasped the edge of it, and then, heart in his mouth, he gave it a quick shake. A clear, high sound rang from it, softer than the bells used from the center of the city to mark the time and summon a meeting.

After a few moments of silence, Lyam rang the bell again. Its sound made his stomach jerk, but his heart was already pattering away with nerves just from being here. It was such an offense to actually be in the presence of sunlight that Lyam already knew he'd be in grave trouble if somebody found him here.

He hoped Annelie had been right about this.

Finally, after a few more agonizing moments of waiting in which Lyam was genuinely afraid his heart was going to do itself in with how quickly it was beating, there was movement from the end of the tunnel. Sand crumbled down, dust filling the air, as the object blocking the edge of the tunnel slowly started to move.

Lyam jumped back, clinging to his lantern and gasping aloud as, with a great wrench and the grating sound of stone grinding against stone, the object was pulled back. With each shift it made, more light came streaming into the tunnel, bright and beautiful and terrible, and Lyam dropped his lantern in favor of throwing his arms up to cover his eyes.

Even through the stiff material of his robes, Lyam could see the bright bursts of sunlight that came streaming into the tunnel with merciless, bounding energy. It was everywhere, white spots dancing behind his eyelids, glaring light filling his vision, pounding against his temples and pressing into his head. The light filled him with an aching burning sensation, warmth hitting his skin full-on. He cowered behind his arms, whimpering.

Footsteps sounded from far ahead of him. A grunt, and then the horrible grating sound again.

The light began to die.

And then, a welcomingly familiar gruff voice: "You can look now, Scribe Lyam."

Lyam hesitated, hiding behind his arms, his head almost fully buried in his robes. He trembled, but then he felt a steady hand on his shoulder, and the vivid light that had pushed him into the corner had gone.

Carefully, Lyam lowered his arms and blinked his eyes open, and he was surrounded by darkness again.

Only the thin beams of light that filtered through the cracks in the opening were there; the stone that covered the tunnel's end was back in place. Lyam let his shoulders fall, tension leaking out of him.

The hand on his shoulder tightened, and Lyam turned to find himself face-to-face with Enoch.

Enoch towered over him, his blue robes flowing down to the sand covered ground, the sandals on his feet caked in it.

Lyam swallowed. Nerves jumbled around in his stomach, tying him in knots.

Enoch regarded him with an unreadable expression, but then

his face broke out into a smile. It changed all his features. The stern furrow to his brow disappeared, the wrinkles on his forehead smoothed, his eyes creased upward with warmth.

"Well, Scribe Lyam," Enoch said, his tone bright. "What a surprise to see you here."

Lyam was smiling back before he realized it. Something about Enoch's expression drew him in, made him feel relaxed. The bright spots of sunlight danced around Enoch's robes, the sunbeam just touching the edge and turning the colors a bright, sparkling blue. Lyam wanted to jump into it, to wrap himself up in the beautiful warmth for the rest of his life.

But he couldn't.

The thought of the Dreamers washed over him, turning his blood cold, freezing his mind until his thoughts were sluggish and heavy. Worry coursed through him, fear twisting inside his gut. *Seven*, in one night. He had to somehow keep Annelie safe.

Looking up at Enoch, Lyam wondered how much he'd be able to help, how much he really knew about any of this. If what he'd read was true, and the Water-Gatherers were as close to the Sun as the Dreamers were, then maybe he knew something. Something the Life-Giver had kept secret so far, or something the Scribes and Designers had been unable to decipher.

He had to take this chance, no matter how dangerous it could be.

"I need your help," Lyam said quietly.

Enoch frowned, but before he could say anything Lyam continued, "Please. Something awful is happening, and I don't understand it. But Anni trusts you, so I'm here."

The crease in Enoch's forehead was back in full form. His voice was flat and stern; serious. "What happened?"

"Seven Dreamers," Lyam answered, doing his best to keep his voice steady. "They were attacked last night."

Enoch's eyes flew wide open.

"There's more," Lyam added, watching the way Enoch stumbled back a step with his heart pounding and his stomach dropping with fear. "Annelie said the Life-Giver is leaving us."

Enoch threw his hand out to catch himself against the side of the tunnel. His eyes were fixed on Lyam, his mouth half-open, shock written into every feature on his face. Lyam felt his stomach clench up tight inside him and his throat constrict. His pulse fluttered in his throat.

Enoch continued to stare at him.

After a too-long moment, Lyam licked his lips. "Aren't you going to say anything?"

Enoch regarded him, and Lyam noticed that he looked unsettled, too.

Lyam felt something break inside him. "*Please*," he almost wailed. "I don't—I don't know what to *do*. The Life-Giver is leaving us, and..."

His throat closed up further the second the words left his mouth. The enormity of them shook his world all over again, flipping his foundations upside down until he didn't even know which way was up. He felt like he hadn't had a chance to breathe in days.

He stared back at Enoch in despair. "Please."

Slowly, Enoch straightened up again. His gold eyes almost glowed in the light of the singular sunbeam that fell on him, just a thin wisp of light, but it was enough to illuminate his broad chin and wide forehead, his long narrow nose. Lyam shuddered again, wondering at how he was seeing actual sunlight direct from the Life-Giver itself.

He couldn't defend himself against blasphemy anymore.

"I will tell you what I know," Enoch said, the words dropping between them like stones in the dark. "But you may not like it."

Lyam swallowed, his throat aching. "I'll take anything at this point. Please. I have to keep my Dreamer safe."

"You're a good one," Enoch responded, his gaze warm as he looked down at Lyam. "I can sense that much. Come with me, Scribe Lyam."

Lyam forced his legs to move, picking up his lantern and following Enoch back down the tunnel, away from the sunlight. A strong longing settled in Lyam's chest, yearning to see the light again, to feel as close to the Life-Giver as he had just then. But he knew it wasn't his place. He was just a Scribe, not a Dreamer. He had no right to seek things above his station.

The tunnel sloped sharply downwards, so Lyam had to brace himself against the sides of the passage and watch every step with care to make sure he didn't slip. Enoch was a big lumbering shadow in front of him, the blue of his cloak faded to an almost dull grey in the darkness that slowly grew around them.

Lyam was beyond grateful he had found his lantern again, although the candle had blown out. Either way, he still clung tight to its metal handle, enjoying the cold steely feeling in the palm of his hand to ground him in the light of what he'd just witnessed. His heart was still racing, panic barely held at bay.

Enoch ducked to the left when they were a little way down the tunnel. Lyam followed him, confused, fingers scrabbling against the rocky wall to steady himself at the sharp corner. In the dark, it was almost impossible to see anything.

There came the scratch of something, then a crackle, and a burst of light appeared in the darkness ahead of Lyam, illuminating a small cave with benches, a few books littered on the floor, and a bright-colored rug decorated with blues and reds placed in the middle.

Lyam looked around with trepidation.

"Don't look so afraid," Enoch grunted from ahead of him, holding a taper. He set about lighting the lanterns set into the walls. "Nothing here bites. Apart from the snakes." He gave a crooked grin.

Lyam swallowed, slowly and carefully entering the small space. With Enoch in the corner, he felt cramped. "What is this place?"

"My home away from home," Enoch answered wryly, and pointed to one of the benches. "Sit. I won't harm you."

Lyam's heart was still pounding, but he carefully lowered himself into the seat anyway. He watched as Enoch bustled around, moving some books out of the way, kicking down the corner of the rug. He only stopped when all the lanterns were lit, creating a warm bubble of light in the small space. Lyam sat back, feeling his tense muscles relax.

Annelie trusted Enoch, and Lyam trusted Annelie. He had to believe he would be safe here.

"Well." Enoch settled himself onto the bench opposite Lyam, his massive frame seeming too big for the space. He fixed Lyam with a stern stare. "It's time you knew what was really happening in your city, Scribe Lyam."

Lyam swallowed. His heart fluttered in his chest as he forced himself to speak. "What do you mean?"

"I mean the curse. It's been building for years, hundreds of years, and we're seeing the end of it now."

"Stop speaking in riddles. Do you know anything?" Desperation tinged his tone, despite Lyam doing his very best to sound calm.

"I don't mean to confuse you. I just mean to prepare you. Something is rotten, and what you believe is based on lies. The Dreamers aren't the only ones who can speak to the Sun."

Something cold trickled down the back of Lyam's neck.

"There are others," Enoch continued, his gold eyes fixed on Lyam's. "Or, there were others. Everyone, in fact, in a time not so long ago."

Lyam frowned, curling his hands into fists in his lap. "You're talking about the myths."

"The myths were reality in ages past," Enoch answered, his tone turning dark. "Not too long ago, either."

"Are you talking about the Water-Gatherers?"

Enoch pinned Lyam with a stare.

"I read about you," Lyam continued carefully, "after what you told me you were. I read that there were many of you, that you...that you walk under the Life-Giver's rays." He swallowed. He'd just seen for himself how true those words were.

Enoch nodded slowly.

"Do you know what's happening?" Lyam asked, desperation clawing its way up his throat. "Please. The Dreamers, they're in danger. Anything you can tell me might help."

"The curse," Enoch rumbled.

"What curse? What do you mean?"

"First, you need some context." Enoch sat back. "You're correct; I am a Water-Gatherer, and I live outside. Above ground."

Lyam couldn't hold back his shudder. Revulsion stuck in his throat.

"I see that you're displeased with that," Enoch continued wryly. "I'm not surprised. Your society teaches you to fear that which is natural, after all."

"What do you mean?"

"I mean that everyone is supposed to be like me. Living above ground, communicating with the Life-Giver, not just through the Dreams."

Lyam's mouth dropped open. He stared at Enoch, tracing his features, looking for some sign of madness to match the words he spoke. "*What?*"

Enoch's wry smile turned into a grin. "That's how things *should* be. If you could feel the sunlight, live in the warmth, the joy. You don't know anything. You've been underground too long. Everyone here has been underground for too long."

Lyam swallowed harshly. "We've *always* been underground," he whispered, his voice cracked. He felt frozen with shock.

Enoch clicked his tongue. "No. You're taught you always have been, but I remember differently. I remember when there were so many Water-Gatherers that our singing could draw a sandstorm. I remember when our work was filled with dance, when we were celebrated for living under the sun, when we worshipped the Life-Giver with our hard work and our devotion and our *whole lives*. Everything we did was under the Sun, and we bathed in the light and the warmth our Life-Giver gifts us with every day."

Lyam was shaking. He stared at Enoch with horror in his eyes. "That's—you're speaking blasphemy. You *can't*—"

"I'm speaking the truth," Enoch cut him off impatiently. "I don't expect you to believe it. But you saw it, today. The light.

There's a reason you can stand by the sunbeams and not be blinded. You have the eyes."

Lyam stared at him in confusion.

"That's why I came to you," Enoch continued. "A gold-eyed Scribe. It gives me hope that things may be starting to change. That maybe the curse can be lifted."

"I still don't understand," Lyam whispered. "A curse? What curse?"

Enoch let out a drawn-out sigh. "It happened long ago. Long before my time. We were once a people who lived above ground. We had a city. It's still there, albeit in ruins now. But it was ours. Until the curse.

"It's hard to piece together exactly what happened. So much has been lost—writings, oral history, our origins. But something happened. The curse came into being, and I have an idea of where it may have come from. And how to stop it."

Lyam stared. "We can stop it?"

"I need to see inside the safe," Enoch rumbled. "That's the only way to end it. End the suffering of the Dreamers, and the fact that so few of us can cope with the light. And I need you to help me, Lyam. The Gold-Eyed Scribe."

Lyam shuddered. His eyes. He hated his eyes, he had for as long as he could remember. They made him an outcast, made people send him sidelong glances. Gold-eyed people were unheard of apart from in the myths. He'd fought against the curse of his eyes all his life.

Enoch, with his own gold eyes, was looking at Lyam with something almost pitying in his gaze. "I don't expect you to understand yet. But listen, and believe. You deserve a different life to the one you've been given."

Lyam took in a quick breath and dropped his eyes to his lap, watching the way his fingers twisted in his stiff green robes. He felt rocked, the foundations he'd always believed in slowly slipping out from under his feet. He couldn't take it in. It was madness.

Slowly working moisture into his mouth, Lyam asked, "What am I supposed to do?"

"The safe." Enoch sat forward, his tone growing eager. "I was given that key by someone with their own suspicions. I'm certain it holds the secret."

A furrow creased Lyam's brow. "What are you saying?"

"I'm saying," Enoch answered, his voice rumbling in the small space, "that you need to take me to that safe, tonight, and then we might find out what's really going on."

CHAPTER

EIGHT

The role of the Designers is not to lead.
They act as the hands of the Dreamers,
Bringing their words to life.
The Book of the Life-Giver, Vol III, Chapter I

L yam made his way back to his and Annelie's hut with his heart hammering in his throat. The whole journey back from seeing Enoch, he'd had to force himself not to run, constantly peering over his shoulder with the lantern swinging wildly from his grip. He was sure he was about to be caught; that somehow the fact he'd stood in actual sunlight that morning was clinging to his skin, the plans he'd made with Enoch wrapped up with his robes.

When he turned the tunnel to his hut and found a black-clad guard standing just beneath the trapdoor, Lyam's heart almost stopped. He froze in place, the lantern knocking into his side with a dull thud that immediately alerted the guard to his presence.

The guard turned, his black tunic and trousers clinging to his frame. He saluted. "Scribe Lyam."

Lyam swallowed, attempting to straighten his robes and stop his heart from clambering out through his throat. "Who sent you here?"

"I'm to guard your hut on orders of Head Guard Tomas himself," the guard replied, and bowed formally. "It's a pleasure to meet you. Rest assured that you and your Dreamer will be safe."

Lyam's mind went blank for a moment as he racked his brains as to why the Head Guard had sent someone to watch over him. Had word of his misdemeanours already spread? How? Had someone seen him go to Enoch? Standing in the sunlight? Even the thought of it made Lyam feel faint.

The guard evidently noticed some of his distress, as he smiled kindly at Lyam. "It was decided at the last Council meeting. All the Dreamers have someone watching over them. I believe Head Scribe Tasmin was supposed to inform you?"

Of course. Lyam sagged a little with relief. It wasn't specific to him; every Dreamer was to have a guard while the Council tried to figure out what to do about the Dreamers' plight. Nobody knew about his meeting with Enoch.

He was safe.

Lyam let out a breath and dipped into a bow to the guard. "Sorry. I remember now. A lot has happened."

If the guard was interested, he didn't show it on his face. He simply smiled again and stepped to the side.

Lyam walked past him slowly, reaching up to pull down the trapdoor and fetch the ladder. The guard watched him calmly, but Lyam still felt uncomfortable as he began to ascend.

As soon as he was inside, Lyam slammed the trapdoor shut behind him, leaning back and taking in deep, harsh breaths to try and calm his racing heart. He felt exhausted, the nights of little sleep itching at the back of his eyelids, the heavy news of his meeting with Enoch weighing him down. He wanted to crawl into his bed and pull the blankets over his head and stay there for days, or at least until the world started to make sense again.

"You look awful."

Annelie's voice sounded from the bed and Lyam jumped, turning to her instantly. She was smiling at him, though the expression looked a little forced. Her round face looked gaunt, her skin glowing slightly. Her Dreams must be leaking through again.

Lyam remembered the beautiful beam of sunlight he'd seen earlier that day and shivered.

"What happened?" Annelie asked, leaning back in her chair. Mima was sitting up beside her, batting at the edge of her blanket with intense perseverance, her pale fur looking sleeker and healthier than when Lyam had first found her. She was growing already.

Lyam shook his head, wondering where to even start. He got to his feet and set the lantern down by the candle on the desk, and then he moved to his bench by Annelie's chair and began to tell her everything.

He told her about finding the tunnel; about the sunlight and his terror and wonder at it; about Enoch appearing and the utter madness of his words. The curse. The idea chilled his heart.

He told her about how they'd planned to meet again that evening, after Enoch had completed his duties for the day (whatever those were) and then they would make their way to the library. Lyam still had no idea how he was going to get Enoch into the Scribes' Hall. Enoch had made it very clear that he wanted to be part of it, and honestly, Lyam didn't feel confident at all about breaking into someone else's safe. He knew he might lose his nerve. Enoch wouldn't.

Annelie sat back thoughtfully once Lyam had finished explaining. Her movements were still slow, her body tired from the stress of the Dreams and the continued worries about the Dreamers. Lyam remembered Adan and shuddered. They had to stop it from happening again.

"I trust Enoch," Annelie said eventually.

Lyam glanced at her, feeling the knot in his stomach unravel slightly. "You do?"

Annelie nodded her head once, slowly, her eyes fluttering shut. "Something about him is familiar. Accept his help. And anyone else's, just—we need all the help we can get. Go to Mirah today, Lyam, and quickly. I can't let another night like last night happen." Her voice trembled over the last few words.

In seconds, Lyam had reached out and grasped her hand. He grounded her as best he could, leaned over so she could see him without having to turn her head, which was heavy against her pillow, her limbs slowed with sluggish tiredness.

She looked haunted.

Lyam swallowed. He reached out and gently placed the back of his hand to her forehead, and he wasn't surprised to feel her burning up. He got back to his feet and fetched the bowl of cool water and the damp cloth, gently patting at her forehead. "I'll trust Enoch. I still don't know how we're going to break into the library."

"You could go at night," Annelie answered, her voice low and tired, but her words clear.

Lyam almost dropped his cloth. "I can't. I have to be with you."

"I can...I can hold off the Dream," Annelie insisted, but Lyam shook his head firmly.

"No. Not after last night, Annelie. I'm not leaving you."

Annelie chewed on her lower lip, her gaze flicking away from Lyam's and down to Mima as she thought. Lyam studied her closely, gently lifting her head with one arm while he washed the back of her neck too. He was stubborn when he needed to be, and he wouldn't leave her.

"The Scribes' Hall will be empty at night," Annelie pointed out slowly. "If you...if you went there late, you have more chance of hiding."

Lyam shook his head, fear crushing him. "I can't. We'll go before, and I'll be back here by night."

"What if you don't have time?" Annelie asked with effort. She lifted one hand, her movements slow, and she winced as she wrapped her hand around Lyam's wrist. "What if someone sees you leaving the Hall with whatever is in the safe?"

Lyam bit his lip. He shook his head. "I don't know. But I won't leave you alone at night."

"I want you to."

"It isn't safe."

"I have to Dream whether you're here or not," Annelie pointed out, her tone surprisingly fierce even as she trembled with the effort of speaking. "I'm the one that has to go through it. You can't come with me, whether you're here or not."

Lyam balked. His breath felt like it had been punched out of his chest. He swallowed, leaning closer and trying to take Annelie's hand, but she withdrew it and faced him, determination clear in the set of her full lips. "Trust me. There's something happening, and...and I can't go and look for myself. So, I'm sending you instead. Take Enoch to the safe."

Lyam closed his mouth. He couldn't really argue with that.

"Alright," he said quietly, and watched her relax. "I'll take him. After I've spoken to Mirah, I'll take him."

෨

L yam put his head down, retreating into his green robes as he made his way back through the maze of tunnels into the city on his way to see Mirah. The South Gate stood tall and ostentatious ahead of him, bustling as ever. Lyam swallowed, nervous about having to get Enoch through here later. He hoped it would be quieter at night. They couldn't risk getting caught. Head Guard Tomas wasn't exactly known for his forgiving nature.

Before he started worrying about that night, Lyam had to get through another meeting with Mirah first. The idea of explaining just how dreadfully wrong everything had gone scared him, simply because saying the words out loud would make them so much more real. Seven more Dreamers, leaving only four still

Dreaming, and they were still in danger too. He just prayed that Mirah had some plan for the night coming; that the Life-Giver had given them some way out of this. Otherwise, Annelie would be walking into danger every time she slept, and there was nothing either of them could do about it.

Perhaps Mirah would have the solution. She always had a way of interpreting the Dream that made sense. Perhaps all hope was not yet lost.

Lyam kept repeating this to himself the whole journey through the city—past the carts rumbling their way through, the donkeys braying, the people nodding at him. His green robes brought him some respect, but he made sure to keep his head down as much as possible for fear of people recognizing his eyes.

Gold eyes. Like Enoch's.

Lyam shook his head, trying to forget all he'd seen that morning; the beauty of the single sunbeam he'd studied. He never should have seen it. He'd cursed himself, blasphemed. And yet it had been so beautiful, so tempting. He'd been taught all his life to resist such things. He couldn't stray from his path now.

He felt completely mixed up. But Mirah would fix everything.

Lyam ducked through some of the smaller alleys of the city, the quieter streets where the only people were messenger youths or children playing hide-and-seek around corners. Dust lay heavy in the air, the lanterns dimmer on the smaller streets. Lyam liked it; the quieter atmosphere, the scents of cooking and the children's screams of delight. Not for the first time, he wondered what it was like to live here. Did these children have any idea what was happening to the Dreamers?

Lyam swallowed. He couldn't rest, no matter how much he wanted to. So he kept directing his steps forward, along the dusty paths until he was back amongst the bustle of the city, leading to the main square.

Lyam turned a corner, and there it was, the beautiful main square of the city paved all in white and gold. The citadel rose up in all its imposing glory on the opposite side of the square. Its beautiful glass walls reflected the lantern light, sending thousands of beams of light bright across the square, sparkles of dust and sand dancing in its rays. All around him, people were marveling at the sight, but Lyam couldn't help but think it didn't stand up to the beauty of the one sunbeam he'd seen that morning.

Blasphemy. He'd be put to death for such thoughts if anyone could hear him.

Swallowing, Lyam made his way across the square, threading through the crowds until he reached the Designers' building. He climbed the few gleaming white steps to the door, feeling eyes of people on his back. His green robes gave him space, at least, as people stepped back to let him through, bowing their heads in a nod. Lyam nodded back, glad to escape to the relative safety of the building once the guards had let him through.

A guard opened the door after a quick check of his robes and face, and Lyam swallowed as he stepped through the large door. The floors inside were still white, but lined with brown that matched the robes worn by the Designers who walked the halls with purpose. Lyam drew in a slow breath and let it out before he started down those same hallways, turning to the first staircase and beginning to climb.

He reached Mirah's office uninterrupted and lifted his hand to knock, but paused when he heard an unknown voice coming from inside.

"...no issues yet, there's no need to raise concerns."

It was a male voice, speaking with unquestionable authority. Lyam paused a moment, hand still raised to knock, when he heard Mirah's answer.

"I know, but if they hear—"

"They won't hear anything," the first voice said with confidence. "There's no need to worry."

Silence for a few seconds, and then Mirah spoke again.

"Izani, you know that I trust you, but I can't help but think this could go wrong."

Lyam froze at the name. *Izani*. The Head Designer. His hand, still raised to knock, began to tremble, his insides twisting as he listened to Mirah continue.

"My Scribe. What do I tell him?"

"I don't care," Izani snapped, and Lyam jumped at the forcefulness of his tone. "Tell him whatever you need to tell him to keep him quiet."

"I'm doing my best," Mirah replied evenly. "But he's smart. They all are. This is hanging on a knife's edge, and I'm afraid."

"This won't be any of your concern soon," Head Designer Izani answered, his voice slightly softer, slightly smoother. "There's a place waiting for you on the Council. You know this. If you want it, all you have to do is keep your head down. This will pass soon. Trust me."

A moent of silence reverberated.

"I have always trusted you." Mirah's voice sounded meeker. "I suppose it's all I can do."

"Good." Izani sounded satisfied. "Don't be afraid. I've got a handle on it, and I've spoken to Speaker Ayanah. Soon everything will be right again."

Mirah made a sound of agreement, but Lyam swallowed, unsettled. He'd never officially met Designer Izani, although he'd seen him at key events and celebrations. He was at every choosing, and with his place on the Council, he'd also been present when the new Speaker had been appointed. It unsettled Lyam to hear them speak about Mirah having a place on the Council. The Life-Giver appointed all their Council members through the Dreams, and with the chaos surrounding the Dreamers, Lyam certainly hadn't heard anything about Mirah.

But then again, he could have missed the news in the chaos, he reasoned with himself. He'd been so afraid the last several days that he hadn't had a chance to focus on anything else.

Lyam almost squeaked when footsteps sounded from the other side of the door, and he stumbled backward as quickly as he could, managing to make it a few steps down the corridor before the door to Mirah's office swung open and there stood Head Designer Izani in all his glory.

Lyam swallowed, trying to calm his racing heartbeat. Head Designer Izani was a tall man, his greying hair and beard neatly trimmed, his dark brown eyes piercing. His nose was upturned and his brows thick, giving him a permanently fierce look. His brown robes swung around his sleek frame, the gold trim marking his place as Head Designer making him imposing and authoritative. He regarded Lyam with a cool gaze, clear in the lanternlight that lined the corridor.

Slowly, Lyam remembered himself, and quickly dipped into a bow. "D-Designer Izani," he stumbled. "Uh, I mean Head Designer Izani. It's an honor to meet you."

Izani tilted his head, studying him. Lyam shivered under the gaze, and he straightened slowly, keeping his eyes down.

There came a rustle from the doorway, and Mirah poked her head out, her expression drawn and tired. She lifted her brows when she saw him. "Lyam," she said, surprised. "I didn't expect to see you today."

"No, sorry," Lyam turned to her, nervously avoiding looking at Izani. "I'm sorry to bother you, it's just...there's been an emergency."

An emergency. Seven Dreamers had been attacked, and it looked as if Mirah had no idea from the crease that furrowed her brow. She looked tired, small next to Izani, who stood tall and proud, almost as tall as Enoch, if not as broad. Lyam couldn't compare them; where Enoch was vast and all-encompassing, Izani was lithe and sure, his gaze sharp.

He hadn't looked away from Lyam once.

Lyam swallowed, unsure what to do under such scrutiny. He curled his fingers in the edges of his robes and shifted his feet, glancing from Mirah down to the ground, deliberately avoiding meeting Izani straight in the eyes. The only Council member Lyam knew well was Tasmin, and she was different as she'd mentored him since before she became Head Scribe. Lyam didn't know what to do with himself around such important people.

He drew in a trembling breath and glanced once more at Mirah. "Please? It's important."

She looked at him blankly for a second before giving her head a shake, as if swatting a fly away, and stepped to the side to wave him forwards.

Lyam walked towards her, but before he could reach the door Izani shot his hand out and caught Lyam's arm.

Lyam froze.

"It's good to meet you, Scribe Lyam," Izani said slowly, his voice as sharp and cutting as glass. "I've heard lots about you."

Lyam swallowed. His arm burned where Izani touched him. He didn't know what to say to that, so he awkwardly bowed his head, still doing his best to avoid looking Izani directly in the eyes. The power behind his gaze was almost too much.

Slowly, Izani released him, and Lyam resisted the urge to shake some feeling back into his hand.

Izani bowed politely. "I'll speak with you later, Designer Mirah. As for you, Scribe Lyam, continue your important work. I hear you're remarkably good at it. And your eyes..." He paused, and this time Lyam didn't look down quickly enough. He was caught looking directly into Izani's eyes.

They were cold, as cold as frozen glass, sending a shiver down Lyam's spine.

"Your eyes are quite something," Izani murmured.

Lyam quickly looked down to the floor again, his ears burning.

Izani contemplated him a moment longer before turning sharply. The door closed with a snap behind him, leaving Lyam alone in the office with Mirah.

Lyam let out a breath and sagged against the doorway.

Mirah laughed at him. "Your first time meeting him, I take it?"

Lyam just nodded, taking off his glasses to rub at his eyes. "Is he always like that?"

"Most of the time," Mirah shrugged. "You get used to it." She went back to her desk, her brown robes swishing around her ankles as she leaned against it, turning to Lyam with an arched brow. "You said there was an emergency?"

"Um...yes." Lyam watched her lean back against her desk with something like fear twisting in his stomach. She looked exhausted already, her face drawn and tired, her body bowed over the desk. Papers were littered everywhere, not her usual neat filing at all. The only thing that looked normal was the view from her wide windows, the Citadel standing proud in the background.

"It's about last night," Lyam continued slowly, reluctant to burden Mirah any more but with no real other option. He glanced away as he said, "The Dreamers. Seven more of them were attacked. Including Dreamer Kiran."

Mirah closed her eyes tight. She bowed her head, and when she spoke, her voice sounded broken. "Seven?"

Lyam shifted on his feet, his eyes fixed on Mirah. Worry sat uncomfortably at the bottom of his stomach, swirling with nerves and a deep-set fear that he'd been carrying since the very first night Scribe Jemme had come to his hut with the news that Rayah was rotting. The foundations of his world were slowly crumbling around him, and Lyam wasn't sure what to cling to anymore.

"Annelie Dreamed it," Lyam said slowly, "and then Scribe Adan came to me this morning. It's definitely seven. Mirah, that leaves only four. This is a disaster. What do we do?"

Mirah kept her head bowed and her eyes closed. Her palms dug into the desk behind her where she was leaning, her muscles tight with strain. She looked a shell of herself.

Lyam wrapped his arms around his middle, tight.

"Seven," Mirah murmured, and gave her head a sharp shake. "This can't go on."

"What was Head Designer Izani saying?" Lyam asked eagerly. "You said yesterday you were taking the matter to him. Has he come up with something we can do to protect our Dreamers?"

Mirah glanced over at him. "What?"

Lyam frowned, but before he could say anything Mirah

collected herself and replied. "Of course. Izani is talking with the Speaker. Something will be done."

Lyam leaned back a little in relief. "So, what do we do now? Should I warn the other Dreamers? I can visit—"

"No," Mirah said sharply.

Lyam jolted, staring at her.

Mirah let out a heavy sigh, watching Lyam closely. "Sorry. Just...your duty has to be to Annelie, Lyam. She's going to need you more than ever right now."

Lyam bit his lip. Annelie was perfectly capable of taking care of herself, as long as he was there to manage some of the physical things. She was certainly coping better than he was right now. Why did it feel like no one was helping them? Why did he feel like he was hanging on a knife's edge, and one wrong move could tip the balance into danger?

But still. Mirah could be right; Annelie was supposed to be his first priority, and he always would put her first. Should he be staying by her side all day instead of coming into the city? But how was he supposed to fix anything for her if he didn't? And she *wanted* him to go out, to do the things that she wasn't allowed to.

It all felt like too much.

"Of course, I'm sorry," Lyam mumbled, folding his arms across his chest. "It's just that it doesn't feel fair, sitting here doing nothing when I know that Dreamers are in danger. And the Scribes left behind must be terrified too."

The thought of the state Adan had been in that morning was enough to shake Lyam. He wanted to help; he *had* to help.

"It's ok," Mirah murmured, crossing the space between them to lay a hand on Lyam's shoulder. She was the same height as him, and met his eyes directly. "I'm taking care of it, I promise. I'll do my job just as you'll do yours, and everything will work out. I promise."

Lyam swallowed. He remembered what Enoch had told him that morning, the madness that said they should live above ground, but also that there was something evil happening around them. A curse.

Fear curdled in Lyam's stomach.

"Ok," he murmured, looking back to Mirah and trying to keep fear out of his expression. "I'll trust you."

The words felt like ash in his mouth

ॐ

L yam was shivering when he left the Designers' Court. His meeting with Mirah left him unsettled, fear gripping him tight and leaving him cold. The thought of having to continue to keep quiet about the danger facing the Dreamers horrified him, but he didn't know what else he could do. If he went around the huts and told the Scribes what had happened, then he'd be directly going against orders from his Designer. While technically the Dreamers had authority over the Designers, Lyam knew it often didn't work out that way. If Mirah caught him then he'd be up against Head Guard Tomas in no time.

Not that he wasn't already in trouble. He'd seen actual sunlight that morning, and he'd thought it was beautiful. That was blasphemy of the highest order.

Lyam swallowed, trying not to let himself dwell on Enoch or any of those problems too much. He didn't want to think about his task for the evening. How he was going to get Enoch into the city, he had no idea. There was no way he'd be able to hide him, resplendent in blue robes and vast as he was, but Lyam had promised. And it might be the only way to learn anything about what was happening to the Dreamers. He had no choice.

Lyam kept his head down as he walked out of the main square, glad that the crowds parted for him after one look at his green robes. The sounds of people chattering and the feeling of tunnel cats slinking past his ankles kept Lyam tied to where he was, but his mind was racing with worry and fear, trying to think through what on earth he could do to keep Annelie safe. He prayed that he would find something with Enoch later, or he was going to have to watch her Dream with the utter terror that it might be her last.

"Lyam! Hey, Lyam!"

The call of his name had Lyam lifting his head, glancing around. The voice was familiar; high-pitched and loud, calling him with an ease of familiarity, dropping the title of Scribe.

He knew who it was before he turned to meet her.

Sure enough, his little sister Sairah was running after him, panting, her sandals slapping against the well-worn path, a lantern swinging from her grip. She had her hands thrown out at her sides for balance, her eyes focused on the ground in front of her, her sleek hair pulled back in a sharp ponytail on top of her head. A cart swung by frighteningly close to her, but she just dodged out of the way and saved Lyam a heart attack.

He smiled, stepping aside in the street to be further out of the way of the constant onslaught of people travelling through the city, and opened his arms wide. Sairah came running into them, throwing her arms around his shoulders and hanging on tight as he straightened and held her close.

"Hey, Sai," Lyam murmured, cradling her in his arms. "What brings you here?"

"Mama said I had to find you."

"Why?"

"Because some men from the Guard came to our house last night." Sairah's voice dropped a bit and she leaned in to whisper in his ear. "They searched your old room."

Lyam went still. His old room? He'd left his parents' house at age nine when he'd been chosen, but they'd kept his room empty, even when they'd had his two younger sisters years after he'd become a Scribe. His old room was mostly a dumping ground for the many objects they accumulated through the years of bringing up his two younger sisters, but there was nothing there apart from old junk.

"What did the guards want?" Lyam asked, his voice dropping to match Sairah's.

She looked him in the eyes with an expression far too serious for her age. "Mama said to tell you they were looking for information about you. They asked lots of questions, but daddy wouldn't answer. They weren't very happy about that. One of the men kept shouting." Her voice wobbled.

Lyam shivered. He hugged her tight.

"Daddy said to tell you that they searched other places, too." Sairah added.

"They did?"

Sairah nodded. "Annelie's parents, and the new Scribe's, and even Head Scribe Tasmin's brother's house."

Lyam almost dropped her in his shock. Tasmin's family? Her brother and his children were her only living relatives; Lyam had met them several times when he was new to being a Scribe. What was going on?

"Are mama and daddy ok?" Lyam asked, shock still seeping slowly through his veins. "What about Kirah?"

"Kiri was crying lots, but mama said she'll be alright," Sairah answered confidently. "Daddy wanted me to come and tell you."

"Thank you. I'll, um..." Lyam paused for a moment, shaking his head. He was utterly bewildered. Why were the guards searching the houses of some of the Scribes? They were supposed to be protecting the Dreamers, not harming the people closest to them. Anger curled hot through Lyam's belly, unusually potent.

"I'll take you home, come on." Lyam set Sairah carefully back down on her feet, and then took her hand. He would get her safely back to his parents, check in on them and find out more about what had really happened, and then he'd return to Annelie before meeting Enoch later that evening.

"Daddy said you should go to Head Scribe Tasmin," Sairah said, clutching onto his hand tight as they began to make their way through the streets.

"Did he?"

"He said she should know about her brother. He was very angry."

"I'll talk to him," Lyam promised.

Sairah bit her lip as she looked up at her older brother. "Are we in trouble, Lyam?"

Lyam felt his heart tug. He thought about the attack on the Dreamers, how there were only four who remained untouched. He thought about Jemme's fear when she'd first come to him, the horror of what she'd said about her Dreamer. He thought about Adan that morning, breaking all the rules by coming directly into Lyam and Annelie's hut, distraught and overwhelmed and with no idea what to do for his injured Dreamer.

Then Lyam thought of his own wrongdoings that morning— going to Enoch, listening to his madness, plotting to bring him inside the Scribes' Hall and breaking all the rules himself.

He thought about the beam of beautiful sunlight he'd seen that morning, gorgeous and tangible and *real*.

He pressed his lips together. "I'll sort it out, Sai. I promise."

"OK," she said, swinging their joined hands.

Lyam wished it was that easy.

§

Lyam hurried through the front door to his childhood home, sick with worry. Thankfully, none of his family had been harmed. He wrapped them all in a hug, still surprised when his mother only came up to his chin now and that his father's back was bent from years of working over a glassblowing desk.

His father hugged him tight before releasing him, and Lyam recognized the worry in his gaze.

"What did they take?" Lyam asked, standing in the doorway of his old childhood room and staring at the mess of books and boxes and old toys and cradles spilling out of every corner. It was obvious that someone had been through who did not love each object; books were spilling pages across the sandy floor, toys broken and carelessly flung away, the floor strewn with bits and pieces that did not belong together. It broke Lyam's heart.

"Nothing," his mother answered from behind him. "They were mostly asking questions, darling."

"About you," his father added darkly.

Lyam swallowed. He turned back to both of them, his heart unsettled. "What did they want to know?"

His parents shared a look that just unsettled him further. He couldn't think why this had happened, why his family had been dragged into the mess that was just getting more and more confusing. Guards, searching his house? A guard outside his hut with Annelie made sense, to protect her, not that they could do much. But guards searching his house? Bringing his family into something that Lyam had been strictly told not to talk about?

None of it made any sense at all.

"They asked about your character," his father told him, his voice just as soft as always despite the stern edge Lyam could hear behind it. "Weren't very happy when we wouldn't tell them much, either."

Lyam's heart fluttered.

"Why did they come, darling?" his mother asked, the lines around her eyes tight as she looked up at him.

Lyam swallowed, debating over how much to say. The honest truth was that he didn't know, but there was a deep-set fear in him that he'd somehow been found out, that they knew about him seeing true sunlight from the Life-Giver that morning, or had overheard his conversation with Enoch. But surely then the guards would have come straight for him, not his family? Even his status as a Scribe wouldn't save him if someone found out about it.

No, not that. But if not that, then what?

Lyam closed his eyes and drew in a slow breath, a hand coming up to rub at his forehead where a headache was starting to form. He just couldn't fathom why the guards had come to his family. What could they possibly have wanted to know about Lyam that they couldn't find out just by asking him? It didn't make any sense.

"Are you alright, Lyam?" It was his father's voice.

Lyam looked up to find him looking at him seriously, his peppered grey hair neatly parted, glasses just like Lyam's perched on the edge of his nose.

"You look tired," his mother added, tucked into his father's side. "Exhausted, actually. Are you eating? Sleeping? Well, as much as you can?"

Lyam felt his heart curl up in warmth at the concern he could hear in their voices. While he didn't see them anywhere near as much as he liked, every time he visited he was made to feel that he had a place, that he was welcome. But he didn't want to drag them any further into the mess that his life was becoming. He couldn't tell them anything. No matter how much we wanted to.

"It's hard," he admitted slowly. "There's a lot happening just now. I'm ok, though. I am, I just..." He paused, and then shook his head. He wasn't even sure what he was trying to say. How did he articulate that lately he'd felt the world tilt on its axis; that nothing made sense anymore; that he'd seen actual sunlight that morning and somehow he was still here?

"Get your rest," his mother said, and hugged him. "And come to us if we can ever do anything."

His father hugged him too, just as soft and gentle as his every other mannerism. He smelt like glass and fire, something so strong from Lyam's childhood that it brought back a rush of memories from his time before being a Scribe, from before he knew Annelie as anything other than the knobbly-kneed girl who lived a few streets away.

He felt like a totally different person to the child he had once been.

"Take care," his father murmured.

Lyam swallowed and nodded. "I will."

He hoped he could keep his promise.

CHAPTER
NINE

The Water-Gatherers are the pillars of our society.
Without them, we are like ants.
With them, we rise to greater heights, and they impart their great
knowledge.
A wise person will always take care to listen when a Water-Gatherer
speaks.
The Book of the Life-Giver, Volume VI, Chapter I

There was one more thing Lyam had to do before he could return to Annelie, and that was to speak to Tasmin. He needed to tell her about the guards searching her brother's house. Maybe she'd have more of an idea about what on earth was going on than he did. It couldn't hurt to talk with her, at least.

The first place he tried was Tasmin's office, but once he reached her door in the Scribes' Hall, he found it empty and her office lantern out. He'd asked around and been told by some of the serving staff that she hadn't come in at all that day, which was so unlike her that Lyam instantly worried. So he found himself leaving the city again after paying a quick call to Annelie's parents to check that they were ok. With his own lantern in hand, he hurried down the tunnels to the north-west of the city until he arrived at Tasmin and Nethan's hut.

Nerves bubbled away in the bottom of Lyam's stomach. He hadn't had occasion to go to Tasmin's hut in several months, but he'd spent so much time coming to her when he was new to being a Scribe that his feet still knew the pathways like the back of his hand. The lights were far dimmer here than in the city, shadows flickering in the corner of his eyes, urgency marking his steps. He couldn't take too long here. Enoch would be waiting.

A guard stood in the corridor below Tasmin's hut. Lyam swallowed down his nerves and bowed his head.

The guard raised her spear. "What's your business here?"

"I need to talk to Head Scribe Tasmin. She's my mentor."

"Your name?"

"Scribe Lyam."

The guard studied him for a second, taking in his green robes and lingering on his eyes, before she reached up with her spear and knocked the flat top against the trapdoor in the ceiling.

Silence reigned for a minute, then there was the sound of footsteps and Tasmin's muffled voice called through the wood. "Who's there?"

"A Scribe to see you," the guard answered roughly.

"It's me," Lyam added, his voice hoarse from the dry sand. "It's Lyam."

There came a scrabbling sound, then the creak of well-used hinges as Tasmin lifted back the trapdoor. She smiled down at him, though there were dark circles under her eyes and her greying hair was spilling out of its tight bun, before rising to her feet and fetching the ladder so she could descend to his level.

The guard watched them silently until Tasmin raised her brows at her. "Give us some privacy."

The guard's jaw worked, but she couldn't refuse a member of the Council. She backed up a few steps and turned her back.

"How are you?" Tasmin asked once the guard was out of earshot, her kind features welcomingly familiar. "Are things going well with your new mentee?"

"Huh?" Lyam asked, his head spinning with so many thoughts that it took him a moment to understand what she was asking him about. Of course. Jorin. Guiltily, Lyam realized that he hadn't even thought about Jorin since the disaster of the seven Dreamers. At least Annelie had said that his Dreamer was one of the ones who survived.

The thought of Adan's distraught face drifted across Lyam's mind again. He felt sick.

Tasmin regarded him with a warm gaze, although he could see the added lines on her face, the worry in the downturn of her mouth. "Scribe Jorin. Is he keeping you on your toes?"

Lyam swallowed. He hated disappointing Tasmin, but in light of everything else that had been happening, his duties as a new mentor had completely slipped his mind.

Something in his expression must have read as guilty, as Tasmin let out a dry laugh and patted him on the shoulder. "Or have you come to me about more distressing matters? You have fear written all over your face, Lyam."

Lyam licked his lips, feeling heat creep up the back of his neck. "Sorry. I just—so much is going wrong. I don't know what to do."

Tasmin sent him a questioning look.

Lyam didn't even know where to begin. Seeing her again wasn't bringing the relief that it normally would, because she looked just as exhausted as he felt, and he didn't even know if she would have the answers he was looking for. But he had to try. She hadn't let him down before.

"Seven Dreamers," Lyam said eventually, leaning close so that his voice wouldn't carry to the guard. "Seven more have been attacked."

Tasmin's lips tightened into a thin line.

Lyam glanced down, studying a spot on the sleeve of his robes as he continued. "I've already been to Mirah about it. She doesn't know what to do either. Although, she says Head Designer Izani is handling it."

"How do you know about this?" Tasmin asked, her tone sharp, though not unkind.

Lyam jumped. He met her gaze again. "Um, Annelie Dreamed it? She saw the seven get hurt, and then..."

He stopped talking before he mentioned Adan's name. He wouldn't bring his friend into trouble. Adan was suffering enough.

Tasmin regarded him, her expression serious. "So Annelie saw everything?"

Lyam nodded his head slowly.

Tasmin looked at him for another moment before she reached out and grasped his arm. "And you've told Mirah? Anyone else?"

"No," Lyam answered, his tone almost turning bitter. "Mirah told me not to." He still wanted to warn the other Dreamers, the only ones remaining, but he knew he couldn't go against a direct order. He almost didn't feel like himself for questioning Mirah in the first place, but he couldn't help but feel trapped, as if he wasn't able to do anything to help. And he wanted to try everything he could to keep Annelie and the other Dreamers safe.

Tasmin clicked her tongue, and when Lyam looked up she was giving him an almost exasperated look. "You and that Dreamer of yours. Always finding out more than you're supposed to."

Lyam blinked at her. "What?"

"No one is supposed to know about the seven," Tasmin answered with a wry smile. "We had a Council meeting. The information is supposed to be kept strictly under wraps, and the Council members have all been ordered to keep it to themselves while the Speaker works out what to do."

Lyam stared at her, taken aback. Even the Council was being asked to keep quiet? What was going on? In that case, what had Izani been doing at Mirah's office? Creeping suspicions were starting to crawl into Lyam's mind, and he didn't like the way it made him feel, as if he was stuck on a path that he hadn't chosen for himself. He felt unsettled.

"Annelie Dreamed about them, though," Lyam insisted. "If she Dreamed about them, then the others did too, right? Shouldn't we be taking it further?"

Not that he knew where else they could go. He'd already told Mirah, and the Council was already aware.

Lyam swallowed. "What are we supposed to do?"

Tasmin let out a soft sigh. She reached forward and ruffled his hair affectionately, making him shake his head and take a step back. "Honestly? I don't know either. I've been staying with Nethan, he needs me right now."

Lyam bit his lip. "Of course. I'm sorry to take you from him, I just—" and then he remembered his real reason for coming to her, and he reached out to grab the sleeve of her robe tightly. "Tasmin, there were guards at your brother's house."

Tasmin blinked at him. "Excuse me?"

"Your brother." Lyam's blood ran cold at the way her face dropped. "And my family, and Annelie's parents, and some of the other Scribes as well. Their houses were all searched."

"When did this happen?" Tasmin's tone was shocked, angry.

"Last night, I think? I was walking back from meeting with Mirah when my sister found me. She said guards came to our house last night and searched my old room, asking questions about me. The same with Annelie's parents, and your brother, and I can only assume it's the same with the other Scribes too."

Tasmin looked shaken. Her brows were drawn low over her forehead, a deep crease in her brow, her lips pursed into a thin line. Lyam didn't like the expression, but he couldn't help but feel grateful that someone was finally taking things seriously. That again, he wasn't the only one scared and confused.

"Why did they do it?" Lyam asked, trying to keep his voice steady. "My family. My youngest sister is only eight. Why would they go to our families?"

"I can only imagine it's some kind of intimidation tactic,"

Tasmin muttered, almost to herself. "Tomas was angry at the Council meeting earlier. He refused to take the matter seriously."

Lyam swallowed. His stomach flipped over in anxiety. "What do you mean?"

Tasmin let out a breath with a low huff, lifting her eyes to meet Lyam's. "I mean, I think Tomas doesn't believe the imminent danger that the Dreamers are in. I think he's searching us because he wants to scare us into letting the matter drop."

"What?" Lyam was horrified. "Why...*why* would we make something like this up? The Dreamers need help, *urgently*."

"I know," Tasmin soothed him, gently placing her palm on his shoulder again. "And we will be there for them. The Council will see, Lyam, don't worry. The Speaker will do something."

Lyam looked at her and wondered whether even Tasmin truly believed the words coming out of her mouth. For the first time in his life, Lyam began to question exactly what the Council was telling him. Keeping quiet just didn't feel like the right thing to do. If he couldn't trust them, then who could he trust?

An image of Enoch flashed through his mind. Lyam tried to dismiss it.

"So, what do we do?" Lyam asked quietly. "It will be night again soon. Annelie has to Dream again. What do I do?"

Tasmin glanced down, and Lyam felt a stab in his chest at how uncertain and exhausted she looked. More of her hair had come down from her bun, strands falling in front of her face, the dark circles under her eyes prominent in the lantern light.

"We stay with them," she said quietly. "We stay with them, and we hope, and we pray."

Lyam swallowed. He wanted to scream that it wasn't enough, that he had no way of keeping Annelie safe when no one was *helping* him. He didn't know what to do. He hadn't known what to do for days now, and every night Annelie grew weaker, more afraid, more exhausted. He was failing at a task he'd been given when he was nine years old and he had no idea where to turn.

Fear wrapped its cold hands around his heart.

"There is hope," Tasmin said softly, and Lyam realized that something of his inner despair must have shown on his face as she reached out and pulled him into a gentle hug. "Believe in the Dreamers, Lyam. Believe in your Dreamer. They are closer to the Life-Giver than anyone; I believe they will be protected."

Lyam shivered. He wanted to believe the words, had never doubted the system before, but there was still a niggling voice in the corner of his mind that was starting to distrust everything he was being told.

He didn't know where else to turn, except maybe Enoch. The safe in the library might hold some answers.

Slowly, as he drew back out of Tasmin's arms, Lyam met her eyes once more and asked, hesitantly, "Tasmin?"

"Hm?"

"Have you... ever heard... of the Water-Gatherers?"

Tasmin jolted, giving him a surprised look. "The Water-Gatherers?"

Lyam nodded his head, trying to read her expression. She seemed surprised, but nothing more than that—not horrified, not shocked, not about to denounce him as a blasphemer. Lyam was surprised by the rush of relief he felt.

"The Water-Gatherers are a myth," Tasmin answered slowly. "There used to be stories about them, oh, years ago. When I was a child. I liked the stories, but they're nothing more than that."

Lyam didn't know what he'd been expecting, really, but at least Tasmin had heard of them. Enoch didn't seem like just a story, though. His presence was undeniable.

"So, you've never met one?" Lyam asked, trying not to reveal too much but desperately seeking answers. He didn't want to trust Enoch. He didn't want to, but he wasn't sure how much of a choice he had. If Enoch could help protect Annelie, and the Council were refusing to do anything, then Lyam would have no choice but to trust him. Plus, Annelie trusted him, and Lyam trusted Annelie's instincts.

Tasmin laughed. "Of course not. And if I did meet someone claiming to be a Water-Gatherer, I'd be quick to send them to a healer. There's nothing right in the head of someone who would do that."

Lyam's blood ran cold.

"It's a story," Tasmin continued, and narrowed her eyes at Lyam. "Have you been spending too much time in the library again?"

Lyam forced out a laugh, hoping it didn't sound as hollow as he felt. "Yeah. Sorry. I found a book, I just...I don't know. I find them interesting."

"I'm not surprised," she answered. "But the stories were old even when I first heard them. I wouldn't trouble yourself about it, Lyam. Focus on your Dreamer. Annelie needs you now more than ever. Nethan has a terrible feeling about tonight."

Lyam's heart sank. Annelie was facing so much danger alone. Surely the Life-Giver wouldn't allow harm to come to her. Lyam had always trusted them before, and something had kept her safe so far. He had to pray that she would remain that way, and that the Life-Giver would not harm her.

He had to believe in something.

Annelie chewed on her lower lip, her expression thoughtful after Lyam had recounted the events of the day so far to her. She was up out of her chair for once, instead seated on one of the rugs on the floor, her legs stretched out in front of her, her back resting against the wall just below the window, the heavy blinds just reaching to the top of her head. She'd been braiding her hair, so it fell in small plaits framing her face. Mima was playing in front of her, batting at a small piece of ribbon. Annelie waved it around, smiling as Mima chased after it.

Lyam sat opposite her on the floor, his legs crossed, out of his stiff green robes and back in his comfortable tunic. He was watching her closely, noting the exhaustion behind her every movement, the sluggish way her hand moved the ribbon, the dark circles under her eyes, the drawn and tired look on her normally cheery, round face. He was worried. Very worried. She was weakening before his eyes and there was very little he could do, other than force her to eat when she could manage it and try and keep her out of bed for a while.

"What exactly did you hear Head Designer Izani saying to Mirah?" Annelie asked, absent-mindedly swirling the ribbon around Mima, who chased it in circles on three legs, her bad paw lifted in the air.

Lyam shrugged, letting out a sigh. "I don't know. I couldn't make sense of it. But there was definitely something about Mirah having a place on the Council. I don't know how the Dream for that could be happening amongst all this mess."

"It isn't," Annelie said quietly.

Lyam stared at her. "What?"

"It isn't happening." Annelie snaked the ribbon across the floor, watching as Mima chased determinedly after it. "The Dreams are all about the Life-Giver at the moment. The Life-Giver l-leaving." She stumbled over the word, struggling. "So, I don't know what Mirah and Izani were talking about, but I do know one thing: it didn't come from the Life-Giver."

Cold seeped through Lyam's veins.

He stared at Annelie, fear rooting him to the spot, his heart beating against his ribcage. "Are you saying that they're, what? Inventing Dreams? You *know* that's impossible!"

Annelie screwed her face up, pausing in playing with Mima. The ribbon hung still. "I know! I know. I can't explain it, Lyam, just—I don't trust them anymore. Not if you heard that, and they aren't giving you any advice about the Dreamers other than to keep quiet about what's happening to us. I don't trust them, and I don't know why!"

Lyam's heart leaped for her. He reached out and gently took her into his arms, closing the gap between them enough that she could bury her head in his shoulder as he held her close. Her plaits swung against the skin of his neck, her familiar scent comforting him.

"We'll do something," Lyam murmured to her, clutching her against him. "I'll do anything to keep you safe. Anything."

"I know," she sniffed, her voice muffled against his chest. "I just—I'm so scared. I'm so scared of Dreaming, I don't know what to do. I thought the Life-Giver—I've always trusted..."

"I know," Lyam hushed her, rocking her gently. "I know."

Minutes passed like that, with Annelie burying her face against Lyam's chest and Lyam holding her as tightly as he could. He would do anything for her. He'd known that from the moment he'd been Chosen as her Scribe. He remembered the day clearly; the knock at his door in the early hours of the morning, his mother stumbling to answer it, the call for Lyam to get out of bed. His father's soft presence as he came into Lyam's room to wake him, the gentle way he held Lyam's hand as Lyam descended the stairs to find strange men at his doorstep—all were as clear to him as if it had happened yesterday.

A Dream had occurred, they'd told him. A First Dream in which a new Dreamer had their first interaction with the Life-Giver. The Dreamers were never the same after that. Not that anyone ever saw them; they were taken to their hut the first instant they awoke from their Dream, and none but their Scribe ever saw them again

Lyam had recognized Annelie's name when they'd told him. He knew her as the gangly girl from a few streets over who played with him sometimes when he wasn't reading books. But he hadn't known she'd be his Dreamer. He hadn't known what a huge part of his life she'd become. She was his sole reason for existing.

Now, as he held Annelie close to him with Mima batting at his knees, he couldn't help but reflect on the years they'd been together. Things had never been smooth, but they clung together. Under Tasmin's tutelage Lyam learned how to Scribe, how to write down everything that happened to Annelie when she slept, and everything she said about her Dreams when she woke. He learned to pass these all on to Mirah, to watch as she made them become reality.

Lyam remembered the first time he'd seen Mirah set something into action purely from his words. It was only a small thing —Annelie had Dreamed that the west wing of the Scribes' library needed looking at, that there were books there that meant something. Lyam brought along his writings to Mirah, and she listened and took them from him. A week later, Lyam had gone to the library to find the west wing closed off, and then a few days later an ancient manuscript that had been thought long lost resurfaced. Lyam remembered the pride he'd felt, how he'd hugged Mirah at their next meeting, how she'd grinned at him with such excitement that they were finally making changes. She was slightly older than him, but not by much. She'd been young, too, when all this started.

Now, Lyam thought of how Mirah had looked that morning —drawn, exhausted, as she sent him away with nothing. She was totally different to how she'd been when they began. Had time done that to her? Or had something else happened to make her so cynical, so broken?

Lyam swallowed. He held Annelie tight against him and resolved to himself then and there that he would do anything to protect the girl in his arms. No matter how uncomfortable or strange or unsettled it made him feel, he would do anything to keep her safe.

Even take Enoch into the Scribes' Library.

"I have to go," Lyam murmured. Silence held between them like the balance of a knife's edge. "If I'm really going to help Enoch, there isn't much time."

Annelie nodded against his chest. "I know. I trust him. I think he knows the Life-Giver even better than I do."

Lyam thought of the glimpse of sunlight he'd seen that morning and silently agreed.

"I wish I could meet him," Annelie said wistfully.

Lyam felt his heart tug. He knew how much Annelie longed for other human contact sometimes, how trapped she felt in her room unable to leave her hut. It was hard when Dreamers were forbidden from contact with anyone other than their Scribe in order to protect their sanctity, but Lyam knew how lonely it made Annelie. She'd cried many tears for it over the years. Lyam wished he could bring other people to her.

"I wish you could, too," he said after a moment. "But—"

"I know," Annelie interrupted with a sad sort of smile. "I know." She sat up straighter and pointed to the wardrobe. "Take your spare robes. Enoch can wear them to get into the library."

"They'll never fit him."

"Do you have any better ideas?"

Lyam snorted under his breath. She made a good point; he had zero ideas, and at least his robes would provide some sort of disguise. Maybe.

He took them before turning to leave the tunnel, kissing the top of Annelie's head even as she swatted him away, laughing, telling him off for being too sentimental when he was going to be late. Mima had clambered back into her lap, so Annelie petted the kitten's head while Lyam turned to leave.

The last thing he heard was Annelie murmuring, "We'll be alright, won't we, Mimi? You and me? We'll be alright together."

⁂

The tunnels felt too quiet as Lyam hurried down the passage that led to Enoch's hut, lantern swinging wildly in his hand. Darkness crowded at his heels as he near-ran, his robes flapping at his ankles. The stale air of the tunnels was slowly dissipating, replaced by a clean, fresh smell that was alien and strange as the passage gradually lightened around him.

Lyam swallowed back fear when he reached the place where the bell was set into the wall and, still there, lay the beam of sunlight, although it wasn't as bright as it had been the day before. Night meant darkness in the land above the tunnels, Lyam knew, but he'd never witnessed it before.

Heart leaping in his throat, Lyam reached out and rang the bell. The sound was clear and echoed through the tunnel, scaring him. If anyone heard that he was here, he would have no defence, no explanation. It terrified him to be acting so obviously against the rules.

It didn't take long for the stone at the exit of the tunnel to begin moving. The awful grating was violently loud, and Lyam instinctively cowered away from it, throwing his hands up over his face to protect his eyesight again. But it wasn't necessary this time. The light that came flooding in was duller, dimmer, though still intense and beautiful to Lyam's eyes.

Lyam stared at it, peeking through his fingers as the stone continued rolling across the entrance. The sunlight splintered into the tunnel, dusky and strange. It spilled across to the area Lyam was standing, and although he flinched it didn't burn him, instead brightening his vision. He reached up with one hand, staring wondrously as the light played across his fingers.

A pleased-sounding grunt sounded from across the tunnel.

With a startled jump, Lyam looked up and saw Enoch standing in the entrance to the tunnel, blocking most of the dusky light from entering. He looked proud, a small smile tugging at the corners of his lips as he regarded Lyam with a warm, calm gaze. "You came back, then."

"I came back," Lyam agreed, though he shook his head. "I must be mad."

"As mad as me," Enoch agreed with humor in his tone. Lyam looked up to find him stepping further into the tunnel, turning with a swish of his long blue robes and pulling the stone back across the entryway. The light disappeared with it, ebbing out of existence as if it had never even been there.

Lyam felt a pang at the loss.

Enoch turned back to him, his robes duller in the lantern light. He regarded Lyam with one eyebrow raised. "Are you sure you're ready for this?"

Lyam swallowed. The question sat heavily in the air between them, and the answer was easily on Lyam's lips. No, he wasn't ready at all. He had no idea what he was doing, and he was terrified that taking this step would leave him with no way back. In fact, he was terrified that he'd already gone too far, that there had been no turning back since the moment the sunlight first fell into his sight. Since the moment Enoch had first come to him with the key.

He gave a quick shake of his head.

Enoch laughed, the sound cynical and hard. "Thought not. You have a choice to make, Scribe Lyam. Either you're ready to go with me and find a solution to this horror, or you can go back to your life and watch the world rot around you. It's easy, really."

"It isn't easy," Lyam argued back, his heart leaping in his throat. He was scared of Enoch, scared of the world he said existed; he desperately wanted to return to life as it had been before.

But he couldn't, something small inside him said. The Dreamers were under attack. Annelie was in danger.

Annelie was in danger.

Shakily, Lyam said, "And you're sure that whatever we find in this safe in the library is going to help the Dreamers?"

Enoch raised both of his hands, palm-out. "I don't know anything for sure, other than we are cursed, and the answer is more likely to be there than anywhere else. There were hailstones again this morning. Our Life-Giver is abandoning us; we must stamp out the evil before it's too late."

Lyam drew in a trembling breath. Pressure built in his head, climbing at his temples. He closed his eyes for a moment.

There was no guarantee that taking Enoch into the library would save the Dreamers. But Annelie trusted Enoch, and if Enoch truly was close to the Life-Giver then Lyam should listen to what he said. But it just seemed so crazy, so alien, to think that something in his city had gone bad.

But then he remembered the conversation he'd overheard between Izani and Mirah. How no one seemed to be helping him try and solve what was ailing the Dreamers. How he felt more alone than he ever had in his life, right at the point where his city was supposed to be helping him.

Lyam swallowed thickly, his throat dry.

"Alright," he murmured, fear making his heart tumble over itself. "Alright. I'm in."

Enoch let out an audible sigh of relief.

Lyam held up his spare green robes, his hands trembling. "I brought these for you. They aren't going to do much to hide you. You're so *noticeable*..."

Enoch gave a hefty laugh. "That's got me into trouble more times than I can count. Don't worry yourself, Scribe Lyam. Your people can't hurt me."

Lyam really wasn't so sure about that. Even if Enoch felt safe, Lyam could definitely get hurt. He didn't much fancy the idea of being thrown in jail.

"You have to stick close to me," he made Enoch promise. "And don't touch anything or talk to anyone. When was the last time you were in the city?"

"Decades."

"Right." Lyam swallowed, nerves tying themselves in knots inside him. "Just...just do what I do, and let me do all the talking. *Please*."

"Am I a sheep?"

"What's a sheep?"

"By the Sun," Enoch muttered, furrowing his brow. "I can't stand how little you know. And you, the most well-read out of them all."

Lyam wasn't entirely sure whether that was a compliment.

"Sheep are animals," Enoch explained patiently. "They live above ground and are notorious for silently following orders without fighting back. I am not one of them."

"I'm not asking you to be." Lyam licked his dry lips, shivering. "Just please—*please*—don't get us into trouble. I'm risking my life taking you inside the Scribes' Hall."

"It's ridiculous that you keep the libraries locked away."

"It's just the way things are."

"All wrong," Enoch muttered, anger marring his face. "No wonder the Life-Giver is leaving."

Lyam didn't want to think about that. He didn't want to

think about the terror in Annelie's eyes, the ferocity that kept her going, desperate to stop the Life-Giver from retreating any further. They couldn't live without the Sun. Their entire society would break down without their guiding power.

Lyam sighed, digging his fingers anxiously into his sleeves. "Come on, then. I want to be back by nightfall."

"We'll move quick," Enoch promised, his voice a rumble over Lyam's shoulder as they started the walk towards the city.

CHAPTER
TEN

The Hall of the Scribes is the center of knowledge.
They keep the secrets of our world on papers locked away,
And only they should be privy to what is hidden between its walls.
The Book of the Life-Giver, Volume II, Chapter IV

With every step they took, Lyam was terrified that guards were going to run to them, that he'd be discovered leading an outsider into their sacred city, or that someone on the street would call them out for the liars they were. But his fears were unfounded. As they moved towards the more populated tunnels towards the entrance to the city, they were joined on the pathway by others; men loading carts, children running errands, women in groups of twos or threes chatting away on their trip into town. Lyam swallowed down his fear and lifted his hood over his head to shield his eyes. Beside him, Enoch hadn't bothered to put up his hood, eyes looking this way and that and attracting a few unwelcome looks.

Lyam's heart beat a little faster every time anyone looked their way.

Getting through the South Gate had Lyam's pulse fluttering in his throat. Nausea roiled in his stomach when he caught sight of the guards standing on either side of the proud entryway, the strong stone archway curving up overhead culminating in a carved image of the sun. There were two guards stationed at either side of the arch, looking across the crowd with a lazy, watchful gaze.

Lyam's heart was hammering, his palms sweating, but he tried to outwardly keep his cool, although he might have ducked farther behind his hood. He prayed that Enoch would hide his face, too, but Enoch still didn't put his hood up, instead looking around with interest as they neared the gate.

Heart in his mouth, Lyam reached over and tugged Enoch's hood up for him.

Enoch sent him a questioning look.

"Your eyes," Lyam said helplessly. "Just...please."

"Alright," Enoch interrupted, his voice completely calm. "I'll follow your lead. It's been a long time since I was in your city."

Enoch was so vast and hulking that it was nearly impossible for them to go unnoticed. The guards eyed him as they approached, but thankfully didn't stop them. Lyam could only hope that the guards at the entrance of the Hall would be as forgiving.

The pathways were much busier here. The buildings of the city grew with each step forward, reaching up several stories towards the top of the cavern way above their heads. Bright lanterns lit the pathway, squabbling children and loud men hauling carts filling the air with sound, the occasional rich merchant passing on a palanquin. The heady aroma of spices wafted out from cafes and restaurants, dark alleyways breaking off from the main path lit by much weaker lanternlight, looking strangely enticing.

Down one such dark alley Lyam led Enoch, one hand on his arm to keep him close by Lyam's side, though he was a little afraid of how Enoch might react to such handling. Enoch kept his silence though, his eyes darting around from under his hood, seemingly taking in everything.

The dark alleys that Lyam led them down were far less frequented, and they only came across a few people on their way to the Scribes' Hall: a couple tucked away in a corner, an old woman using a knobbly stick to carry most of her weight, a few children playing catch. Lyam kept his eyes down and did his best to keep his feet slow, although everything in him had an urge to run. He knew he'd cause much more of a stir if he ran, and he was worried about losing Enoch. The way to the Scribes' Hall was a winding one.

Enoch's expression lit up when they finally broke out of an alley and into the main passage before the Scribes' Hall. The building remained imposingly tall, built out of strong stone, the words carved into it scattering all the way round to the back.

"I'd heard tell of it," Enoch murmured, "But I have no memories here. What a building, what a place! The curse begins here, in many ways, although it ends somewhere else."

Lyam twisted to send Enoch a confused look, bristling despite himself. "Here? But it's sacred..."

Enoch regarded him, his gaze warm and strong. Lyam felt vulnerable under that gaze, carefully taken apart until Enoch could see right to the center of him, and then clumsily put back together again.

"I fear you will understand soon enough," Enoch answered.

Lyam shook his head, certainly not understanding. He felt strung too tight, his head pulsing with an ache, his heart fumbling in his chest. The hardest part was coming up now, getting Enoch inside the Scribes' Hall without notice. Lyam's mouth was dry. He'd never done something like this before, but he knew well enough that now was his final chance to turn back. Once he'd brought Enoch inside, he'd have officially broken the law. He could be put to death. He'd never see his family again.

Enoch watched him closely.

Lyam took in a shuddering breath. Panic was clouding his

vision, making his thoughts tremble and fall over themselves. He didn't want to do this. He didn't want to take Enoch inside.

But he thought of Annelie. Of the Dreamers. Of how little help Mirah and the Council had been.

Lyam swallowed down his fear and straightened his back. His choice was clear. He would do whatever it took to keep Annelie safe.

"Follow me closely," Lyam murmured, glancing to the side to make sure Enoch was listening. "Don't look at anyone directly, and keep your hood up. People know there's only one Scribe with gold eyes. They'll recognize me, but not you. I'll cover for you, just don't say anything, please?"

Enoch eyed him closely. "I said I'd follow you, Scribe Lyam, and follow you I shall."

Lyam nodded, feeling helplessness cling to his skin.

Squaring his shoulders, Lyam let his arm drop from around Enoch's and stepped out from the alley into the main street. He crossed quickly, keeping his head down. Most of the traffic had died down. It was less busy as the Scribes' Hall was tucked away from the main square. Lyam preferred it that way.

He led Enoch around the side of the building, to the servants' entrance he usually liked to go through. The usual black-clad guard lounged against the wall, one hand on the handle of his sword tucked close to his hip. His hood was down, showing lanky limbs and sandy hair, muscles obvious under his cloak.

Lyam steeled himself, took Enoch's arm, and walked as steadily as he could to the entrance.

He wasn't surprised when the guard stopped them. He kicked one foot out in their path, not pushing off the wall, just eyeing them both with an almost amused expression. "Wait. You I know, but I don't recognize him."

Lyam swallowed, lifting his head high. He tried to fight the fear clogging up his throat, aiming to keep his voice steady. "He's my friend."

"Well, I've never seen your friend before, gold-eyes." The scribe finally eased himself upright and took a step closer, blocking the entrance from both of them. He eyed Enoch closely. "Never seen anyone as big as him go in here before."

"He's...new," Lyam said desperately, taking a chance. "Scribe Jorin. He only became a Scribe a few days ago."

Enoch stood impassive, and Lyam prayed that luck would be on his side and this guard wouldn't know Jorin well enough to recognize him by sight yet. Enoch couldn't look any more different to Jorin if he tried.

The guard narrowed his eyes. "I haven't heard that name before."

"He's very new," Lyam pressed, pulse bubbling in his throat. "I'm his mentor. Head Scribe Tasmin gave him to me, so I'm just showing him the library."

"Name of his Dreamer?"

"Elinah," Lyam said without hesitating. "She was chosen earlier this week."

"He's old to be newly chosen."

Enoch grinned, showing his crooked teeth. "The Life-Giver works in mysterious ways."

The guard raised a brow. "And you know about that, do you?"

"Of course not. No one truly understands the Life-Giver, though I strive to learn."

"Yeah," Lyam cut in, tightening his hold on Enoch's arm. "He's learning, and I'm going to teach him."

He prayed that the guard didn't hear Enoch's low scoff.

The guard watched them suspiciously for another long moment before finally, *finally,* relenting. He stepped to the side and gestured them in. "He's your responsibility, gold-eyes. If there's any trouble, it will be on your head."

Lyam swallowed. His stomach was a mess of knots, tension holding him stiff in its hands as he made his way forward, Enoch trailing after him. He knew well enough what would happen to him if this went wrong.

They stepped inside, and it was done. Lyam was officially a criminal.

The corridor was empty, thankfully. Lyam took a deep breath

to try and allay the constant pounding of his heart, but nothing he did seemed to calm his racing pulse or the nausea curling through his stomach. Bile rose up his throat.

Lyam kept his thoughts as ordered as he could as he walked through the long, winding corridors of the Scribes' Hall, following paths he knew better than the back of his hand. He took no detours or short cuts, instead just making his way straight for the library.

They passed a few people on the way, mostly staff cleaning up for the day, although there was one other person in the green of the Scribes' robes. Lyam recognized him immediately. Seth, someone he'd only spoken to once or twice. Seth nodded at him, but seemed distracted, hurrying on his way forward without even sparing a second glance to Enoch's hulking form.

Lyam thanked the Life-Giver as he hurried on past, and then prayed hard that they'd make it to the library without incident. Although, he thought bitterly, most Scribes would be tucked up close to their rotting Dreamers with bigger problems than someone breaking into the library.

They turned the last corner, and there was the door to the library right in front of them, innocuous looking. Lyam paused and turned to Enoch, who had been staring around with avid interest the whole time despite Lyam's pleas to him to try and fit in.

"Silence from here," Lyam whispered, his voice audibly trembling.

Enoch nodded once, his eyes clear and bright with curiosity.

Lyam swallowed, turned, and pushed open the door.

The library greeted him like an old friend. The smell of musty parchment and hazy lanternlight washed over them from the moment they entered, Lyam setting down his own lantern in favor of picking up one of the specialized library ones. He paused a moment, just taking in the familiar sight of the shelves of books and rows of aisles. It calmed him, being in his favorite place.

Enoch let out a low exclamation beside him, sounding awed.

Lyam smiled before he could stop himself.

After a moment, Lyam started forward, Enoch following close behind him as he led the way past all the shelves, right to the very back of the library where the corners grew more shadowy and the lanterns fewer and further between. The smell of damp and mould was stronger back here, the scrolls and books less disturbed.

"Do you remember where the safe is?" Enoch hissed from behind him.

Lyam nodded once. He remembered where he'd gone looking for Jorin. He turned down one of the very last aisles, passed the myths where he remembered waiting, and there—

There—

In a corner, tucked out of sight, lay the safe.

With shaking fingers, Lyam pointed towards it.

Enoch made a low sound of approval. He moved forward straight away, showing none of the hesitance that Lyam was feeling, and Lyam produced the key from within the folds of his green robes.

Lyam held his breath as he handed it over.

There was a rustle, then a click as Enoch slid the key in, and then the hinges opened smoothly, the two snakes reaching up the sides of the safe parting easily. There wasn't even a squeak.

Well oiled, a small voice inside Lyam told him. Well cared for. Someone visited this safe a lot.

And now Lyam was helping to break in.

Enoch stood back once he'd opened the hinges, crouching to see inside. He gestured for Lyam to hold the lantern closer, which he did with his heart in his mouth, terrified that someone was going to turn the corner and catch them in the act. Shadows flitted around them as Lyam lifted the lantern higher, and the light fell upon the piles of scrolls inside the safe that Lyam had seen before.

They shared a look before Enoch reached into the safe and drew out a handful of the scrolls.

Lyam drew back a step, unable to help himself. He felt so

wrong, looking through parchments that weren't meant for his eyes, taken from somewhere that Lyam was clearly not supposed to be. Enoch, it seemed, had no such qualms, as he leaned over the pile of scrolls without a moment's hesitation, going through them roughly. Lyam couldn't read the writing from where he stood, and, while curiosity bit at him keenly, he preferred to stay back. He didn't want to think too much about what he was doing.

Enoch glanced up and beckoned Lyam closer.

Lyam hesitated.

"Come on," Enoch hissed, "I can't read these on my own. I don't understand what I'm looking at."

Lyam stared at Enoch's broad, frowning features and struggled internally. He didn't know what to do for the best, and he only had a split-second to decide. Any time they wasted here was more chance of them getting captured.

Enoch glared at him, frustrated.

Lyam drew in a shaky breath and shook off the fear as best he could, taking a step closer. He held a hand out.

Enoch instantly dropped a pile of parchment into Lyam's hand before he turned back to the safe.

Heart beating in his throat, Lyam crouched and spread the scrolls out before him, his eyes skimming the words, and felt his brows pinch into a confused frown.

He recognized the handwriting.

He'd seen it before in his Scribe meetings, in the registers that Tasmin took, in notes passed between the Scribes. It belonged to a fellow Scribe, older than Lyam although not by much, a quiet man—Yenn, Lyam thought his name was. He'd thought nothing of him before, just that he was a Scribe who had been chosen while Lyam was still young, and had kept about his business quietly. Lyam had spoken to him a handful of times, maybe. He didn't know him well.

Lyam's brow furrowed as he sifted through the parchments, all written in Yenn's handwriting. Sentences ran together, not making much sense, with dates at the top of each page, carefully noted and underlined.

A horrible thought came to him.

These scrolls were Dreams.

He turned back to the parchment in his hands, eyes quickly skimming the words. If they were Dreams...if they were Dreams, then the dates made sense. They would be the night that the Dreams happened. The reason the sentences were so cryptic and confusing would make perfect sense if they came from the Life-Giver. These were supposed to be for the Designer's eyes only, as the Designers were the only ones chosen to decode the words the Life-Giver spoke to the Dreamers every night.

Lyam was holding another Scribe's Dreams in his hands.

"Shadow's eye," Lyam cursed for the first time in his life. "These are—these are *Dreams.*"

Enoch turned to him roughly, his brow pinched. "What?"

"They're...they're from another Scribe. These are another Dreamers' Dreams."

"That's impossible."

"I know." Breath hitching with fear, Lyam's hands trembled, almost dropping the precious parchment in his hand. His voice sounded wheezy as he whispered, "But these are supposed to be seen by the Designer only."

Lyam's blood ran cold.

Yenn, the Scribe who wrote these, his Designer is Head Designer Izani.

"What?" Enoch near-barked at him, his head snapping in Lyam's direction.

Lyam jumped. His fingers tightened around the parchment, smooth against his fingers, feeling the ridges of the inked words under his skin. He swallowed. "These are from Scribe Yenn."

"Who is that?" Enoch asked. "Why are his Dreams here?"

Lyam shook his head, his mouth dry. "I don't know, but his Designer is Head Designer Izani."

Enoch went very still.

Lyam's breathing sounded fast to his own ears. He couldn't

begin to untangle the web of confusion—that Scribe Yenn would have a secret safe in the library where he kept his Dreams, that his Designer just happened to be Head Designer Izani. It made no sense. Was Yenn not giving them to his Designer? Or was Head Designer Izani somehow involved in keeping them hidden?

That thought made coldness wash down Lyam's spine, sending a shiver in its wake.

"This Scribe," Enoch said softly, keeping his voice down. "Who is his Dreamer?"

Lyam swallowed, his fingers shaking as he held onto the parchment. "Um, Emery, I think his name is. Yes, Dreamer Emery. He's...he's one of the four of us left."

Enoch nodded slowly, then turned back to the Dreams in his hands. He looked just as confused as Lyam felt, crouched there holding parchment that he should never have seen. Sacred parchment straight from the Life-Giver.

"We need to read them," Enoch said roughly.

Lyam choked. "We...we *can't*. That's *blasphemy*."

"Larger things are at stake here than the lives of you and me," Enoch hissed. "There's a *curse*, Lyam. This might be our only chance to find out what it is!"

Lyam swallowed, staring down at the forbidden parchments in his hands. He felt dirty touching them. They were private—sacred. They shouldn't be out in the light like this.

Then why had Yenn stuffed them into a safe?

Curiosity gripped Lyam, squeezing his insides. Reluctantly, he nodded, dropping down to the floor of the library and starting to go through the scrolls one-by-one. "Dreams are always hard to decipher."

"I can help," Enoch said impatiently. "I know the words of the Life-Giver."

Lyam nodded. He picked up the earliest dated Dream he could find and began to read, Enoch crouched at his shoulder, breathing heavily in his ear.

Hours could have passed and Lyam wouldn't have noticed. He grew absorbed in the written words—words of the Life-Giver that had never been brough to light. Enoch pointed out certain words and phrases, translating them for him, and Lyam's blood ran cold as they began to piece the story together.

"*The old ones retreated when the Great One came,*" Lyam read aloud, furrowing his brow. His glasses were steaming up from the lantern that he had to hold close over the pages. He wiped them irritably.

"Old ones. That refers to the city above us," Enoch explained. "The people who once lived there. As we should be."

"So, what's the Great One?"

"Old leaders were sometimes referred to as Great," Enoch shrugged. "That would be my best guess."

Lyam nodded, reading further. "So, the people retreated underground because of a leader. It looks like they were trying to protect themselves? Look." he pointed to another passage. "*The Great One warned of a distant foe, and the Old Ones believed. But I could no longer reach them. I could no longer save them.*"

Enoch pursed his lips. "The Life-Giver is speaking in first person. Read on."

"*I could only watch as corruption took them. The curse began in the Great One's heart, passed down from generation to generation, and I could no longer protect them. The darkness came. I can do nothing when my people flee from me.*"

Lyam stopped reading, surprised. "The Life-Giver didn't want us to go underground?"

"No," Enoch grunted. "It's unnatural. We belong in the light. Keep reading."

With trepidation making his tongue feel heavy, Lyam forced himself to read. "*I try to reach you. I call to you in Dreams, but the darkness is reaching there, too. I can only give the gift of gold to a few. I rely on them. Find them. They must undo the curse.*"

Lyam frowned. "The gift of gold?"

"Eyes," Enoch rumbled, slapping a sweaty palm on Lyam's shoulder. "You and me, kid. We're the gift of gold."

Lyam's stomach clenched. He shifted uncomfortably; his legs were cramping from crouching on the dusty floor so long.

"Er," he said slowly, "Right. But what are we supposed to do? How do we stop the darkness?"

Enoch hummed, skimming back through the documents. "The curse originated with the Great One—the old leader. It looks like it passed down their bloodline. Whoever their current descendent is must be the one causing all this to happen."

"But that could be anyone!"

"I don't think so," Enoch said thoughtfully. "They have power. They must, to be able to manipulate things as they are. They must have hidden these dreams somehow."

Lyam's heart clenched in realization. "Head Designer Izani."

Enoch shot him a dark look.

Slowly, everything clicked into place. Lyam's fingers went slack, the documents toppling to the ground in piles of sheets, the low *hiss* of paper echoing through the silence. Izani was the one who should be dealing with the Dreamers, and yet nothing was happening. Lyam heard him speak to Mirah earlier that very day, plotting a place on the Council that hadn't appeared in the Dreams. And Izani was the Designer who must have seen these Dreams.

"It's him," Lyam said, his voice quailing. "It...it has to be. Only he and Yenn must have seen these Dreams. And he's powerful. He's on the Council. He's supposed to be helping the Dreamer's right now and he's doing *nothing*!"

Just then, a noise sounded from further in the library, something that sounded awfully like footsteps.

Lyam cut himself off in a panic.

Enoch wouldn't stop looking at him. "Head Designer Izani, you say?"

"Hush," Lyam hissed. "We can't talk about this here." In a rush, he gathered up the scrolls and shoved them in the safe, turning to Enoch and snatching the paper right out of Enoch's hands when he didn't move.

Enoch raised a brow at him, unhurried. Lyam hated him just a little in that moment.

Hastily, Lyam shoved the rest of the parchments in the safe

and just managed to close the door, turning the key to lock it before he grabbed the key to shove in his pocket.

Footsteps rounded the corner to their aisle, and Lyam span around just in time to see Adan appear.

Lyam's eyes widened.

Adan looked haggard. He was unshaven, his usually-smiling mouth a grim line, and his green robes rumpled and stained, hanging awkwardly off one shoulder. He'd lost weight; the broadness of his shoulders sagged. There were dark bags under his eyes, and his expression was dejected.

When he looked up and saw Lyam, there was anger in the set of his lips.

Lyam couldn't stop the shiver that rippled through him. He remembered all too well the last time he'd seen Adan, when he'd broken *inside* Annelie's hut and stood there, in Annelie's presence, distraught and furious and full of emotion that Lyam couldn't fully understand.

Now, standing under the weak library lantern light, half in shadow, Adan looked... broken.

"Lyam?" Adan's voice was still strong, but there was a waver to it that wasn't usually there.

Lyam flinched. He stood conspicuously close to the safe, but there was no way he could edge away without bringing even more attention to it. Lyam was also painfully aware of Enoch by his side, his hood down, his face unrecognizable and his gold eyes there for anyone to see.

Adan's eyes skimmed across Lyam to the man beside him, and his expression shifted into one of confusion.

Lyam felt frozen in place. He worked moisture into his mouth, stepping forward and grabbing Enoch's arm, swallowing hard when this made Adan send him an even more confused look.

"What's going on?" Adan's eyes narrowed suspiciously. "Who is he?"

Lyam had nothing to say.

"Please," he managed to whisper, staring imploringly at Adan. "Just—we're just, um...."

Adan looked right back at him, and there was no forgiveness in his hollow features.

Swallowing, Lyam tried to change the topic of conversation. "How is your Dreamer doing after—?"

"Don't you dare mention him," Adan hissed, his voice dropping instantly. His expression shifted, melting into despair so strong that Lyam almost turned away.

Lyam's heart stuttered. Despite everything, Adan was still his friend. It hurt to see him look so distraught, so angry, so broken.

"Is there anything I can do?" Lyam asked, taking a step forward and reaching a hand out to Adan. "Anything, I...I want to help you."

"Yeah, well, you can't," Adan said bitterly, looking determinedly at the floor. His shoulders were hunched over, and he wrapped both arms around his own chest, as if he was holding himself together.

Lyam felt torn. He desperately wanted to reach out to Adan, wanted to explain that Lyam *was* helping, or at least he was doing his best. He had to protect the Dreamers, had to get to the bottom of what was harming them, and he couldn't help but feel like the answer may lie much closer to home than he was comfortable thinking.

"Adan, listen," Lyam lowered his voice, took another step closer. He could touch Adan's arm now, if he reached out. "I'm going to fix this, I swear. I won't let any other Dreamers get harmed."

"And what about the ones that already are?" Adan huffed, lifting his head so his eyes met Lyam's again. Lyam's heart shuddered at the distress he found in Adan's gaze. "What about us? Kiran is—" he broke off with a shake of his head, glancing away.

Lyam took in a careful breath. "Kiran is what?"

Adan's face screwed up in pain. "He's rotting from the inside out. The smell—and his veins are *black*. I—" he broke off again, curling into himself with a shuddering breath.

Lyam couldn't help himself. He reached out and touched Adan's arm, wanting to do so much more—to hug him, comfort him, tell him everything would be ok.

But Lyam wasn't sure it would be ok.

"I'm doing everything I can," Lyam promised softly.

"There's nothing anyone can do." Adan shook his head, curling his hands into fists. He gestured to the room around them, the endless shelves of books, ancient knowledge piled above their heads. "I thought coming here might help, that there might be something written about it, but—"

"There's nothing," Lyam continued softly. "It's never happened before."

Adan nodded his head, dejected.

Lyam looked at Adan closely—his friend whom, he realized, he'd let down—and made a split-second decision. He had to tell Adan what was happening. He deserved that much at least, when Lyam had failed him. He opened his mouth. "Listen, Adan. The Life-Giver—"

"Scribe Lyam," Enoch rumbled warningly from behind him, but Lyam ignored him.

Adan deserved to know the truth.

"The Life-Giver is leaving," Lyam pushed on, fixing Adan with a near-desperate gaze. "That's why the Dreamers are in danger. The Life-Giver is leaving us because of a curse, and we have to find a way to stop it."

Adan looked at him in astonishment.

"I know it sounds unbelievable," Lyam pushed on, trusting his instincts and praying that Adan would believe him. "But Annelie has seen it. That's why I'm here. I have to find out what's really going on."

Lyam could feel Enoch's glare on the back of his neck. He daren't turn around, fear climbing up his throat with every second that passed.

Adan stared at him in utter disbelief. "The Life-Giver is *leaving?*"

"I swear it," Lyam answered, digging his nails into his palms. He was trembling. "I wouldn't be here if not."

Adan shook his head, staring at Lyam hard for another moment before his attention shifted to Enoch. He gestured at him. "And I suppose this person is helping you? I know he isn't a Scribe."

Lyam swallowed. "You can't tell anyone. Please."

Adan narrowed his eyes. "Just what are you up to, Lyam? This isn't like you—hiding out in corners, bringing strangers into the library. It's against the *law*."

"So is breaking into a Dreamer's hut," Lyam answered quietly. "But I haven't reported you."

The reaction was instantaneous. Adan drew back as if he'd been hit, shrinking in even further on himself. He squared his jaw, looking down.

"I'm sorry about that," Adan murmured, his voice dropping to match the hush of the library. "I didn't...I didn't mean to scare you or Dreamer Annelie." He dropped into a bow.

Lyam gently pushed him back upright with a hand on his shoulder. He looked directly into Adan's eyes, even though his broken expression was hard to hold, and straightened his spine. "We're doing everything we can to fix things. I just need you to keep quiet. Please."

Adan regarded him for a moment, standing frozen under Lyam's hand on his shoulder. Lyam's heart was racing, pattering against his ribcage, and his stomach clenched tight with worry. If this didn't go right, then everything he was hoping for could be over before it had even started. If Adan told someone that he'd brought a stranger into the library...

Adan moved suddenly, reaching up to place one hand over Lyam's.

Lyam's breath stopped.

"Alright," Adan murmured softly after a long moment. "I'm trusting you, Lyam. I don't know why the hell I am, but I'm trusting you."

A relieved sigh left Lyam's lips. He closed his eyes, bowing his head. "Thank you."

Adan nodded once before his expression closed off. He stepped back, Lyam's hand falling from his shoulder, and drew himself up. "You'd better get out of the library if you don't want to get caught."

Lyam swallowed. He turned back to Enoch, who was sending him a cold look, and nodded.

Adan stepped aside, and Lyam reached out and grabbed the sleeve of Enoch's borrowed robe, tugging him forward and turning to leave the aisle. As Adan had said, no one else was there. The route to the door was clear.

Enoch was stiff next to him, but still followed as Lyam led them both quickly through the library, trying not to rush their steps too much in case that drew more suspicion. All he really wanted was to run, to escape the Scribes' Hall and be back out of the city where there would be no one to question Enoch's presence. But they couldn't run. That would only draw more attention.

So Lyam kept his pace slow and dropped his hand from Enoch's arm, trusting him to walk with him out of the library.

Thankfully, the corridors of the Scribes' Hall were quiet when Lyam pushed open the door to the library and stepped outside with Enoch in tow. There were a few staff members tidying shelves, but no one else was there. It was unusually empty, but it was also close to nightfall. The Scribes should all be with their Dreamers, even if only four could still Dream. He didn't like to think of the state the others were in.

They were still in danger of getting caught. Lyam walked quickly through the Scribes' Hall, almost too quickly, until finally he broke outside of the side entrance again and stepped into the fresher air of the cavernous city, Enoch close behind him.

Lyam waited until they had darted into one of the alleys to let out a deep sigh of relief. His eyes fluttered closed, his knees shaking. He felt spread too thin, as if too much had been taken out of him, leaving him hollow.

Enoch let out a huff from beside him as soon as he'd checked that they were alone down the darkened alley where they stood. Then he whirled on Lyam, pushing him back against the wall, usually proud features contorted in anger.

Lyam choked, surprised.

"What in shadow's name did you just do?" Enoch demanded, his deep voice rumbling threateningly. "Who was that Scribe?"

"A friend of mine," Lyam explained hastily. His back hurt where it scraped against rough brick.

Enoch didn't let him go. "Why did you tell him about what we're doing? It's dangerous! We can't trust anyone in this city."

"I trust him," Lyam answered stubbornly. "He lost his Dreamer last night. He's in bits, I *needed* to give him some hope."

Enoch's browfurrowed. He still looked angry, but this was one thing Lyam wasn't giving in on. He lifted his head with the last of his courage. "You heard him. He won't tell anyone, Enoch. I had to do it. He deserves to know."

Enoch held his gaze for another long moment, hard and not showing emotion. Lyam swallowed. He was still unused to seeing gold in someone else's eyes.

"Alright," Enoch finally gave in, stepping back. "But don't do that again. I almost had a heart attack."

Lyam bit back a smile. He felt as if he'd taken a step in the right direction, as much as he had no real idea what he was doing. He straightened his robes carefully. "I need to get back to Annelie."

"Yes, of course, but first," Enoch fixed him with a serious look, "those scrolls. They were Dreams. I don't know much of your system, but I believe they are supposed to go to Designers, not locked away in libraries."

Lyam nodded, fear clamping around his heart again as he remembered what they'd found. He let out a breath. There had to be a reason that Scribe Yenn would hide these Dreams that told so much of an ancient, forgotten curse, and it couldn't be a coincidence that his Designer was Head Designer Izani.

That thought terrified Lyam.

"I don't know what to do," Lyam whispered. "What those Dreams said. What Yenn must know..."

"We need to ask him," Enoch said, far too nonchalantly in Lyam's opinion.

Lyam nearly choked. "Are you mad? We can't just *ask him*."

"Well, I can't," Enoch agreed, and there was almost a glint of humor in his eyes as he turned to Lyam. "But you can."

Lyam froze.

He couldn't. The idea of confronting another Scribe terrified him, especially when he didn't even know Yenn very well. Never mind the fact that his Designer was *Head Designer Izani*. Lyam couldn't risk word getting back to him. It could put his entire life in jeopardy.

Panicked, Lyam shook his head. "I can't."

Enoch frowned at him. "What else can we do?"

"I don't know, I just—I *can't*." Lyam's voice went high-pitched, his breathing short.

Enoch leveled him with a serious look. "We don't have much choice, Scribe Lyam. You said that this Scribe's Designer is the Head Designer?"

Lyam hushed him, glancing around with terror in his eyes. "That's what *scares* me. I don't know what to *do*."

Enoch straightened up. His face was set as he looked at Lyam, his voice unwavering. "You still have not made your choice. If we don't find out more, there's nothing more we can do."

Lyam quivered.

He couldn't do it. Head Designer Izani was in such a position of power, and although Lyam was suspicious of him, Lyam didn't want to do anything to draw attention to himself. Not after his family had been involved. The guards searching their house hadn't gone forgotten by Lyam.

He shook his head quickly. "My family. I can't risk it."

Enoch's expression softened. He reached out and placed a warm hand on Lyam's shoulder, squeezing. "I would do it for you if I could, child. You shouldn't hold such a burden. But the Life-

Giver has blessed you for a reason. I believe in that, if nothing else."

Lyam swallowed. He felt unsettled, on edge, like he didn't quite know what he had let himself in for.

But it was too late to turn back now.

"I have to get back to Annelie," Lyam murmured, "I... I can't decide right now."

Enoch nodded, releasing him. "Come find me in the morning."

Lyam bowed his head in response, his fingers trembling as he turned to lead Enoch out of the city. His heart hammered, fear creeping along his veins.

There was too much to think about. He didn't know how to cope. But perhaps Annelie would have some answers after her Dream tonight, if she survived it.

Lyam shook his head. She *had* to survive it. He believed in her. He believed in the Life-Giver.

He just hoped his faith wasn't misplaced.

&

Annelie wasn't sitting in her chair when Lyam got back from the city.

He was panting, scared from leading Enoch back out to the tunnels, bidding him goodbye at the juncture of the tunnel that led out to the sunlight. The memory left a dull ache in Lyam's chest—a longing that scared him. He couldn't long for sunlight. It was wrong.

But Lyam had led an outsider into the library. He was wrong, too.

With a shudder rippling up his spine, Lyam managed to keep himself together enough to nod at the guard stationed outside his hut before pulling the ladder down and climbing inside. When he shut the trapdoor behind him and turned around, he found Annelie sitting on the floor beneath the window blinds, her head down. She'd pulled all her plaits out, so her hair stood up in tight curls around her face. Mima was curled up asleep in her lap.

Lyam swallowed. He settled onto the floor opposite her. "Hey. How are you doing?"

She barely lifted her head to look back at him. She looked exhausted, her eyes half-lidded, her arms hanging heavy by her sides. Her hands were curled into the edges of her favorite red blanket, faded with age, which she'd dragged over to the corner under the window and curled herself under, as if she was a stray tunnel cat herself.

Lyam let out a low sigh. He reached forward and brushed a couple of strands back from Annelie's forehead, feeling the heat radiating from her skin. He murmured, "You're burning up. Let's get you back to your chair, hm?"

Annelie barely acknowledged him. With slow, heavy movements she lifted her head to meet his gaze, her arms twitching by her sides as if she wanted to move them, but the effort was too much.

"Are you sure?" she slurred, her hands buried in Mima's fur. "I'm not—I don't...The Dream—"

"I know. We're going to do our best to keep you safe." He leaned closer, wrapping an arm around her shoulders. She felt frighteningly frail under his touch as she moved with him slowly, leaning heavily against him.

"Hold onto Mima."

"...Al...right."

Lyam slipped his other arm beneath her bent knees and scooped her into his arms, standing slowly with her cradled against him. Annelie buried her head into his chest, Mima cradled under her chin. She was warm, almost too warm, glowing lightly. She was being marked by the Dreams; they were bleeding through into her reality.

Lyam swallowed. It was dangerous. He was scared for her; he had no idea how she'd be able to Dream when she was as frail as she was just then.

Carefully, Lyam crossed their hut and laid Annelie down in

her chair. She'd clung onto her favorite blanket so that it travelled with them, and Lyam helped her gently tuck it in under her chin, falling down across her torso and legs and joining the myriad of other blankets that covered her chair. Mima resettled herself on top of Annelie's stomach, curling up and purring loud enough for the sound to reverberate around the hut.

Lyam drew a few more of the blankets up, covering her, and then took his seat on his bench beside her. Then he told her everything he and Enoch had found out.

Annelie was quiet for several seconds before she spoke. "I'm going to try and find out what's going on this time," she murmured after a few moments, her voice thick with effort. "If... if Scribe Yenn really is the one who wrote those Dreams, then Emery must know about it. I can ask him."

Lyam ran a hand through her hair. "You're already doing enough."

"But we need to *know*. I need to know." Anni sniffed, her voice breaking. "I've trusted the Life-Giver all my life. The Dreams are hard, I know they are, but I've always thought they were serving a purpose, you know? That being able to visit the Life-Giver every night was a gift. Now, it feels like a curse, like this curse has been happening since before we were even born."

Lyam licked his lips, swallowing. He couldn't help but feel like she was right. Everything screamed at him that they had to be wrong, that the Life-Giver was their savior, the only one keeping them alive. He couldn't help but question how the curse could have taken hold so well if that was true.

"I'm going to make them tell me tonight," Annelie said, determined. "The Life-Giver, I mean. They're going to give me some answers. They owe me that much."

"If anyone can do it, you can."

"I hope so."

Lyam took her hand; squeezed her fingers. "I believe in you. There's no one I'd put my life in the hands of other than you, Anni."

She smiled back at him, the deep circles under her eyes

painfully obvious. "I'm going to do my best."

"That's all I would ever ask."

Her eyes fell closed within moments, and her breathing evened out. Lyam thought she was actually sleeping, though, not Dreaming. She was too still—looked too calm. He hoped she was able to get some rest. With the chaos of the past few days, Lyam knew he hadn't been taking as much care of her as he should have been. His every waking moment should be dedicated to her, and yet he'd been out of the hut and in the city every day, chasing other people, being told a web of lies that he still didn't know how to uncover.

It was all too much, too confusing. He didn't know who to trust anymore, and that terrified him more than anything.

With Annelie resting as peacefully as she could, Lyam leaned his elbows on the edge of her chair and pressed his face into his palms, taking off his glasses and massaging his closed eyes for a moment. His head hurt, his bones aching with weariness. He couldn't remember the last time he'd been able to sleep. The night before had been a rush of fear, of getting back to Annelie in time and then being late, her painful screams as she awoke.

At least this night he was back before her Dreams started.

His eyes itched. His head pounded.

Mima stirred on Annelie's stomach, her eyes blinking open, one bright blue, the other filmy and grey. Lyam reached out and petted her gently, her soft fur inviting. Her eyes half-closed and she purred, nuzzling her head into his hand.

Lyam fought to stay awake, but his eyes kept closing. He jolted with sleep, his thoughts sluggish. Images of the library, of Enoch's sharp, golden eyes, of Jorin, of Yenn, the Scribe who for some reason was hiding his Dreams away in the library, all flashed before his eyes in a mixed up jumble he couldn't make sense of.

It was all too much.

Lyam didn't notice when his eyes closed and his head fell forward, pillowed on his arms on the edge of Annelie's chair, as he fell heavily into sleep.

PART FOUR

THE DEATH OF A DREAMER

T he Dream formed around her like she was coming home. Annelie opened her eyes to find herself floating. She felt light as air, as dust dancing in the lanternlight, her movements free and without pain. In the Dreams, it was as if the brokenness of her physical body faded away.

Around her, three other orbs popped up; the three other Dreamers who survived.

Elinah, the newest Dreamer, was next to her, quivering in fear. Annelie's heart tugged. She couldn't even imagine being thrown into this new world during such a tumultuous time, when everything was overwhelming anyway. Elinah was only young. It wasn't fair.

Annelie floated closer, sending out a protective rush of energy, the golden glow of her own form covering some of Elinah's.

Emery popped up next, behind both of them. He was pulsing with anger, his light throbbing rhythmically, like a raised heartbeat. He always had been one of the more powerful among them. He reached out with his light too, meeting Annelie and Elinah's, and Elinah's trembling lessened slightly.

Emery?

Yes?

Annelie swallowed, nervous. For a second, she wondered if she should even ask him about what Lyam had found in the library; if he knew that his Scribe was hiding his Dreams. Was it even safe to ask? Dreams were tricky things; sometimes, she could barely even sense the other Dreamers.

The Life-Giver's burning surface floated just out of reach. Annelie glanced down at it, her heart racing. What should she do? Ask first?

Could she even trust the Life-Giver anymore?

Swallowing, Annelie turned back to Emery. I have to ask you something.

Oh? Emery's ball of light was close to Elinah's. Annelie hated the thought of scaring her, but what choice did she have? She needed to know what was going on.

My Scribe found your Dreams.

Silence.

Emery reared back in shock, his light pulsing. What?

In the library.

What are you talking about?

What are they doing there? Is your Scribe hiding them? Why?

Emery's light pulsed, his orb shrinking visibly. Elinah squeaked, shifting closer to Annelie, and she reached out to her as comfortingly as she could. She never intended to make things worse, but she had to know. Dreams should never be hidden.

Suddenly, a fourth ball of light burst into view, Nethan appearing at Annelie's shoulder. Annelie trembled with relief. Nethan would know what to do.

What's going on?

I don't know, *Annelie answered truthfully.* But Lyam found something today that doesn't make any sense.

Nethan sounded serious. Explain.

Annelie told them everything that Lyam had found out. She skimmed over Enoch's presence, because although she trusted him, she knew his existence left too many questions, and she needed her fellow Dreamers to understand the urgency of the situation. She needed to know how much Emery knew, if anything, about what was going on.

When she was finished, silence reigned for a long, long moment.

202

Then Emery groaned.

The sound was heart-breaking; a great, keening moan that ripped through the vacuum like a clean break of bone. Emery's orb pulsed, his light fading so much that he shrank down smaller than Elinah.

It was Elinah who spoke next. I thought Dreams had to go straight to the Designer? No one else is allowed to see them, are they?

That's how it's supposed to be, *Nethan confirmed.* Isn't it, Emery?

Emery's orb flashed, light fluttering at the edges as if he was coming apart at the seams. I've been telling him not to do it. I've been telling him for years.

Years?!

Annelie's heart sank. She was trembling. What do you mean, years?

Emery shivered, his orb pulsating. The faint smell of smoke and incense from the Life-Giver's surface was growing sharper, and Annelie didn't think they had much time before the Life-Giver would draw them towards the surface. She spoke quickly. Tell us. Please, you have to tell us. Why?

She wasn't able to finish her sentence before she felt a bruising grip wrap around her middle, forcing her backward.

She shrieked, kicking, but the Life-Giver held tight, drawing her firmly backward and away from the other Dreamers. She could hear Nethan calling out for her, Elinah screaming, and she struggled desperately to return to them.

Her effort was useless. The Life-Giver determinedly dragged her down until she was buried among the rising flames, tongues of fire licking against her. The horrid inky blackness that attacked the other Dreamers crept through the air, struggling to fight through the flames.

She could feel tears of frustration and terror evaporating on her cheeks.

Be still, child. *The Life-Giver's voice was as soft as it could be, but still powerful enough to shake her ribcage. She cried, thrashing.*

I need to talk to them.

There is too much danger. I fear we are out of time.

What do you mean? *Annelie was trembling, but she finally relaxed, letting the Life-Giver cradle her amongst the flames, burning warmth crisping her skin. She could smell fire and incense everywhere, sticking in her throat. Her hair stuck to her forehead with sweat.*

The surface of the Life-Giver was almost unbearable.

Emery is in danger.

What?

Heart in her mouth, Annelie watched as the Life-Giver gathered Nethan and Elinah close to the surface, wrapping them up in flames just as they had to Annelie. They were dragged to the surface kicking and screaming, their orbs weakening, but Emery stayed distant, pulsing bright with anger.

He must leave, now. He cannot be here.

What are you talking about? *Annelie swallowed, her throat thick, a touch of accusation leaking into her tone.* You haven't stopped the rest of us when we've been in danger.

Silence.

Emery's bright light pulsed, but the Life-Giver lashed out at him, raining fire and smoke on him until he shrank back, crying out. Annelie shivered at the heart-wrenching sound. She tried to get up, to force herself to her feet and back into the vacuum, but only the Life-Giver decided when she was allowed to leave.

Why are you doing this?! *Annelie all but screamed, battling the flames that tightened around her wrists and ankles like bonds.* I want to help him.

He is beyond our help. He must wake, now.

What?

Emery's orb of light retreated from the barrage of flames attacking him, Nethan and Elinah screaming somewhere in Annelie's vicinity, but she couldn't take her eyes off him. His orb throbbed, light pulsing and retreating and pulsing again, and then—

Then he screamed.

The sound was full of pain so strong that Annelie physically felt it. Emery screamed loud enough that her ears throbbed, her head pounding, and as she watched his orb started to... to come apart.

There was no sign of the inky blackness that oozed across the Life-

Giver's surface. Instead, Emery's orb seemed to split in half, a jagged, gaping hole opening in his center. Light poured out of him, streaming across the black vacuum, and his screams grew even louder as he was carved in two.

Annelie shrieked, desperately fighting her bonds, but the Life-Giver held her firm. The flames that had been pummelling Emery quickly changed, caressing him instead, cradling him as his orb split in half, the two pieces falling to the sides and growing smaller and smaller as light continued to drain from him, evaporating into the darkness. His orb of light shrunk until, with the quietest pop, his screams stopped and his orb disappeared.

Horrible, overpowering silence surrounded them.

Annelie could hear nothing other than her own harsh breathing. Her chest felt tight, her muscles bunched until her whole body was one tense ball. The flames of the Life-Giver had loosened, cradling her, but she couldn't move anyway—couldn't take her eyes off the patch of vacuum where Emery had been.

Nethan's voice sounded from somewhere very far away. What happened to him?

The Life-Giver made a low, mourning sound. **He is gone.**

Annelie swallowed, fear creeping up her throat. Gone?

Murdered.

Annelie froze, a shock of cold hitting her as if ice-cold water had been dumped over her head.

She couldn't believe what she'd just heard.

Listen. *The Life-Giver spoke with an urgency Annelie had never heard before. Her skull rattled with it.* **We are out of time. You must not return here.**

What?!

You must not. It is not safe. Do not return here alone, my child.

Annelie couldn't believe what she was hearing. She shook her head slowly, confusion clouding her mind, still rattled from Emery's screams. You're not making any sense.

Do as I say. Do not come here alone, do you understand me? Not alone.

Annelie didn't have time to question any further before she felt the familiar tug under her arms and around her middle, lifting her up and away from the Life-Giver's surface. She struggled, but she felt drained, her body weak and sore as it was when she was awake. She groaned. And as she was lifted up into the vacuum, she sensed another shift in the air, her heart breaking as the Life-Giver shifted further away once more.

The Life-Giver was still leaving.

Annelie shivered, crying as she was dragged up into the freezing ice of the vacuum, the inky black tendrils still obviously writhing across the Life-Giver's surface. At least none of them had been hit by those this time. At least they were spared that.

Emery's screams still pierced her ears as she was pulled out of the Dream.

CHAPTER
ELEVEN

Should a Dreamer come under threat,
Then the entire city must rally around them.
Dreamers hold true power and are to be protected,
Whatever the cost.
The Book of the Life-Giver, Volume I, Chapter VI

There was a distant, incessant noise in Lyam's ear.

A scream, perhaps? Or a sob? High-pitched and desperate, full of wheezing breaths and terrified cries. A voice that was familiar to him, as familiar as his own breathing. It tugged at his ears, pulsing in his head. He thought he was imagining it.

Lyam opened his eyes and found himself staring at Annelie's blankets. They twisted and moved in his vision.

He'd fallen asleep. *How* could he have fallen asleep?! He was supposed to be vigilant, taking care of Annelie. She needed him. He shot upright so fast that he felt his back click, his shoulders jolting.

Annelie lay before him, her eyes still closed, twisting and writhing in apparent pain. The noise was coming from her. She was crying, tears rolling down her cheeks, her breathing hitched and loud—wheezing and sobbing. Mima was standing over her yowling in her tiny high-pitched voice.

In seconds, Lyam leaned over her, shaking away the last remnants of sleep from the corners of his mind. He reached out and grabbed one of her hands, feeling her weak grip tighten around his fingers, clenching and unclenching. Her head was flung back, her neck exposed, her eyes squeezed tightly shut.

As he watched, another sob wracked through her, sending her shuddering, and Mima yowled. He reached out with his free hand and smoothed Annelie's hair back from her forehead, feeling the intense heat there, the way she burned with unnatural power, glowing out of her pores. The Life-Giver, leaking through her Dreams.

Then Annelie screamed.

Lyam dropped her hand and ran across the hut, pouring a bowl of water. He brought it carefully back to her side, watchful not to spill a drop, and placed it down beside her before picking up a cloth and gently wetting it. He placed the cloth on her forehead and held it there as she writhed, hoping it brought her at least a little relief.

This Dream was one of the most intense Lyam had ever seen her have.

Her expression was twisted in pain; her body twitched and writhed. He held the cloth to her forehead and glanced over to the desk where the pendulum clock sat, noting the time inching its way towards morning, and he worried. Intense Dreams couldn't go on for too long. They left her so drained she could barely move. He hated seeing her like that, and she'd already been exhausted when she went to sleep.

The Dreams tore her apart.

As she twisted, the heavy smell of burning descended over the hut, and fear gripped Lyam's heart. The Life-Giver was here, leaking through the Dream. Terror thrummed through him at the thought that Annelie might be next—that whatever was happening to the Dreamers might be happening to her. That soon she wouldn't be able to move or speak at all, she would be trapped rotting, webbed with black, and there would be nothing he could do but watch. He shuddered with fear.

Before his thoughts could get too dark, Annelie twisted violently and cried out, her lips stretching into a scream, and her eyes flew open.

Lyam breathed out a relieved sigh. He grabbed her hands, grounding her, and started murmuring comforting words that he knew would bring her back from her Dream, while Mima pressed herself up against Annelie's side and purred as loud as she could. Annelie thrashed wildly in Lyam's hold, screaming, but he held on tight and kept murmuring, hoping it would calm her soon.

It didn't.

Once she glanced over and recognized his face, her screaming only got louder. She suddenly grabbed his hand in both of hers, gripping so tight with a strength she didn't normally possess, her nails digging painfully into his palm until his skin broke.

"Help!" she screamed, holding him desperately. "Go, run, run! *Help*!"

"What happened? Annelie, *what happened?*"

She was never like this. In the immediate aftermath of a Dream she might be afraid, or confused, or upset even, but she was never like this. This time, she was incoherent.

Lyam did the only thing he could think to do and held her, wrapping an arm around her shoulders, but she shook him off with another loud yell and sobbed. "Please, you have to go now. I can't—this can't be happening!"

"What's happening?" Lyam asked urgently, feeling the back of his throat burn in response to her tears. He stood over her, trembling, desperate to calm her down. "You have to tell me what's happening, or I can't help you. Please."

"Emery," she sobbed, grabbing for Mima and holding the kitten up to her face, crying into her fur. "Emery. Emery."

Lyam froze at the name.

"What happened?" Lyam whispered again, dread and panic building in his gut. "Annelie, what happened to Emery?"

Annelie sobbed louder. "Go, you have to go to him. Go to him now!"

Panic bubbled in Lyam's throat at the next words she said. "*Dead. He's dead.*"

§

L yam ran through the tunnels with abandon, the lantern in his hand clanking as the metal crashed against his hand at his fast pace. He was headed east this time, away from Enoch and the city, instead rushing towards the tunnel that he knew led to Emery and Yenn's hut. As he ran, Lyam was terrified that he was doing the wrong thing in leaving Annelie alone. She was still inconsolable, barely coherent—a crying, terrified mess—but he had to know what was happening. He had to see for himself what was going on.

The tunnels filled with smoke because he hadn't closed the lantern properly, but Lyam paid it no mind when he started to cough. His thoughts were racing. It was *Emery*. Out of all the Dreamers to be harmed, it was the Dreamer of the Scribe who'd been leaving Dreams in the library, something he and Enoch had only just discovered. Furthermore, their Designer was Head Designer Izani.

It couldn't be a coincidence. Much as it terrified Lyam to think, it *couldn't* be a coincidence.

Lyam ran until he came to the tunnel that led to Yenn and Emery's hut. He reached up with scrabbling fingers to find the trapdoor set into the tunnel's sandy roof, and when his fingers met wood he knocked as loudly and fervently as he could, until his knuckles burned.

The trapdoor was pulled open, and the terrified face of a Scribe Lyam barely knew stared back down at him.

Scribe Yenn was a tall, thin, wispy man, older than Lyam, although his face didn't show it. His hair was longer than most men's and pulled up into a tight bun at the top of his head, leaving his gaunt features bare and exposed. His nose was long and pointed, his jawline sharp, his eyes narrow. Except just then, they were wide, the whites showing, fear clearly written all over his face.

Scribe Yenn stared down at Lyam and instantly went to slam the trapdoor shut.

"Wait!" Lyam cried, his voice echoing too loudly in the tunnel. His voice shook. "Wait, please! My Dreamer...my Dreamer saw something awful, and...and I have to—"

Yenn paused in pushing down the trapdoor. His voice, when he spoke, was wispy, barely-there. "How awful?"

Lyam swallowed. His fingers shook around the lantern, causing light to spill in irregular intervals around the tunnel. "Awful enough to send me here. Worse than the other Dreamers. Your Dreamer. Emery—"

At the name, Yenn broke. His thin features screwed up, his eyes squeezing shut, and it was then that Lyam saw the glisten of tear-tracks on his face.

"Please," Lyam said again. "You have to tell me what happened. Please!"

"I *can't*." Yenn groaned, dropping the trapdoor so it lay open and pressing his face into both his palms. "Shadow's eye, I *can't*."

Lyam trembled. He pushed forward, holding his smoky lantern up to better see Yenn, taking in the lines on his forehead, the stains on his tunic.

"Let me in," Lyam said desperately. "I'll help you. I'll do whatever I can. Just, please, let me in."

Groaning, Yenn shook his head. "It's *you*. I *can't*. They told me not to trust the gold-eyed Scribe."

Lyam's blood ran cold. He swallowed. Fear gripped his heart, and he wasn't even sure he wanted to know what had happened to make Yenn look as terrified and broken as he did.

But Lyam couldn't leave another Scribe in distress. He just couldn't.

"My Dreamer," Lyam started, licking his lips. "She said she saw that Dreamer Emery is...is no longer alive."

The words dropped between them like stones.

Yenn dropped his hands from his face. He stared at Lyam in broken astonishment. "You...you know?"

"Please," Lyam tried again, "Let me help you. What happened? Is it true?"

Yenn trembled, squeezing his eyes shut. Instead of answering, he stepped aside and dropped the ladder down.

Lyam climbed with fear and trepidation squeezing his insides, panic building.

He was entering another Dreamer's hut. Breaking another law.

Swallowing down guilt and bile, Lyam clambered into the hut and then instantly wished he was back down in the tunnel.

The scent hit him first, a stink of poisonous death. The inside of the hut was a scene of destruction. The desk in the corner was strewn with paper, ink spilling sideways, a tray of leftover food thrown haphazardly onto the rugs. The glass full of water had smashed, leaving droplets spilling into the sandy floor and bits of glass mixed in with the grains of sand. Lyam eyed it with care from his place crouched by the trapdoor, utterly frozen in place.

The bench by the side of the Dreamer's chair was on its side. And in the chair itself lay a man that Lyam didn't recognize, dressed in the white robes of a Dreamer, his eyes shut and his face contorted. His body was twisted into an unnatural position, his arms thrown out around him, his hands frozen in half-formed fists. His mouth was open, and there were traces of foam around his lips.

"I should ring the alarm bell," Yenn's broken voice sounded from behind Lyam. "The bell, I should—the bell."

Lyam couldn't look away from the body on the chair. The

Dreamer was quite clearly dead. Even if the stench wasn't enough, there was no sign of breathing, and he was frozen in an unnatural position. The blankets were wrapped tight around his legs, as if he'd been writhing in them.

Bile rose in Lyam's throat and he turned, barely managing to fall to his knees before he was throwing up.

Dead. A Dreamer was dead. A Dreamer was dead and Lyam was inside his hut, witnessing it—witnessing something that should never, ever have happened. Not ever.

Dreamers didn't have long life spans, as a general rule. Dreamer Nethan was the oldest currently, but he'd been exceptionally strong. Most didn't make it to their thirtieth birthday. Their life was a hard one. The Dreams took too much out of them, left them without enough energy to keep their own bodies going.

Their Scribes would usually outlive them, but they never returned to normal society. The bond between Scribe and Dreamer was so strong that Scribes were often inconsolable after losing their Dreamer, and unable to function in normal society. Known as the Grey Ones, they were taken to live in a community to the north of the city, together in their shared grief with the only other people who understood the dreadful pain they felt.

Lyam didn't think of it often. He couldn't imagine a life where he didn't have Annelie by his side.

His stomach heaved. Lyam leaned forward and threw up again, until there was nothing left in his stomach but acid and the stench lay heavy in the air. He rocked back onto his heels and groaned, squeezing his eyes shut so he wouldn't have to look at the body on the chair any longer.

Just then, a loud, shrieking chorus of bells rocked through the air.

Lyam jumped violently. The loud wailing of the bell continued, tolling through the air and rocking the tunnels underneath the hut. Lyam clapped his hands over his ears and span, finding Yenn in the corner, his hand over the alarm bell.

"I had to," he stammered under the chorus of nerve-wracking noise. "I have to tell them."

With three quick strides, Lyam crossed the hut to stand right in front of Yenn, shouting to be heard over the clamor. "What happened here? What happened to your Dreamer?"

Yenn stumbled until his back met the wall of the hut. His eyes were wide, his lips trembling.

Lyam grabbed his wrists and held on tight, fear and panic making him move without thinking. "*Please.* You have to tell me. What happened?"

"The guards," Yenn whispered, his voice trembling. Lyam ducked closer so he could make out the words. "Th-they held me back, and poured...something down his throat."

Lyam's blood ran cold. The *guards*? The guards did this? But—

Footsteps sounded from the tunnel where the trapdoor still lay open. Running footsteps, echoing louder and louder with each passing second, shouted voices soon joining them.

Lyam recognized the voice of Head Designer Izani.

He froze. Fear ran through his veins, panic making his actions clumsy. He dropped Yenn's wrists and stumbled backward, his sandals scraping across the sandy floor.

Yenn stared at him, eyes wide, his whole frame shaking. "You...you can't be here."

Yenn was right. Lyam couldn't be caught inside the hut of another Dreamer, not even in such exceptional circumstances as these.

With panic running through him, Lyam turned and ran across the hut, to the adjoining room that contained the wash tub and wardrobe. He span around just before slamming the door shut, mouthing to Yenn, "Please don't tell them I'm here. Please."

All he caught was one terrified glance from Yenn before Lyam slammed the door shut, hiding himself from sight.

No longer able to see the dead body, Lyam's stomach turned as he began to understand everything that he'd just witnessed.

His mind was a mess of racing thoughts, dizziness clouding his vision. Annelie had warned him, but he hadn't been ready to *see* Emery lying there contorted—deformed.

Dead.

No sooner had Lyam slammed the door shut than raised voices sounded from the other side. Lyam pressed himself against the door, shaking, tremors running through him.

He could instantly make out Head Designer Izani's voice. "Yenn, stop that noise."

There was a scuffle, then the alarm bells stopped ringing. Deathly silence settled over everything for a moment, then Izani's voice sounded again. "Stand back. Out of the way, quick."

Yenn was Izani's Scribe. They had to be close, had to know each other, but Lyam couldn't detect any note of true concern behind Izani's words.

Yenn's quavering voice sounded through the silence, quickly turning into sobs. "H-he—"

There was a stumble of footsteps. Lyam squeezed his eyes shut, standing in the pitch dark. His lantern, where had he left his lantern? what if one of them saw it?

After a short silence, Izani stated, "Tomas, examine him. And the bed."

Tomas. Head Guard Tomas, it had to be. Lyam froze when he remembered Yenn's terrified words to him. *The guards, it was the guards.*

An unfamiliar voice spoke up, gravelly and rough. "He's dead. Not long. An hour, at the most."

The voices were muffled by the wood of the door, but Lyam could still hear them well enough. He was still shaking, his breathing sounding terrifyingly loud in the small, quiet room he found himself in. The lantern. He'd left the lantern.

"How?" Izani's voice was clipped.

Yenn whimpered.

Footsteps sounded from the other side of the door, followed by a rustle of blankets. Then, the unfamiliar male voice sounded again, deep and grating. "Poison. Ertroot. As we planned."

"How can you tell?" Izani's voice again, sharp and cutting.

"I can smell it on him," Tomas grunted.

Yenn was crying, words barely making their way through his sobs. "I saw. It was...I saw—"

Izani hushed him roughly. "Stop. We need to keep this from spreading. Tomas, disguise the Ertroot. Quickly. Help me move him. Yenn, *stop that noise.*"

A louder sob, quickly muffled.

There was a grunt, some rustling of sheets, and Tomas muttering a few choice swear words under his breath. Lyam stood frozen, his eyes wide, breathing harsh, desperately trying to stay still.

"There," Izani spoke up again finally. "Yenn, wash his mouth. Get that disgusting smell out of here."

A louder whimper, then Yenn's voice. "You. Did you—"

"Get yourself together," Izani hissed. "Do you want us all caught?"

Yenn's voice was a barely-there tremble, but his words chilled Lyam to his core. "You did this, didn't you? The guards. It was—"

A loud smack sounded through the room, jarring Lyam even through the wood of the door.

"Shut your mouth." Izani's voice was low, cutting—cruel, even. "Pull yourself together, before I get rid of you too."

A terrified silence was the only answer to his words.

"Washcloth," Izani said, curt.

Footsteps, shuffling and slow.

Lyam held himself absolutely still when the footsteps came closer to him. He squeezed his eyes shut, leaning his forehead against the door, digging his nails into the palm of his hand.

The footsteps paused for a moment, and then there was the sound of glass clinking. Then footsteps started up again, this time away from where Lyam stood behind the door.

Lyam let out a shaky sigh of relief.

There were a few more sounds—harsh breathing, sheets rustling, the occasional clink of glass.

Then Tomas spoke again, gruff and irritated. "Shadow's eye, Izani, there's vomit over here."

"Yenn," Izani's voice sounded disgusted, "Could you not keep it together?"

Lyam held himself utterly still.

Silence, and then, "Yes. Yes, it was me. S-sorry."

"Well, you can damn well clean it up yourself." Izani sounded irritated, but not fazed. "Get a move on with washing him, too. Tomas and I have to get to the Council."

Another whimper, high-pitched and afraid, and then more sounds of rustling sheets.

Lyam felt his legs trembling. He prayed that he could manage to stay upright for just a little longer. His stomach roiled, panic and fear melting into a potent mixture. He felt light-headed; dizzy.

"That's enough," Izani commanded. "Get away from him now. Don't you *dare* let anyone else in here until we return with the Council."

More footsteps, this time away from the door completely.

"And, Yenn," Izani's voice was silky smooth. "I don't need to remind you not to tell anyone about this, do I?"

Silence.

"No." Yenn's voice was defeated. "I—No."

"Good."

More footsteps, and then the sound of the trapdoor closing.

Lyam stayed behind the door, his breathing ragged, until silence had held for what felt like an agonizingly long time and he was sure that they had gone. Then he pushed opened the door and tumbled back into the room, gasping for breath, his eyes flicking wildly around.

The hut was empty save for Yenn, who was curled up in a corner with his head hanging low. The chair was arranged beautifully. Dreamer Emery's body looked as if he might be sleeping. He was covered in blankets up to his chin, his hair brushed and combed, his face wiped clean. He looked peaceful.

Lyam felt sicker than ever.

Stomach turning, he turned to Yenn with wide eyes. "Thank you. For not telling them about me."

Yenn moaned, covering both his eyes with his hands.

Lyam's insides twisted. He hurried over to Yenn's side, hands fluttering, wanting to comfort but not having the faintest idea where to begin.

"Look," Lyam said desperately. "Look, whatever they're doing, whatever hold they have over you, I'm going to fix it. Ok? I'm working on it."

Yenn just groaned. "I can't *talk* to you."

"Did they tell you not to?" Lyam asked, hot anger building along with fear inside his stomach. "Look, Yenn, I...I know about the safe in the library."

Yenn stared at him through his fingers, expression terrified.

"Do you know what it is?" Lyam asked, heart in his throat. "The curse? Why are you hiding the Dreams?"

"You need to *go*." Yenn's voice was thin and scared, and he weakly pushed at Lyam's shoulder. "Go, now. You can't be here."

Lyam bit his lip, hard. Yenn was crumbling before him, and Lyam couldn't even begin to imagine what he was going through —couldn't even consider the grief he must be feeling. He was right. It was dangerous for Lyam to be there. Izani and Tomas were coming back with the Council, from what it sounded like, and Lyam couldn't be found there.

"I'll come back for you," Lyam promised, squeezing Yenn's hand. "I'll find some way to help you. I promise."

Yenn shook his head, thin face and hollow cheeks gaunt. "Go. Before they come back. *Go*."

With fear swirling in his stomach and sadness slowing his heart, Lyam turned and scooped his lantern up from the floor. Thankfully, the glass hadn't broken, although the flame was long since out.

Letting out a breath, Lyam turned to the trapdoor and helped Yenn pull it open, and then Yenn shoved the ladder into his hands, his fingers trembling and cold where they brushed Lyam's.

Lyam paused once more before descending. He looked into Yenn's eyes and felt something in his chest tug. "I'm sorry. I'm so, so sorry."

Yenn just shook his head and waved Lyam away.

Lyam had barely taken two steps in the tunnels when he heard the trapdoor snap shut behind him.

TWELVE

The Healers are a separate sect.
They are to be called on for practical matters,
But all manner of spiritual healing must go through the Designers,
Who may contact their Dreamers for advice.
The Book of the Life-Giver, Volume VII, Chapter II

Annelie was a shaking mess by the time Lyam returned to her side and finished explaining everything that had happened. She was sitting in her chair still, exhausted from the night's harsh Dream, her body barely able to move, her chest fluttering with every breath. She wouldn't let go of Mima. Lyam sat over her, one hand holding hers, the other keeping a cool cloth on the back of her neck.

Lyam watched her worriedly. There was a faint smell of burning lingering in the hut, the same as when Annelie was Dreaming intensely, but it had never happened when she was awake before. Annelie herself had her eyes closed again, her breathing ragged. Mima was in her lap, batting at her fingers, and Annelie had one hand always on her fur. She looked weak again, frail, as if he could break her if he touched too hard.

"It's true, then," Annelie murmured, her voice low. "I mean, I knew it was true, but... Emery. He's really..."

"He's gone," Lyam confirmed, clutching her hand tighter, though gently.

Annelie let out a low cry. "I knew it. In the Dream, he...he started screaming, and struggling, and the Life-Giver reached out to him, but he...he was split in half."

Lyam shuddered in revulsion. His heart was hammering. "Do you...do you really think that the guards killed him?"

"I don't think it can be anything else. Scribe Yenn wouldn't lie about his Dreamer's *death*, Lyam. Would he?"

Lyam shook his head. He thought he knew his fellow Scribes well, but evidently not well enough. He could remember Yenn from meetings, seeing him every week in the Scribes' Hall with all the others, with Tasmin leading. He couldn't recall ever having a one-on-one conversation with him before.

"All I know for sure is that Head Designer Izani and Head Guard Tomas—it must have been him—they were covering it up." Lyam swallowed, trembling. "They made Emery look like he hadn't been poisoned, but it doesn't make *sense*."

"They're planning something," Annelie answered in a monotone.

Lyam shuddered. He almost dropped the cloth from Annelie's neck, catching it last minute before it could fall onto her robes or Mima, who recoiled from the water with a low hiss.

"We have to stop them," Annelie said, carding her fingers through Mima's fur. "Whatever they're doing. We have to stop them."

Lyam shook his head. "Izani is the *Head Designer*. He's too powerful. Maybe we're wrong, maybe...maybe he isn't the one bearing the curse, maybe he's trying to help."

"By covering up Emery's death?" Annelie shook her head, the movement slow and sluggish. Her skin seemed to glow for a moment, the scent of burning lying heavily in the air.

221

Lyam paused in his movements, looking at her closely.

"I don't trust them," Annelie murmured, her eyes fluttering shut again. "In my Dream, I saw the Life-Giver move further away from us, even though they were in pain, even though I was screaming for the Sun to stay. But they aren't. They're leaving, and I'm sure that everything is connected to what's happening here."

Lyam shook his head. "What do we do?"

Annelie remained silent. She curled up on her chair, her head flopping forwards as though her neck could no longer support the weight. Mima licked her fingers, her good eye glowing blue.

Lyam eased the cloth out from the back of Annelie's neck and brushed her hair back from her forehead. Her skin was hot to the touch, glowing with a strange golden light that seeped out of her every pore.

Just then, the silence was broken by the loud, bright pealing of a bell, making them both jump violently and Mima yowl.

Annelie turned to Lyam, wide-eyed. "That's the High Council bell."

Lyam's heart stuttered.

"That's the call for a meeting." Annelie sat up straighter, groaning at the pain. "You have to go to the city."

"If you think I'm leaving you for a *second* after a Dreamer just got *killed*—"

"I'll be fine," Annelie insisted. "Go, quickly. You have to know what they're going to announce."

Just then, a knock sounded from the trapdoor.

Lyam stared at it, fear clouding his thoughts.

"Scribe Lyam!" It was the guard who was stationed under their hut. "Scribe Lyam, you've been summoned. You must go urgently!"

Lyam shook his head, torn.

Annelie tugged on his arm insistently until Lyam turned to look at her. "Go. You must. Go."

Lyam screwed his eyes shut, squeezing her hand. "I'll be back. Fast."

Annelie smiled gently at him, one hand still in Mima's fur. "I know."

🐾

The central square of the city was packed by the time Lyam finally made it there.

People crowded in every corner, dressed in all different colored robes, the sounds of chanting and calling echoing throughout the square. The Citadel stood tall and proud before them all, reflecting the light from the giant lanterns lit periodically through the square, forcing the shadows to retreat with bright lines of blinding light. Lyam couldn't see much over the heads of the people, short as he was with his glasses sliding down his nose in the heat, but he could hear the clamor of voices, feel the panicked energy that ran through everyone in the crowd.

The High Council bells were hardly every rung. Only in cases of extreme emergency to call everyone together.

The sound of the bells pealing rang through the square, echoing in the giant cavern until it was painfully loud, resonating through the crowd. Lyam pushed his way forward as much as he could, ending up behind a balding man not much taller than he was who was clutching the hand of a little boy. Lyam hovered behind them, wringing his hands, fear pounding through him.

He hadn't been able to rid himself of the image of Emery's dead body. Not since the second he'd first seen it. His stomach twisted violently.

Eventually, the bells stopped pealing, and a strange silence settled over the crowd. A few stragglers joined at the corners, but otherwise everyone stood still and silent, facing the raised steps into the Citadel.

Lyam, just like everyone else, watched as the giant glass doors to the Citadel slid open, gliding soundlessly, revealing the members of the Council standing in a line behind them.

The Head Scribe, Designer, and Guard stood together, in their green, brown, and black robes respectively. Lyam was too far back to properly make out Tasmin's face, but he caught a glimpse of the green of her robes as she stepped forwards, flanked by the other two. Lyam tried not to look at Izani in his brown robes, or Tomas in the black.

On either side of those three stood the First and Second assistants, dressed in the ordinary red robes of the Council. And behind all of them, dressed in resplendent red and gold, stood the leader of the city herself: Speaker Ayanah.

Lyam had only seen her a handful of times. She hadn't been present at Lyam's choosing, as that had been before the previous Speaker passed away. In fact, Ayanah had only been Speaker for a matter of months. Lyam shuddered to think of the amount of responsibility thrust upon her when the Dreamers had come under attack.

Speaker Ayanah stepped forward, Tasmin and Izani separating to let her pass between them as she stepped into the light from the lanterns that flooded down onto the steps of the Citadel. She looked young, but strong, her voice firm as she addressed the crowd. "My people. Thank you for gathering so suddenly."

Silence rippled across the crowd from the front to the very back as she started speaking. Lyam craned his neck to better see, his heart pattering quickly in his chest.

"My people." Ayanah's voice carried clear and sharp across the crowd. "I called you here today for a very grave reason. There is no easy way to say this, but I urge you not to panic. We are under attack."

Lyam noticed movement out of the corner of his eye; guards, clad in black, making their way around the perimeter of the crowd, spears in hand.

"We are under attack," Ayanah repeated, and another ripple ran through the crowd. "We are being hit where we are most vulnerable; our Dreamers. Eleven Dreamers are rotting in their huts, and I have the grave news to report that one Dreamer was found dead in his bed this morning."

Shocked cries rang through the crowd.

Ayanah held up a hand. Lyam couldn't make out her expression from so far away. "Our greatest fears have been realized. Our Dreamers are under attack, and with them our very society is threatened. We depend on them for everything: for our homes, our food, our buildings, even our Council. Everything is decided through the Dreams from our Life-Giver. But that has come under threat."

Silence settled heavily over the square.

"So how has this happened?" Ayanah continued. "Our Dreamers are the most protected members of our people. They are secluded, loved, protected in their huts by their Scribes and Designers. We follow the Book of the Life-Giver to the letter. They should be the most difficult to attack. So how is this happening? How are our Dreamers, as protected as they are, being harmed? There is only one explanation. The Life-Giver themself is attacking them."

Lyam froze in shock.

Murmurs of dissent ran through the crowd, whispers and shocked cries echoing in the square. The guards around the perimeter stood up straighter, their spears crossed, keeping the crowd penned in.

Lyam swallowed, uneasy.

"There is no other explanation," Ayanah continued from her place at the doors of the Citadel. "The Life-Giver, for whatever reason, has turned against us. One by one, the Dreamers have come under attack in their sleep. They rot. Their skin turns black. I have seen this for myself; I do not speak of this lightly.

"But now the Life-Giver has gone too far. Last night, in the midst of Dreaming, Dreamer Emery was attacked and killed. His body has been burned beyond recognition. It is the work of the Life-Giver. There is no other explanation. Head Designer Izani himself found him this morning, and he confirms everything I am saying to you now."

Lyam's blood ran cold.

"We are left with no choice." Ayanah straightened, her resplendent robes billowing around her. "The Life-Giver is attacking us through the Dreamers. There are only three remaining unharmed. I am calling for those Dreamers to be protected. The Healers have brewed a draught that will allow them to sleep without Dreaming. The three remaining Scribes must come to the Citadel immediately to collect it, and then give it to their Dreamers straight away, before they Dream tonight. That way, the Life-Giver will not be able to reach them too."

Lyam jerked, fear clamoring inside of him. He stared up at the steps of the Citadel, saw Tasmin step out from her place in line to reach out for Ayanah, only to be stopped by Head Guard Tomas.

"Head Scribe Tasmin is already here," Ayanah was saying. "I am now calling for Scribe Lyam and Scribe Jorin to join us here, on the steps. The draught is ready for collection."

Lyam's breathing sounded far too loud. The people standing near him withdrew, the balding man glancing around and immediately stepping back when he caught sight of Lyam, drawing his child in close to him. Lyam swallowed, looking around to find himself in the center of a makeshift circle of emptiness.

Everyone was staring at him.

Lyam felt his ears grow hot. Anger was bubbling away inside of him; anger that Ayanah was blaming the Life-Giver for Emery's death when he *knew* that it had been poison—that the guards had poisoned him. Now, the Speaker was asking for the remaining Dreamers to be silenced. Everything within Lyam rebelled at the thought of giving Annelie something to make her sleep. He wouldn't do it. He *wouldn't*.

"Scribe Lyam."

The voice jolted Lyam, and he turned to find a guard standing at the edge of the circle of people around him, one hand outstretched, the other holding a spear. "Come with me."

Lyam swallowed. He didn't want to, but what could he do? Run? The guards had already surrounded the perimeter.

Fear gripping him, Lyam nodded once and stepped up to the guard. He caught hold of Lyam's arm, the grip casual but firm, and began to lead him through the crowd towards the Citadel.

Despite the vast number of people, they had no trouble reaching the Citadel. Everyone took one look at Lyam's green Scribe robes and his gold eyes and they instantly made way.

Lyam stumbled when they reached the steps of the Citadel, his knees trembling. He didn't want to do this, didn't know *what* he was going to do. All he knew was that the Speaker was *wrong*. The guard caught him, holding him steady, and Lyam struggled for a moment, trying to break his grip, trying to get *away*.

He turned his head and saw the vast array of people splayed out behind him. Everyone was watching. There was nowhere for him to go.

Defeated, Lyam allowed the guard to pull him up the final steps to the doors of the Citadel where the Council were standing. First Assistant Symon gave them a nod, stepping aside as the guard pulled Lyam up the first step and led him towards Speaker Ayanah herself.

Lyam's heart stuttered in his chest for a moment. She was beautiful, her face calm, her eyes serene. She regarded Lyam with a distant, almost cool gaze, her resplendent robes in red and gold flowing down her body to the floor. She gave him a long, hard look under which Lyam trembled, his knees shaking, his hands clutching at his robes by his sides. He felt like she was looking right through him.

Finally, Speaker Ayanah stepped aside and gestured behind her, to where Tasmin and Head Designer Izani were standing. Lyam looked at Izani for a moment, noticing his carefully expressionless face, his immaculate brown robes, the gold trim glinting in the lanternlight. He looked stern, but at peace. There was no trace of the hard, cruel words Lyam had heard that morning.

Swallowing, Lyam moved passed him quickly until he reached where Tasmin was standing, her green robes falling off one shoulder, her hair tightly pulled into its bun but her eyes wild with distraction.

Lyam stared at the fear he found in her face and instantly felt unsettled.

"Scribe Lyam!"

Lyam turned at the call, seeing Jorin tripping up the steps below him, accompanied by another guard. Jorin's eyes were bright, but he looked confused. "What's happening? Is Dreamer Emery really dead?"

Lyam's stomach turned at the memory of the body he'd seen that morning. He turned his head quickly to the side and squeezed his eyes shut, trying to control the bile rising in his throat.

A hand touched his shoulder. Tasmin's voice, calm and familiar. "Not here. We will speak, but not here."

When Lyam opened his eyes again, Jorin had joined them, his youthful face looking confused. They were surrounded by guards who had closed in and joined the guards standing with Jorin and Lyam until there was no path left for them other than to enter the Citadel.

Ayanah gestured to the Citadel doors pleasantly. "Go ahead. The Healers are waiting for you."

Lyam didn't know what was going to happen, but a terrible feeling was growing in his gut, gnawing at his insides until he felt chewed up and beaten. Tasmin's expression had smoothed into something calm and impenetrable, and Jorin had made his way to Lyam's side, rocking on the balls of his feet, bunching his hands in his robes with a kind of restless energy that Lyam wished he had.

Lyam stared at the vast, imposing doors of the Citadel, at the line of guards showing them a pathway into it, and felt something deep within him crumble.

Tasmin stepped forwards first, her head held proudly high, green robes swirling behind her as she strode confidently forward. Lyam wished he could mimic her, but he walked with hunched shoulders and hesitant steps as he started following her into the Citadel. The doors stood vast above his head, the glass patterns intricate and reflecting back the lanternlight.

The smell of incense and perfume was overpowering as Lyam took his first step into the Citadel. He could hear Jorin gasp from behind him, and he wasn't surprised as he took in the room before him. A sweeping staircase stood proudly front and center, gliding gracefully upwards and lined with thick red and gold rugs. The colors of the Life-Giver spilled out from every corner. The walls were painted a fiery orange, the glass chandeliers hanging down from the ceiling intricately designed with stylized sunrays and beams.

The ceiling was high above their heads, the foyer wide and welcoming, but it didn't stop the trembling in Lyam's knees. They came to a stop at the foot of the staircase, and the doors to the Citadel glided closed behind them, sliding soundlessly shut.

Lyam swallowed. There really was no way out.

Tasmin stood on his left, Jorin on his right, bouncing on his heels. Lyam wanted to reach out and stop him.

Was it a coincidence that it was the three of them who had Dreamers left? Lyam's mentor, and Lyam's mentee?

Lyam didn't want to think too much about that. It made the knot in his stomach tighten.

A guard appeared at the top of the staircase, descending quickly and fluidly and absolutely silently. Lyam couldn't stop himself from taking a step back, his fingers shaking. Tasmin reached out and laid a steadying hand on his shoulder.

"Follow me," the guard told them, and turned to Lyam's right. Stumbling, Lyam obeyed, accompanied by Tasmin and Jorin, towards an innocuous looking brown door set into the wall. There was a set of much grander glass doors at the back of the foyer which looked to lead to a grand sort of meeting room, but Lyam didn't look too closely. His heart was pounding out of his chest. He was in the *Citadel*.

The guard swung open the brown door and waited for them to go inside. Jorin stepped through first, eyes wide, and Lyam followed him with Tasmin comfortingly at his back. The room

229

they stepped into was small, full of long lined tables. At one of the central tables sat a woman with wrinkled skin wearing the yellow robes of the Healers. Her back was bent, her hair standing up in thin wisps around her head.

Lyam recognized her. Lara, head of the Healers.

Upon their entry, she got to her feet, her back bowed. Despite this, she walked with sure footsteps towards them, her eyes intent where she peered at each of them individually. When her eyes rested on Lyam, he felt as though she pierced right through to his core.

"The Scribes." The Healer gave them all another hard look, her eyes narrowing. "The only ones whose Dreamers I have not needed to see."

Lyam swallowed, his lips dry. He felt Jorin quivering beside him. Tasmin stood calm, strong and firm as wax before a candle had been lit.

"You're here for the draught." The Healer turned her back on them and hobbled back to the table, where Lyam could see three clear vials of liquid balanced in a tray. His blood ran cold at the sight.

The Healer, Lara, picked the tray up with assured hands, waving away the guard when he tried to help her. Slowly, she walked back over to the three of them, holding the tray of vials steadily before her.

"I do not give you these lightly," Lara said, her voice hoarse and thin, cracking a little. "It has been a long time since I have needed to make such a thing. Use it sparsely. Three drops will do, and your Dreamer will sleep. If they show any signs of stirring, then another drop, used sparingly, to settle them."

Lyam felt sick to his stomach. The idea of sending Annelie into sleep—a sleep she couldn't wake from—was abhorrent. The thought of it made his insides curdle.

"Each of you must take one," Lara continued. "And keep it somewhere cool and dry. As little direct lanternlight as possible. Even being in this room for so long will have warmed the mixture too much, and it works best when it is cold. Keep it that way. And do *not* give more than three drops at any given time."

Lyam's knees were trembling.

"Take a vial now, each of you." Lara held the tray up with steady hands.

The vials contained clear, thick liquid that looked viscous. It refracted the lanternlight into odd shards.

Lyam didn't want to take it.

Tasmin moved first. She bowed to the Healer, then reached out and carefully lifted one of the vials out of its slot on the tray. The liquid moved sluggishly as she tilted it, edging towards the corked top with a slow, certain movement.

Jorin went next, following Tasmin's movements exactly. He bowed too, stuttering out a quick thanks before reaching out and taking the vial on the right, leaving only the central one behind.

The one for Lyam to take. The one meant for Annelie.

Lyam's fingers trembled as he clenched his hands into fists by his sides.

"Scribe Lyam." Lara's raspy voice had him looking up, and she was staring directly into his eyes.

Lyam felt pinned in place. Lara's piercing gaze submerged him in terrified thoughts, knowing that this was *wrong*. All of this was wrong. The Dreamers didn't need to be afraid of the Life-Giver, it was Izani, Izani and Tomas, they'd been the ones to cover up Emery's death.

"Ah," Lara said, her tone a little saddened. "The gold-eyed Scribe."

Lyam tore his gaze away from hers at that, staring down at the ground by his feet instead. He didn't want to hear what she'd have to say about his eyes; didn't want to deal with the talk about it. He wanted to scream, to scream that the world was all confused and wrong and he needed somebody to set it right.

"Old blood runs through you," Lara said. "There is hope yet, where the gold eyes still run in our people."

Lyam swallowed. He glanced back up hesitantly and saw

Lara with her gaze fixed on him, though it had turned slightly gentler.

"Take it now, child," she said, and held the tray out to him. "It is time."

Lyam swallowed. He glanced once at Tasmin, who nodded with her own vial in her hand, her face grimly set.

Jorin nudged him in the side.

Taking in a breath and fighting all of his instincts, Lyam reached out and took the vial. It was cold against his fingers, the liquid thick and clear.

Bile rose up his throat.

Lara nodded, setting the tray down on the table by her side. She turned back to Tasmin with her piercing gaze peering out from her wrinkled features. "You know what to do."

"I do," Tasmin said stiffly, bowing once.

Lyam fought a wave of dizziness as the guard stepped forward to lead them back out, out of the Citadel and to their huts. He wouldn't force Annelie to sleep—he *couldn't*. It would break him, the thought of her sleeping and never waking again. His stomach clenched and curdled, his limbs trembled, his vision blurred. He couldn't do this. He *wouldn't*.

A steady hand landed on his shoulder. Tasmin's perfume wafted over him as she leaned in close, murmuring into his ear, "We'll talk. Hold yourself together for just a little longer."

Lyam swallowed back bile and fought for his balance. He trusted her. She'd seen him through everything in his life as a Scribe, and she had never let him down before. He could trust her.

Tasmin's hand left his shoulder once he was stable again, and Lyam took a shaky step forward, the vial still clutched unwillingly in his hand. He slid it into one of the inner pockets of his robes, trying not to think about its weight as he focused on walking out of the room after Tasmin and the guard. Jorin was just behind him, but Lyam didn't look at him. He couldn't face anyone just then, not when the world was tilting around him.

THIRTEEN

The Speaker of the Sun is the leader of the Council,
And, therefore, the leader of the People.
But the Speaker must take care to listen to the Dreamers,
And would do well not to forget where true power lies.
The Book of the Life-Giver, Volume VI, Chapter I

T hey didn't leave the Citadel the same way they'd come
in. Rather, the guard led them down a confusing mix of
twisting, winding corridors, to a side entrance where no
one would see them leaving. The guard informed them that he'd
be escorting them all to their huts where they could administer
the draught to their Dreamer. Revulsion weighed Lyam down,
but he held his tongue. He couldn't speak around the closing of
his throat or the racing of his heart.

He had to trust that Tasmin had a plan, some way out of this.
He knew one thing for sure: the draught was never touching
Annelie's lips. Not while Lyam still had life in his limbs.

They stepped out of the Citadel into the fresh air of the

cavern, the lanternlight brighter. Lyam could see the grey peppering Tasmin's hair, the fraying of the sleeve of his own green robe, the shine of the guard's spear.

Jorin appeared at Lyam's shoulder, his eyes wide. "Can you believe we just met the oldest Healer?"

Lyam turned to look at him and saw a mix of emotions on Jorin's face—disbelief, curiosity, confusion. He looked so young. Too young to have to deal with any of this. Lyam's heart tugged in sympathy for him. At least he hadn't had to witness his young Dreamer come under attack.

Or die. Lyam remembered Yenn's horrified trembling from that morning and shuddered. His stomach clenched inside him. He couldn't let that happen again.

The guard hurried them through some of the back alleys away from the square to avoid the people staring at them, led by the guard. But after they'd gone a few steps into the darkness, Tasmin stopped abruptly and held up a hand.

The guard turned to her with a questioning look.

"We must stop by the Scribes' Hall first," Tasmin said, her voice steady and firm.

The guard hesitated. "My orders are to see you all back to your huts."

"And you may do so," Tasmin agreed, "After we have met in my office. There is some business we must yet discuss."

The guard looked uncertain.

"You may accompany us there," Tasmin firmly stated, and then turned on her heel and led them back through the alley.

Lyam looked after her, his heart hammering in his chest. Jorin had perked up the moment she spoke, and he went scurrying after her instantly, questions burning on his tongue. Lyam, however, hung back a moment. He still felt sick, the world spinning a little beside him, and he didn't know what Tasmin was planning

He had to trust her.

"I'm not sure this is supposed to happen," the guard said uncertainly, looking at Lyam with a curious gaze.

"None of this is supposed to happen," Lyam answered, his voice flat, and then he started after Tasmin.

They caused a bit of a stir once they stepped out onto the main streets, people stopping to look at them in their Scribes' robes, the gold trim around Tasmin's robes and the gold of Lyam's eyes easily identifying them. The guard scurried after them until he was walking side-by-side with Tasmin, who had her eyes fixed firmly forward, her steps assured.

Lyam followed just behind her, Jorin by his side. Jorin was still eagerly bouncing on the balls of his feet, questions spilling from him at every turn. "What do you think we're going to discuss? Can you imagine the *actual Speaker* called us forward? Us! And we're the only ones who have Dreamers who haven't been attacked, why do you think that is? Why us? There must be a reason."

Lyam listened as well as he could with his own thoughts tumbling over themselves. He envied Jorin's enthusiasm, his slightly naïve view of what was happening. Lyam was trembling, knowing that none of this should be happening. It had to be something to do with Izani and Tomas covering up Emery's death, although he couldn't fathom why they would. He was itching to tell Tasmin, to make it clear to her just exactly what they were up against.

He hoped she was going to give him a chance to explain. If not, he would have to force her, somehow.

They entered the Scribes' Hall, the familiar narrow corridors lined with books going some way towards easing Lyam's restless heartbeat. He breathed in the scent of musty parchment and tried to calm his racing thoughts, the familiar territory easing him slightly.

The path to Tasmin's office was up just a couple of flights of stairs, and when they reached it Tasmin opened the door to let the others in, standing aside. Jorin rushed in first, and Lyam ducked in after him. Tasmin came in behind them and calmly shut the door in the guard's face.

She turned to them, and her usually friendly face crumpled

into lines of worry, her brow creasing, her eyes narrowing. She ran one hand over her forehead.

Lyam felt his stomach clench. She looked just as worn down as he felt.

Jorin, on the other hand, was still bouncing with enthusiasm.

"Well," Tasmin began, dropping her hand back to her side to survey the two of them. "We have a lot to do."

She led them over to her desk, Lyam and Jorin taking the two seats on the other side as she rounded to sit behind it. She leaned her elbows on her desk and rested her chin in her palms, surveying the two of them closely.

Much to Lyam's surprise, it was him that Tasmin turned to first. "I am not surprised to see you here, Scribe Lyam. Dreamer Annelie is strong. I expected her to survive the chaos of the past few days."

Lyam wet his lips nervously.

"And you," Tasmin said slowly, turning to Jorin. "You are so new, so young still. Perhaps the Life-Giver has spared you thus far because of that, but...ah, I don't know. I don't know why the Life-Giver is attacking us."

Lyam took in a harsh breath, feeling his insides squirm. This wasn't the Life-Giver's doing. He felt it within his bones, knew it from the way Annelie spoke of the Dreams, had seen it in whatever Tomas and Izani had done that morning with Emery's body. Something was *wrong*. Something cursed.

Lyam swallowed down his nerves and said, as bravely as he could, "The Life-Giver isn't harming anyone."

Tasmin straightened up in surprise.

"There's a curse," Lyam continued, determined despite the shake he could hear in his voice. "But it isn't caused by the Life-Giver. I know...I know it isn't."

Jorin turned to him with wide, shocked eyes. "But Speaker Ayanah said—"

"I know what she said." Lyam clenched his fists in his lap, looking down. The tips of his ears were hot. "But she's wrong."

He could feel both their eyes on him.

"That's a bold claim," Tasmin said slowly, and when Lyam risked glancing up she was giving him a serious look.

Lyam swallowed around a dry throat. "I know. But I-I've seen it. Evidence. And Anni says the Life-Giver is leaving. We should be trying to get the Sun to return to us, not cutting ourselves off even more. If we send the last three Dreamers into sleep..." he choked up, his voice trailing into silence.

Silence rang through the room.

Eventually, Tasmin laid both her hands down on her desk with a dull thump, sitting up straight. "You're lucky that I happen to agree with you, Lyam, or you would be put to death just for *suggesting* that the Speaker is wrong."

Lyam's breathing grew high and wheezy. He *knew*. He knew that what he was thinking was blasphemous, but every bone in his body was telling him that things were *wrong*. He couldn't leave things to go on as they were. Not if it meant silencing Annelie. That was his last straw, his breaking point. He couldn't do it.

"I can't give the draught to Anni," he said softly, his voice shaking. "I know how much trouble this is going to get us in, but it's *wrong*."

"I agree," Tasmin murmured. "But keep your voice down. The guard is just outside."

Lyam felt as if someone was stepping on his chest. His breathing sounded high and ferociously loud to his own ears.

Jorin stared between them, his eyes wide and his expression terrified. "Are you...are you saying we shouldn't give our Dreamers the draughts? But what about what the Speaker said? It isn't safe for them to Dream anymore, is it?"

Lyam let out a shaky breath. His fingers were trembling in his lap, so he clenched them into fists, studying the loose fraying threads at the end of his left sleeve.

"It isn't safe, no," Tasmin said slowly. "But I happen to agree with Lyam that silencing the Dreamers isn't the way forward."

"Then what do we do?" Jorin sounded totally enthused, not even slightly afraid. Lyam wished he had that kind of bold belief in something, but he felt totally at odds with the world he'd grown up in. He didn't know who to trust anymore.

Tasmin leaned back in her chair with a low, troubled sigh. "I don't know. But we can't do as Speaker Ayanah suggests. We three represent the last Dreamers; we can't let them be silenced too."

Lyam closed his eyes in relief. His stomach bubbled unpleasantly, his insides squirming.

He could sense Tasmin's eyes on him.

"I don't think it's a coincidence that it's the three of us that are left," she said quietly.

Lyam looked up to meet Tasmin's eyes.

"You're the link, Lyam," Tasmin said lowly. "I'm your mentor. Jorin's your mentee. You're the link between us."

Lyam frowned at her in confusion.

She continued to look at him steadily, and Lyam felt himself unwind a little. At least she agreed with him. But he didn't know what she was trying to suggest.

"If anything, Annelie is the link," Tasmin continued thoughtfully. "She keeps letting you know about things you aren't supposed to know about. Like the second attack, not that it matters now. We need to know how to protect our Dreamers. I agree that the draughts aren't the way forward, but we have to do something. The Life-Giver killed Emery last night."

"No, that isn't what *happened*," Lyam said bitterly, and dropped his head into his hands. He was trembling, whole-body shivers, his eyes squeezing shut.

"It is," Jorin disagreed, puzzlement in his voice. "Speaker Ayanah said—"

"Speaker Ayanah is *wrong*." Something inside Lyam broke. He felt it, his throat loosening, the words finally spilling out the story that had been trapped inside him. "I went to Dreamer Emery's hut this morning."

"You *what?!*" Tasmin sounded shocked.

Lyam drew in a shuddering breath. "I went, and Scribe Yenn was there, he was...he was a mess, honestly. Shaken and terrified.

I went inside their hut. I know I shouldn't have, but Anni sent me there saying Emery had been killed, so I went. And Dreamer Emery was...he was dead, on the chair." Lyam shuddered, remembering the contorted way Emery's body had been lying, the stench, the dried bits of froth at his mouth. Bile rose up Lyam's throat, his stomach cramping.

"The Life-Giver must have done it," Jorin said hesitantly. "Nothing else could touch a Dreamer. Right?"

"But it wasn't the Life-Giver that killed him!" Lyam exclaimed. "I asked Scribe Yenn, and he...he told me that the guards came in and poisoned Dreamer Emery while they held Scribe Yenn back."

His words dropped liked stones into silence.

Lyam looked up, scared, to see Tasmin staring straight at him. Her eyes were wide, a few wisps of hair escaping her tight bun, the lines on her face creased in shock.

Even Jorin had gone deathly quiet.

"But then Yenn rang the alarm bell," Lyam continued miserably, "And I had to hide. I hid in the washroom. Head Designer Izani and Head Guard Tomas arrived and made it *look* like the Life-Giver had killed Dreamer Emery."

Silence rang through the room again.

"That's impossible," Jorin murmured in awe. "*Impossible.*"

Lyam wished it was impossible. He wished he hadn't gone there this morning, wished that Dreamer Emery had never died, and that he could go back to believing in the system again instead of being suspicious of the Head Designer. He wished Enoch hadn't told him about the curse, and that Dreamer Rayah had never been attacked in the first place.

It was all too much.

"You're saying some very dangerous things," Tasmin said lowly.

Lyam swallowed. He knew. He knew what he was saying would have him killed if Head Guard Tomas ever heard of it, but he'd been quiet for so long and nothing had gone right. Lyam felt as if his world was collapsing around him, like the foundation stones had been removed and now everything was crumbling.

He took in a shaky breath.

"Izani and Tomas, you say?" Tasmin said again, and Lyam looked up to find her looking intently his way.

Gathering his courage, Lyam nodded. "They came to Yenn and Emery's hut and made it look like Emery died in his sleep. But I saw him before...before—"

"What did he look like?" Tasmin asked.

Lyam held back a full body shudder at the memory. He closed his eyes. "Um. Contorted. There was foam at his mouth, and... and the *smell*—" Lyam cut himself off, screwing his face up. The memory spread revulsion through him, aching in his bones.

Tasmin pursed her lips. "It sounds like it could be poison."

"It *was*," Lyam insisted, shuddering. "I saw Yenn, the look on his face. He was telling the truth."

Tasmin made a low sound.

Jorin was staring between them, his mouth open, showing the gap between his teeth. "Emery was *poisoned*? By a guard? Why?"

"I don't know," Lyam said quietly, brokenly. He squeezed his eyes shut. "Yenn said it was the guards, but I don't know how that can be true."

"The guards answer to Tomas," Tasmin said grimly. "And Tomas is loyal to Izani. Neither of them have shown any desire to help the Dreamers at any of the Council meetings I've attended."

Jorin and Lyam both turned to her, shocked.

Tasmin put her head in her hands for a moment, raking her fingers through her hair. She spoke so quietly that Jorin and Lyam had to lean in close to hear her. "Tomas and Izani have been trying to keep this quiet in every single Council meeting we've had. I have demonstrated, time and time again, that we are in a state of crisis, that our Dreamers are under attack, and they have blocked me at every turn. The only allowance they made was to have a guard stationed outside every hut, for what little good that did. Perhaps that wasn't safe at all, if Tomas is truly somehow behind all of this."

Lyam's blood ran cold.

Jorin's eyes were wide. "Are they the ones behind the attack on the Dreamers?"

"They don't have that power," Tasmin answered grimly. "Or at least, I hope they don't."

Lyam pressed a hand to his temple, feeling the throbbing beginnings of a headache. He'd barely slept, hadn't eaten. He was too caught up in what was going on, in figuring out how *any* of this could be possible. A Dreamer had died. A Dreamer had died, Annelie wasn't safe, and Lyam had no idea what to do.

"I think only the Dreams will show us the truth of things," Tasmin said, her voice still as quiet as possible, highly mindful of the guard stationed outside their door. "That's why the draughts aren't the answer. I can't believe I'm saying this, but we can't do as the Speaker has instructed us."

Lyam held back a shudder. Blasphemy, uttered by Tasmin, but it was making him feel *safe*. He felt impossibly relieved. He knew he would never give Annelie that draught. Whatever it took.

Tasmin reached inside her robes and extracted the vial she'd been given by Lara. The clear, viscous liquid remained unscathed, glittering dully in the lanternlight.

Lyam held back a shudder of revulsion.

"Take out your draughts," Tasmin said, her voice low.

Lyam reached inside his cloak and brought out his own vial. It felt disgustingly wrong between his fingers, cold and lifeless and awful. He couldn't look at it, keeping his eyes turned away. Beside him, Jorin was looking curiously at his own glass vial, holding it up to the light and tilting his head.

Tasmin looked them both in the eye. "We will never give this to our Dreamers."

Lyam nodded his agreement, felt Jorin beside him do the same.

Eyes blazing, Tasmin opened her palm and let the glass vial smash to the ground.

Lyam jumped. He stared down at the ground where the vial had smashed into a thousand glittering pieces, the thick clear liquid oozing across the marble ground under the desk.

Tasmin met his eyes. "Your turn."

Sucking in a breath, Lyam held out his own draught and dropped it too, watching as it fell down through the air, wincing at the loud crash as it collided with the marble floor. He watched the liquid seep out, mingling with what was already there from Tasmin's vial.

From beside him, Jorin also released his own vial, and it smashed along with the two of theirs.

Tasmin let out a loud breath.

What they'd just done was enough to see them put to death, and yet Lyam felt giddy with relief. Annelie was safe from that at least.

"So," Tasmin said briskly, dusting her hands over the desk. "That's that. But we're still left with the question: what do we do now?"

Jorin let out an excited breath and leaned in over the desk. "If the Dreams are really going to give us the answer, I read about a joint Dream in an ancient myth. A Dream where the Dreamers sat together and held hands, and it, like, combined their power."

"We don't have time for myths," Tasmin said impatiently.

Jorin shrank back in his seat, but his words sparked something in Lyam. He remembered the myth Jorin was talking about —a time when there had been a great drought, and they'd been desperate for any way to find water. The Dreamers had joined together, all of them, sitting in a circle holding hands and turning their faces to the sky, to their Life-Giver. The Dream had ended with a new spring being discovered and the drought coming to an end.

Lyam bit his lip.

"We must keep this from Tomas," Tasmin was saying, quickly and quietly. "Don't say anything to the guards stationed outside your huts. Only tell your Dreamer about the draught, but we're not giving it to them. We need our Dreamers now more than ever."

"That's why Jorin might be right," Lyam said slowly. He thought of the myths again, remembered reading about the one Jorin had talked about, and felt something like hope beginning to unfurl in his chest.

Tasmin paused, looking at him with a question in her eyes.

"The joint Dream," Lyam said, leaning forward and gripping the sides of his chair tight. "If we had our Dreamers Dream together—"

"It would be like the myth," Jorin interrupted excitedly. "The drought ended. We'd find the answer."

Tasmin looked between them slowly.

Lyam swallowed around a dry lump in his throat. "If we can contact the Life-Giver, it might tell us once and for all what's going on with Head Designer Izani and Head Guard Tomas."

Tasmin met his eyes, her gaze steady.

Silence reigned for a moment.

Eventually, Tasmin gave a slow nod. "We need to find out what they're planning. Izani and Tomas plotting together does not surprise me, but I hadn't realized the scale of their corruption. We need to stop them, and fast."

"This could be the quickest way," Jorin said, wriggling in his seat. "We can bring our Dreamers together. They can have a joint Dream. It'll let the Life-Giver really speak to us."

Lyam felt his pulse speed up. He leaned forward in his seat a little, looking between the two of them. Jorin was so excited, his eyes wide, and Tasmin looked exhausted but was finally beginning to show some interest.

"We'd have to be careful," Tasmin warned. "How do we even get our Dreamers together? They can't leave their huts."

Jorin closed his mouth, chastened. He sat back in his seat, and Lyam felt his chest tug at the sight of it. He wanted the joint Dream to happen. Jorin was right, it was the best idea they'd come up with so far. There was just so much to think about. How would they bring their Dreamers together? How would they do it without any of the guards finding out? Would a joint Dream even work? Lyam thought of Annelie, of how frail she'd become. He wasn't sure she would even last another Dream, although her inner strength had never failed her before.

Tasmin furrowed her brow. "Can we take that risk when we're not even sure a joint Dream would work?"

"It worked in the myth," Jorin piped up. "The Dreamers working together let more of the Life-Giver's message come through. The Scribes were there too, of course, and the Designers, and so they could search for the spring straightaway."

Tasmin looked to Lyam, who nodded. "That's what I remember reading, too. I really think we need to try."

Tasmin pursed her lips. "Then we will make it happen."

Something sharp spiked in Lyam's chest.

Jorin let out a cry of excitement, and Tasmin leaned in closer. "But we need somewhere safe. Somewhere out of sight of the guards, a place we can safely move our Dreamers to outside of everything we know."

The words flickered in Lyam's brain, and slowly, he glanced up at Tasmin and Jorin. Quietly, he said, "I think I know exactly who we can go to."

Jorin shot him a curious look.

"How easily can we get past that guard?" Lyam asked.

Tasmin tilted her head, studying him. "Easily enough, depending on what you need."

"We need to go to the Southernmost tunnel."

Jorin frowned. "What?"

"Trust me," Lyam implored, looking between them with hope and fear clamoring for attention in his chest. "Just...just let me take you both there. I know someone who can help."

Tasmin clicked her tongue. Slowly, she nodded. "I'll deal with the guard. Go ahead, Lyam. Show us the way."

&

Enoch looked between the three of them, his arms crossed over his chest, and harrumphed.

Lyam held his breath. From beside him, he could feel Jorin trembling. Tasmin stood tall and proud on Lyam's other side, her chin jutted out, serene calm on her face despite the fact that she'd been shocked at hearing Enoch even existed less than an hour ago.

"The three of you," Enoch said eventually into the painful silence, "expect me to agree with some hare-brained scheme you've all cooked up together?"

Lyam swallowed. His heart felt like it was dropping through his stomach.

"Mad, the lot of you," Enoch shook his head. "And they call *me* crazy."

Lyam felt the tiny tendril of hope he'd been nursing shrivel up and die. "Enoch, please."

"And *you*, Scribe Lyam," Enoch let out a noisy breath. "I'm guessing you're the one that brought these two to my door?"

Lyam had to hold back a shiver. He hadn't led them right to the entrance to the tunnel that led out to the light. He hadn't needed to. They'd been walking towards the tunnel when Enoch appeared, somehow silent in the darkness, massive and unbending before them. Lyam had been so sure that he'd help.

"It's our only chance," Lyam tried again. "Please."

"You think a joint Dream is the way out of this mess?" Enoch clicked his tongue. "Have you ever tried one of them before? How do you know it's safe? If you care so much about your Dreamer—"

"I *do*," Lyam interrupted, voice strong. "I do."

Enoch surveyed him closely, his gold eyes deep and intense.

"I've heard of a joint Dream before," Jorin piped up into the awkward silence. "In a myth. It worked then, why wouldn't it work now?"

Finally, Enoch removed his gaze from Lyam. Releasing a low

245

breath, he turned instead to Jorin who instantly shrank against Lyam's side.

"A myth, hm?" Enoch pursed his lips. "I'm assuming you're referring to the drought?"

Hesitantly, Jorin nodded.

Lyam watched the changing expressions flit across Enoch's face—concern to incredulity to confusion to questioning. He seemed unsettled, and for once not the calm, collected presence that Lyam had always seen from him before. Lyam wasn't sure whether that was a good thing or not.

"It worked," Jorin said bravely. "The drought ended."

Enoch clicked his tongue. "It could still be completely foolish. Do you know what would happen if this Dream also failed? How much more damage could be caused if the Dreamers are linked, made vulnerable to each other?"

"But it's the only way," Lyam said desperately. "We need to talk to the Life-Giver. All of us, together."

"And it isn't any safer for the Dreamers to Dream alone," Tasmin quietly said from beside him.

Enoch's attention shifted to her. "That may be true. Ah, that may be true." He closed his eyes and brought one hand up to his forehead, shielding his eyes for a moment. It was harder to read his expression like this, so Lyam simply drew a long breath into his lungs and held it there, hoping.

Praying.

"You're mad," Enoch said finally, "The three of you. Barking mad."

Lyam closed his eyes, defeat swirling through him.

"But I'm as mad as any of you," Enoch said, and Lyam's eyes flew open again to see Enoch sending him a knowing gaze.

Jorin drew in a breath from beside him.

"You'll do it?" Lyam asked, hope bleeding into his tone.

Silence held for an uncomfortably long moment, but then Enoch dipped his head in a nod.

"Mad, all of us," he laughed, the sound sudden and shocking in the tunnel. "But I'll help you."

CHAPTER

FOURTEEN

When Scribes lose their Dreamers,
They lose their lives and become Grey Ones.
They go to grieve in community,
Away from the daily lives of the city,
For none but their own can understand the pain of losing a Dreamer.
The Book of the Life-Giver, Volume II, Chapter VII

L yam peered around the corner with trepidation, his pulse
fluttering faster in his throat.

Tasmin had told him where to go, but Lyam still felt
fear tighten nauseatingly in his chest. They'd made plans with
Enoch earlier to get the Dreamers out of their huts and to a safe
space for the joint Dream. Even the thought of it was terrifying.
Dreamers outside their huts. Lyam was secretly excited to tell
Annelie that she'd be leaving her hut for the first time since she'd
been a little girl.

But before he could go back, there was somewhere else he
needed to be.

Tasmin had agreed with his plan, saying she would have gone with him if she didn't need to go and speak to the Council to try and find out more about what Head Designer Izani and Head Guard Tomas had been plotting. Lyam didn't wish that task upon anyone, but if anyone could do it, then Tasmin could.

Not that the task he was undertaking was really any easier. Lyam had never been down these tunnels, but Tasmin had told him that if he wanted to talk to Yenn, then he needed to come here—to the House of the Grey Ones. The community of Scribes who'd lost their Dreamers.

The tunnels to the North of the city were much the same as the ones to the South, but they felt colder and darker to Lyam as he stepped forward, lantern in hand. The light bleeding into the tunnel felt feeble. Lyam was still scared. He dreaded every step, but he didn't once consider turning back. He needed answers, and the only one who could give them to him was Yenn.

Lyam rounded the last corner and his jaw dropped.

The tunnel split into a cavern not unlike the city itself, though it was maybe half the size. The path went steeply downward from where Lyam was standing, leading to a blank grey wall that looked formidable and unapproachable. The path was littered with rough stones that pricked his feet even through his sandals, and the air smelled stale. From his vantage point, Lyam could see that the wall carried on in a rough circle, hiding whatever was behind it from view. If Lyam stood on his tiptoes, he could just about make out the roof of what might have been a building in the middle of the wall, almost like a fortress, but he couldn't be sure.

The path led to an entryway set back into the wall, and that was it. Nowhere else to go.

Lyam swallowed around a dry throat.

Carefully, he stepped forward, despite the threatening blank face of the wall making him want to turn and run far away. He had never seen anything look so uninviting. The path was steep, and Lyam had to clutch onto handholds built into the wall of the path to stop from tumbling down to land in a heap before the entrance to whatever it was the wall was hiding. His feet skidded on uneven ground, loose rocks, sand, and dust tumbling down around him, echoing loudly throughout the otherwise silent cavern. It was eerie.

Eventually, Lyam made it to the bottom of the path. The wall looked far more formidable from down there, and Lyam craned his neck backward, peering up to where the wall was swallowed by blackness.

The only light came from two lanterns set in the wall on either side of the entrance, which was a large stone doorway with words carved into the center.

Here we come to mourn, our lives no longer ours.

A shudder ran down Lyam's back. The air was colder down here, biting at his skin, and he was grateful that he was still wearing his thick, stiff Scribes' robes. The darkness clung to his ankles, flanking his sides, and Lyam brought his own lantern in closer to his chest, the shadows leaping around him.

Gathering as much courage as he could, Lyam lifted a hand and knocked on the smooth stone surface of the door. The sound rang out around the cavern, and Lyam flinched, instinctively drawing his hand back to his chest. He swallowed.

It took several moments of eerie silence for the door to begin to open. It swung open with a deep grating sound that rattled Lyam's bones, revealing a dark hollow space that seemed crammed into an area too small for it.

Lyam hesitated.

Then a great, bright light suddenly crashed into view, making Lyam stumble back a step with a shout. He put his hand up to his eyes. The light reminded him of seeing actual Sunlight for the first time in his life, in Enoch's tunnel. It held the same almost fluid quality, trickling through the air before him with pale, hollow warmth.

Lyam dropped his hand and was met with the face of a man he'd never seen before.

A shaggy beard, hollow eyes, sparse hair—the man was old, his face wrinkled and creased, the scraggly hair of his beard grey-white and coarse looking. The smell that accompanied him was of something old and rotting, a gust of stale air blowing out from the space behind the man brushing cool air against Lyam's face and hands.

The man was taller than Lyam, though not by much, his back bent. He peered down at Lyam with hollow dark eyes. "Ah. Someone new. Bad news, is it?"

Lyam blinked, surprised at the scratchy quality of the man's voice. Before he had a chance to speak, the man leaned down and waved his lantern in Lyam's face, almost blinding him.

"Tired and sad," the man said bluntly. "News of hollow things. Loss and darkness; we know these well. Aye, but you have something else. Gold eyes? Never seen those before. Not outside of fairy tales."

Lyam stuttered, confused by the man's rambling. He tried to draw back another step, the light from the lantern still almost blinding him, but before he could move the man reached out and grabbed him.

Lyam cried out, but rather than closing around his wrist, the man's fingers instead pinched Lyam's robe, bringing the lantern close to it.

Lyam squinted, just about making out the look of sadness on the man's face.

"Not your time yet." The man shook his head, peering at the green of Lyam's robes. "We just had one. Can't take another yet. No, can't be your time yet."

"It isn't," Lyam said hastily, trying not to flinch when the man pressed his face in close to Lyam's, his stinking breath almost making him cough. "It isn't my time yet."

The thought made Lyam shudder. He would come here one day, when Annelie had passed, but he couldn't imagine it. Losing Anni was unthinkable.

To his great relief, the man relaxed a little, and a crooked smile appeared on his face. He peered intently at Lyam. "Ah, no, not your time yet. Good. Full and tired, we are. Crowded and old. Not a place for a young man. Not a place for you."

"But I'm here to visit," Lyam said quickly. "I need to see someone."

The man's eyes narrowed.

"Please," Lyam continued, shivering. "I need to speak to someone who just came here. Scribe Yenn. It's really important."

"No Scribes here," the man said blankly. "Just Grey Ones."

Cold sweat was gathering at Lyam's temples. He swallowed. "No. I'm sorry. He...he *was* a Scribe. He only came here this morning. Please, I must speak to him."

"Not purified yet," the man shrugged, his expression guarded. "No visitors. No people. Certainly, no *Scribes*." The word left the man's lips almost like a curse.

Lyam quivered. "It's *really* important."

"No," the man said, and turned to shut the door.

"It's to help the Dreamers," Lyam said desperately, lunging forward and pressing a hand against the cold stone of the door. "You remember them, right? The Dreamers?"

The man's expression almost cracked, but he recovered quickly, his face as impassive as the stone door he was trying to close.

"They're in danger." Lyam fixed his eyes on the man's. "All of them. Something's coming for them, something sinister and awful, and the only one who knows anything about it is Yenn. Please. It's our only hope. I *have* to speak to him."

The man's expression crumbled, bleeding into something deep and sorrowful and *old*—the wrinkles around his mouth turned down, his eyes creased, his forehead tumbled in on itself. He looked pained, and sad, and ancient, and Lyam didn't know how to react.

The man surveyed him for a long, silent moment.

"Alright," he finally caved, and stepped aside, beckoning Lyam closer. "You want in? I will let you in. Not easy, but I will let you. For the... for *them*."

Lyam let out a shuddering breath. Relief flooded through him, but it was tainted as the door inched further open, the stench of rotting and old things wafting out from the revealed blackness. He bit his lip. Nerves jumped in his stomach, tightening his already tight chest until it was hard to breathe.

He thought of Annelie; of all the Dreamers; of Jorin and Tasmin who were waiting on him, and he found enough courage to take his first step forwards.

The blackness encircled him as he stepped onward, his lantern light feeble against the encroaching dark. The stench of old rotting things hung heavy in the air, and silken strands of cobwebs caught on Lyam's outstretched hand where he clutched at his lantern. The light flickered weakly, hardly making a stain on the inky blackness within.

The man stepped confidently ahead of Lyam, continuing to ramble into the darkness. Lyam only caught the odd half-word he tossed behind him. *Lightless. Dreamless. Half-living.* Nothing broke through the fear that had gathered around Lyam's heart.

The sounds opened out around them, echoing, and suddenly Lyam found himself in a vast dark space filled with people. He couldn't see them, really. He could only make out half-shadows —the corner of a cloak, the profile of someone's nose and mouth, a sharp finger snagging on air. But he could feel the eyes on him. Hundreds of eyes peering through the darkness as the people stopped what they were doing, turning to watch him step forwards with a thin, dead gaze.

The man who was leading Lyam paused, and Lyam instantly froze. His every muscle was heavy with tension, fear slowing his thoughts and clouding his mind. The man fiddled with something set into the wall, and then sudden light started to appear in pinpricks in the corners of the vast hall.

Slowly, as the lights grew brighter, Lyam started to make out where he was. And then he instantly wished for the darkness again.

Hundreds of people surrounded him. People dressed all in grey, long robes that swept to the floor, tied with grey braids and with grey hoods that most of them were wearing pulled down low over their heads. But he could sense their eyes. They were all gathering around him, drawing together in a fluid, silent mass, the weight of their gazes heavy on Lyam's skin. The few people who were without hoods had gaunt, thin faces, long noses and straight lips, hair pulled back, eyes fixed on him.

Lyam swallowed and curled as much into himself as he could.

The man leading him continued walking through the crowd as if nothing was wrong, and he was right. This was probably normal for this place. The place Scribes came to die, to live out the rest of their lives without their Dreamer.

The thought of it made the hair rise on Lyam's arms.

The air shivered cold around them, stale and still, as Lyam hesitantly walked after the man leading him. The crowd hovered just outside his circle of lanternlight, the grey of their cloaks merging with the darkness that held the vast hall in its grip. He felt trapped. He tried not to meet the eyes of anyone, but one woman caught his gaze. Her eyes were pale grey, drained of color much like the rest of this shadowy hall.

Lyam quickly reverted to staring at his feet.

Their footsteps echoed loudly up to the high, vaulted ceiling, the fortress-like place cold and unfeeling. It almost felt unlived in, which was concerning considering the number of people currently surrounding Lyam. He focused on his feet and walked after the man leading him, one foot in front of the other, until the man came to an abrupt halt.

Lyam stumbled behind him, his lantern swinging, and looked up to see a hunched figure sitting over a stone table tucked into the wall.

Lyam swallowed. He recognized him instantly, even with the grey robes and the deep hood. Yenn's face was burned into his memory, torn apart with grief. Here, Yenn looked small. His back was bowed, chin tucked into his neck, and eyes downcast.

The man leading Lyam coughed, and reluctantly Yenn looked up.

Lyam's eyes widened. His face had been thin and gaunt before, but now he looked almost skeletal. Wrinkles that had not been there before folded his forehead and tugged at his cheeks, his mouth turned down in a thin, sad, line, his eyes dark and blank. He looked empty.

"Well." The man leading Lyam turned to face him, his wrinkled face impossible to read. "You asked for him. I did as asked. Your problem now."

Lyam swallowed. Silence rang through the vast room, painful and pressured. The man stepped aside, clapping one bony hand on Lyam's shoulder before he disappeared into the dark mass that still surrounded them.

Lyam glanced at Yenn, who was looking at him blankly, and then to the mass of undulating bodies surrounding them that still had their eyes fixed on Lyam. It made all the hairs on the back of his neck rise, a deep sense of foreboding sitting heavily over him. He hated this place. He hated how it made him feel; how slow dread crept over him like wax dripping down a candle; how he felt inevitably like he was looking into his future.

Lyam shook off the thought and focused on Yenn. He needed to get his answers.

"Scr— Yenn." Lyam tried to keep his voice even, though even he could hear the wobble in it. "Can I talk to you?"

Yenn lifted his head to meet Lyam's gaze directly. He looked uncaring and blank, like the atmosphere of this place had already anchored itself in his bones.

"It's important," Lyam added more firmly.

Slowly, Yenn dipped his head in a half-bow. "If you must."

Lyam swallowed. His legs were aching from the cold, his fingers frozen around the handle of his lantern. He leaned forward and set his lantern down on the table, and then forced his slightly-trembling body into the seat opposite Yenn.

"It's about what happened to your Dreamer," Lyam said lowly, noting the way Yenn stiffened, sitting up straighter. "I need to know the truth."

"You shouldn't have been there." Yenn's voice was quiet, raspy.

Lyam bit his lip, glancing down at the rough stone table

before he glanced back up at Yenn. "I know that something deeper is going on."

Slowly, Yenn shook his head. "I'm sorry, but there's nothing for you here. I have no answers for you."

"But you *know* how your Dreamer—how he died." Lyam said the words reluctantly, hating how Yenn flinched before him. He shouldn't be forcing Yenn to relive this, but there was nothing else Lyam could do. They were running out of time. Night was approaching faster than ever.

"The Life-Giver turned on my Dreamer," Yenn said tonelessly.

Lyam hissed, lowering his voice and leaning in close. "We both know that isn't true. The guards..."

"Don't do this." Yenn's mask slipped, just a little, and he peered at Lyam with something like desperation hiding behind his eyes. "Please. Don't do this."

"I have to," Lyam said. "I have to, or my Dreamer is going to end up like yours."

Yenn's eyes tightened. "It's not your time yet."

"I know," Lyam answered, refusing to think about a time where Annelie was gone from his life. "But I need your help."

Yenn turned his face away, hunching up smaller in his seat. Lyam took in his trembling form with fear clutching at his heart. He hated seeing Yenn like this, so different from the proud Scribe he'd once known.

"Please," Lyam said softly. "You're the only one who knows what's really going on. Please, talk to me. We need you."

Yenn squeezed his eyes shut. "You're better off not knowing."

"How can you *say* that?" Lyam placed both palms flat on the table and leaned closer, right into Yenn's face, until the faint stench of rot surrounded him. "They took your Dreamer from you. They abandoned you here, Yenn, please."

"They had no choice," Yenn hissed back. "Emery knew. He knew what they were doing. What *I* was doing. And...and he was going to stop them. They couldn't let that happen. They have to have control, or their plan will fall apart."

"What plan?" Lyam asked breathlessly.

Yenn opened his eyes again and fixed Lyam with a distraught gaze. He shook his head.

"*Please.*" Lyam leaned in close, dropping his voice so that the mass of people around them couldn't hear. "I know that it involves Izani and Tomas. I know they made it look like the Life-Giver took your Dreamer, when really it was the guard. And I know that you've been hiding your Dreams in the library. Dreams that show the curse."

Yenn shrank back.

"Tell me," Lyam whispered. "What is the curse? What does it mean?"

Yenn shook his head, face stiff. "Emery was the one who knew about it. He's been Dreaming about it for years."

"*Years?*"

Yenn nodded stiffly. "I know I shouldn't have hidden them," he said brokenly, so quiet Lyam was struggling to hear him even with how close he was. "But I...I couldn't. Izani was changing them. I knew he was, and I couldn't let him have the Life-Givers words." Yenn's face suddenly drew closed; angry. "He shouldn't be allowed anywhere *near* the Life-Giver."

Lyam swallowed, disbelieving. "He was—he was *changing Dreams?*"

The Dreams were the word of the Life-Giver. The Dreams shaped their very society, were filled with power and authority beyond what any one of them could comprehend.

The thought of changing them made Lyam feel sick.

Yenn's expression was twisted as he continued. "Izani sees the world as something he can mould. He wants power. He longs for it, hungers for it above anything else. He would, and will, do anything for it. And he's not the first one."

Lyam's blood ran cold. "What do you mean?"

"Dreams have been changed for generations," Yenn murmured. "Izani is just the latest. He knows how to use his influence to manipulate the Council."

"Is...is he the one hurting the Dreamers?" Lyam whispered.

Yenn shook his head. "He doesn't have that power. But I think the corruption that's been going on for so long is polluting the Dreamers' relationship with the Life-Giver."

"What do you mean?"

"Emery talked about it, sometimes," Yenn said, his voice breaking and turning wistful. "He could feel a disconnect in the Dreams. Like he couldn't reach The Life-Giver anymore. I think Izani's actions here are impacting the Dreams."

Lyam swallowed. He remembered the blackness that Annelie described oozing through the Dreams and shuddered.

"I hid the Dreams from him." Yenn glanced down, curling his fingers into fists. "Izani told me to destroy them, to destroy the true Dreams so that he could write his own. But I didn't destroy them. He wanted me to set them on fire, but I stood there with my lantern flame above the papers, and I *couldn't*. It was like a vast warmth filled the room, and it singed my arms and burned my tongue, and I couldn't destroy the Dreams. I *couldn't*."

Lyam couldn't even imagine it.

"How did you find them?" Yenn asked, finally meeting Lyam's gaze again. His mask had completely slipped; he almost looked human again.

Lyam bit his lip. "I had some help. Someone gave me the key to your safe."

Recognition flashed in Yenn's eyes. A slow, sure smile stretched suddenly across his lips. "Ah. Enoch."

Lyam's eyes widened.

"I found him," Yenn said slowly, quietly. "I was shocked. A Water-Gatherer? I thought the curse already got rid of them all."

"The curse?" Lyam asked, confused. "What has the curse got to do with the Water-Gatherers?"

"It has to do with everything." Yenn leaned closer, dropping his voice even lower until Lyam had to place his ear right by Yenn's lips. "It's been here for centuries. Since before we came underground."

Lyam swallowed. "The city. The one above us."

Yenn nodded. "There was a leader. You'll know if you've read the Dreams."

"I couldn't read all of them."

"Did you read about the Great One?" At Lyam's nod, Yenn continued, "He was the origin of it all. He wanted power, but he wasn't chosen as a Dreamer, and he resented it. So he moved us underground. Convinced everyone that Sunlight was sacred, that we aren't supposed to see it."

"How?"

"He was a Designer, and he changed Dreams. Just as Izani is doing now."

Lyam's stomach turned.

Yenn nodded grimly. "He made the Dreamers convince the Speaker at the time to bring us underground. To separate the Dreamers from the rest of society. It isn't supposed to be like this. Dreamers are supposed to live among us, to teach the rest of us how to communicate with the Life-Giver. But now we can't. The curse has gone on too long. Corrupting the Dreams has changed us too. We can't see above ground anymore. Sunlight hurts our eyes. We have to use all these rituals to speak to the Sun. Even the Dreamers have set phrases they're supposed to use."

"Anni hates them," Lyam murmured. "She just says what she likes."

"Maybe that's why she's still alive," Yenn said dully. "All this has meant the Life-Giver has grown distant from us, which only allows the curse to spread. And the descendants of the Great One have been changing dreams all this time. Izani is just the latest."

Lyam sucked in a sharp breath. "Why? Why would he do this?"

"For power," Yenn shrugged. "He has the ear of the Speaker. It was supposed to be Symon, the First Assistant. But Izani changed the Dream to Ayanah, who is a close family friend. He's like an uncle to her."

Lyam rocked back from the table. "He *what?*"

"This runs too deep," Yenn said. "It's been happening for centuries. What's happening to the Dreamers is the final stage of removing power from the Life-Giver and putting it in the hands of the Council. They will rule alone, and we will be trapped here forever."

Lyam's heart clenched. He drew in a shuddering breath. The thought of losing Annelie—all the Dreamers—ripped his soul to shreds, until he could hardly breathe.

He couldn't let that happen.

"Enoch is helping me," Lyam said in a fast, hushed voice.

Yenn stirred. He smiled. "Enoch. I hoped he would do something. I gave him the key to the safe."

Lyam blinked, stunned. "You?"

"I don't want Izani to change Dreams," Yenn murmured. "He asked that I burn the true ones and replace them with false ones. But I couldn't do it. So I hid the true ones away in a safe, and when I discovered Enoch's existence, I gave him the key. The last of the Water-Gatherers. It gave me hope."

Lyam nodded fiercely. "We're planning something. We're going to stop them—Izani, Tomas. All of them."

Yenn sent him a look that was almost soft. "I wish you the best. I wish I could have done more. I protected Emery as best I could, but Izani—" Yenn shuddered. "He is not a man who suffers others gladly."

"We have a plan," Lyam said stubbornly. "A way to get back in touch with the Life-Giver. To bring us back above ground."

Yenn was looking at Lyam again, watching him with a heavy gaze. "Whatever you're planning, I hope it's something big."

Lyam swallowed. He thought of their plan for the joint Dream, their last bid at saving their Dreamers, but now he saw that it ran deeper than that. This was about bringing them all out into the light.

"I can see in Sunlight," Lyam said softly.

Yenn dropped his fist onto the table with a dull *thud*. He stared incredulously at Lyam.

"It's my eyes," Lyam explained. "Like Enoch's. I can see up there, and I'm going to find a way to bring everyone else up with me."

Yenn looked ashen. Slowly, he reached up, one cold finger brushing Lyam's face.

"Gold eyes," he breathed.

Lyam nodded. "We're going to do this. We have to."

Yenn regarded him as his mask fell back into place. "I hope you're strong. You're going to have to be."

CHAPTER

FIFTEEN

Designers must not, in any circumstance, speak over their Dreamer.
To do so is punishable by immediate death without trial.
To speak over the Dreamers is worse than evil.
The Book of the Life-Giver, Volume III, Chapter I

L eaving the House of the Grey Ones was more of a relief
than Lyam had felt in a long time. As soon as he was in
the tunnels again, he felt at home, although the heavi-
ness of the grief and rotting and cold from the fortress clung to
his skin like shadows. As Lyam walked through the city, he felt as
if he stood out, like he drew eyes everywhere he went. He hurried
along with his head down low and his hood covering his face,
especially his eyes.

As he passed through the main square, by the Citadel, he
looked up and saw a familiar figure entering the Designers'
Court.

Mirah.

She was dressed in her usual brown robes, though they were

drawn tight around her. Her head was low, her curly brown hair falling in her face. Lyam couldn't see her expression.

He felt a pang. Mirah was someone he'd relied on almost all his life, since he became a Scribe and was thrust into this life that he didn't understand. He'd always looked up to her. He wasn't ready to believe that she could be working against him; that she'd had some other agenda this whole time.

Maybe she didn't know about Izani's plan. Maybe she wasn't part of any of it.

Before he could properly think through what he was doing, Lyam found himself hurrying across the square after her. He felt like he drew a lot of attention, but in all honesty the bustling crowd that filled the square was probably full of people who were too focused on their own tasks to worry about him. Still, Lyam felt anxious. He kept his hood pulled all the way up as he ducked inside the Designers' Court, low enough to shield his eyes from view.

The route to Mirah's office was painfully familiar. Lyam kept his eyes down whenever he passed someone, knowing he was on borrowed time. He couldn't rouse any suspicion before nightfall and had to make everyone believe he was doing as the Speaker had asked.

Apart from Mirah. He needed to talk to her.

He knocked on her office door once, but then walked in without asking.

Mirah glanced up from where she was crouched behind her desk, rummaging through a drawer with her hair falling into her eyes. She looked surprised to see him, but she didn't stand up.

Lyam closed the door behind him.

Mirah frowned. "Lyam, now really isn't a great—"

"I need to talk to you," Lyam interrupted, his voice wavering a little.

"I'm sorry, if you make an appointment—"

"It's really important. Please. I wouldn't ask, but...please."

Mirah looked up and met his eyes. Her expression was hard

to read, but Lyam found some softness there. Something in her looked at him fondly. He had to trust in that.

She rose to her feet and tucked her hair behind her ears, then gestured for him to sit.

Lyam sat, watching as Mirah closed the drawer before taking the seat opposite him. She placed her hands carefully on the table before meeting his eyes again. "What is it?"

Lyam swallowed. He wasn't sure where to begin, only that he had to give her a chance. He had to believe that maybe she didn't know what she was involved in, that perhaps Izani was manipulating her the way he'd been manipulating Yenn.

He had to give her the chance to change things.

"I might need your help," Lyam said quietly.

"As ever, I will do anything I can," Mirah answered, her tone clipped; neat. "But I believe you were summoned by the Speaker earlier. Has Annelie had trouble with taking her draught?"

Lyam felt sick to his stomach. A wave of nausea rolled over him, forcing him to close his eyes for a second. "No, I'm not here about that," he answered delicately, trying not to let his voice waver as he thought of the smashed vial lying on Tasmin's office floor. "I need to ask you something. It's...it's about Head Designer Izani."

Instantly, Mirah's posture changed. She sat up straighter, her hands curling into fists on the surface of the desk, and her expression went carefully blank. "Do you need me to call him here?"

"No! No, there's no need for that."

Mirah arched a brow at him, her face perfectly impassive. "Then what is it?"

Lyam swallowed. "He— I...I went to see Yenn today."

Mirah hummed. "So sad, that. I hope he is settling in well."

Lyam held back a shudder at the memory of the fortress full of broken, mourning Scribes, and prayed that the day he entered their number remained far, far away. "He is as well as can be expected. But he told me something. Something about Head Designer Izani—his Designer—something that worried me."

Mirah held his gaze. "What was it?"

Lyam licked his lips, nerves swallowing his stomach. "He...he told me that Head Designer Izani has been changing Dreams."

Mirah went very still.

"He told Yenn to destroy his real Dreams and allow Head Designer Izani to replace them," Lyam continued. "And that the Speaker wasn't appointed by the Life-Giver. That Izani appointed her instead. I think—"

"These are very serious claims," Mirah interrupted, her voice soft—dangerously soft. "You're taking some very big risks, Scribe Lyam."

Lyam swallowed. "It's just...if Yenn's correct, then we have to do something."

"And what would you suggest we do?"

Lyam took in a quick breath. "Go to the Council. Or...or to the Dreamers. Yenn told me the true Speaker should be Symon. If we appoint him instead—"

"You're talking about uprooting our entire city," Mirah said coolly. "Throwing away everything we hold dear, we hold *sacred*. It's impossible, Lyam. What you're saying is impossible."

Lyam stared at her helplessly. "But the Dreamers..."

"The *Dreamers*." Mirah laughed, a cold, derisive sound. It chilled Lyam to the bone, making him shrink back in his seat. "This is *better* for the Dreamers. My sister, she was a Dreamer, taken from us when she was twelve. By her sixteenth birthday she was dead."

Lyam sucked in a shocked, harsh breath.

"The Dreams destroyed her," Mirah continued, her voice a low hiss. "My baby sister. Better for her had she never been chosen. Better for *all* of them. No, Lyam, Izani is doing the right thing. The Dreams should have been stopped centuries ago."

Lyam stared at her. Remnants of shock, horror, and fear mixed together in his stomach, jumbling his thoughts, confusing his emotions. Mirah looked different. She looked *frightening*. Her eyes were dark, her features contorted.

"You know, don't you," Lyam said, gathering all his courage. "About the curse. The city above ground."

A crease appeared in Mirah's brow.

"Have you known all along?" Lyam was breathing heavily. "All this time? You've been— You *want* Anni to be hurt, don't you? You could have warned us!"

"I don't want to hurt her," Mirah disagreed, her jaw working.

"Then you should have *done something!*" Lyam cried. "All this time Izani has been spreading this curse. Why did you help him?"

"I don't know what you're talking about," Mirah said flatly.

Lyam stopped short, confused. He eyed Mirah closely, taking in her closed-off expression, her tight lips and sharp nose. Behind her stiff expression, she seemed genuinely confused.

Maybe she really didn't know.

"We're not supposed to live like this," Lyam said eventually. "None of us. We're supposed to live above ground. The Dreamers aren't supposed to be locked away like they are. We're all supposed to be together, but the curse stopped us. And Izani is the one keeping it going."

Mirah was quiet for several moments. Then, she pursed her lips. "I don't know about any of this. All I know is that Izani is working for the good of us all, you included. But now you know too much, Lyam. You're too dangerous."

Fear flooded Lyam's body. He got quickly to his feet, almost tripping on his robes. "I—"

"Guards." Mirah raised her voice, the look in her eyes as cold and distant as granite. "Take him."

Lyam's heart leaped in his throat. The door opened behind him, and he only had enough time to see two black-clad guards entering the room before he ducked his head and ran. He pushed past the guards, hearing one give a shout, but he didn't stop, his feet skidding against the perfectly smooth flooring. He ran faster than he ever had in his life, adrenaline pumping through him, his heartbeat pounding in his ears as he tore through the corridors of the Designers' Court, making for the back entrance. He could hear footsteps behind him, the shriek of a passing servant as he ran around a corner and almost barrelled straight into him.

Lyam threw an apology over his shoulder before he was running again. He slid down the narrow, stone stairs that led to the back entrance, almost tripping on the corner of the red rug, and then threw himself at the door. It opened and he tumbled out onto the street, surprising a group of young children playing ball.

He didn't stop to see their reaction. Instead, he just ran, their screeches following him, his feet taking him back around to the square. Vaguely, he was hoping he'd be able to lose the guards in the crowd, but he could hear shouting behind him and thundering feet. He didn't dare look back.

Lyam burst out into the square and dove straight into the crowds of people, tripping over feet and dodging reaching hands. A shout rose up behind him. "Stop him! By the order of the guard, stop him!"

Then, Lyam realized his mistake.

The crowds of people in the square would all listen to the guard. As far as anyone knew, the guards were the ones looking out for their safety and wellbeing. They would listen to them over a fleeing Scribe.

Instantly, hands started reaching for him, fingers clutching onto his robes, feet trying to trip him up. Lyam dodged as best he could, tearing himself free, hearing his robes rip. He kept his head down and struggled on, running along the edge of the crowd, trying to find another alley he could dodge down.

"Lyam?"

The voice was wonderfully familiar, if a little unexpected. Lyam snapped his head up and saw Adan standing at the mouth of a small side street, his hands full of books, his mouth slightly open.

Lyam didn't think twice. He dove down the side street, shouting, "Run!" as he tore past.

The footsteps behind him didn't linger. Lyam had no time to breathe before something whistled past his ear and he saw with jolting shock that an arrow had embedded itself in the wall a few centimetres from where he'd just been. He had no time to stop or linger on that thought, not with guards still chasing him. He put his head down and ran, his breath coming in short gasps, panic tingling under his skin.

It only took a second for the pounding feet coming after Lyam to catch him up. He caught a whirl of black out of the corner of his eye, heard the hiss of steel as one of them raised his spear. He had run out of time.

He squeezed his eyes shut. The world swam around him for a moment when he opened his eyes again to find himself at a dead-end.

No way out.

And then, a hand clasped Lyam's wrist.

"This way," Adan hissed into his ear, and tugged Lyam to the left.

Lyam stumbled, tripping over his feet as Adan dragged him through the tiniest crack between buildings on the edge of the side street. The rough dirt beneath the soles of their shoes caused a cloud of dust to rise around them and Lyam coughed, struggling to breathe.

A hand clapped over Lyam's mouth. Adan pulled him further into the crack and pressed him against the wall, still holding a hand over Lyam's mouth.

Lyam simply stared at him, wide-eyed.

They stayed wedged in the crack, out of sight from the side street, and Lyam listened as the first guard chasing him continued to run down the street, more and more black-clad guards pouring after him. The sound of people shouting and calling to each other rang from the square, disembodied voices floating through the darkness.

So much for not arousing suspicion.

Lyam had lost his lantern somewhere in the chase, so he stood there, sweaty and with his robe ripped to shreds, lost in the darkness. He studied Adan's face in the light from Adan's lantern, pressed close against him. Adan was standing with a straight back, his expression pinched as he listened. They were wedged so close together that Lyam could feel Adan's body heat, could see how much weight he'd lost. More lines had appeared on his face, his forehead creased, his eyes dark. He looked like a shadow of Lyam's best friend; a memory.

Lyam couldn't even begin to imagine what the last few days had been like for him.

Eventually, the sounds died down. Adan kept them still, though he lowered the hand that he'd kept clamped over Lyam's mouth. Lyam swallowed, his breathing fast, his pulse still thudding in his ear, and he gently let his head fall forward until his forehead was resting on Adan's shoulder. Panic and fear from the chase washed over him, exhausting him until his legs felt like jelly and his chest hitched with every breath.

"Shadow's eye, Lyam," Adan said into the silence when the noise of the guard was long gone. "What have you got yourself into?"

Lyam breathed out a laugh. He squeezed his eyes shut before lifting his head out from Adan's shoulder and pushing his glasses up his nose, running a hand through his sweaty hair. As he lifted his hand, the rips in the sleeves of the robe became even more apparent, shreds hanging from his sleeve.

Adan saw it and winced. He motioned for Lyam to stay still while Adan wedged his way back out of the crack, glancing up and down the street before he beckoned Lyam forward. Lyam stepped towards him, his legs feeling shaky. He felt horribly exposed even in the small side street.

"Come here." Adan shrugged out of his warm outer cloak, a plain grey color, which he'd been wearing over his official green robes. He held it out to Lyam.

Lyam looked at him blankly.

"To hide you," Adan said, exasperated, and shook the cloak at him. "Take it."

Slowly, Lyam reached out and took the cloak, wrapping it carefully around his shoulders. Adan helped, muttering something under his breath about Lyam's robes being too ripped to be decent and how he should be grateful for Adan's cloak, not standing there like a pillar.

Lyam shook himself and worked moisture into his mouth. "Thank you. Sorry."

Adan snorted. "Some thanks that is."

Despite himself, a smile found its way onto Lyam's lips.

"And what are you sorry for?" Adan huffed, stepping back and brushing down Lyam's shoulders.

Lyam winced. "For running into you. Making you hide with me."

"Whatever you're up to, I know it's important," Adan shrugged, but there was a glint in his eye as he surveyed Lyam. Out in the light of the alley, it was even easier to see how haggard Adan looked. His hair was limp, his skin a sickly yellow. But he was looking at Lyam with intensity.

Lyam nodded his head, glancing around and shivering.

"I saw you earlier," Adan added, "In the square. Not when you were running. When the Speaker called you forward."

Lyam winced. Had everyone witnessed that? He hated being center of attention, feeling more exposed than ever. At least he had Adan's cloak to hide him a little. Nervously, he pulled the hood up over his head.

"But I don't think that's all there is to the story," Adan continued, his expression growing steely. "I think you're up to something. I don't think you're just going to give Dreamer Annelie a draught to shut her up. Not if I know you at all."

Lyam worried his bottom lip with his teeth, glancing around again. The alley they were in was deserted, the bustle of the square tucked away. He'd already made a mess of things by drawing so much attention to himself. He never should have gone to see Mirah.

He remembered her cold voice as she'd sent the guards after him and shuddered. He had to hold off his questions about their relationship, about how deep her betrayal had run, how much she'd truly known. For just then, his priority had to be keeping the Dreamers safe.

But Adan had already lost his Dreamer. Surely Lyam owed him some answers.

Lyam let out a rough sigh and pushed his glasses back up his nose, his sweat making them slide right back down. "I'm not giving Annelie the draught. None of us are. We destroyed them."

Adan's eyebrows shot up.

"And," Lyam continued, "We're planning a joint Dream. Tonight."

Adan stared at him, confusion marring his gaze. "A joint Dream? What's that?"

"Like in the myths," Lyam said, straightening his back until he stood at his tallest height. Which was still only up to Adan's shoulder, but still. "We think that if the Dreamers are together when they Dream, there's less danger."

"You *think?*" Adan stepped closer, his tone disbelieving and shocked. "You're going to *bring the Dreamers out of their huts* when you only *think* that something's going to work?"

"It's our only chance," Lyam insisted. "Our only hope at stopping them from getting hurt too. And it might tell us how to reverse what happened to the rest of the Dreamers."

Adan paused. An expression of impossible hurt crumbled across his face.

"You think you could..." he trailed off, shaking his head.

Lyam stepped forward and pressed a hand on Adan's shoulder. "We could help Kiran. I hope we can help Kiran."

Adan drew in a breath, pressing his lips together. He took a moment to compose himself again before he looked down into Lyam's eyes. That steely glint had returned.

"I want in."

§

They were headed to Enoch's tunnel.

Lyam had decided that the safest place for him and Adan to go, if Adan really was intent on joining in their plan, was to the tunnel that led outside—the tunnel that no one else knew about. Enoch's tunnel. Enoch had always known what to do. It was strange how Lyam used to be terrified of him but now sought him out at a time he needed comfort.

Lyam would be lying if he said he wasn't happy about Adan's company, too. The quiet, confident strides of his friend next to him helped Lyam stay grounded, stopped him from panicking as they walked through the city back to the South Gate. Lyam still felt horrendously conspicuous. Even wrapped in Adan's cloak as he was, the tears in his green Scribes' robes and the gold of his eyes would reveal exactly who he was to anyone who looked close enough.

"So this Enoch," Adan said, a pinch in his brow. "He's helping you?"

"Yes." Lyam pulled Adan's cloak closer around himself and kept his eyes focused on his feet, stepping carefully along the street. It was getting busier as the city was readying for night, people who worked in the city all attempting to leave through the South Gate at the same time. Lyam itched to be free of the city, to run from the guards who he knew would still be looking for him, but he knew that would ultimately arouse more suspicion. Adan was right; if they went slow and stuck together, they should get out just fine.

"Is he a Dreamer?" Adan sounded confused. "You said he walks outside."

"He's a Water-Gatherer," Lyam answered, keeping his voice low. "I didn't know what that was when he first told me, either. But yes, he walks outside."

Adan gave a low whistle.

Lyam winced. He reached out to tug on Adan's sleeve, glancing around skittishly. "Can we please not talk about it out here?"

Adan caved, though reluctantly. They continued moving forward, slowly, until finally they were at the Gate itself. The next step was getting past the guards.

Lyam kept his eyes on the ground and his hood pulled down low, sticking to the middle of the path where it would be more difficult for the guards to see him. Adan stood up taller, linking his arm with Lyam's, making it very apparent that they were together. The guards were looking for one Scribe, after all, not two.

Much to Lyam's horror, a spear crossed their path just as they were under the wide expanse of the Gate.

A guard surveyed them, a quick up-and-down sweep, and then he said roughly, "Where have you come from?"

"The Scribes' Hall," Adan answered easily, not even a tremble to his voice. "I was doing some research."

"Name?" The guard asked.

"Scribe Adan."

"And your friend?"

Lyam didn't dare look up.

He felt Adan's grip tighten on his arm, but then Adan said smoothly, "My cousin. He's visiting, so I said I'd take him around the tunnels for a bit."

The guard grunted, stepping back and withdrawing his spear. Lyam still held his breath as they continued walking forward though, all the way until they were on the other side of the Gate and safely passed the guards.

Adan chuckled under his breath as soon as they were far enough away. "Look any more frightened and you'll get mistaken for one of your alley cats."

Lyam laughed despite himself. He didn't look up as he answered, "Easy for you to say."

"Yes, I suppose I'm not the one directly going against the Speaker's orders," Adan agreed easily. The casual way he said it made Lyam blanch, but he couldn't argue. It was true, after all. By this point, Lyam had enough black marks against his name to get sentenced to death three times over.

They continued through the tunnels, Lyam taking the lead the deeper they got. He was the one who lived here; Adan and Kiran's hut was further to the north west. Lyam hated to think what they would find if they went to his hut. What sort of state was Dreamer Kiran in? What happened to the Dreamers, after they were thrown forcibly out of their Dreams?

He shook the thought away. The sooner they got to Enoch, the better. These tunnels still weren't devoid of guards.

Adan grew instantly wary when Lyam went to lead them down Enoch's hidden tunnel. He paused, and when Lyam looked over at him, he was eyeing the dusty, cobwebby entrance with obvious suspicion.

"It gets wider," Lyam assured him, already half-way through the tiny hole. "Come on. I need the lantern."

Adan muttered something under his breath about the state of Lyam's sanity, but he followed him anyway.

Lyam climbed the steeply-inclining tunnel as best he could; his arms braced either side of the wall. He could hear Adan puffing and panting behind him. The lantern swung wildly, the light scampering from place to place, chased by the ever-present shadows. But as they travelled further and further along, the lantern light grew weaker and a different, warmer, brighter light grew stronger.

Lyam paused, making Adan crash into him. "Sorry. Just...I need to warn you about what you're about to see."

Adan huffed. "Stranger than this rat hole?"

"Something like that." Lyam felt the corner of his lips quirk upwards, fighting back a smile. "Adan, you're about to see sunlight."

Silence rang around them.

Then, Adan laughed, but the sound was nervous. "Sunlight? You can't be taking me *outside*."

"I'm not," Lyam promised. "But Enoch walks outside. We have to summon him. There's a bell a little further on, but there are cracks in the tunnel up there. Sunlight gets through."

Adan breathed out a swear word.

Lyam laughed under his breath, remembering his own terrified reaction the first time he'd come here, but this time he wasn't afraid at all. This time, his body thrummed with anticipation, humming with desire to see the beautiful, dancing sunbeams again.

A few steps further, and the light grew brighter and brighter. Adan made a pained sound from somewhere behind him, but Lyam was too caught up with seeing the light again to turn around. Instead, he hurried on, standing up as the tunnel grew tall enough, and tumbled around the last corner until—

There.

The crack in the giant round stone was still there, letting through a singular, perfect, fragile beam of sunlight.

Lyam's breath was stolen away. He walked hesitantly up to it, standing just out of its reach and admiring the way it danced against the rocky walls of the tunnel, dust and sand floating through it. He wanted to touch it, but he was afraid of the consequences.

On the other hand, the last time he'd been here he had been bathed in complete sunlight from when Enoch rolled the stone out of the way, and nothing had happened to him then. Even the crippling fear of being caught had gone. Lyam knew, somehow, that he was safe here—that the guards couldn't reach him, that nothing could surprise him, that he was exactly where he was supposed to be.

Cautiously, he reached out a hand and brushed his fingers through the sunlight.

It was warm on his knuckles. The light brown of his skin drank it in greedily, the fine bits of dust and sand gently bypassing him. The sunlight caressed him, warm and soft and almost like liquid, running through his fingers as he turned them over. Lyam was transfixed; entranced. He couldn't look away.

Then he heard a pained whimper from behind him.

With effort, Lyam tore his eyes away from the sunlight and whipped around to see Adan hovering back down the tunnel, a hand up in front of his eyes.

"What's the matter?" Reluctantly, Lyam stepped away from the light and closer to Adan. With the next few steps, he could see that Adan had his eyes squeezed tightly shut. Lyam frowned. "Are you alright? Open your eyes, come on. Look."

"How can you bear to see?" Adan hissed, keeping one hand pressed over his eyes.

Lyam paused.

Adan gave a low moan, curling up and turning around, keeping his eyes screwed shut. "It's too bright up here, I can't *see* anything."

"But the sunlight," Lyam said slowly, confused. He turned around and saw the perfect sunbeam still hovering in place, illuminating the tunnel with a soft, warm light. It didn't hurt his eyes at all. "It's fine, Adan. It's the sunlight."

Adan whimpered again. Much to Lyam's shock, he turned his back on the sunbeam and looked back down the tunnel, still with his eyes squeezed shut. "Whatever it is, it *hurts*."

Lyam stared at him, confused. He didn't know what to do.

"Just...just summon this Enoch person," Adan muttered, wincing. "Do whatever you have to do, and then get us out of here."

"I— Alright," Lyam said, still looking at Adan with surprise. He turned and walked to the side of the tunnel where the bell to summon Enoch still sat, and he rang it firmly so that it chimed three times. The sound bounced around the walls of the tunnel, a pleasant, light note that warmed Lyam's insides. He couldn't believe how terrified he'd been the first time he'd come here. This time, it felt like coming home.

Barely two minutes passed before the rock at the exit of the tunnel started to groan with movement.

Hurriedly, Lyam ran to Adan's side and whipped his cloak up, covering him in as much shadow as he could. "Close your eyes," Lyam said urgently, watching as Adan hunched over and pressed both fists over his eyes. "It's going to get brighter. Just close your eyes."

Adan whined as the tunnel flooded with brighter and brighter light. Even with their backs to the exit, their surroundings became bathed in sunlight, warm and dancing and inviting.

Lyam wanted to stay in it forever; it warmed his insides filling him with burning energy.

Adan, however, was groaning, hunched over with both hands pressed over his face.

"What's this?" Enoch's booming voice sounded, and Lyam could sense his warm, vast presence behind them. "Lyam, did you bring someone else?"

"It was an emergency," Lyam said, craning his neck around until he could catch sight of Enoch's face. Enoch looked... angry. Worried. His forehead was furrowed, his lips pursed, his long blue robes rippling behind him as he studied Adan's hunched-over form.

Slowly, Lyam began to get the feeling that he shouldn't have brought Adan here.

"He's a friend," Lyam explained hastily. "He helped me. There's been a problem."

Enoch made a low noise in the back of his throat. In two quick strides he was beside them, crouching down and touching Adan's shoulder.

Adan whimpered.

"Keep your eyes closed," Enoch hissed, and then span back towards the entrance to the tunnel. "Keep him down, Lyam! And then you will tell me why you brought someone without gold eyes here."

Lyam blinked. His mouth dropped open.

But then Adan whined from beside him, and he instantly crouched back down by his friend, sheltering him with his cloak as much as he could.

A grating, groaning noise sounded behind them as Enoch began rolling the stone back over the entrance. It grew gradually darker and darker, and Lyam felt a pang as he watched more and more sunlight disappear from view, until the tunnel was back to its semi-dark state, only muted grey light surrounding them from the few cracks in the stone and the flickering of Adan's lantern.

Then, Enoch was beside them again, reaching into his cloak

and grumbling. He crouched down on Adan's other side and handed him a bottle. Lyam caught a whiff of something sharp and sour.

"Drink this," Enoch grunted. "That's it, there you go."

Adan's throat worked as he took a couple of sips, and then he gagged. Lyam touched a hand to his shoulder, something like fear and worry sitting heavy in his gut.

"What happened to him?"

"The curse," Enoch rumbled. "You should know better, Lyam. He doesn't have our eyes."

Lyam's eyes widened. Of course. The curse. The reason they were all forced underground. Adan must be affected too. He hadn't even *thought*. He was so foolish.

"Now." Enoch turned his head and *glared* at Lyam, cutting off his racing thoughts. "Explain."

So Lyam did. Haltingly, and feeling far more nervous than he'd thought he would, Lyam explained everything that had happened, from going to Yenn and learning that Izani had been changing Dreams—which made Adan look sick to the stomach —to going to Mirah, to being chased out of her office when he found out that she was working on Izani's side, to being rescued by Adan, and bringing them both here.

Enoch surveyed him when he was done, the three of them sitting on the dust floor with their robes gathered about them. Lyam was still wearing Adan's cloak. He shrank into it under the withering stare Enoch sent him.

"You are a fool for going to your Designer," Enoch said bluntly.

Lyam winced. Obviously, with hindsight, he could see what a mistake that had been, but at the time it was the only way to try and get through to someone he considered an old friend. Mirah had been such a staple in his life for such a long time, it was hard for him to believe that she was the one who'd sent the guards after him.

But he'd seen it with his own two eyes. He couldn't deny it.

"I know," he murmured eventually, eyes down on the sandy

ground by his feet, tracing patterns in the dust. "But I had to at least try."

Enoch harrumphed. He leaned back and turned his hard stare onto Adan instead, who quickly drew himself up as tall as he could.

"And how are you feeling now?" Enoch asked.

"Better," Adan answered, matching him stare-for-stare. Lyam almost despaired at his posturing, knowing it to be entirely unnecessary. And yet, he still felt a little proud of his friend just then.

Enoch gave an approving nod. "Good. Not many could stand the amount of light you just saw. You must be strong."

Adan's lips twitched into something that might have been a smile.

Enoch turned back to Lyam. "I have prepared everything as agreed. We can fetch the Dreamers whenever you're ready."

Lyam's heart stuttered at those words. He knew what they'd been planning, had been there earlier with Tasmin and Jorin and Enoch when they'd made these plans to fetch the last three Dreamers and bring them together. Out of their huts. Out of the *tunnels*.

"I want to help," Adan said suddenly, drawing himself up again.

Enoch turned to him in surprise. "You do? What part do you have in all of this?"

"I know you're helping the Dreamers. My... my Dreamer..." Adan stopped, swallowed, before continuing, "he was attacked. I want him back. So I'm going to help you with whatever you're doing, and nothing you can do or say is going to stop me."

Once again, Lyam felt fierce pride rise up somewhere within him.

Enoch remained still, his face unreadable, before he eventually gave a terse nod. "Very well. You may join us. But I'm warning you that it isn't going to be easy."

"I'm ready," Adan said determinedly.

Enoch pursed his lips. "Lyam, get him up to speed. I'll go and fetch the chairs." Without another word, Enoch rose to his feet and headed back up the tunnel, pausing to add, "Shield him from the light again. The antidote will still be working, but he needs protection."

Adan bristled at those words, but the minute the grating sound of the stone being rolled away again echoed through the tunnel he ducked his head, covering his eyes with both his hands.

Lyam felt guilt eat away at his stomach. He shouldn't have taken Adan here. He should have realized that the sunlight, which seemed so beautiful to Lyam, was going to harm Adan. The curse had to have something to do with it—the reason they were forced underground.

The Dreamers had to be his priority. Annelie was always his priority. She was going to be so excited about leaving her hut. His heart ached from missing her.

Once the stone had been rolled back across the entrance to the tunnel, Lyam turned to Adan and quickly explained their plan. That they were going to take the Dreamers outside their huts and bring them to a safe place Enoch had outside the tunnels, above ground. Adan promptly choked at that.

"You mean you're going to *walk outside*?!"

"It's the only way," Lyam answered, wincing at the shock and horror painting Adan's features. "Enoch has made three wheelchairs from resources above ground. We're going to use them to move the Dreamers. They need to preserve as much strength as possible for the night."

"And this...this *curse* is what's attacking them? My Kiran—"

"Yes," Lyam said softly. "Izani is the one keeping it going. We have to stop him so we can go back above ground."

Adan shook his head. "You're actually crazy. You do realize that, right? All of this is crazy."

"I know," Lyam mumbled, placing his head in his hands. His temples were throbbing. He couldn't remember the last time he'd slept. "I know that all of this is unbelievable. But what am I supposed to do? We have to stop them—stop Izani—before the Life-Giver leaves and everything we have is lost."

They sat in silence for a moment, the weight of Lyam's words sitting heavy in the air around them.

"Well," Adan said bracingly. He climbed to his feet and reached out to pull Lyam up with him, and then suddenly Adan's crooked grin was back on his face, his sickly-tinted features pulled into a shadow of his old self. "We'd better get around to saving the city, then, hadn't we?"

CHAPTER
SIXTEEN

Dreams are difficult.
Dreamers suffer as a result.
Scribes should give them ointments to ease their pain,
But there is no cure.
To be a Dreamer is to be isolated and in pain,
But to see the surface of the Life-Giver is a blessing beyond all else.
The Book of the Life-Giver, Volume I, Chapter IV

Adan, Lyam, and Enoch walked through the tunnels slowly, their footsteps too loud in the silence that surrounded them.

The three of them each pushed a chair fashioned out of wood and rubber, wheels attached to make the glide over the sandy floor as smooth as possible. Lyam clenched his fingers around the wood. They were headed to Annelie first. He was dying to see her again.

Enoch had returned from the outside covered in white flakes that Lyam had never seen before in his life. He'd read about it, though. He knew what snow was, and hadn't needed the explanation Enoch gave him and Adan. Snow was falling outside. The Life-Giver had moved dangerously far away.

They needed to act fast.

The guard standing outside Lyam's hut made the three of them pause in the tunnel. But they knew what they needed to do, had planned for this. It was Adan who stepped forward and quickly grabbed the guard from behind, slapping a hand over his mouth and digging his elbow into the pressure point in the guard's neck, knocking him unconscious. He carefully dragged the guard's body out of the way and laid him on the ground, then stood up, wiped his hands, and grinned his crooked smile.

Lyam found himself smiling back as he stepped forwards, even as wild and strange as everything was.

He knocked on his own trapdoor and in seconds it was flying open and Annelie's face stared down at him. He felt something jolt in his chest at seeing her again, his arms instinctively reaching up for her.

Her entire face lit up when she saw him. "You *idiot!* You've been gone so long! I was going out of my mind with worry!"

"I'm sorry," Lyam interrupted hastily, and dodged the piece of blank parchment she threw at his head.

"Oh, sure, *sorry*," Annelie huffed, but she was laughing, and crying, and so was Lyam. He could feel tears at the corners of his eyes.

He reached up for her again, and this time she let the ladder down, and he climbed it as quickly as he could until he was back in their hut—*home*—once again.

Annelie threw herself at him the moment he was upright. He caught her with easy familiarity, swept her up in the tightest hug he'd given for a long time. It felt like masses of time since he'd last seen her even though he knew it had only been a couple of hours. Too much had happened in between. Everything had changed.

Annelie tucked her head into the crook of his neck and clung on, her fingers wrapped tight around the soft dark material of

Adan's cloak that Lyam was still wearing. She drew back with a frown, fingering the material and glancing at Lyam. "This isn't yours."

"No, it's...it's Adan's." Lyam answered haltingly.

Annelie gave him a close look.

"It's nothing," Lyam continued, swallowing, and beckoned her closer. "So much has happened since I was last here."

"I know," Annelie answered simply. "The Life-Giver showed me."

There would never be a day that Lyam didn't blanch at how easily Annelie spoke about their Sun.

"You're not giving me the draught," she continued, stating it as easily as she might say the tunnels were dark. "You smashed it."

Lyam swallowed. He nodded, feeling tears clinging to his lashes. The thought of giving her something to make her sleep, the thought of forcing her into rest that she would not wake from, it made him feel sick.

Annelie clung to him again, hugging him tight, and he bowed into her despite her being a fair bit shorter than him.

"I would— I would never," Lyam stammered out, his shoulders shaking. "I wouldn't!"

"I know you wouldn't," Annelie whispered. "I know you wouldn't."

They clung to each other for another long moment, in which Lyam sank into her, basking in her familiar scent and the warmth of her body against his. She had been the one constant in his life for as long as he could remember, and she remained constant still. Unchanging and strong and stubborn and feisty as she always had been, despite the world changing around them.

"We have a plan," Lyam said finally, lifting his head out of her hair to speak.

Annelie glanced up at him. "We?"

"Yes." Lyam swallowed, and quickly brought her up to speed about Tasmin and Jorin and he coming up with a plan; how they'd taken it to Enoch, who'd agreed; how Adan had appeared just in time to save Lyam.

Annelie stared at him, her eyes huge. "A joint Dream?"

"It would give you more strength," Lyam confirmed. He grimaced. "Or at least, that's what we're hoping for. We can't be certain, but—"

"But it's the best chance we've got," Annelie finished for him. She shook her head, her expression shocked. "But how will it even work? It's impossible for us to be in one room."

"No, it isn't," Lyam answered gently, and drew back enough to hold her at arm's length, meeting her eyes. "Enoch and Adan are waiting right outside. There's a wheelchair for you. And then we'll go and fetch Dreamer Nethan and Dreamer Elinah, and go outside to a place Enoch has prepared, where you'll be out of reach from the city and closer to the Life-Giver."

Annelie's mouth dropped open wide. Her expression had progressed into completely gobsmacked, and she stared at him as if he'd grown three heads, as if what he was saying didn't make sense.

It didn't, he supposed. Nothing about any of this was making any sense. It went against everything they'd ever believed in to bring Dreamers out of their huts. But they were left with no choice.

"It's the only way we can come up with," Lyam added, nervously rubbing his hands together. "It's the only chance we've got."

"You mean—" Annelie's words were stuttered, dropped into the air like she thought they would break. "You mean I-I'm going *outside?*"

The last word was whispered like it was too precious to speak.

Lyam nodded his head. He smiled softly at her. "You can go outside. If you're ready."

"I was ready nine years ago," Annelie answered, and got to her feet, trembling a little. Lyam was instantly by her side, drawing her against him, letting her lean heavily on his arm. "But...how?"

"There's a chair waiting for you," Lyam answered. "I'll push you. And I'll help you down the ladder."

Annelie looked like she might argue for a moment, but then she nodded vigorously and leaned against him. "Alright. And Enoch and Adan are down there?"

Lyam nodded. "Oh, and a guard that Adan had to take out, but he's unconscious, so you don't have to worry about him."

Despite everything, Annelie snorted. "Right, so I leave you alone for five seconds and you go and knock someone out."

"Hey, I did it all for you," Lyam huffed, though he was grinning.

Everything was going to work out as long as they stuck together.

"You still shouldn't have *knocked someone unconscious*," Annelie grumbled, but she was smiling too. There was excitement visibly brewing in her; it was there in the way she held her head, the brightness behind her smile, the sharp glint in her eye. Lyam's heart warmed to see it.

"Oh! Wait." Annelie turned to her chair, where Mima was curled up sleeping, her twisted leg stretched out comfortably. Annelie petted her gently, making her stir. "Wait for us here, darling, okay? We'll come back for you. When everything is safe again, we'll come back for you."

Lyam bit his lip. He was beyond relieved that he'd rescued Mima that day in the tunnels. She'd brought Annelie a lot of comfort, and she needed more of that in her life. Especially now when they were about to do something so ridiculously dangerous. But it was their only shot.

He walked over to her and brought her close to him, squeezing once before releasing all but her hand. Annelie moved with him, leaning into his side as he gently brought her across until they were standing by the trapdoor. He pulled it open and fetched the ladder while Annelie leaned against the wall, staring down at the open trapdoor with a keen, glowing expression.

Lyam laid the ladder down carefully.

A voice called up to them; Enoch. "Are you ready, Scribe Lyam?"

Lyam glanced across at Annelie, who's whole face had lit up. She glanced back at him, smiled brightly, and called back, "We're both ready."

There was a startled gasp from the tunnel.

Lyam went to the ladder first, beckoning Annelie to come down right in front of him where he could catch her if she fell. She leaned heavily against him, and he used one arm to support her weight, the other to climb down the ladder. Once they were at the bottom, she grabbed his arm and hobbled around him, wobbling slightly, her eyes fixed on the two occupants of the tunnel.

Enoch smiled broadly at her. Adan hung back a little way, next to the fallen guard.

"Dreamer Annelie." Enoch swept into a steep bow, his blue robes flowing. "It's an honor."

"Enoch," Annelie answered, grinning, and tugged Lyam forward until she could stumble into Enoch's arms. Enoch held her with a deep, rumbling chuckle, hugging her tight so that she was engulfed in his blue robes.

"You little troublemaker," Enoch laughed. "Ah, what have you been putting me through? Shadow's eye, girl, but what the Life-Giver has done to us both."

"It's all going to be ok now," Annelie answered, her voice muffled, and she appeared from the midst of his robes with a grin. "We're going to fix everything. All of it."

"With you among us, I can almost believe it," Enoch rumbled in response. He stepped back and beckoned to Adan, who cautiously wheeled forward one of the three chairs, his eyes deliberately on the ground and avoiding Annelie's gaze.

Annelie hummed as he drew near. "You've been in my hut before."

Adan flinched. He kept his eyes fixed on the ground, his hands clutched tight around the arms of the wheelchair until his knuckles went white, a stark contrast to his light-brown skin. His green robes fit him more easily than Lyam's did, but he still managed to look somehow small, shrunken into himself with dark circles under his eyes and a desperately fierce air about him.

Annelie made a low, upset noise. "How is Kiran?"

Adan's face screwed up. He ducked his head even lower, his eyebrows furrowing and his hair falling into his eyes, his expression filled with pain.

"He's..." Adan started, then cut himself off with a shake of his head. "He's still rotting."

The words were chilling even in the warm dusty air of the tunnels.

Annelie took a couple of wobbly steps towards him. Reaching out and up, she patted his shoulder. There was a small look of wonder on her face, but she hadn't touched anyone other than Lyam since she was a small girl.

Adan jumped as if he'd been stabbed.

"We'll figure out how to help him," Annelie said stubbornly. "We will. I swear it."

Slowly, Adan lifted his head until he could meet her eyes. He still looked crestfallen, as if the world might crumble around him without him desperately trying to hold it up, but there was something in his eyes—something close to the steely glint Lyam knew him to have.

Annelie smiled at him.

"Not to hurry you along," Enoch rumbled, "But night will fall soon, and we have two more Dreamers to collect. Come along now, all of you."

Adan's eyes widened. He jumped back away from Annelie's hand immediately, then gestured to the wheelchair. Lyam stepped forward and wrapped his arm around Annelie, helping her to hobble backward until she could settle comfortably into the cushion Enoch must have provided for the chair. It was red, her favorite color. Lyam approved.

He took up position behind the chair, Adan stepping across

to push one of the other two. Enoch took the last, and they started their slow and strange procession through the tunnels.

Annelie stared around with wild curiosity, drinking in every inch of the tunnels they moved through. As they got closer to Jorin's hut, excitement began to wriggle through her body, and she shifted about so much in the chair that Lyam had trouble pushing it. She just laughed when he told her to sit still, though, and twisted around to send him a big grin.

"Your fault for taking me outside," she said simply.

Lyam rolled his eyes, but he'd be lying if he said he wasn't happy. Seeing Annelie like this, looking truly free for the first time in almost their whole lives, warmed his heart.

Soon, they were outside Jorin's hut, and Enoch knocked loudly. The guard had already been sent away, as had the one outside Tasmin's hut. Tasmin had made sure to make up some form of Council business to keep them both busy. So Lyam watched, still standing in place behind Annelie, as the ladder lowered to reveal Jorin, closely followed by a young girl with short, fuzzy dark hair and dressed in a long flowing white robe that was far neater than Lyam had ever seen Annelie in.

Annelie immediately jumped up from her chair, wobbling, as she cried, "Elinah!"

The girl startled, turned, and broke out into a wide smile. She pushed away from Jorin enough to hobble across to Annelie, sturdier on her feet than Annelie was, but then she hadn't been Dreaming as long. Both girls hugged each other tight.

Lyam smiled, but caught Jorin staring at them in surprise. "You know each other?"

"The Dreamers can sense each other in their Dreams," Lyam explained, smiling as Jorin turned his wide-eyed look to him. "They've known each other just as long as I've known you."

"It's like sensing their whole being," Annelie filled in, her voice muffled by Elinah's shoulder. "We know each other far better than we could after a whole century of talking."

Elinah nodded fervently, then murmured something low in Annelie's ear. Annelie instantly ducked closer to her and held her tighter, and Lyam smiled at the sight, knowing how protective Annelie felt over the younger girl, how she delighted in the Dreams with her.

When they finally broke apart (after a pointed cough from Enoch), Elinah settled into a wheelchair which Jorin instantly went to push. Adan relinquished it and came silently to stand beside Lyam.

Lyam reached out and squeezed his hand.

They continued on, although this time it was more difficult. They had to circle all the way around to the Northern tunnels to fetch Tasmin and Dreamer Nethan. Enoch led them on a winding path that not many knew, so they hopefully wouldn't run into anyone else, but Lyam's heart remained in his mouth for the whole journey.

When they approached Tasmin's trapdoor, there was no sign of the guard. Lyam still felt his throat close up as he watched Enoch leave behind the one remaining empty wheelchair to knock authoritatively on the trapdoor. Sand and dust rained down around his fist, catching in his resplendent blue robes.

There was silence for a moment.

Then, footsteps sounded from above and the trapdoor was roughly pulled open, and Tasmin peered down at them all. A smile lit up her face, smoothing out the tired, worn expression covering her features.

She turned her head to call over her shoulder. "They're here."

In the wheelchair in front of Lyam, Annelie sat upright, excitement making her wriggle. "Oh, it's Nethan. It's really going to be Nethan. Oh!"

Sure enough, more footsteps sounded from ahead—slower, but sure. Tasmin appeared again, climbing down the ladder slowly with all her attention focused on the person climbing down after her.

A man. A man with a shaven head, wearing a long white robe, his head bowed and his arms shaking with the effort of bringing himself down the ladder. At the bottom, Tasmin reached up and bodily lifted him, bringing him carefully to the ground at her side. They were of equal height, but the man was thin and frail and trembling, a contrast to Tasmin's sturdy, broad frame.

Annelie squealed, holding out her arms, and Lyam instantly wheeled her forward until she could stumble upright and fall into the man's arms.

The man chuckled, falling back against Tasmin, who supported both their weights without batting an eyelash. Annelie buried her face in the man's chest, and the man held her tight, though his body was still shaking with the effort.

"Nethan," Annelie said, whispering the words against him in a repeated mantra, as if it was the only thing she knew. "Nethan, Nethan, *Nethan*."

The man rocked her a little, as much as he could without knocking Tasmin over. "Little Annelie. What a delight to finally see you, hm?"

His voice was thin, but melodious, and it rocked with the power of the Sun. His voice seared through Lyam, not loud exactly, just with *authority*. It was impossible not to feel chills. Lyam felt the need to bend to him.

Annelie just held onto him tighter.

Lyam watched them with warmth unfurling in his gut. He couldn't even remember all the countless times Annelie had talked about Nethan over the years—how she used to wake a little calmer from her Dreams because she said Nethan had stayed close beside her; how she chattered on about how bright he was, how close he was to the Life-Giver, how he showed her the way to the surface in her very first Dream.

As Tasmin had acted as mentor for Lyam, so Nethan had acted as mentor for Annelie. Both of them owed the older pair a lot. Lyam knew for a fact that they wouldn't have survived their broken, hurried childhood without their guidance.

It warmed his heart, seeing Annelie held in Nethan's arms.

Enoch was once again the one to break them up. He stepped forward, bowing deeply, greeting all three Dreamers with a bow at first, and then rumbled, "We have to hurry."

That was all it took for Annelie to stumble back into her chair, and for Tasmin to lead a trembling Nethan to the final spare wheelchair.

And so their procession started up once again.

This time, Lyam felt nerves begin to clamor inside him for real. They climbed up his throat, stopping his heart and making his breathing struggle, jangling in his belly like he'd eaten something bad. If they were caught now, there would be no talking their way out of it. Three of the Dreamers were outside their huts, and not just any Dreamers, but the only Dreamers remaining who could still speak with the Life-Giver. Dreamers who were supposed to be drugged and asleep. There would be no fair trial, no sense of justice if they were caught. Anyone who defied the Speaker's word so obviously was sentenced immediately to death.

Lyam glanced down at Annelie every time these thoughts overwhelmed him. One look at her head, at her hands clenched tightly in her lap, at how she excitedly twisted to see Nethan and Elinah as much as she possibly could, kept him focused.

For her. She was the only one who could save them; he had to keep going for her.

Eventually, they were back in the Southern tunnels, and then Enoch led them as quickly as possible to the tunnel that led out to the light. Getting the wheelchairs through the entrance was a very tight fit, but it was doable, although Enoch was the only one with enough strength to get the chairs through the tight, narrow hole in the wall and then up the steep incline to the exit. He pushed each Dreamer through one by one while the Scribes hung back, gathered together in a tight group.

"This is really happening." Jorin looked as though he couldn't contain himself. He was bouncing on the balls of his feet, his hands clenched into tight fists by his side. "We're going *outside.*"

Lyam was still filled with fear at the thought. He caught Tasmin's look of fond exasperation, and Adan just shook his head. Lyam bumped his shoulder against Adan's side. "For Kiran, remember."

"You don't need to remind me," Adan muttered.

Enoch returned soon after, holding a handful of banded blue cloths out to each of them. "Tie these over your eyes. Lyam and I will lead you through the tunnel."

Lyam blinked, glancing at him.

"Gold eyes," Tasmin murmured. "Well. There always was something about you, Lyam."

Lyam glanced down, shifting awkwardly on his feet.

Adan huffed, tying the cloth over his eyes and grabbing firmly onto Lyam's robes with his free hand. "You'd better not walk me into a wall."

Lyam stuttered out a laugh despite himself.

They all joined hands, with Lyam at the front and Enoch at the back. He could feel Adan close behind him, his slightly sweaty fingers slipping a little in his grip, and it eased Lyam's nerves a bit. The group of them were together and almost out of the tunnels. They could make it, but then the Dream would start and none of them really knew for sure what was going to happen after that.

Lyam kept his eyes in front of him, walking slowly enough that their group could stay together. The light grew gradually lighter and lighter around them, but it still didn't hurt Lyam's eyes. Instead, he felt something inside him break free, joy and calm and comfort surrounding him all at once, an intense feeling of safety surrounding him.

The light grew brighter and brighter until Lyam saw that Enoch had left the stone at the entrance rolled away. As such, bright, intense light flooded the tunnel, lighting up every corner, bringing out every detail in the sandy walls and the gritty floor. It filled Lyam with happiness at the warm sensation against his skin. He glanced down, watching his robes ripple with bright, vivid green underneath the grey cloak Adan had lent him. Even that did not seem so dull anymore.

"Lead us on, Lyam," Enoch called from behind him, making

him realize he had paused frozen still in the sunlight. "Everyone else, keep those blindfolds tight."

Lyam obediently stepped forwards again, glancing up. Ahead of him, the tunnel exit gaped wide and jagged, lit up by bright streams of sunlight. Lyam could pick out every detail of the rocky entrance—every jagged spike, every worn edge, and every dusty corner. And beyond it...

Lyam could see a vast expanse of dusty sand accompanied by a wide vault of blue that stretched impossibly high and impossibly far, so far that Lyam couldn't see an end to it.

He swallowed. Fear clutched at him until he felt frozen, immobile.

"Lyam?" Adan's voice sounded rough behind him. Fingers squeezed around his own.

Lyam couldn't take his eyes off the massive space that stretched out from the exit to the tunnel.

"Lyam?" Another voice called his name this time—a higher, lighter voice that was achingly familiar to him, that sounded bright and happy and *warm*.

Annelie.

Sure enough, when Lyam managed to tear his eyes away from that frightening expanse of blue, Annelie was waiting at the exit to the cave. She was holding herself up against the side of the stone wall, uncaring of the sharp stones that tore at the corners of her robes. She was looking at him and beaming.

Lyam felt himself smile back automatically.

"Come on," Annelie said, reaching out a hand.

Lyam stepped forward automatically and felt Adan move behind him. After the first step, and if he focused on Annelie instead of the vast space behind her, it was much easier to move.

Soon enough, Lyam stepped up beside Annelie, who pointed out at the space behind her. "It's beautiful, isn't it?"

Lyam took in a deep breath, stepped outside the tunnel, and looked.

The space was *vast*. There wasn't a word big enough to describe it—massive, immense, limitless, boundless. It started from the very exit of the tunnel and spread out endlessly which-ever way Lyam looked.

Directly in front of him, the space was broken by some sort of large monument. It was made of white stone and stretched up impossibly high, the cracked, broken emblem of the sun sitting proudly at its top. Behind it, a steeply-sloping hill led down to what looked like the ruins of a city. More buildings of the same white stone rose from the sandy ground, although they were fractured and damaged, lying in pieces or huddled together in sharp, jagged shapes that Lyam couldn't make sense of.

The thing was, he *recognized* it. He knew the shapes; he'd seen them proud and tall in the illustrations of all the books, although they now lay in near-ruins. But the layout, the basic structure, was the same.

This was the City of the Sand. The City from the myths.

He drew in a sharp, ragged breath, his eyes impossibly wide. He'd never seen shapes like it in reality before, never really thought it even *existed*. But there it was, right in front of him and impossible to deny; the city from the myths.

"Isn't it amazing?" Annelie murmured from his side.

"Yeah," he breathed, and then turned to her in surprise. "Wait. You aren't wearing a blindfold?"

"We don't need to," Annelie answered, pointing to Nethan and Elinah who were sitting in their chairs a few paces away, heads bowed together in conversation. "This is what we see in our Dreams."

Lyam stared at her in awe. Her skin was glowing brighter than ever, light oozing out of her as if she were carrying the Sun within her own chest. He shook his head, staring back out with shock. "Is this real?"

Annelie laughed lightly. She reached out and touched him. "As real as we are."

Lyam shook his head again.

"What is it?" Adan asked impatiently behind him, and then Lyam remembered that he was supposed to be leading them out. He twisted, his fingers still entwined with Adan's, and saw the blindfold that easily covered half of Adan's face. The banded blue cloth was thick.

"Well?" Adan continued impatiently, squeezing Lyam's fingers. "What do you see?"

Lyam just shook his head. He turned and moved forward again, over to where Nethan and Elinah were sitting in their wheelchairs outside one of the few buildings that remained intact. It was in the shadow of the huge monument to the Life-Giver; a small hut made of pale white stone.

"This is my hut," Enoch rumbled. He stepped forward, past the three blindfolded Scribes up to Lyam's side.

Lyam stared at him. "You *live* out *here*?"

"And why should I not?" Enoch raised a brow at him. "It's our home, after all."

Lyam stared at him. He wondered if he'd ever stop being surprised by Enoch. Probably not. Enoch was a man full of twists and tricks, nothing about him simple or even, and the more time Lyam spent with him the more confused he became.

"The door is around the other side," Enoch said, and took off with long strides across the sand. It was all Lyam could do to follow, keeping Adan and the trail of blindfolded Scribes behind him. The interior of Enoch's hut was full of blue—blue rugs, blue art on the walls. The great vast blue that stretched high above them apparent outside the windows.

The sky. It must be the sky.

Lyam went to one of the windows and peered out. Looking up was hard. It was bright, and while the light didn't hurt his eyes, it did make him squint. The sky stretched above him, endless, reaching unbroken from one side of the window to the other. It should have been impossible. All of this should only exist in the myths and in the Dreams.

Yet there he stood.

He leaned further out of the window, taking in as much as he could. It was, without a doubt, the most beautiful thing he'd ever seen, but he was also afraid. Afraid of the wide, open areas; the unending reach of the City; how the sky held the Life-Giver itself somewhere within its depths.

That was the one difference. In the myths and in the Dreams, the Life-Giver was an undeniable constant presence, filling the sky with flames of red and yellow and orange, heating up the whole city. But there was no sign of flames whichever way he looked, and he wasn't warm. If anything, he was a little chilly, unused to the way the air moved and shifted around him.

Wind. It was wind.

Sensing a presence behind him, Lyam whirled around to find Enoch standing there, the three blindfolded Scribes behind him settling into seats. They would remain blindfolded until nightfall, when apparently it would be dark enough for them to be safe.

Enoch was looking at Lyam with a strange expression on his face. Lyam swallowed, bunching his hands in the sides of his cloak.

Eventually, after another long moment, Enoch beckoned him over. "Come with me."

Hesitantly, Lyam stepped forward. "Are we going to bring the Dreamers inside?"

"They asked to stay out in the sunlight a little while longer," Enoch answered. "I think we can give them that much."

Slowly, Lyam nodded his head. They'd been trapped in their huts all these years—in their huts *above ground* but forbidden from opening the blinds. The huts had been part of the ancient city. The current laws stated the Dreamers must live above ground to be closer to the Sun, but they weren't permitted to see the Sunlight.

This had been just outside their door all this time.

"Come." Enoch led him back out of the door and into the great, wild, ruined expanse of the City again. "There is something I want to show you."

Lyam swallowed. He stuck close behind Enoch as they walked through the City. It made Lyam feel strange, being around so many old, ruined buildings. The white stone stood out sharply against the sandy earth, the same sand that made up the tunnels beneath their feet. But the City rose proudly to the sky, even as it lay in ruins. The broken buildings and cracked walls and dusty, eroded stone felt old, yet fresh at the same time; older than anything Lyam had encountered before, as old as the most precious, broken parchments in the library; and yet fresh, new, filling him with fear and awe and a strange, growing feeling that, somehow, he was supposed to be out here.

Here, amongst the half-built ruins, was where he truly belonged.

Enoch led him down the cracked remains of what once must have been the main street of the City. It was lined with white, uneven stones that tripped him unless he carefully watched where to place his feet, sweat making his glasses slide down his nose no matter how many times he pushed them back up. The buildings rose around them, half with their ceilings caved-in, others with boarded up and shuttered windows, or doors that swung half-open, showing their empty, broken interiors. It was eerie, being the only source of sound in a whole city. The scent was fresh and wild, flowers and weeds creeping up where Enoch had evidently not been able to maintain the whole city himself.

As they walked on, a tunnel cat appeared from one of the side-streets. It paused, watching them with bright baleful eyes. Lyam stopped automatically and bent down, extending one hand towards it, which it sniffed without taking its eyes off him.

Lyam smiled.

The cat continued to stare, but moved forward just enough to bump its head against Lyam's palm. Lyam obligingly rubbed between its ears, his smile widening when he heard purrs begin to emanate from the cat. It was a tiny, skeletal thing, couldn't be more than a year old. If he was at home, he would feed it.

"Scribe Lyam." Enoch's rumbling voice made him jump, and he glanced up to find Enoch watching him fondly. "There is not much time before nightfall. Come."

"Sorry." Lyam hurried back to his feet, giving the cat one last pet before he set off after Enoch. "Where are we going, anyway?"

"I want to show you my work," Enoch answered mysteriously, and said nothing else.

Lyam bit his lip. He stepped after Enoch, trying to take in as much of the city as he could, even though he was terrified to be standing on its streets. This was the city of the myths, the city of the Life-Giver. The fact that the myths were coming to life around him was partly terrifying, but partly invigorating at the same time. He had never felt so alive.

Eventually, Enoch took them down a street that was emptier than the others. The only remains were of feeble stone walls that leaned dangerously to one side, and there were no buildings. Instead, the land opened up around them, vast swathes of sand extending as far as Lyam could see. The ever-present, heavy weight of the blue sky continued to throb above them. Lyam did his best not to look up.

As they continued on, Lyam began to hear a strange noise. It sounded like the rustling of fine papers, but at the same time it was angrier, heavier than that. It grew louder and louder with every step they took, echoing hollowly out around the sandy plane, rushing and rustling and eventually growing to a roar.

Lyam paused, fear clutching at him, but Enoch beckoned him onward, so onward Lyam walked.

They reached the crest of a dune, and in front of them—

Before them lay a river, water rushing with the current, small white tufts appearing at its surface with the force with which it was moving. Lyam had never seen running water like this before. It was nothing like the small brook that ran underground. No, this was angrier, rougher. The water tumbled down the ground ahead of them as if it was being chased. Currents whirled visibly, cresting along the rocks that lay at the side of the riverbed. He couldn't see how deep it was.

"Look where it goes," Enoch rumbled from beside him. "Look at what it leads to."

Trembling, Lyam tore his eyes away from the tumbling river and instead looked to his right, following the current. And then he blinked several times, not believing what he was seeing.

The river cut through the sand in a sharp arc, leading to an open space of interlocking streams in one of the most complex patterns Lyam had ever seen in his life. Water rushed every which way, the currents running together so quickly that Lyam couldn't follow them with his eye. The waterways criss-crossed over each other, spreading out so far that Lyam couldn't see the end of them. The city lay behind them, silent and still in the distance.

The sound of the water rushing along the carved-out waterways was deafening.

"This is my work," Enoch boomed, sweeping one arm in an expansive arc to include the wide array of waterways. "This is how you are sustained, you who exist underground. This is your lifeblood."

Lyam stared out at the water, astonished. "This— What?"

"I am a Water-Gatherer," Enoch continued. "I tend to these waterways, and they feed your little stream underground. Did you think your water just magically appeared to you?"

Lyam felt completely blindsided. "I...I didn't think—"

"No, none of you think," Enoch harrumphed. "That's why we're in this mess. None of you thought to *question* what you were doing underground."

Lyam didn't know how to respond. Instead, he stared back out at the water, taking in the way it glimmered in the Sunlight, occasional bright flashes winking out at him. The myriad of directions the water was going in confused his eyes. He tracked one for a while until it intercepted with another one, and then another one twisted and turned its way across it until all he saw was a blurred mass of water.

"It's beautiful," he breathed, and then said, "But do you really tend to this all on your own?"

Enoch nodded his head. He let out a melancholy sigh. "It's too much for one man. There were supposed to be hundreds of us."

Lyam swallowed. "What happened? Why are you the only one left?"

Enoch's expression darkened. He turned to Lyam with a strangely hollow gaze, his eyes sharply focused. "The Dreams. We are supposed to be chosen in Dreams, just like the Dreamers and Scribes and Designers and Council members. We're supposed to be chosen, but the choosing just... stopped."

Lyam was chilly. He wrapped his arms around himself, grateful that he was still wrapped in Adan's cloak. "What do you mean?"

"I have my suspicions." Enoch's tone was unforgiving. "Your Head Designer, and those before him, have been changing Dreams for a long, long time."

Lyam shivered. It was still hard for him to wrap his head around the fact that the Head Designer had been writing his own Dreams and ignoring the ones that Yenn was giving him. He believed it, though. Yenn had been in no state to lie when Lyam spoke to him.

He looked back out over the waterways, taking in the breath-taking beauty of it, the soft babbling sounds that built up and up and up as the currents rippled along their way. The water reflected back the blue of the sky, tinged red with the beginning of sunset. Lyam had read enough to recognize what was happening around him, even though actually *witnessing* it was making him tremble.

Sunset. He daren't glance up to see the terrifying, unending reaching of the sky, but the very air around him trembled with anticipation, streaked red and pink and orange so bright that it almost hurt Lyam's eyes.

He wondered how the others felt; if they knew what they were missing, the blindfolds hiding all this from them.

"Come," Enoch rumbled. "It is time to get back."

Lyam nodded and turned, following the folds of Enoch's long blue robes across the cracked paved path that led back to the city. If it was sunset, then that meant night would soon be falling, which meant the Dreamers needed to be safe and settled inside the hut. He wondered what they would be bearing witness to tonight. Nothing could prepare him for it.

Nothing but his own instincts and his sense of fear and trepidation.

Lyam swallowed. He wasn't impulsive. This was the kind of thing Adan would do, or Jorin with all his curiosity, or Tasmin with all her resolve. It wasn't for Lyam. This kind of task wasn't meant for him.

But Annelie was strong enough. As always, he could lean on her.

They stepped back inside the hut to find the blindfolded Scribes settled in different corners. Tasmin sat in the center of a patterned red-gold rug, her legs crossed, her arms settled by her sides. Beside her sat Jorin, his head twisting with every sound. Adan was standing a little away from them, in a shadowed corner, his lips pulled down.

Lyam glanced around. "Where are the Dreamers?"

"Still outside," Tasmin answered. "Enjoying the sunlight, I believe."

"What does it look like?" Jorin asked, breathless. "Is it beautiful? Like in the myths?"

Lyam held his breath. He glanced at Enoch, who merely raised his eyebrows, nodding at him as if to say *you answer it, this one's for you.*

Lyam swallowed around a dry mouth, drawing Adan's cloak tighter around him as he answered. "Yes. It's so beautiful."

Jorin sighed wistfully. "I wish I could see it too."

"All in due time," Enoch cut in. "Come, Lyam. It is time to bring the Dreamers inside."

When they stepped outside again, the whole world had turned orange. The light was tinted red and pink, streaks of color flooding the air, reflecting off the eroded white stone of the city. Darkness crept behind it—darkness and the promise of night, the scent of moss and mould lingering.

Lyam tried not to think about it as he followed Enoch across to where the Dreamers had taken shelter. The three wheelchairs were pushed close together, and it looked like Nethan was talking, Annelie and Elinah both bowed in close to listen to him.

They looked so fragile, barely held together, and yet so much was resting on their shoulders.

They were the last hope.

"It is time," Enoch rumbled as soon as they were close enough. Annelie's head snapped round instantly, and she beamed at Lyam, who found himself automatically smiling back. She looked more alive out here than he'd seen her look in years. Her skin was still glowing golden, emanating that eerie shining light, although accompanied by the streaks of red and orange from the sunset, she blended right in.

Elinah was staring at him with wide eyes, and Nethan sat back a little, smiling. He glanced at Enoch. "We'd better hurry. It's almost night."

Enoch muttered something under his breath about teaching grandmothers to suck eggs and reached for Elinah's wheelchair.

Lyam pushed Annelie, and Enoch went back for Nethan, until the three Dreamers were safely inside the hut along with the blindfolded Scribes. The space felt crowded, too full, like there was no room to breathe. Lyam shrunk into a corner.

It was dark enough now that Enoch instructed the Scribes to take their blindfolds off. Lyam watched through the dusky, warm air of the hut as they each untied the strips of cloth from over their eyes. Annelie was beaming as she glanced around the hut, watching Jorin blink and Tasmin take in her surroundings and Adan stare sullenly at the floor.

"How are we going to do this?" Tasmin asked.

"On the floor," Annelie answered immediately. "We should be touching each other."

"Holding hands," Elinah said.

Nethan nodded. "It'll strengthen the Dream if we can feel each other."

Lyam shared a look with Tasmin and Jorin. They both looked just as unsure as he did about the whole thing, but the Dreamers at least sounded confident.

"Then that's how we'll do it," Enoch stated. "Let's clear some space."

Together, they cleared the rug in the center of Enoch's hut so that there were no chairs or tables or cushions cluttering it up. Then, Lyam went to Annelie just as Jorin and Tasmin went to Elinah and Nethan, and they gently helped the Dreamers up from the wheelchairs.

"You scream if anything starts to go wrong," Lyam murmured in Annelie's ear as he took most of her weight, bracing himself against the ground. "Whatever it is, if you start to feel like anything isn't as it should be—"

"I'll call for you," Annelie answered. She squeezed his hand. "I know. I'll come back to you, Lyam. You know that."

Lyam nodded slowly. He trusted her, but it still hurt, knowing that the Dreams had brought only danger recently. He feared for what was going to happen. A joint Dream meant that the Dreamers would have a stronger chance of contacting the Life-Giver, yes, but it also meant they would be that much more vulnerable. With a Dream amplified like this, in the current circumstances... it was hard not to be frightened.

Still, they had made their decision. Lyam led Annelie over to the rug where Elinah and Nethan had already settled, Nethan in the center, Elinah slightly to the side. They were both cross-legged.

Lyam lowered Annelie carefully to the ground, minding her sore legs, her cramped muscles. Her skin glowed against his, the golden light softer, but the brightest thing in the room just then. Darkness had come, but Annelie still shone.

In the corner, there came the sputtering of a lantern, and a feeble light flickered into being. It illuminated Enoch's face, the whites of his eyes showing. Adan was merely a hulking shadow in the corner.

Lyam made sure Annelie was comfortable before he stepped back. The three Dreamers formed a circle on the floor, their knees touching, their white robes rumpled and stained with the outside for the first time ever. They looked at each other with gentle gazes that were far too familiar for people who had just met for the first time that day. Their bond was physically palpable.

Nethan reached over and took Elinah's hand. Elinah smiled at him, her face smooth, her amber eyes glowing. Annelie reached out and took her other hand, her shining skin reflecting off Elinah's arm.

Nethan looked at Annelie. Annelie looked at Nethan.

Lyam held his breath.

Nethan reached his hand out, palm-up. Annelie looked at it for a second, then up at Nethan's face. He gave her an encouraging smile.

Annelie reached her hand out.

Lyam couldn't stop himself. "If *anything* goes wrong—"

"I know," Annelie murmured. She twisted to send him one last glance, and he could read a lot in her eyes—fear, but also awe. Amazement that the world had led her here. She looked strong.

Annelie reached out and took Nethan's hand, and instantly the three Dreamers' heads bowed.

Jorin shifted from his place behind Elinah, his hands bunching nervously in the sides of his robes. Adan remained hulking in the corner, while Tasmin stood with her head held proudly, the only sign of stress the tight lines around her eyes.

Lyam swallowed. He hadn't taken his eyes off Annelie, but she was still, her head bowed forward, her hands tightly clasped to the other Dreamers'. Then, suddenly, the glow of her skin began to spread, bright sparks shooting from the ends of her fingers to wrap around Elinah's wrist, Nethan's elbow, tracing so fast up their arms that it was impossible to follow with his eyes.

Lyam stared, astonished, as glowing light surrounded the three Dreamers in the center of the hut.

The joint Dream had begun.

PART FIVE
THE LAST DREAM

THE LAST DREAM

I t was easy to reach the vacuum this time.

Annelie opened her eyes to darkness. The Life-Giver floated far below, distant, and it was cold enough that Annelie shivered, wrapping her arms tight around herself.

Annelie stepped forwards and found herself floating. Everything moved sluggishly around her as if it was an effort to hold everything together—as though the Life-Giver might break apart if she made the wrong move. Fragile and beautiful and so, so distant.

Something was different this time. The light was brighter, the air hotter. Everything felt more real, more substantial, as if it had presence in reality outside of the Dream. Annelie knew that could be dangerous. She knew from experience that any injury sustained here would hold out there, too.

Slowly, she became aware of two bright spots of light in her periphery. The one to her right glowed meekly, almost apologetically —unsure. Uncertain of her right to be there. Annelie recognized her instantly. Elinah. But, again, something was different this time. She glowed brighter, her shape more recognizably human, so close that Annelie could almost make out the features on her face inside the bright, glowing orb she became here.

Annelie tried to speak, but her lips felt sealed together. The air pressed against her, forcing her still. She was going to have to tread carefully.

The glowing light to Annelie's left felt much more certain of itself. His shape was more forceful, more apparent, and he shone brighter yellow, so bright that it was hard to look directly at him. He blended with the orange in the air as if he belonged.

Nethan.

Annelie smiled. She remembered. They were Dreaming together— a joint Dream, where they sat in each other's presence and held hands. She was holding hands with two people at once. Warmth trickled through her, pricking at her skin, bubbling her insides until she felt lighter than air.

She reached out to her sides, but the heat emanating from Nethan and Elinah was too much. She couldn't touch them, couldn't speak to them. They didn't even look like they were moving.

They were with her, but she still couldn't touch them. That was ok. She would still try her hardest.

Casting her eyes down, Annelie saw the Life-Giver's surface raging below her. Its rays were in every possible hue of yellow and orange and red, bathing them in moving, golden light. Annelie's reaction was automatic; she reached out to it, and the Life-Giver answered.

As she did every night, Annelie felt an invisible pull, and she followed it with easy familiarity. As she stepped forward, she was pulled down closer and closer towards the surface, flames rearing red-orange-white around her.

The light was all she could see. And as she drew closer, the light began to take shape. Familiar large flames roared off the surface of the Life-Giver. They called out to her, reaching for her, and she answered, lifting both her hands up to embrace them.

Impossible heat prickled over her skin. She was already glowing, but now the flames licked around her too, curling over her wrists and up her arms, reflecting off the white of her robes. Sweat pricked at her temples. Her hair crisped around her, seared by the heat, and she felt as if she were melting.

But she wasn't. The Life-Giver never harmed her, the magic of the Dream somehow protecting her.

She floated closer. The flames roared on all her sides now, crackling and whispering and cradling her whole body. She reached out and brushed one hand through the red tip of one flame, feeling the searing heat under her fingertips.

Then, abruptly, she landed. Her feet found solid ground too quickly and she stumbled, throwing out her hands to balance herself. Hundreds of flames caught her, wrapped around her, helped her to stay upright again without even the thought of falling.

Annelie closed her eyes and smiled. Peace and comfort settled in her heart. She was with the Life-Giver again.

My daughter. I thought I told you not to return.

The voice was as achingly powerful as ever. It pulsed inside her head, pressure building at her temples that she was never quite sure she could take. She opened her eyes again to find her vision had turned completely white like the center of a candle flame.

She swallowed around a dry mouth. It felt like there was no moisture left in her. I needed to come back.

And you are not alone. *The Life-Giver sounded amused.*

Annelie smiled. Delighted, she looked to her sides to find Elinah and Nethan there, buried in the midst of their own Dreams, but by her side. Closer to her than they'd ever been before.

I'm holding their hands, *she told the Life-Giver excitedly.* We're sitting together.

The myths are not dead yet, then. *The Life-Giver sounded melancholy. It tugged at Annelie's heart, the voice in her head pulsing with something close to sorrow.*

Annelie bit her lip. Lyam still thinks we're in danger.

Your Scribe is intelligent. *The Life-Giver's voice grew even stronger, beating about her temples. Annelie closed her eyes for a moment, breathed through the pain, curled her hands into fists by her sides.* **This was his idea?**

Jorin's, I think. *Annelie answered. She grinned.* I met him today for the first time. I think he's scared of me.

Ah, he is following in Lyam's footsteps already. A deep, musical, throbbing laugh sounded inside Annelie's head.

So we're not too late? *Annelie asked. She bent down where she stood amid the flames, reaching one arm out to watch the way they writhed around her arm in a streak of red-yellow-orange.* You're not out of reach yet?

A deep sigh resounded in Annelie's head, bouncing off the edges of her skull. **I do not wish to leave you, daughter. You know this.**

But you are leaving. Aren't you? I saw it for myself today. The city is covered in snow.

A low, mournful sound echoed in Annelie's head.

Annelie closed her eyes for a moment. When she opened them again, she reached her hand out and placed her palm flat against the hot, solid surface of the Sun beneath her. White-hot heat enveloped her, searing her skin, melting her fingertips, and yet she remained unharmed.

Come back to us, *Annelie said.* Please.

I cannot. *The Life-Giver sounded regretful.* **There are still those who work against me.**

We're fighting them! *Annelie cried out, frustrated. She pressed down harder with her hand, felt the impossible heat pulse against her palm.* We want you. I want you, Life-Giver. I *need* you. *Her voice broke over the last word, and she squeezed her eyes shut again, frustration bubbling up inside her.*

Oh, my daughter, *the Life-Giver replied.* **If only you spoke for your city.**

Annelie swallowed. She opened her eyes again and looked up, at where the figures of Nethan and Elinah still hung suspended in the air. They were unmoving. She looked back down, at where the flames curled around her, rearing up high above her head, forever shifting and changing. She swallowed. Is it the curse? Is that why you're leaving?

One flame detached itself from the roaring fire before her. It wrapped itself around her like a cloak, until she was surrounded by intense warmth, feeling it pulse against her back and her arms and her neck. The sound of it rushed and roared in her ear.

He still works against us, The Life-Giver whispered in her ear.

In the corners of her vision, Annelie saw familiar inky blackness begin to creep into view.

She shivered, pulling her thin white robe around her and bringing the flames with it. They encased her until she burned, but her skin remained unharmed. Sweat prickled at her forehead. The darkness brought with it a rush of cold air, a rotten and horrid stench sweeping through the air. The flames reared back from it.

Annelie swallowed. She glanced up to check on the white-gold silhouettes of Nethan and Elinah, still suspended in the air above her. She was the only one to have landed on the surface again.

Tell me how to help, *she said desperately, watching the blackness seep onto the surface, coloring the flames grey-black. In other places, the fire sputtered out completely.*

Annelie drew back a step, tucking herself into her robes until she was as small as she could be.

It is almost time, child. The voice throbbed in her head again, brazen and bold and beautiful. **You will have my strength. You will have my voice. All my will is yours.**

The blackness was growing ever stronger. It dripped into her vision, freezing the flames where it brushed them. She watched, sickened, as it raged across the surface of the Sun, turning flames grey and still, coming ever closer.

Until it was almost upon her.

All my will is yours, the voice repeated in a whisper.

Annelie shrieked and bowed down, the flames encasing her raging up. They wrapped around her body and lifted her. She was ripped bodily from the surface of the sun and catapulted up into the air again, the flames releasing her as soon as she was floating on her own. She tried desperately to stay, reaching out her arms and fighting with ever last piece of strength in her body to return.

The blackness almost covered the whole surface. It was worse than before. It was the worst she'd ever seen it. The surface of the Life-Giver looked mottled and sickly—grey frozen flames shattering, the tiniest peeps of red-gold the only sign of life.

Next to her, Annelie saw the forms of Nethan and Elinah. They *remained suspended, but—*

But the blackness was too close.

It followed the course of the flames up into the air, greedily sucking in everything it could. It didn't stop when it reached Elinah's arm. She writhed, a scream echoing from somewhere distant. Annelie could only watch in horror as inky darkness chased up Elinah's arm, engulfing her. The bright light dimmed instantly.

Annelie cried out for her, writhing and pushing forwards, but everything felt sluggish as she was dragged backward. Her arms felt heavy as she struggled.

The blackness engulfed Elinah completely, until she winked out.

Horrible, roaring silence.

And then the blackness turned its attention to Nethan.

Annelie could only watch in horror as the same thing happened to him—the tendrils racing up his arm and down his chest and encasing his legs. She screamed and struggled and wept and called out to him, but it made no difference. With every desperate movement, she was forcing herself backward until all she could see of him was a distant, bright dot above the blackened, sickened Sun.

Then Nethan winked out, too.

Annelie was frozen, her breathing sounding too loud in the desperate, echoing silence. She floated, still, above the horrific image of the diseased Sun beneath her, the blackness seeping into every corner of her vision. They were gone.

She felt suddenly, horrendously alone.

She was still being propelled backward. The inky darkness reached hungrily out to her, but she was too distant, too far out for it to reach.

Lyam. She had to get back to Lyam.

She turned, writhing. She couldn't suffer the same fate as Nethan and Elinah. She had to wake up, to see if they were alive, if they were breathing, if the inky blackness had followed them into the waking world. She stopped fighting the current dragging her backward, moving with it instead as the horrid blackness chased her.

Annelie squeezed her eyes shut.

You will have my voice, the Life-Giver whispered into her ear just as she felt herself falling.

CHAPTER
SEVENTEEN

Dreaming is only to be done in the presence of a Scribe.
Dreams are dangerous by nature.
Not just to their Dreamers, but to everyone around them.
This is why their isolation is essential.
The Book of the Life-Giver, Volume I, Chapter VI

L yam was nervous.

The Dreamers had been still for what felt like hours. The darkness outside had grown more and more solid, the air colder, a chill biting them even inside Enoch's tiny hut. The one lantern sputtered away pitifully in the corner, barely lighting up anything.

Lyam sat tucked up against the wall, his knees drawn into his chest. The frayed edge of the rug was in front of him, its tasselled ends lying limply against the mud-sand walls of the hut. His robes were covered in dust. He drew the cloak he had borrowed from Adan close against him, trying to take comfort in the soft material when every inch of him was tightly-strung, waiting on edge for Annelie's return.

He had a bad feeling in his gut.

Adan sat against the wall beside him, but his gaze was fixed on the floor. He hadn't said a word since they'd entered the hut. Lyam couldn't blame him. He would be the same if his Dreamer was injured and he had to watch others Dream. Lyam couldn't even imagine it. Nothing could happen to Annelie under his watch. He could never, ever forgive himself, or survive alone without her.

The other Scribes were sat leaning against the opposite wall —Jorin at Tasmin's elbow, his eyes fixed on his notebook where he was determinedly writing down everything that happened. Enoch sat against the door, just outside the lanternlight, his bold golden gaze fixed on the circle of Dreamers in the center of the hut.

And then there were the Dreamers. They hadn't moved an inch since they'd started to Dream. Their hands were clasped, their heads bowed, Nethan in the center with Elinah to his left and Annelie to his right. They were all glowing softly with the golden light that streamed from Annelie's skin, risen to wrap around the three of them in a benediction of light and warmth.

Lyam hadn't taken his eyes off Annelie once.

He had to believe in her. She'd promised that she would come back to him, and he held onto that belief like it was his life-line. The Dreams had always been hard, but they hadn't always been so terrifying. Not since the Dreamers had begun to be picked off one by one until there were only these three left.

They would come back. They had to.

Suddenly, the light around the three Dreamers flickered. Lyam sat up straight, eyes trained on Annelie, but she hadn't moved. Rather, the light on her skin and surrounding the other two Dreamers had flickered out for just one instant and then come back.

Under his gaze, it happened again; the light winked out and then came back. It looked weaker—paler.

Enoch growled from beside the door. "Something's wrong."

No sooner had the words left his mouth than the light around the three Dreamers flickered out again, and this time when it came back it only covered Nethan and Annelie.

Elinah flinched. Her body shook, falling backward until she crashed to the ground, her eyes still tightly shut, her limbs flailing. With horror, Lyam saw something dark appear at the tips of her fingers, inky blackness racing up her arms, along her veins, sinking underneath her skin with dire speed. Her limbs froze where the blackness crept, her fingers stiffening into half-formed fists, her legs kicking. Her mouth opened in a scream that tore through the hut.

From beside him, Lyam heard Adan murmur, "Just like Kiran. It's just like Kiran."

Dread flooded through Lyam's stomach.

"Don't touch her!" Enoch cried, but it was too late. Jorin, horror written all over his young face, had run straight to Elinah's side, his hands automatically going to her. He grasped hold of her wrist and everything exploded.

Bright, blinding light flashed in Lyam's eyes, so bright his head hurt. He squeezed his eyes shut and dropped his pulsing head into his hands, fingernails digging into the skin of his forehead as he groaned low and loud. The light was gone as soon as it had appeared, but he couldn't lift his head straightaway, pain throbbing through his skull.

He heard a deep, desperate whine, followed by a sob.

Dread filling him, Lyam opened his eyes to see Jorin crouched over Elinah's body, held tightly in place by Enoch. Tasmin was beside them, her face frozen in shock in a way Lyam had never seen before. The sight of her—Lyam's mentor, the person he'd always gone to for help—so distraught disturbed him in a deep way.

Then he turned his eyes down and instantly felt sick.

Elinah was lying flat on the ground, her whole body blackened, poisoned with the inky darkness that tainted her. Her veins webbed out under her skin, visible because they were pitch black; rotten. The stench of something old and dead wafted from her, tinged with the sear of impossible heat that often came after Dreams. The remnants of the Life-Giver, Lyam had always thought, but with a scene so horrible spread out before him he couldn't believe it.

He felt sickened.

The light surrounding Annelie and Nethan flickered again, sputtering, shadows leaping around it. It went out, and when it returned, it just surrounded Annelie, her skin glowing, her eyes still tightly shut.

Nethan was left in the darkness.

He cried out, falling back and holding his arms over his face, but it was too late. The inky darkness was already corrupting him too. His arms turned black, his legs jerking, rot spreading up his arms and his neck and over his face, right to his hairline. He shuddered and fell still, frozen in place where the inky black had infected his veins.

Tasmin made a low, horrid sound filled with utter distress.

She ran across the hut and fell down on her knees beside Nethan's still form, leaning over him with her hands fluttering.

"Don't touch him!" Enoch warned, still holding Jorin. "Don't!"

Tasmin's hand found Nethan's arm, hovering above it. She clenched her fist and dropped her head, saying through gritted teeth, "Explain why I cannot touch *my* Dreamer when he...he's—"

"He is rotting," Enoch said sharply. "You will only hurt yourself, and us at the same time."

Tasmin sucked in a raw, harsh breath.

"Do not touch him," Enoch snarled.

Lyam was only partially aware of the scene unfolding before him. His attention was fixated solely on Annelie. She remained upright, her hands still extended as if she were holding the other two Dreamers by her side, but she was alone. Her skin shone with glowing golden light that throbbed in time with her pulse, extending above her in the pale, ghostly shape of a flame.

The light flickered again.

Fear clenched Lyam's heart. He sprinted to Annelie's side and wedged himself in front of her, his fingers itching to cup her face, to hold her close, but Enoch's warning had found its way into his skull. Plus, he knew that touching her when she Dreamed was dangerous. He could bring her back too early, forcing her to fall, injuring her.

He prayed with every single cell in his body that she would come back to him unharmed.

The light flickered, sputtered, and winked out.

Lyam cried out before he could help himself. He grasped desperately for Annelie, grabbing her hands, studying her skin for any sign of the blackness, the rotting that had taken over the other Dreamers.

There was nothing.

Annelie drew in a great, shuddering breath, and then her eyes flew open.

She was glowing.

Lyam rocked back, shocked, and dropped her hand in fear that she would burn him. Light streamed from her eyes, from her skin, every pore shining with bright light that encompassed the entire hut in a hazy glow. She turned her head to him, and then she smiled light streaming out between her teeth.

Lyam stared in shock at Annelie. "What— Are you okay?"

"I am everything," Annelie answered, her tone awed.

Lyam swallowed, watching as she reached out and took his hand in her own. She was warm, impossibly warm. "What?"

"I have all the Life-Giver's strength," Annelie said, and her voice sounded stronger, resonating with something new. Something forceful. "I have the Life-Giver's voice. The Life-Giver's will is mine."

Lyam stared at her, his eyes wide.

"It was the Dream," Annelie said, her gaze clear and sharp as she met Lyam's eyes. "It's time, Lyam. It's time."

Before Lyam could ask anything else, before he could even try and understand what was happening, Tasmin cried out low and long. With a jolt, Lyam turned and found her cradling Nethan's still, rotting body against her. Jorin had his face buried in Elinah's hair, and Enoch stood watching them with tight lines creasing the edge of his eyes.

Lyam turned away, shuddering, and met Adan's eyes.

"What happened?" Adan demanded.

Slowly, Lyam turned back to Annelie. She was staring down at her own hands, one still clasped in Lyam's, a look of awe on her face. When she spoke, her voice rumbled with strange power.

"It's time. Time to end this." She turned to Lyam with her face set and her tone fierce. "I'm ready. Let's bring them all back."

Lyam squinted at her, confused.

"The Life-Giver is here." Annelie held out her hands and spread her fingers, light shining between them. "They're with us."

Enoch uttered a curse.

Lyam could scarcely believe his ears. He stared at Annelie—his Anni—and was astonished to see someone *else* looking through her eyes. She was still there, but behind her familiar dark eyes and snub nose lingered something other.

Something powerful.

Lyam shifted onto his knees. "Life-Giver."

Adan took in a sharp breath, but Enoch was the one who moved, dropping to his knees beside Lyam and touching his forehead to the floor.

Annelie shook her head impatiently. "There's no time. We need to go to the one who bears the curse."

Enoch sat up slowly and hissed. "Izani."

Annelie nodded. "If I get to him, I can heal the Dreamers."

"Wait." Adan's voice sounded strained. He crossed the hut, dropping to his knees in front of Annelie, his shoulder brushing Lyam's. "You can bring him back?"

Annelie reached out and touched his face with her glowing hands. "Yes. Kiran is still alive. They all are."

Lyam felt the shudder that ran bodily through Adan.

Annelie turned to Jorin and Tasmin, who still lingered over the blackened, rotten bodies of Elinah and Nethan and reached out to them. The light spilling from her skin washed over them.

They both turned to her, hopeless.

"I'll bring them back," Annelie promised, her voice stronger than ever. "Take me to Izani, and I can bring them back."

Jorin blinked rapidly, wiping at one eye with the dusty back of one hand. Tasmin never took her gaze off Annelie.

Lyam swallowed. "So, we...go to Izani?" He didn't mean for it to come out like a question, but it did.

Annelie turned to him and nodded. "I can reverse all of this once I find him. He's the root of the curse."

"How are we supposed to do that?"

"What time is it?" Tasmin asked, her voice hoarse and rough.

Lyam glanced towards the door, still closed firmly to keep out the light. Enoch followed his gaze, strode to the window, and peered through the blinds. "It's a little past dawn. Our Life-Giver rises again."

Annelie's glowing skin pulsed.

"Right." Tasmin didn't move from her place crouched beside Nethan, but her eyes were fixed on Annelie. "The Council will be meeting in their chambers. Izani will be among them."

"Who else?" Lyam asked.

"Speaker Ayanah and the first and second assistants. Head Guard Tomas. I'm supposed to be there."

Lyam swallowed, his throat feeling stuck. The most powerful people in the city gathered together, and Annelie wanted to confront them. But Lyam knew he couldn't hide from this anymore. He had to face the consequences of what he'd done— what he knew. They couldn't leave Izani unchecked.

He nodded stiffly. "Then let's go."

Annelie gripped his hand tight.

"Wait." Adan cut in, staring around with wide eyes as the rest of them began to get to their feet. "You can't just—we need a *plan.* Shadow's eye, you can't expect to just *walk into the Council chamber."*

"I have access," Tasmin said grimly.

"You still need a plan!" Adan pointed out. "Tomas will have guards swarming everywhere. Izani will never risk anything effecting his power. Never mind the *Speaker* is going to be there!"

"She needs to know, too," Annelie said quietly. "I don't think she does."

Lyam's stomach clenched. Adan was right. The enormity of what they were attempting didn't escape him, and they couldn't walk blindly right into the enemies' trap. They might as well walk into a nest of snakes.

He crouched beside Annelie and murmured, "I think we do need a plan."

Adan let out a relieved sigh.

"What do we do about the guards?" Jorin asked, still hunched over Elinah's body.

"I... have an idea." Lyam took in a careful breath. "There are people who would do anything for the Dreamers."

"Who?"

"The Grey Ones."

Jorin stared at him, wide-eyed. "The past Scribes?"

Lyam nodded. "Yenn is among them. He knows all of Izani's crimes better than anyone. They would come to our aid. They outnumber the guards."

"Then we'll go to them," Adan said firmly. "Jorin, you should come with me. Lyam needs to stay with Dreamer Annelie and... and the Life-Giver."

A stunned silence followed his words.

Annelie just smiled. "We need to go to the Council chamber as soon as we can, "We've wasted too much time already. The Dreamers can't suffer any longer."

"I'll take you," Tasmin said. She glanced down at Nethan's body, face tight. "What's one more act of treason?"

Lyam shuddered.

"I'll come too," Enoch rumbled from the door, his thick brows furrowed. "I would like to have words with Head Designer Izani."

"But we can't leave them," Jorin whispered. Lyam turned to find his gaze fixed on Elinah, his youthful face crumpled in pain.

Annelie crawled her way towards him, arms trembling. Lyam supported her while she reached out to touch Jorin's hand. "Don't worry. We won't abandon them."

Jorin turned to face her, tear tracks staining his cheeks. Annelie let him go, then turned to Elinah and Nethan, her lips setting in a thin line. She shifted onto her knees, then held out both hands and gestured upwards.

Instantly, the bodies of Nethan and Elinah rose up into the air.

Lyam choked, scrambling backward. The two rotting, blackened bodies of the Dreamers floated in the air before them, rising with Annelie's gesture until they hovered just above the ground, their toes dragging over the rugs.

Jorin drew in a trembling breath. Tasmin's face was tight.

"They'll come with us," Annelie said. "To show the truth of what's happened to us."

A small silence followed before Enoch let out a low, dark chuckle. "Well. That's one way to get them to listen." He clapped his hands. "Hurry now. Let's put an end to this."

They parted ways in the tunnels.

Lyam and Enoch led the blindfolded Scribes back underground, Lyam pushing Annelie in her wheelchair. The bodies of Nethan and Elinah floated eerily before them, Annelie animating them with one hand lifted.

The image was bone-chilling.

Adan and Jorin left to go to the House of the Grey Ones before they reached the Southern Gate, disappearing into the shadows.

Tasmin led the rest of them, grim-faced, through the tunnels, her features set and her eyes sharp as shards of glass.

Terror clawed at Lyam's throat. Annelie turned to him, reassuring, the glow from the Life-Giver still shining from her pores. Her expression was fierce.

Lyam gathered his courage and pushed her forward.

When they entered the city through the Gate, everything was eerily silent. Their group clung together, Annelie in the center with Lyam pushing her, Enoch and Tasmin walking at their flanks. The animated bodies of Elinah and Nethan floated before them, Annelie lifting them with one hand.

Lyam tried not to look at them as they treaded the familiar path through the city. His stomach roiled.

A low cry from one of the side streets made him startle. He looked up sharply to see a boy standing in the mouth of an alley, stunned. He shouted again when he made eye contact with Lyam.

"The traitors!"

"Keep walking," Enoch rumbled, and Lyam obeyed, forcing himself to put one foot in front of the other.

The boy's cry drew others, and soon enough the streets were lined with confused crowds, merchants and glassblowers holding lanterns high, trying to get a glimpse of the strange procession, but not daring to approach when they caught sight of the floating bodies of Nethan and Elinah. Lyam thought of his own family and felt a pang. Had they heard of his treason yet?

Tasmin laid one hand on Lyam's shoulder, her jaw clenched tight.

Lyam put his head down and kept walking.

The Council chamber was in the central square, opposite the Citadel. The gleaming glass walls reflected bright light as they stepped into the square, but Lyam wasn't as impressed, not after he'd seen real Sunlight and the wonders of the city above ground. The Citadel held nothing to the sky.

Beside the Citadel sat the Council chambers, a fleet of black-clad guards lining the steps. The chambers were encased in a squat building, white marble the same as the rest of the city—the same as the city above them, Lyam realized with a jolt. The materials that built their city must have come from somewhere, after all.

The clues had all been right before their eyes.

Tasmin marched up to the steps, her eyes hard.

The guards all crossed their spears.

"I will have entry," Tasmin ordered, her voice strong and harsh. "I am Head Scribe Tasmin, and you will let me in."

"You are a traitor," the guard said, eyeing her with contempt.

Tasmin's nostrils flared.

Before she could respond, Annelie lifted a hand, and the floating bodies of Nethan and Elinah rose higher in the air.

The guard's face drained. He stumbled.

"You'll let us in," Annelie said, her voice light and melodic. The glow from her skin illuminated the guard's face as Lyam pushed her closer.

The guard swallowed. He took in her white robe, her unknown face, and his jaw went slack.

Annelie glared at him. "Let us in, or you'll become like them."

The guard's eyes flickered up to Nethan and Elinah again, and he visibly shuddered. He wavered, but the other guards stepped forward, crossing their spears over his.

Annelie barely moved, just tilted her head to the right and a burst of golden light shot from her skin, enveloping the guards in an instant. A smell of smoke and incense followed her, the roaring flames distantly audible, and the guards shouted and took cover, fleeing behind the building.

Lyam drank in the sight, astonished. The light was undoubtedly sunlight. Tasmin had been forced to turn away, shielding her eyes.

"The Life-Giver walks among us," Enoch rumbled.

Lyam swallowed.

"The Life-Giver would like to enter the building," Annelie

said, a touch of amusement in her voice. She twisted in her seat to send Lyam a cheeky smile.

Lyam shook his head, biting back a laugh, and pushed her to the building.

The steps had a ramp curling around the side, and Lyam pushed her up to the doors, pausing when he reached them. Tasmin opened them for him, striding inside, and Lyam took a deep breath before following her.

He wasn't permitted to be in here, but with all his other crimes, it hardly mattered now.

The two people sitting at the desk inside scrambled as their procession entered. They stumbled to their feet, rushing to block the path, but one look at Nethan and Elinah had them backing away with terrified screams.

Tasmin didn't even spare them a glance. She opened the next set of doors and led them down a winding corridor, barely wide enough for Annelie's wheelchair. The ceiling was low enough for Enoch to have to bend almost double. Lyam was, once again, thankful for his short height.

The door at the end of the corridor was outlined with gold. Faint incense floated through the air from its cracks, cloying Lyam's nose, and there were audible voices from inside. A motto was inscribed over the door: *Duty, Honor, Sanctity.* The motto of the Speaker.

Lyam almost wanted to laugh.

"Well." Tasmin turned to Annelie, her hand on the door. "Are you sure about this?"

Annelie nodded, her eyes bright. "Izani is in there. I can feel it."

"Then let's put an end to this once and for all," Enoch rumbled. "The curse starts with his ancestors and ends with him."

Annelie glanced up at Lyam.

He nodded to her, surprised when his voice came out steady. "Let's end this."

"And quickly," Tasmin added. "Those guards won't wait long before they come back with reinforcements."

Annelie drew in an audible breath. She straightened her spine, sitting proud in her wheelchair, and lifted one hand higher so that Nethan and Elinah floated directly before her.

She nodded to Tasmin.

Tasmin pulled open the door, and Lyam pushed forwards.

CHAPTER
EIGHTEEN

The Life-Giver is ultimate power.
Our warmth, our light, our life source.
We worship the Life-Giver to the end of our days.
The Book of the Life-Giver, Volume I, Chapter I

The Council chamber was lavishly decorated.

Gold lined everything—the large round table taking up most of the space, the padded chairs lining the outside, and the rich curtains that hid the chamber from view when the Council was in session. Ornate golden dishes and glasses were laid out neatly, glistening in the light from the lanterns bracketed to the walls. Shadows flickered in the corners. The scent of incense lay thick in the air. Lyam wrinkled his nose.

All around the table, people stared at them in shock.

The Council members were all wearing their official robes—Speaker Ayanah in resplendent yellow, her First and Second Assistant flanking her protectively. Head Healer Lara sat primly beside the Second Assistant, her hands folded. Tasmin's usual seat was conspicuously empty, and on the other side, Head Guard Tomas in his gold-lined black robes sat beside a familiar close-shaven beard, sharp, proud features, and a stare as hard as rock.

Head Designer Izani.

Lyam's blood ran cold when he saw him. He froze in the doorway, hands on Annelie's wheelchair, struck by a sudden rush of *hatred*. This man was the source of all their pain, all the suffering the Dreamers and their Scribes had been subjected to. Everything could have been avoided if he'd come forward, if he'd *stopped*.

"The bearer of the curse," Enoch growled from Lyam's side.

His words seemed to finally kick the stunned chamber into action. Chairs scraped as the Council members leaped to their feet, Tomas' spear springing into his hand as he strode in front of Ayanah, blocking her from view.

In the corner, Izani stood, his brown robes flaring around him. His eyes were calculating as they landed on Lyam.

"What's the meaning of this?" Speaker Ayanah asked sharply, stepping around Tomas.

Tasmin stepped forward and bowed. "Speaker. We are in danger. The Dreamers—"

"Tasmin?" Ayanah interrupted, frowning. Her long hair fell into her eyes; she pushed it back irritably. "You should be watching over your Dreamer. The draught—"

"My Dreamer is here," Tasmin said. Lyam could tell that her voice was near breaking.

Ayanah blanched. "What? He's *out of his hut?!*"

"There," Lara rasped, and pointed to the door.

They all turned to see the bodies of Nethan and Elinah rising slowly from the ground, entering the chamber. The black corroding their veins had grown thicker, and the stench of rotting wafted through the air.

Ayanah retched, stepping back.

"The Dreamers." Lara studied them with almost scientific

curiosity even as her colleagues turned away, choking. "The curse is true."

"What curse?" Izani spoke, his deep voice authoritative. He stepped up beside Tomas, who was staring up at the Dreamers with grim, beady eyes. "These Dreamers were supposed to be protected. Why are they out of their huts? What treason is this, Tasmin?"

"Treason," Tasmin hissed. "*You* dare speak of treason?"

Izani regarded her coolly.

"What's going on?" Ayanah insisted, folding her arms so her robes flared around her. "I will have the truth of this. Tell me, Tasmin. I'm sure there's a good reason Dreamer Nethan is not sleeping, as the draught should have made him?"

Tasmin's throat bobbed as she swallowed. She straightened her back. Lyam had never felt prouder of her. "I didn't give him the draught."

Silence.

Ayanah's lips tightened. "I'm sure you have a good reason for disobeying a direct order?"

"We've been wrong about everything," Tasmin continued. "The Life-Giver is not the one hurting our Dreamers."

"The Life-Giver is leaving."

"To *protect* us," Tasmin insisted. "From the curse that has trapped us underground for centuries."

Izani audibly scoffed. He crossed the chamber, laying a hand on Tomas' shoulder when he went to block his way, and surveyed the rag-tag group of them with an arched brow.

Lyam's gut flared with hatred.

"You've lost your senses," Izani said. "Mad with grief from your Dreamer's affliction."

Tasmin snarled.

Before she could say anything or leap for Izani with her nails like claws, Enoch stepped forward, towering over Izani with a threatening rumble.

Izani's gaze jumped up to him, and his face slackened in shock.

"We meet at last, Curse-Bearer." Enoch hummed, tilting his head. "You're smaller than I thought you'd be."

Izani's jaw was hanging open. He snapped his mouth shut, drawing back a step, and gestured for Tomas to step between them.

Enoch laughed. "Scared now? Because you didn't manage to get rid of me?"

Izani glowered.

"Who are you?" Ayanah asked, looking to Izani with a crease in her brow. "Uncle, what's going on?"

"Traitors," Izani growled. "This man walks under the Sun."

A shocked silence rippled through the chamber.

Enoch's square jaw worked. He took another step forward, ignoring the spear that Tomas thrust at him. "Do you want to tell them, or shall I? How you've locked us all underground and doomed us to a life of darkness and rot?"

"Treason," Izani snapped. "And lies. All of you. You're known liars. I see Scribe Lyam is among you. He's currently a wanted criminal."

Lyam quaked when all eyes turned to him.

"Strength now," Annelie murmured to him, perfectly poised. "Just a little longer, Lyam."

"Arrest them," Izani snapped, stepping back to Ayanah's side. "Now."

Enoch growled and Tasmin drew in a sharp breath, but the guards were already swarming forward, Tomas leading them with his spear held aloft. Everything happened too fast for Lyam to keep up. Suddenly, Enoch was right in front of him, grabbing the point of Tomas' spear and flipping it, jerking Tomas' wrist so the spear clattered across the floor. Tomas snarled, aiming a kick at Enoch's stomach, and Enoch dodged clumsily, grabbing for Tomas' elbow and twisting hard.

Behind the grappling pair, Tasmin was surrounded by three black guards circling her with their spears aloft. When they moved, it was as one, and Tasmin spun and dodged as best she could, crying out when a speak cracked across her ribs. One of the guards grabbed her hair, triumphant, but Tasmin roared and grabbed the other end of his spear, forcing him back through sheer force of will.

Lyam spun Annelie's wheelchair around, desperately looking for somewhere to shelter, when hands grabbed at his back and dragged him away. He fought, crying out, kicking back with his right ankle and hearing a satisfying *crunch*. But then more hands were on him, forcing his arms behind his back. He watched as Annelie's wheelchair was swamped with a swarm of black.

"No!" he cried desperately, kicking and writhing in the hold of the guards. The door to the chamber burst open again and a new flood of people entered—a sea of grey.

Lyam could have cried with relief.

The Grey Ones.

They swept in with their hoods pulled up, their fingers wrinkled and decrepit, their backs bent and their eyes dull. But there were enough of them to swarm the guards and pull them back. Lyam almost sobbed as the guards holding him were overcome, freeing him so he was dropped, coughing, to his knees.

A hand touched his shoulder.

Lyam jumped, spinning in terror, only to find Yenn standing there looking at him with something determined in his eyes.

Lyam's mouth dropped open. "You..."

"We came as soon as Scribes Adan and Jorin told us what was happening," Yenn murmured, at the same time as a new voice rang out, echoing through the commotion. Lyam got unsteadily back to his feet with Yenn's help and found himself in front of the old man who had let him inside the House of the Grey Ones.

"Ah, safe you were not," the man said. Lyam realized he had never asked his name. "But now things will be correct again. Time not to argue. Time to *act*."

"You really came?" Lyam asked breathlessly, his heart racing in his throat.

The old man smiled at him, showing his crooked, toothless

mouth. "Help. You woke us up. Time to act now, Scribe Lyam. For you and your Dreamer."

Lyam took in a trembling, shaking breath, spinning around to survey the room. The guards were being held back by the sheer number of hooded, grey-cloaked people, all the Scribes who had lost their Dreamers coming together in their numbers to force the guards back. The room was overwhelmed with grey.

Lyam span on his heel and found Annelie surrounded, the Grey Ones forming a protective circle. He let out a relieved breath and took a step towards her, but Yenn suddenly took his arm in an iron grip.

Lyam turned, surprised, and found Yenn staring in terror at Izani.

Izani stood mere feet away. His expression was cold, his proud features contorted in fury as he glared right at Yenn. The clamor of the chamber seemed to die away until all Lyam could hear was Yenn's trembling breaths.

Izani advanced, and Lyam acted without thinking. He stepped in front of Yenn.

Izani paused. His gaze flickered between them, and then he grinned, a terrible expression. His teeth were perfectly even.

"I should have known," Izani murmured, gaze locked back on Yenn. "Should have done away with you at the same time as your pathetic Dreamer."

Yenn snarled, the sound almost inhuman. He lunged forward, but Lyam caught him, holding onto him tight while Yenn struggled.

Izani watched with delight.

Lyam felt sick. Part of him wanted to let Yenn loose, to do what he wanted with Izani, but he didn't want Yenn to deal with any more grief. So, he held on tight and twisted, craning his neck for Annelie.

He met her eyes where she was still surrounded by Grey Ones. Her skin glowed.

Suddenly, a pulse of bright light cracked through the chamber, silencing everyone. When it cleared, Annelie sat in the center of it, hair and eyes wild with light.

Yenn stared in astonishment.

Izani snarled. "*Annelie.*"

Annelie regarded him with a blazing gaze.

"This is all your fault," Izani hissed, stepping closer. "Both you and your troublesome Scribe. Sticking his nose in where he shouldn't, no doubt on your instruction. You couldn't have just stayed *quiet*, could you?"

"I don't have to," Annelie answered sharply. "It's my purpose to speak. Not yours."

Izani's cold smile widened, his teeth glinting. "Mm. I'm changing your purpose, sweetheart. No need to trouble yourself anymore. Your Scribe should have just given you your draught like he was supposed to. Then you'd be out of the way, and I wouldn't have to do this. Too bad he's the worst Scribe to ever grace our People."

"Lyam is the best Scribe I could have asked for," Annelie snapped, her fingers curling into fists. Lyam felt a shiver of pride.

"Don't worry yourself, little girl," Izani said soothingly, still approaching. "It will all be over soon."

"Yes," Annelie agreed, her eyes burning back at Izani. "It will."

A chill raced down Lyam's spine at those words. The chamber had fallen silent, everyone watching as Izani approached the final Dreamer. He caught a glimpse of Adan and Jorin among the crowd, watching with set faces. Adan had a grip on Head Guard Tomas.

"I know what you've done," Annelie said, her voice growing in strength and volume. "I've seen it all. In the Dreams."

Izani snorted. "*Dreams.* What have they to say now? The Dreamers are corrupted and gone, and *you* are the only one left. You expect us to believe the word of a child?"

"I expect you to believe the word of the last Dreamer."

Izani raised both brows, folding his arms across his chest.

"Alright. Impress me. You won't be Dreaming for much longer, after all."

Annelie's brow creased, her lips pursing into a thin line. "You're wrong. You're so, so wrong, and you don't even realize it."

"Excuse me?"

"You've been out of your depth for a long time, Head Designer Izani."

Izani's steps slowed.

"I'm sure you had good intentions when you started," Annelie continued. "I know you became a Designer with the intent to do good. You are a lover of tradition, and you wanted to make our city greater. You were thrilled when Dreamer Emery's First Dream appointed you as Designer. You thought your time had finally come. But it hadn't, had it? It wasn't at all like you expected it to be."

Izani's expression darkened. His lips twisted, his eyes shadowy and cold. "Watch your tongue, child."

"That's just the problem," Annelie said, almost pityingly. "You never understood the balance of power. Designers might be the most visible of our system, but they are far from the strongest. They interact the most with the rest of our people, yes, but only on the word of the Dreamer. Everything comes back to the Dreamer, who is only heard through the Scribe. Designers are the least powerful in the system. You're irrelevant. You despised that, didn't you? Despised having to listen to a mere boy tell you what to do.

"But you weren't satisfied to just do your assigned work as the rest of us are. No, you wanted more. You wanted *power*. And you found it when you discovered the curse, didn't you?"

"I know nothing of a curse," Izani hissed.

Annelie shook her head. "It's been happening for a long time. Centuries. I presume the previous Curse-Bearer chose you because of your ambition. Showed you how to change Dreams. How to take the power you so desperately craved. Yenn never stood a chance."

A shocked gasp rippled through the crowd. Izani looked livid.

"Just small changes to begin with," Annelie continued. "Odd things here and there that wouldn't draw too much attention. An expansion of an east tunnel instead of south; assigning different books to the school curriculum; continuing to rid us of the Water-Gatherers. Did you think they'd all gone?"

Izani hissed. "No Dream has chosen a Water-Gatherer in decades. That man is a fraud."

Enoch laughed. "Not so, Curse-Bearer. I was chosen in my cradle. Before you were even born."

Izani's jaw visibly clenched.

"You've gone further than other Curse-Bearers," Annelie added, tilting her head almost curiously. "You decided that you needed someone in power that you could control. Someone who wouldn't argue with you; someone you could influence. I believe that Ayanah has been a friend of your family since she was young, correct? Her mother and you practically grew up together. She trusts you like an uncle. And she was already Second Assistant. Would anyone really question it if she was chosen to be Speaker over Symon even though Emery's Dream showed that the Life-Giver had chosen him?"

A choked gasp sounded from the crowd, cries of disbelief tumbling from every corner. Ayanah, from her place surrounded by guards, looked horrified. Lyam wondered how much she'd actually known about Izani's true intentions.

"You have no proof," Izani growled, his tone low and dangerous.

"I don't need it." Annelie voice was sad. "I see it in the sickness of my friends; the way the Dreamers have fallen. I *know* that it's true. You've been changing the Life-Giver's words."

"The Life-Giver!" Izani barked out a harsh laugh. "You *fool.* Your precious *Life-Giver* is the one that's caused all this! They *left you.* The Life-Giver corrupted the Dreamers and left them for dead, and you still expect us to listen to you? This would never have happened if we didn't have *Dreamers* in the first place!"

Annelie's nostrils flared. The glow emitting from her skin

sharpened, growing brighter until it was almost painful to look at. Her face remained calm, but she lifted one hand, pointing imperiously at Izani, and the light followed her movements, illuminating him in a cold, bright way that left nothing to the imagination. The creases and crevices in his skin stood out like shadows, his wrinkled face and peppered grey hair suddenly making him look a lot older than he appeared.

"You've always been clever at twisting words," Annelie murmured, still clear enough to be heard throughout the chamber. "That's how you got away with it for so long. People want to believe you. You can twist them around and around until they don't know how to think for themselves anymore. But the Life-Giver sees through you. The Life-Giver knows your very soul; every corrupt, blackened, filthy inch of it. And you are nothing but rotten inside."

Izani's jaw clenched. He stepped forward, lunging for Annelie, but Lyam moved in a flash and dragged her wheelchair back, spinning until she was behind him and he could look Izani right in the eyes.

Izani spat at him. "*You*! Worthless, useless Scribe, so *humble*, do you do nothing to control your Dreamer? To stop the lies she's spitting out?"

"She isn't lying. You are."

"Insolent little *brat*!"

Izani grabbed the front of Lyam's robes and lifted him high in the air, cursing in his face. The thick fabric tightened around Lyam's throat, rough against his skin, and he coughed and spluttered, gasping for air. Black lights swam in his vision, his fingers tingled and began to go numb.

Stop!

A bright, burning flash of light streaked through the air, accompanied by a throbbing, powerful voice, deep but warm. Intense heat ran through the chamber, searing Lyam's skin. Sweat broke out on his forehead. The smell of incense swam heavy through the air, perfumed by cries and screams of terror and awe.

Izani dropped Lyam. He crashed to the ground, his legs giving out, gasping.

Twisting as best he could, Lyam saw Annelie behind him, sitting straight up in her wheelchair, her eyes blazing gold. They were *gold*, just like his and Enoch's, no trace of her usual deep brown in sight.

Her skin was glowing. Golden light burst from her, radiating in a wide circle and bathing the rest of the chamber in bright light. Shadows retreated, flickering at the very edges of the chamber.

Annelie's eyes were golden, and when she opened her mouth to speak, light poured out of it, seeping from every pore of her skin.

This is not the way. The voice that echoed from Annelie's lips was not her own. *My children. This is not the way. This was never supposed to be the way.*

Silence rang through the chamber once Annelie had stopped speaking. Even Lyam stared in awe. She looked otherworldly; alien. Not the girl he'd grown up knowing, the person closest to him in the world. She looked... awe-inspiring.

"Life-Giver." Enoch whispered breathlessly.

Shock was almost palpable in the air. Ayanah had gone ashen, and she sank to her knees in an impossible slow movement, dropping forward to touch her forehead to the floor. The rest of the Council members quickly followed suit, as did Enoch and Jorin and Adan, then the Grey Ones, a ripple running through the crowd as everyone dropped to their knees.

Lyam shuffled around until he was facing Annelie, his throat tight, and touched his forehead to the floor.

Annelie's glowing eyes were soft. *Do not be afraid. I have never wanted you to fear me. My children.* Annelie span her chair in a slow circle, glowing hands on the wheels, the stinging scent of incense wafting with her. *You have been trapped here for too long. Underground, away from me, locked in a system I did not intend. It is time we changed it. It is time for everything to change.*

Lyam couldn't breathe. His chest felt tight, his throat still burning from Izani's assault, and he couldn't believe what he was hearing.

The Life-Giver. Inside Annelie. Speaking with Annelie's voice; glowing out of her skin.

His Annelie, the Life-Giver.

It is time to change, the Life-Giver repeated, just as Annelie came to a stop, her wheelchair directly facing Izani who was standing, grey-faced, the only Council member not on his knees.

And to change, we must cut out the curse.

A bolt of light burst from Annelie's fingers, and she lifted her hand, palm-out, and flicked the tips of her fingers. A web of light burst from her, spanning out into a net of jagged beams of solid sunlight that wrapped around Izani's form, trapping him in place. He screamed, writhing, but the lights just tightened around him as his skin began turning black.

You. The Life-Giver's—Annelie's—voice was cold and harsh, devoid of all emotion. It shocked Lyam to the core, freezing him in place. **You are the source of it all. Did you think I wouldn't know? That you could change my Dreams and murder my Dreamers without me raising a hand to you?**

Izani thrashed, tripping over his own feet and rolling against the ground. "I don't know what you're—"

Do not lie to me! The Life-Giver's voice cracked, harsh and boiling over, and steam began to fill the room—thick, burning tendrils of it bleeding through the air, covering their noses and mouths and clinging to their skin. Lyam dragged himself up to his knees breathing in and feeling the steam gather inside of his lungs.

I know what you are, and I know what you have done. Annelie guided her wheelchair forwards, the glow emanating from her spreading wider, illuminating the whole chamber with white light. The shadows trickled away in the wake of the steam.

Izani stood, shaking, at the foot of Annelie's wheelchair.

You have been working against me from the very start, the Life-Giver said quietly, the voice still loud in the silence of the room. *I never should have chosen you. I knew you had a possibility of corruption, but I chose to believe in you. I chose to give you a chance. But I know now that I was wrong. Your corruption has bled through to my Dreams and poisoned my relationship with my people. The Dreamers have been attacked because of you. Your constant deception and manipulation of my words led to the curse infecting the very Dreams themselves.*

Slowly, Annelie lifted her hand, and Izani's tangled, golden-wrapped form started to rise. He was lifted into the air, thrashing and screaming and fighting his bonds as Annelie held him perfectly in place, until he was even with the two Dreamers who still hung in mid-air, their rotten, blackened bodies still and silent.

Annelie regarded them both with sad eyes.

Nethan. Elinah. Kiran, Hathor, Mollah, Forst, Islah, Lori, Alissah. Charis, Ash, Imri. Rayah.

Emery.

You are responsible for all of them. And yet you pinned the blame on me.

Annelie abruptly tightened her hand into a fist, and the bonds around Izani tightened until he was yelling out a hoarse, tight cry, going still. Inky blackness spread across his skin.

Now, you will restore what you have taken.

The room thrummed with power, a loud, high note ringing like a bell through the air as warmth surged through the chamber, steam blowing thick and the hot smell of charcoal cinders sitting heavily in the atmosphere.

Lyam craned his neck back, watching in shock as Izani writhed, screaming, before blackness began spreading faster across his skin. It froze on his face, rotting and eating at his skin until darkness spewed from every corner of his body. His eyes widened, his mouth opening wide in a silent scream that also spewed blackness into the world, seeping from his mouth and rotting the air with the stench of burning flesh.

As the blackness grew on Izani's skin, Lyam looked away, sickened, and stopped when he caught a flicker of something from the corner of his eye. Looking up, he saw the two Dreamers hung in the air, Nethan and Elinah, slowly turning...lighter?

Blackness oozed out of their bodies, hovering in the air and evaporating where the beams of glowing warmth radiating from Annelie met them. The scent of rotten burning lay thick in the air, but the glowing sparks and cinders from Annelie's fingers blew it away, the thick steam winding around Lyam's nose and mouth to protect him from the smell.

The blackness oozed out of Nethan and Elinah and seeped into Izani until they were free and he was desecrated.

His eyes, wide open and terrified, were the last to turn black.

The next second, the Dreamers drifted to Annelie's feet, laid down carefully, and then Annelie bent forward and touched each of them on the top of their heads, the glow from her hands spreading to them.

Nothing happened for a second.

Then, slowly, their eyes blinked open.

Nethan stirred first, groaning long and low, his skin without a blemish. He turned his head slowly, glancing up at Annelie, and froze. Awe flitted across his face.

Elinah moved a moment later, lifting her head, her curly hair streaked with mud and dust, and gasped.

"Life-Giver."

My children. Annelie smiled, but her voice was still not her own. **It is safe now. I am sorry.**

There was a rustle of movement in the crowd and then Jorin broke forth, tearing into the center of the chamber with a sob and all but throwing himself at Elinah. She fell sideways with a squeak, but when she realized who it was, she gave a delighted laugh and wrapped her trembling arms firmly around him, burrowing into his neck.

It only took a second longer for Tasmin to join them. She crouched by Nethan's side and petted his head and rocked him as if she couldn't decide whether she wanted to kiss him or slap him.

Hesitantly, Lyam got to his feet, drawing closer. His body

ached for Annelie, his soul terrified that something had happened to her too, but but there she sat. Still in her wheelchair. She turned her burning golden eyes on him.

Lyam froze in place.

My son. The voice rumbled deep in Lyam's chest, reverberating through his bones, its power echoing in his head. He recognized the power from his writings of Annelie's Dreams and couldn't help but wonder at the fact that this had been the voice he'd been writing about all these years.

You have done well. So well, my child. You are brilliant, and in you and Annelie I know I chose well.

Lyam swallowed and bowed his head, overwhelmed. The Life-Giver, talking to him, *directly* to him with no barriers and no Dreams. It was beyond belief.

And yet, it is true. Annelie was smiling wide, her crooked tooth glinting in the sunlight. *This is how it is supposed to be. You know that. You have studied the myths; the tales of my earliest People.*

Lyam swallowed. "We should never have come underground."

No. I gave you golden eyes so that you might better see. I trusted you to guide my people back to me, and you have done better than I ever could have asked of you. The sight has returned to all of you now the curse is broken. Return to me, my children.

Lyam trembled as Annelie reached out to him and lightly grasped his fingers. Her touch was searing, burning, and yet he remained unharmed.

It is over now, my child.

As if on cue, there was a small commotion at the side of the chamber, and a new figure stepped through the crowd and into the light. He was waif-thin and wobbly, hesitant. His dark hair was long and tangled, hanging to his shoulders, and he looked about the chamber with confused dark eyes.

Lyam had never seen him before, but before he could wonder any further, Adan gave a cry so full of emotion that it reverberated in Lyam's chest. Adan crashed through the crowd and straight towards the young man, wrapping him in a tight hug.

"Kiran!"

Lyam's heart leaped, his blood boiling back to life. A giant smile broke out over his face. Adan's Dreamer! Adan's Dreamer was unharmed.

He was alive, clean of the blackness, and held tight in Adan's arms.

My Dreamers. Come to me.

A loud cry sounded from the crowd as more and more people drifted in from the edges of the Chamber—Scribes Lyam recognized accompanied by faces he'd never seen before of all ages and genders, their skin clean and a healthy, glowing brown without an inch of rotting in sight. He recognized Jemme leaning on the shoulder of a tall, slender girl with sleek black hair and deep brown eyes who must be Dreamer Rayah. The Grey Ones looked on with warmth and an odd kind of longing, Yenn in particular, his eyes damp.

It is finished, Annelie said in a strange, deep voice, not as loud nor as powerful as before. She tightened her fingers around Lyam's, the glow around her growing bright for one second as she smiled. *It is done.*

Then, the light winked out, and Annelie slumped forward, unconscious.

PART SIX

IT IS FINISHED

You are finished now, my daughter. It is complete.

Annelie was wrapped up in unending, soft comfort, flames flickering gently around her as she lay cradled on a soft, solid surface.

You did so well. I am so proud of you. It is your time now.

Memories came back to her in bits and pieces. Nethan and Elinah rotting. Lyam staring at her with terror. Enoch's desperation. Tasmin's grief.

Ayanah and her horror.

Izani, the source of the curse.

A rumbling sound echoed in the back of her head. **You do not need to worry about him. I have taken care of it.**

What?

He can't hurt you anymore. He has taken the curse onto himself. It is him who will rot for eternity now.

Annelie shuddered even in her exhaustion. Her joints hurt in a way they usually wouldn't in a Dream.

This is not a normal Dream, child.

Annelie didn't understand. She was speaking to the Life-Giver, *and though she couldn't feel the crisp, burning flames, she was sure that if she opened her eyes she would see the surface of the Sun.*

If she just opened her eyes...

Rest, my child. *The Life-Giver's voice was gentle, cradling her.* **All is well now.**

Don't leave me, *she thought, tired but desperate to hold onto the voice.*

A low chuckle resounded in her head.

I will always be with you, my daughter. Sleep now. I will be here when you wake.

Slowly, slowly, Annelie closed her eyes, her mind sinking into oblivion. The feeling of soft comfort persisted, even as she felt herself falling, even as her heart jumped to life in her chest and reality crashed down around her again, her bones aching and sore and exhaustion steeped deep in her soul.

"—*ni! Anni! Anni!*"

Distantly, Annelie listened to the voice calling her name, but it wasn't the same deep, heart-aching voice that she usually heard in her Dreams. This one was softer, higher, lighter, and wonderfully familiar, even though it was soured with obvious distress.

"*Anni, please. Please.*"

The feeling of hands on her shoulders, shaking her until she felt her bones rattle. She tried to find herself, to fit herself back into her body so she could open her eyes, and when she finally managed it, familiar gold eyes looked right back at her.

Lyam.

He sucked in a harsh breath as soon as he saw her eyes were open, and before she knew it she was crushed against his chest. "*Anni! You scared me! I didn't know— I thought— I thought you'd—*"

"*'M'here,*" *Annelie murmured tiredly, her eyes half-closed and heavy.* "*I'll always come back to you, Lyam. I promised, remember?*"

Lyam's bright, gold eyes, damp and glistening and with tear-tracks staining his cheeks, stared at her as he wrapped her up in a hug.

"*I know,*" *he murmured into her wild curls, clutching tight.* "*I know. I love you.*"

"Love you, too." Annelie buried her face in the comfort of Lyam's shoulder and allowed herself to be held, her body slowly coming back to her.

CHAPTER
NINETEEN

Above all else, we must remember that the Life-Giver is ours.
We are here to be with them,
And in return we are gifted life and land and warmth and light.
Our relationship with them is paramount.
The Book of the Life-Giver, Volume VIII, Chapter I

Lyam took in his first deep breath of clean air, feeling as if he'd aged a thousand years.

The city above the surface was in ruins, as ever, the buildings eroded and crumbling, the once-great sculptures chipped and ebbing away. And yet, it was still beautiful. The snow that had been lying thick on the ground had disappeared, melted away in some last move by the Life-Giver to allow them a fair chance at rebuilding their lives in a habitat in which they could survive. As a result, the waterways had swelled, close to bursting their carefully-monitored banks.

Somewhere behind him, Lyam could hear Enoch swearing. He grinned.

Wrapping his cold fingers around Annelie's wheelchair, Lyam pushed her forward across the rocky ground, being as careful as he could. Mima was sitting in Annelie's lap, staring about herself with her good blue eye wide, her filmy eye gleaming dully. Her tail was swinging back and forth, Annelie petting her back.

Lyam smiled as he continued forward, minding the bumps as best he could. Annelie grumbled a bit from her seat. "When we rebuild this, we're putting flat roads in. My ribs are complaining."

"I'm sure your ribs will be top priority."

"*Hey*, I didn't ask for your sarcasm."

"I'm joking, Anni," Lyam reassured with a small grin, freeing one hand to pat the top of her head. "I think all the Dreamers are going to want everything to be flat and comfortable, so no hills or flights of stairs or bumpy roads for us."

"Good."

Lyam was still smiling as he surveyed the land around them —the ancient city that they would have to rebuild. They would have to relearn how to work the land and survive the weather. But it would get easier. This was how things were supposed to be. The farmers could tweak their techniques, and the glass-blowers could still work in the fresh air. The Dreamers could Dream among the rest of the people, no more need for isolation.

Crowds of people drifted in sections across the ground, taking in the landscape wondrously. Everyone could see above ground now. Once the curse broke, filtering into Izani from the Dreamers, the shadows lifted from the other's eyes and now they could all see in sunlight. A final gift from the Life-Giver. Lyam spied his sisters playing by the riverbank, his parents watching over them. He smiled.

He looked up, far above in the deep blue sky where the Sun was hovering by the horizon. The Life-Giver was returning, just as promised, visibly moving closer. Streaks of red and pink touched the sky, and, if Lyam squinted and looked hard enough, he swore he could see flames.

"They're beautiful, aren't they?"

Annelie's voice was low, pitched under the chattering and excited conversations and slight wonder of the rest of the people, most of whom were stepping out above ground for the first time in their lives.

Lyam glanced around at them all: at Adan, who hadn't let go of Kiran once since his reappearance and remained plastered to his side, introducing him to Enoch; at Elinah and Jorin and Nethan and Tasmin, gathered in a circle sitting on the floor. Yenn was standing with the old man, surrounded by the Grey Ones who all stared around themselves with wonder. Lyam could hear their excited chatter all the way from over here. Yenn still looked gaunt, but there was a new hope in his eyes as he joined the other mourning Scribes in examining their new home.

Ayanah and Symon stood together not far away. Symon was wearing Ayanah's red and golden robe.

Mirah and Tomas, along with a selection of other Designers who knew that Izani had been changing Dreams, were gathered before them, hands in chains. Lyam wasn't sure what would happen to them now, but, by the grim look on Symon's face, it wouldn't be anything good. They certainly wouldn't be Designing anymore.

Izani himself was still trapped underground, his body stiff and frozen, blackened by the curse. Lara had checked, but found no pulse.

No one was mourning.

A breeze ruffled through Lyam's hair, the sensation still refreshingly new, and Mirah turned her head to look right at him. Her expression was stiff, but her eyes were sad, though they sharpened as soon as they landed on him.

Lyam dipped his head in a small bow. She'd been his friend for almost ten years. That wasn't something that just went away no matter what else had happened. Respect wasn't lost so easily, not for him.

Mirah simply pursed her lips, impassive, before turning her back on him.

Lyam let out a sigh. A soft touch to his hand made him look down, and he found Annelie glancing up at him, her eyes—back to their usual dark brown—narrowed with concern. Exhaustion still weighed heavily on her, but she was *alive*, and Lyam couldn't be happier.

Lyam leaned close and dropped a kiss to the top of her head, winding his arms around her small frame in the wheelchair. Her body was warm against his as they both looked back up the sky, where the Sun, their Life-Giver, continued to draw closer, painting the horizon with red and pink and yellow. It was the most beautiful sight that Lyam had ever seen.

"See?" She smiled at him. "Beautiful."

"Yes," Lyam said softly, resting his head against Annelie's. "Yes, we are."

THE END

ACKNOWLEDGMENTS

How do I even begin coming to terms with the fact that this book is now complete?

There are not enough words to describe how the end of this journey feels. This book has been through many iterations, countless changes, and endless edits since the first time these characters walked into my head when I was 15 years old. They have stayed with me through some of the best and worst years of my life, quietly keeping me company, biding their time, waiting for their moment.

That moment is now, as this book sits in your hands.

The fact that this story exists at all is the fruition of many years of hard work, and not just on my part. I would not have come anywhere close to having my story make the arduous journey from a teenage daydream to a fully-fledged novel without the help of many people, and though they are too many to thank, I'll do my best to cover as many as I can.

As I previously mentioned, Anni and Lyam first popped into my head when I was 15 years old. I was given a piece of creative writing coursework to do under the title 'A Sacred Place', and this world, with a Life-Giving sun god that people could visit in their dreams, formed as a result. Huge thanks to Miss Butler, my English teacher at the time, for reading that coursework and telling me that it read like a page out of a novel. This is that novel, finally finished more than a decade later. I hope it makes you proud.

To everyone at WriteNowLive 2018 for explaining the confusing, intoxicating, terrifying, beautiful world of publishing and convincing me that I had a place among its wildness, in particular Sharan Matharu, the first person to believe that the word document sitting half-finished on my laptop had legs.

To Michael Langan and The Literary Consultancy for offering me a Free Read and giving me the confidence to make this book as good as its potential. Your notes shaped the beginning of this novel and made me a better writer. Who knew that edits *do* make writing better, as much as I hate to admit it?

To everyone at Parliament House Publishing, for seeing something in my story and being the juggernaut behind bringing it to life. There are too many of you wonderful people to thank, but in particular: Mary Westveer; Mike Feeney; Alyssa Barber; Chantal Gadoury for all your hard work; Malorie Nilsen for taking the reins and making me feel so at home and welcome; Shayne Leighton, for your kindness and unbelievable cover designing skills (that day I opened the email with the mock-up for my cover remains one of the most thrilling of my life); Cindy Kilbourne, for liking my tweet pitch that started this incredible journey, and for your careful and thoughtful edits that turned this story into something far better than I could have imagined.

To my wonderful friends who kept me sane throughout this process, cheered me on at every success, commiserated with me through every failure and rejection, and, most importantly, reminded me that even when I'm too unwell to write, I'm still a writer. In particular, thank you to Milica for always being on the other end of a message, for your wonderful editing skills and constant encouragement, for the endless memes and cat pictures when I needed them, and lastly, for lending me your nickname, Mima.

To Jayne, the best writing friend anyone could ever wish for. Thank you for reading my entire draft in one sitting and telling me exactly what you thought, for your constant support and help, for your excellent hair-dyeing skills, for talking me down when I'm on the verge of giving up, and for also giving me the joy of reading your work. One day, your books will sit on a shelf beside mine.

To Charlotte, for always being there.

To Stacey, for supporting my writing since day one, and for lending me your beautiful art to bring my characters to life. Here's hoping you'll continue to draw my OCs forever.

To my dad—this entire book is dedicated to you. You instilled a love of reading in me from before I could walk, and it's thanks to you that I write as well as I do now, and also that I have the drive to continue to improve. Thank you for being my biggest fan, the best cheerleader, and always reminding me that I have you on my side.

To Michael, my brother and best friend. I hope that when you eventually read this book, it meets the expectations I've set over the past couple of years. Thank you for being my voice of reason.

To bookstagram and book twitter—I owe this community a lot, but especially, thank you for introducing me to the magical world of writing bullet journals.

To the disability community on twitter, who taught me so much about the importance of good representation. Us disabled people struggle in this world that isn't built for us, and I hope that my words might provide an escape, at least for a little while.

To my guinea pigs, Noodle and Tofu. Your happy squeaks are a welcome distraction from staring endlessly at a word document for hours and hours.

And finally: to any and all aro/ace teens out there who aren't quite sure where they fit. I hope that this book shows that love without romance is just as beautiful as a traditional relationship. Sometimes, particularly in YA, it can feel like romance is the only option, and I wanted to show, in my own small way, that there are other ways to lead a happy life. Lyam and Anni have each other for the rest of their lives, and you will find your people one day. I know. I was once you. Hold on, breathe, and stay. Your chosen family is waiting for you.

ABOUT THE AUTHOR

Jase Puddicombe is a fantasy author based in Nottingham, UK. They write quiet, introspective fantasy with a focus on characters and relationships, especially platonic or familial. Their debut novel, The Life-Giver, is due out March 29th 2022 with Parliament House Press.

Jase is nonbinary, asexual, and greyromantic, and uses they/he pronouns. He's also disabled with severe ME and HSD. When not writing, he can be found curled under an electric blanket with a hot chocolate, or playing with his guinea pigs.

www.jasepuddicombe.com

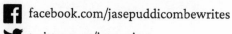 facebook.com/jasepuddicombewrites
twitter.com/jasewrites
instagram.com/jasewrites

ANNELIE AND LYAM STILL NEED YOU

Did you enjoy The Life-Giver? *Reviews keep books alive . . . Annelie and Lyam need your help!*

Help them by leaving your review on either GoodReads or the digital storefront of your choosing. They thank you!

THE PARLIAMENT HOUSE

THE PARLIAMENT HOUSE WWW.PARLIAMENTHOUSE-PRESS.COM

Want more from our amazing authors? Visit our website for trailers, exclusive blogs, additional content and more!

Become a Parlor Peep and access secret bonus content... JOIN US!